VICKIE, I APPRECIATE YOU
TAKING THIS TIME OUT TO
REVIEW MY BOOK. GOD BLESS.

ANDREA

LOVE IS ALL
WE'RE AFTER

ANDREA' PORTER

Publisher's Cataloging-in-Publication
(Provided by Quality Books, Inc.)

Porter, Andrea'.
Love is all we're after / Andrea' Porter. — 1st ed.
p. cm.
LCCN 2008905240
ISBN-13: 978-0-9818263-0-1
ISBN-10: 0-9818263-0-X

1. Marriage—Religious aspects—Christianity—
Fiction.
2. Man-woman relationships—Religious aspects
—Christianity—Fiction.
3. Love stories, American.
4. Christian fiction, American.   I. Title. II. Title:
Love is all we are after.

PS3616.O77L68 2008   813'.6
QBI08-600195

Printed in the United States.

Acknowledgements

First off, I want to give thanks to God who planted this story in my heart. I am thankful for His guidance as He orders my steps and shows me each day that love comes to us all. I also want to thank so many others who have helped to make this book possible. Curtis M. Johnson, Linda R. Broussard, Monica M. Polk, Angel Tyler, Tiffany Ambroise, Jonathon Greenaway, Lisa Venkatesan, Montrae Y. Chretien, Cindy Motsko, Chad Porter, Phil and Pam Young, June Sonnier, Emma A. Antoine, Verna B. Mosby, Jo Anne Greene and Patricia Eaglin, you each took a leap of faith and supported my dream. Thank you all. I am immensely grateful for your generosity and encouragement.

Shatonna Williams, of www.shatonnasphotography.com, you did such a great job with my photograph. You captured me beyond my imagination.

Holly D. Robertson, what can I say? Many a night, I shared my uncertainties, dreams, and visions with you. You listened and inspired me to keep reaching for all that I hold in my heart.

Monica and Anubhav Tagore at RootSky Creative, thank you for your editorial skills and for the design of my book cover. Monica, you have been a guiding light and an encourager when I have wanted to give up. I truly believe that God placed you in my life for such a time as this. God bless you, and I hope we will be working together for years to come.

To the two very important men in my life, Chanz Porter and Diandre Stevens, thanks for being the fuel in my fire.

CHAPTER ONE

Candy

It is the end of the day and my last customer has left me reeling from the one-sided conversation. He is a head case. I talk to some of the richest people in the world on a daily basis, top of the line clients, but some of the people I encounter are about as dumb as a box of rocks. He fits this category. He asks questions he already has answers to, and seems to be hearing the answers for the first time each time I respond.

But I push him from my mind as I close my Sony laptop, unplug the cord and stick it into the travel case. I grab Dean Frazier's file from the stack on my desk and shove until I squeeze it into the overflowing cabinet. I've made this man a lot of money over the years. I give him great advice and steer him in the right direction, the same thing I do for all my clients. But he's so ungrateful.

The bulging filing cabinet needs attention, but I sure am not going to clean it this evening. It will wait until Monday. It's been a tough day. Dean Frazier has just questioned my competence and given me the third degree about two stocks I advised him about two months ago. I told him they were duds, and not to get them, but he has some hotshot friend who told him otherwise. Dean took the friend's advice.

Now the stocks are losing money and he's grilling me about why I made the buy. I wanted to tell his crazy behind that he told me to do it, even after I told him it wasn't a good idea, but of course I couldn't do that. Simple-minded clients never remember the good advice you give. Only the bad moves they make — and blame you for.

"Candy, I thought you left already," Shelly says. Her appearance in my doorway can only mean one thing — Miranda is still in the building. A tight-nosed she devil who wears pinstripe suits and Blahniks. She is also my boss.

"No, I'm still here. Weren't you meeting up with Tom tonight?"

"Yes girl, but he had to go to Barnes & Noble to pick up

1

that Harry Potter nonsense everyone's been raving about." Her sunny voice does nothing for my mood.

Shelly has a bubbly personality, a trait I admire, but not at the moment. I just had my rear end chewed out and handed back to me. The last thing I need is her happy-go-lucky attitude.

"Is Miranda still here?" The words come out a bit sharper than I intend, but I don't think that even registers with Shelly. She ignores my question and goes into compliment mode.

"Wow! You will have those men following you around, trying to get next to you. I don't understand why a woman who looks as good as you do is still single."

I ignore the compliment and repeat. "Is Miranda still here?"

Again, Shelly ignores my question and pries further into my business. My impatience is lost on her. "Who are you meeting up with anyway?"

I sigh. "I'm meeting up with the usual suspects, Lisa and Mona."

"Dressed like that?" Shelly asks, her eyebrows shooting up. She looks me up and down, taking in the skin-tight dress, the possessive hug of the material on my body, and the split running up the side.

I can tell she is not buying it and this is not the hour to convince her otherwise. Shelly thinks there is a man hidden in my life somewhere. Sometimes I wish I were hiding someone. Ever since I shed the devil's cloak and started living right, all the men have disappeared. I looked around one day and they were gone.

Impatience saturates my tone. I respond, "Yes dressed like this. Did Miranda leave or not?"

Shelly shoots me the evil eye, and would have given me the finger too, but she's trying to be respectful of my Christianity. "Miranda left a few minutes ago. You're grouchy."

So, my mood has registered with her.

"Sorry, my last client was a jerk," I apologize. "I didn't mean to take it out on you."

She inches further into my office, until she stands next to my desk. Hipbones resting against the sharp edge, she folds her arms and stares me down. I know that look; I've seen it many times. It's the I am going to get all up in your Kool-Aid look. Shelly eyeballs my mahogany desk, taking a mental inventory of the items on it; I ignore her.

She waits a beat, then asks, "You taking this entire work home with you?"

Shelly flips through the first file and clucks. I know what she is thinking and she is right, I am a workaholic. I did not get where I am by giving only a hundred percent. I learned three things in this business: Never leave before my boss. Always give a few percent more of my time. And make this time here count for something.

"I need to catch up on some work I didn't get to finish today," I say, eying her as she flips through the paperwork.

"More power to you. Saturday cannot come soon enough. All those naked men and me, woo hoo!" Shelly fans her face. "Let me calm down."

I laugh. "Yeah, you need to calm down with your hot tail."

Shelly's bachelorette party is this weekend and she has talked nonstop about it since we orchestrated it. Listening to this constant talk about weddings is a reminder that I am a single, celibate woman with the odds of getting married bleak. Being single has its charms, but hearing someone else talk constantly about getting married can make you wish for things to be different. Like Prince Charming, baby and carriage, and a house on the hill with a white picket fence.

"I think I've hit my sexual peak," Shelly confesses to me. "I can't stop dreaming about men and their anatomy, and my dreams are vivid. I wake up in heat in the middle of the night, frantic. Has that ever happened to you?"

Choosing my words carefully I say, "That's normal. You're probably nervous about the wedding. Are you having second thoughts about this marriage?"

Shelly puts a finger under her chin. "Yes and no. Could this be the reason why I have those dreams? I mean, I get to see what Tom is working with all the time. I would like to see what other men are working with, too. Tom and I have been dating since high school, and I've never been with anyone else. Just once, I would like to be with somebody who wants to try out positions other than missionary."

She grabs me by the shoulders and starts shaking me, then says in exaggerated tones: "Candy, help me! I'm bored!"

Her comment humors and frustrates me. If I tell her how I really feel she's going to call me a hypocrite, because I've been there, and if I don't say something she'll think I'm Miss Goody Too Shoes. "You need to quit," I tell her. "You need to be thankful you have a faithful, loving man who worships the ground you walk on. Do you know how many women want what you have? If it ain't broke, don't fix it."

I am ready to change the subject, so I give her a wink. "Since you're here, help me look for my attaché case."

Somewhere in this pile of junk is my attaché case, but I can't remember where I last saw the brown beat-up, second-hand briefcase I bought when I got my first job. I can afford to buy a new one, but this one has sentimental value.

"You sound like my mom. She says I should be grateful for Tom. Anyway, are you bringing Mona to my party tomorrow?" Shelly asks as she stoops down to look under my desk. "You should bring her. She is lots of fun." She uses her foot to nudge a box out of her way in her search for my attaché case.

"Maybe. I haven't told her about it yet." I take that same box she moved and place it on a rattan chair.

"Whyyyyy? You had a month to tell her about my party."

Shelly's rueful whine irks me. I tune it out and check my purse for my cell phone, the charger, and car keys.

"Tell her tonight," Shelly carries on. "Do it. Don't forget. I want her to come. She's a little crazy, but the woman is a riot."

I laugh at her understatement in her description of Mona. "I'll ask her, but I can't make any promises she'll come with me. Does Tom know what you're up to this weekend?"

"No, and I won't dare tell him," Shelly says quickly.

"He would be there acting like a police officer patrolling everything and spoiling all my fun. I told him I was going to a bridal shower the girls were throwing for me."

"Look at you lying," I say with an eye roll. "You better not get caught."

"I won't." Shelly's response is confident, and she has every right to be.

Tom thinks Shelly wouldn't harm a fly. In his eyes, she can do no wrong and in my opinion, he's too gullible.

I force a smile to my lips. "Then I can't wait to party it up with you on Saturday." Shelly's face melts into a smile.

"Have fun tonight, and don't do anything I wouldn't do," she says.

That leaves very little to the imagination. The woman does nothing. More than likely, she is going home to Tom to cuddle up and watch sappy movies or squabble over Monopoly. Shelly talks about wanting to experience another man, but I don't think she will do anything to betray Tom. Shelly and Tom have something a lot of people envy; I top the list. Their deep-seated love and respect for each other radiates to everyone around them and for people like me, it can be very annoying. I need to leave. I open my mouth to say goodbye and close it when Shelly's phone rings. She looks at her cell, then back at me.

"That's Tom calling. I better get this. Talk to you later." Her phone's steady tone is insistent in its demand. She answers. "Baby, I'm on my way."

Shelly throws her arms around me.

"Tell Tom I say hello," I say as she releases me.

Shelly races out the door leaving traces of perfume in her wake. I fluff my hair and look around my office once more for my attaché case. I give up and move on to stacking the loose papers on my desk. I toss them into the empty file bin, and a single leaf of paper flutters to the ground next to the briefcase hidden between the love seat and the end table. We just finished tearing this place upside down searching for this thing, and it shows up when I least expect it.

Life constantly surprises me that way.

CHAPTER TWO

Mona

Standing at six foot four, John towers over me.

"You got a body on you, you know that?" he says and licks his bottom lip, then pulls it in.

John removes my blouse. The flimsy material slides to the floor. As I unbuckle his belt, he begins to remove my bra. We play follow the leader until we're completely nude.

"And it's all yours," I say smiling up at him. The light from outside is hardly muted by the threadbare paisley curtains. The tiny motel room has a faint musty smell and the bed creaks, but for now, it's a haven for us. "I love being here with you."

I circle my arms around John and rest my face against his chest. I feel heat radiating from him, and his heart is beating at a rapid pace. The blood coursing through my veins is like liquid fire. I stroke his torso, running imaginary lines between the split of his pecs to his sculpted shoulders.

"There's no place I'd rather be than here with you," he says and devours me with his eyes. "I love the way you love me, Mona. I thought about this moment all day. Come and lie with me, baby."

I exercise the power I have over John. I say, "No you lie down. I've been practicing some new tricks for you."

"You like this power you have over me too much woman. I like it," John says with a grin.

The only time I have control over John, is in the bedroom. It's the only time I feel like I'm in charge. It's an illusion, yet every chance I get I feed into the lie.

"You brought protection?"

I shake my head. "No, I thought you were gonna bring it."

"Let me see if I have any in my wallet." John bends to pick his pants up, rummages through the pockets, and removes a condom.

Someone's car alarm goes off outside our window. The

noise is so deafening we jump and turn our attention to the window. Glad for the diversion, I take the condom from him and drop it to the floor. I refuse to let him rob me of the pleasure I get from having him skin to skin, to feel his body jump and twitch when I take his soul.

"You don't need this," I say, eying the tiny packet I've just dumped.

He stares into my eyes and asks, "You still on birth-?"

Shaking my head in protest, I place a finger on his lips. "No questions."

He bites at my finger playfully and draws me close.

"You have all the power," he says in a low voice. "When do we reverse the roles?"

"We don't."

John pretends to sulk. My inner being charges with adoration for him.

"I love you, John." I caress his face, nuzzle his neck, and cup the back of his head.

"I know." For once, I wish his lips would say the words I want to hear.

I brush my hair from my face. "Are you ever gonna say it back?"

"Why? You know how I feel about you." John stretches out his hands in surrender. "Here I am. Do as you like."

Ooh, I love this cocoa brown, big, strong stallion. It's a shame I have to share him with his wife. His goody two-shoe of a wife cannot satisfy him in the bedroom as I do.

John asks, "Are you going to keep me waiting?"

Lights, camera, action! The scene is set. This is where I pretend it's only the two of us. The time we spend with each other is always short. Today it's even shorter, but we make it work.

I push John to the bed, and he takes me with him. The bed jerks with our weight when we land. The look in his eyes reveals all the things he wants to do to me. I know his pleasures, and he knows mine.

He asks, "You're enjoying this aren't you?"

I say, "I am. I can't get enough of you."

John mutters into my ear. "Mona baby, tell me you love me again. I like when you say it."

"I love you baby, you're my king." John grows sentimental with every word and every touch. I can't reach his mind, the place where his soul lives, but I can use the wiles of my womanly skills. He is my puppet on a string. I talk dirty to him; this is John's weakness. His dirty little secret. These are the things his wife can't and won't do for him.

For these moments, John is all mine.

CHAPTER THREE

Lisa

"You've reached John Boutari. Leave a message, and I'll get back to you." The voicemail instructs, and I sigh.

"John, where are you?" I say into the phone, and my tone is sharp, even to my own ears. I can't believe this is happening to me all over again. John left work hours ago, according to his secretary. I have called him six times, left six voice messages, sent three text messages, and I haven't heard from him once.

John and I have been at each other's throats all week. I haven't slept in two days and the drink I'm holding will be the first I've had in years — but from the looks of things, it certainly won't be the last. I'm so stressed by the strife between my husband and me, that I'm looking for any way to calm my nerves. Things have gotten so bad between us that I don't think we're going make it this time.

The man sitting on the stool next to me has been staring me down since I got here. I avoid making eye contact. I look everywhere but at him, because I don't want to give him the impression he interests me.

"Hi, are you waiting on somebody?" he turns to ask.

I narrow in on his face. "Yes." I thought he would take the hint and leave me alone.

"If I were the guy you are waiting on, I wouldn't keep you waiting." His breath smells like old cheese.

I smile reluctantly. "Hmm."

He looks at me incredulously. "You don't believe me? Are you willing to give me a try?"

"I'm married," I say flatly. He glances at my ring finger knowingly and smiles. "It's at the cleaners," I say before he can question.

"Most rings are, sweetheart. I won't tell your husband if you don't."

I ignore the man and go back to sipping my drink.

"If this is your first time we can take it slow," he says, leaning a little too close to me. His offending breath almost makes me gag.

"Look Don Juan, I'm not here to cheat on my husband," I snap. Even though it's a half lie, he doesn't know the truth. I sure as heck wouldn't mess around with him even if he were the last man on this earth.

He tsks. "But you thought about it, that's why you don't have a ring on your finger," he says knowingly. I shoot him a cutting glare. "That's all right little mama, I'll leave you alone."

He turns to the two women who walked in and took the seat beside him and they brush him off. "See you around, Ms. I'm-Not-Here-to-Cheat-on-My-Husband. Dang prude."

"Whatever," I shush him. "Go sit down somewhere."

"Go get your ring from the so-called cleaners, and stop wasting a brother's time."

"I see somebody forgot to send you the memo that gold chains and starched pants are out of fashion," I spit back at him, shooting a disdainful look at his outfit.

He throws me a disgruntled look and rushes off to the other end of the bar to disgust some other woman. Better her than me. If I'm going to cheat on John, it's going to be with someone who looks better than him, not some fuddy-duddy.

The diamond Tacori ring John gave me on our wedding day is not at some jewelry cleaners as I had claimed earlier, but at the house. I took it off this morning and placed it in the box it came in. It should be collecting dust by now.

"Are you running our customers off?" Jack asks, as he places before me the meal my mouth has been watering for since I got here. "Here is your Cajun Cacciatore."

But when I examine it, I see it's not what I wanted. Disappointed I say, "That's not what I ordered."

Jack's eyebrows rise. "Then what did you order?"

I huff. "I get the same thing every time I come here, and you still manage to mess it up some how."

Jack thumps the table impatiently. "What you want to eat, woman?"

"Bring me the same thing, but without the mushrooms."

"The mushrooms are the best part," he says.

I glare at him and he sighs. "Picky, picky, picky."

"I'm not being picky, unless you want me to blow up like a blowfish. You better get me something else," I say matter-of-factly.

"Yes, ma'am." Shaking his head, Jack takes the plate. "One Cajun Cacciatore coming right back up."

Jack is one of the owners of Zane's and is recently divorced. He caught his wife of fifteen years in bed with another man. He took the kids and left her high and dry. Apparently, she only married him for his money. The man she had the affair with was more than willing to give up the goods on her for a few extras dollars.

Even as I give Jack a hard time about my order, I feel as if he and I are somehow kindred souls. I could be among the divorced myself, pretty soon, if things keep going the way they have been.

I touch the spot where my wedding ring should have been. Sadness makes my heart heavy.

CHAPTER FOUR

Mona

John looks so peaceful sleeping. He always falls asleep after we make love. I don't know how he can go to sleep with all this noise outside. We are in a seedy motel on the wrong side of town where people sell household items out of the trunk of their cars and the street corners are used for peddling dope. Two blocks over from here is the headquarters for hookers, pimps, crack heads, and whatever form of low life living you can find.

I nudge John on the shoulder. "Wake up, baby. We have to leave." He turns over on his side.

He mutters, "Give me thirty more minutes."

I stick my finger in his ear. "We don't have thirty minutes; well you don't have thirty minutes."

"Shhh, stop talking and just lie here with me." He covers my mouth, and pulls me close.

"I have cottonmouth. I'm getting some water; want some?" I ask between the spaces of his fingers.

He clears his throat. "Yeah bring me some."

John chose this place because he doesn't want to risk running into anyone he knows. Personally, it matters little to me if we do. There can only be one queen to a throne, and it is time for me to reign. I grab the bottle of Dasani they charged me an arm and a leg for downstairs. I take a big gulp.

"Aw." I sigh and smack my tongue. "That was some good water."

John asks, "Where are you guys going tonight?"

His question catches me off guard. "Huh?" Where did that come from?

I hand him the rest of the water and he repeats. "Where are you ladies going tonight?"

"I don't know. Some new Jazz club Candy wants to check out. You know her. You've never cared about where we're going before, why the sudden interest?"

"I'm only making conversation. Come sit by me." He pats

the spot next to him. I lean against the cold wall instead.

"You have any plans tonight?" I look at him; I mean really look at him. Our eyes connect, each trying to figure out the other.

"I'm heading home to bed."

I ask, "Are you nervous about me hanging out with your wife?"

"Should I be?"

Instinct tells me this is no time for a power trip. Ego dismisses common sense, and I proceed full speed ahead like a freight train out of control.

I ask, "Are you afraid I'll slip up and mention to your wife that I slept with you before joining them?"

John crushes the water bottle and pitches it into the garbage bin. "I know you're not that stupid." His face takes on a sickly appearance.

"You don't have to worry about me telling your wife anything." Common sense takes over again and I assure him his secret is safe.

"Good girl, now give me a back rub," he says, gesturing for me to approach. "I'm soar."

Talk about killing the mood. This is what those questions were about — preserving his marriage.

I tell him, "Turn over on your stomach." I climb on top of him, twist his arm behind his back, and pop it. I consider wringing his neck with his own hands. "Does it feel any better?"

He grunts. "I don't think I can move. I think you dislocated my hips, too."

"Me? You were the one acting like Tarzan. Where's my bra?" I ask feeling around on the bed for my pink Fredrick's of Hollywood under garment.

"I didn't hear you stopping me, Jane."

"I thought you had it under control, ape man."

I find my bra stuffed between the headboard and mattress. I slip it on and motion for John to snap it into place.

He gets cocky. "A brother always has it under control, sweetie."

He ain't lying. He has skillz w/ a — Z. "Uh-huh. We still on for tomorrow?"

John puts on his pants and tugs the zipper shut. The simple movement distracts me. John's body is beautiful artwork, lean and muscular like a body builder. I know every inch, every mole, and every scar.

"Unless old girl trips on me, I don't see why not. Let's play it by ear though. If something changes I'll call."

I look up from buttoning my top. "Want a demonstration of why you should meet me tomorrow?"

"Baby you keep putting those moves on me, and you're going to send me to an early grave."

I smile a silent victory, knowing he will not have any energy left for his wife when he gets home. Lisa and I went to college together, but we stopped being friends a long time ago.

"You sure you're not ready for round two?" I joke.

"I want to, but I have to get to the house."

"I want you to stay, spend more time with me." I look at him with seduction in my eyes.

"You know I can't do that; Lisa will get suspicious." His tone is matter-if-fact.

"How long are you going to use the same old tired excuse?" My tone lets him know I'm growing weary of this game.

"Do you walk around with blindfolds on your eyes? I'm married, Mona, and my obligation is to my wife right now," he says staring at me, hard.

I take a deep breath. "We can't keep sneaking around like this. I want more from you than a casual roll in the sack."

"And you'll get more. Just give me some time, OK?"

We all need a little happiness, and this is what I seek from John. When John touches me, he sets my soul on fire. I hate to see him conflicted because of me. He is the air I breathe, to deny him is to deny myself.

I prod, "How much longer?"

"Soon, I promise. Just wait on me." I wrap my arms around him and hold for as long as I can. "Come on baby girl, finish putting your clothes on."

I feel his disconnection, even before he peels my hands from around his neck. He trails small kisses across them, and then lets them fall loosely. This is hard for me, knowing he is leaving me to go home to be with her. This is when jealousy rears its ugly head. Desperation makes my heart beat faster, shoving logic from my mind.

I pull my lip in and tug on John's belt buckle. "John, please stay," I plead, my eyes begging even more than my words.

"Why do you have to act this way all the time? I already told you I can't; now let's go."

"Then go," I say and motion to the door. "I'll be fine."

"Mona, you know I'm not leaving you here. So stop fooling around and put your clothes on, woman."

I sit down on the bed, pouting.

I say, "Go, John, I'm not ready to leave."

John's tone is low, even, and threatening. "Mona, get your clothes on right now. Why do you always want to start a fight when I get ready to leave? You know the deal. You know I can't stay."

"I'm tired of living this lie, John. Tired of feeling like a whore, as if the only thing I'm good for is being on my back. There is more to me than sex. I am not going to allow you to sleep with me and then toss me to the side anymore. You're the only one having any fun, getting the best of both worlds with a wife at home and a mistress on call."

John's expression darkens and from the look on his face, he wants to wring my neck. "Where do you come up with this stuff? Don't I treat you good? I buy you all these fancy things... take you to nice places... I treat you like a queen and what do I get?"

"You call this whorehouse the good life?" I ask waving my hand around dramatically. "Look around, John. I might as well be walking up and down the boulevard like the prostitutes outside. If you have to leave, leave. I'm not ready to go."

John paces the room like a caged animal. Watching him wears me out. We give each other the silent treatment. Seconds roll into minutes.

I say, "I'm not trying to be difficult, John. I want this to work, but I like nice things. This trailer park lifestyle is not me."

"Mona, I've already explained to you why we come here. The last time we were at the Ritz Carlton we ran into Lisa's aunt. Do you want me to be caught cheating on my wife? Is that it? Mona, I have a wife at home who nags me enough. I don't need this, if this is the way it's going to be between us then we might as well end it now."

His arrogance rubs me the wrong way. I dig my heels in ready to fight with him, and I say whatever comes to mind.

"Then don't let the door hit you where the good Lord split you." I hurl the bouquet of flowers he gave me at him. It hits him in the center of his chest, bounces to the floor and there goes a nice bunch of flowers.

He tsks and says, "Suit yourself." John brushes his shirt off, turns on his heel, and walks out the door.

"You selfish jerk!" The words spew from my mouth, but John is already gone.

I imagine plowing John over with my car for leaving me in this rundown motel in the ghetto. I look around the dingy room and suddenly the room turns cold and I feel like it is caving in on me. I punch the bed and fight back bitter tears threatening to fall. The pain in my chest is too much. I let the tears fall. After a few minutes of feeling sorry for myself and loathing John, I build up the strength to leave the motel room.

The devil is up to his old tricks again. The evening grows interesting when I walk upon three men hanging out by the Dumpster playing dice, listening to loud rap music and puffing on marijuana. Fear rises in my gut.

Lord, what have I gotten myself into? Why do I have to be so stubborn? The afternoon's emotions wash over me with full force. I have been having sex with a man who is somebody else's husband. I've been letting this "relationship" control me and I seem only too willing to keep letting it continue. I want a man of my own. Lord, if you just get me out of this situation, I promise I will live right. I will start going back to church. I will tithe. I will be kind to my neighbors. I will —

"Hey baby girl, come over here for a minute." One of the men by the Dumpster invites and moves toward me. He's the biggest of the three.

Terror blocks my airway, my heart pounds wildly against my chest, and sweat runs from my head to the sides of my face. I look around to see if anyone is watching.

I manage to say, "I don't think so, pal."

His smile makes my skin crawl. "We got us a feisty one here, Parker."

Someone needs to give him a toothbrush and toothpaste. His perverted smirk reveals badly stained teeth. He continues to swagger toward me, black pick comb sticking out of his hair and torn jeans sagging down to his hips.

Aggravating John into leaving me here was not smart. I'm on the wrong side of town with no one in sight, ambushed by a bunch of punks. If I hadn't switched purses this morning, I would have my Mace as a last resort. I'm in a dilemma and every fiber in my being tells me to make a run for my car, but judging by the distance between them and it, I know I won't make it.

I'm petrified. Like a hunter after its prey, this thug senses my fear. "Hey don't be scared, we won't hurt you. Ain't that right, fellas?" the ringleader says.

Their chuckles blend.

The ringleader continues. "Naw, we won't hurt you. I just want to talk to you for a minute. Won't you step into my office?" he motions to the dark alley behind him.

The scene is straight out of the movies, and I'm the victim. Never in my wildest dreams would I have fathomed something like this happening to me. I put myself in this danger and now I must get myself out of it. A bluff is all I have.

Loud enough for his two buddies to hear me I say, "Do you know you can get ten to fifteen for substance abuse? How much of that stuff do you have on you? Do you mind if we search your car? Oh, my partner is upstairs. He'll be down in a minute."

His face goes still, all signs of his earlier humor are gone, and bewilderment replaces cockiness. I take three steps closer to them.

"I think she's Five-O," he tells his friends and puts distance between us. "Are you Five-O lady?"

I have to convince them that I'm a cop so I reach into my

jacket, as if I'm reaching for a gun. I know if I give them a scare they will leave me alone. I'm in control again and it's funny to see them squirm.

"Do you really want to stick around to find out? Today is your lucky day. I've got bigger fish to fry."

They shake their heads vigorously.

One of them speaks up. "No, ma'am. We were just leaving, weren't we man?"

They all nod their heads in agreement. I watch them fall over themselves to get in their car. The ringleader is the only one still standing in my face with a scared look on his face. I should slap him just for good measure.

"Don't let me see you around here again, understood? If I do, I'm gonna lock you up and throw away the keys."

"I'm gone," he says and in two swift steps, he sprints to the waiting car.

I keep an eye on them until their car disappear from my sight. I climb into my car and the shock of it all hits me hard. Hunched over the steering wheel, I cry my heart out one more time.

I could have easily become the next rape victim, killed, and stuffed in a dumpster. Thank God, tonight I won't end up on the 10 o'clock news.

CHAPTER FIVE

Candy

Satisfied I have everything I need to get me through the weekend, I shove my laptop into its case and lock the door to my office. The service elevator leading out to the parking lot is deserted. Everyone is gone, and it's quite spooky being down here alone.

Tony the security guard is nowhere around. A loud crashing noise echoes from the far corners of the parking garage, scaring me half to death. Looking around for the culprit who made the noise, I miss a step and trip. I curse something ugly under my breath. I'm sorry, Lord, I pray a speedy apology. I've been trying to watch my language since I got saved, but sometimes...

Construction workers slave away on a road opposite our building. Orange cones and ugly hazard signs section off the right lane. They have been working on this road for months and I still can't see any improvements. These are my tax dollars at work.

Tail lights flash all the way up to thirty-five. Shelly's directions to that side road would do some good right now. The men stop to watch me as if I'm some kind of picture show. I smile politely, acknowledging their favorable stares and nods. I am a beautiful woman and that is putting it mildly. Most men say I am fine with a capital F. Maybe too fine for my own good. Maybe that's the reason I can't find a decent man. Then again, maybe it is because I'm too picky.

The man I want to spend the rest of my life with has to make three times as much as me. He has to be tall, athletic, intelligent, and have a relationship with God. My mom calls it "The ideal mate impossible list." She told me I'm chasing a ghost, and moms know best. What can I say? I am an idealist. Perfectionism propels me to have high standards and to accept nothing less. This is why I'm down here in this parking lot struggling with work from the office.

Balancing the files in one hand, I reach into my purse for my car keys with the other. I almost lose them to the dusty ground, but catch them in time.

"You are always struggling to get in your car," Tony says, appearing out of nowhere.

"I swear you have ESP," I say, "I thought you took off and left me here to fend for myself."

"Naw, I had to check the perimeters. Let me help you with those."

"You don't have to do that, I got it."

"I know I don't have to, give them to me anyway," he says and grabs for the files.

I hand over my load and locate my car keys. They jingle noisily in my hand. I marvel at technology. One press of a button, and my door unlocks. Tony puts the files on the backseat, and checks my tires. He's such a good person, sweet, cute and happily married. I used to think he was flirting with me because he's always so nice to me until I found out I remind him of his little sister.

"Have a nice weekend, Tony."

"You have a nice weekend too, Ms. Cameron." He still addresses me by my last name even when I've told him a thousand times to call me by my first.

I place my purse in the seat next to me, hang my jacket on the back of the seat, and put my shades on. I turn the keys in the ignition of my custom-built BMW Roadster and the car purrs to life. With ease, I maneuver it in line with the rest of the traffic, top down, and the wind blowing through my hair. The breeze strips away the stressful day I had at work, filled with boardroom meeting after boardroom meeting.

It is the middle of September and a new season is on its way. The leaves are already changing colors, going from green to red and yellow to honey brown. Even the wind has a different feel. The clouds cover the sun's brilliance, diminishing it to a rustic hue. I inhale fresh air deep into my lungs, and release it. God and all his glory surround me.

I hit the disc player on my stereo and Cece Winans comes on crooning her latest hit "Hallelujah to the King" from her Throne Room album. It's 7:15 in the evening and traffic is bad, because of all this construction. This one-lane business forces us to move at a snail's pace.

LOVE IS ALL WE'RE AFTER

Traffic is moving along as slowly as my love life has been growing lately. I sigh.

CHAPTER SIX

Lisa

My cell phone vibrates, flashing green. Candy's number pops up on caller ID. I answer on the second ring.

I ask, "Hey girl, are you on your way?"

"Yeah, where are you? You made it to Zane's already?"

"Yes I'm at Zane's. It is a really nice restaurant slash jazz club."

"You got there early." Candy says, sounding a little surprised.

"Yeah I got off work early today. I didn't want to go to the house to face off with demon seed."

Candy laughs and says, "I hear that."

"Do you know where this place is?" I ask.

She yells over the music instead of turning it down. "I think so."

"Do you need directions?" I turn the volume on my phone down. I'm already deaf; I don't need to speed up the process. It's still loud. I put her on speaker. Too much static makes me take her off speaker.

"Isn't it off 119th Street and Metcalf?" Candy asks. "Hold on, someone's beeping in on the other line."

I wait and wait some more. I watch my Sprint minutes climb to three minutes then she comes back to the line.

"Lisa, is this place in the same plaza as Phil's Restaurant?"

"Yes, you can't miss it," I assure her. "When you come to Metcalf and 119th Street, look to your left and you will see Zane's and hurry, I don't like being here alone."

"OK, then I'll see you in a few minutes."

"I'm sitting at the bar. See you when you get here." I rush her off the phone, to preserve what little hearing I have left.

The bartender serves me a fresh drink. He is nice looking. We exchange smiles. He wipes the moisture from the counter, collects the empty glasses, and empties the cigarette trays. After the Cajun Cacciatore ordeal, Jack left me to fend for myself. He said I'm too bossy — me, bossy?

Candy, Mona, and I haven't hung out together very often since college. There is the occasional dinner party I throw yearly, but I wouldn't label that as hanging out. The three of us met when we were sophomores. The school messed up and double booked their dorms and we ended up sharing the same room. We were inseparable until I met and married John. I always thought the three of us would get married at the same time, be one big family, and live happily ever after. That was a fairytale. Fairytales don't come true.

***

Candy

Friday night is singles' night at the church and that's where I usually go right after work. Lisa threw a monkey wrench in my plans when she called to invite me out to eat. I wouldn't be so skeptical if she had asked me out to a charity function, to one of the many boring seminars she frequents, or to one of her over-the-top dinner parties. The people she rubs elbows with think eating caviar and drinking thousand dollar bottles of champagne is the norm.

Lisa told me John's up to no good again. This isn't the first time he has cheated on her during their four years of marriage. The man gives new meaning to the word "dog." Cheating plus conflict is the perfect recipe for a divorce. She talks about leaving him, but she never does. Lisa would rather have a piece of a man than no man, just to save face. I don't know who she's trying to impress more: All those people she eats caviar with, or her mother who expects perfection. The only thing keeping these two together is a piece of paper with some dried up ink. Ink that wasn't even dry on the marriage certificate before John started showing his true colors. He fooled her but his charms never worked on me. I dislike the man, God forgive me, but it's the truth. Lord, you nailed it on the head when you said: "Charm is deceptive, and beauty is vain, but a man who fears the Lord, he shall be praised."

John is nothing but smoke and mirrors. He's too flipping sneaky, tries too hard, as if he's trying to cover up some flaw.

I've studied him long enough to recognize his flaw. He has wandering eyes. I figure he would be cross-eyed by now.

Someone honks a horn at me for cutting them off at the light. The driver waves angry hands at me. I switch lanes to get out of his way and the driver next to him gets road rage and cuts me off. Tires screech as I hit my brakes. I miss running into the back of a Benz by mere inches. Four teenage girls glare at me. I smile and raise my hand in an apology, but the gestures didn't soothe their angry stares.

Shaky hands grip the steering wheel as I make an effort to regain my composure. Flashbacks from my last accident grip my stomach. I reach for the bottle of water in my cup holder and take a sip. It's warm from sitting in the car all day.

I ride Metcalf all the way up to 119th street. Zane's wasn't hard to find. Before getting out of my car, I spray some perfume on, taking care not to get any on my dress. Silk and perfume don't go well together. I selected this dress tonight because of its flirtatious subtlety. I have my hair up in a chignon and the gold chandelier earrings sparkle like stars in the dark.

The faint sound of Anita Baker's voice, sensual like a lover's touch, singing "Sweet Love" welcomes me to the door. Lisa sits at the bar with her head down. I almost don't recognize her because her hair is cut.

"I made it. Girl, I love your new 'do," I announce and give her a hug. "Lucky for you I can scope out your giant head anywhere. Why didn't you tell me you cut it?"

She smiles. "Thank you. I had it done last Saturday. I forgot to tell you about it," she touches her hair with one hand. "You really like it?"

"I love it! Keep your hair this way; it makes you look different, more alive, and fresh. We will probably have to beat the men off you with a stick tonight. You're making it hard on us single gals to find Mr. Right."

She says, "Girl please, I'm not studying these men."

I work the room, resting my eyes on a few possibilities. I notice the missing wedding ring on the fourth finger of her left hand. Lisa claims she's not studying these men, yet she's out here ringless and half-naked.

"Where's the rest of your dress?"

Lisa blushes slightly and shrugs. "At home," she replies and tugs the hem down, as if doing so will make extra material miraculously attach itself to the dress.

I laugh, and tug at her dress too. Unless she can pull a Houdini, this dress isn't getting any longer.

She swats at my hand. "Quit it, what do you want to drink? First round is on me. I already started a tab. Just let the bartender know what you want."

Hmm, I sure could do with a nice drink. Temptation beckons me to get one, and I can almost taste the alcohol on my tongue. The accident I almost had five miles north of here is the perfect persuasion to indulge. But my newfound desire to live right battles with my initial response. No, God has been too good to me. And I'm trying to do better to honor him. I don't need that poison to have a good time.

"That's OK, I'll pass."

Lisa insists, waving her hand toward the array of alcohol behind the counter. "They have drink specials. One drink won't kill you."

Then she taps her forehead. "Oh shoot, I'm sorry. I forgot you don't drink anymore."

"Your company showed up." The bartender announces to Lisa.

"Uh-huh. Now maybe people will stop sending me pity stares."

He smiles and charms her. "They look because they think you're pretty." Turning to me, he asks, "What can I get you to drink?"

You. But aloud, I say simply, "Yes. Um... I'll take a virgin daiquiri."

Before he turns to leave, I ask. "Have we met before?"

I am seriously attracted to him. I have never had such strong attraction to a man in my life, especially not to a white man, but he's fine. He puts Brad Pitt to shame.

The bartender grins and his blue eyes twinkle. "I'm sure I would remember you." He winks and repeats my order. "One virgin daiquiri coming up."

Déjà vu surrounds me. I know him from somewhere, but can't seem to recall the place. I study him, trying to pull out some answer to the how's and why's of where we've met. Nothing comes to mind. Maybe he is just one of those people with a familiar face.

"You are such an outrageous flirt, and these men just eat it up," Lisa chides. "Poor little fools."

I'm inclined to agree with her. I do have a way with the opposite sex, however I do not agree with her description of them. Men are not fools. I've been around too many to agree.

I say, "You call that flirting? I think I've met him somewhere before. I'm not sure where, but I know his face."

"You always think you know somebody. Well, I like free drinks so keep working your jelly, Miss Thang."

"I am not flirting with this man to serve you alcohol. I thought you quit?"

"I did, and now I am taking it back up," she declares with malicious intent. I hold my tongue. "You would be drinking too if you lived with the devil."

I cannot imagine a man not being happy with only her. Lisa is a beautiful, intelligent, well-rounded woman who has a lot going for her. She is a very successful part owner of a private firm. You would think a woman who has all that going for her would be flying on top of the world, but she is messed up in the head like the rest of us.

"Lisa." I pause. I want to ask about her situation with John, but I don't think the timing is right.

She crosses her legs and looks at me expectantly.

Hesitation slows my speech. "When you ah... when you called yesterday, you mentioned you and John are having problems. It sounds a lot worse this time."

She rolls her eyes as if this is the last thing she expects me to ask her. Seeing her pain, I wish I never asked.

Lisa leans her head back, then turns to look at me. "Girl, I don't even want to talk about that two-timing loser right now."

"I know. It's just that you haven't been yourself lately, and I'm worried about you."

Visible stress lines show under her eyes. The makeup she wears doesn't do a good job of covering them up.

"John's up to his same old tricks. He's not at work when he is supposed to be there and he's coming home late. He starts petty arguments with me just so he can leave the house. Oh, and let's not forget the hang up calls."

Her pain sounds familiar. Her small, delicate face mirrors the same misery I had not so long ago with Mikhail.

I ask, "How do you know that he is cheating on you this time?"

"I know, Candy. I just know... don't ask me how I know. A wife knows when something is amiss."

"Maybe he's under a lot of pressure. Didn't you tell me he just signed some big contract with the company Mona works for?"

"Girl please, John's not under any pressure at work. How do you explain the hang up calls and all the other things that doesn't make sense? Take this for example: John has a gym membership he purchased over a year ago." She sips from her glass and continues.

"He has been to the gym say maybe once or twice since he signed up for the darn thing. The other morning I caught him sneaking out of the house at dawn. When I asked where he was going, he had the nerve to say the gym, looking guiltier than a burglar caught stealing. I know my husband, Candy, and I know when he is up to no good. John's not going to the gym."

"Do you think maybe you're reading too much into it? You have accused John of cheating many times over. Have you ever caught him red-handed? Do you think maybe you're overreacting a little?"

She glares at me. "What is it with you people always telling me that I'm overreacting?"

Her raised voice turns the heads of the other patrons at the bar. Lisa notices and continues softly. "No, I have never caught him. That is the problem. I am always accusing him, but never have anything to back up my accusations. This time, I will. I hired one of the PI's from my firm to follow him around. If John so much as takes a leak, I'm going to know about it."

Why go through all that trouble? I know better than to say that to her. When Lisa makes up her mind about something, it is hard to talk her out of it. I listen to her ramble about her plans to hire a PI. If I thought she might be losing her mind before, I'm convinced now. Throwing away her money on some private investigator is crazy to me. Where I'm from borrowing a friend's car to drive around town to check out every hotel, motel, and restaurant parking lot from here to Tahiti is how we do our investigation. I guess you can afford to do stupid things when money is no object.

"This guy is very reliable. We use him when we want to get information on people we cannot get ourselves. We used him in a lot of our high-profile cases, and he's very discreet."

She shocks me and I don't hide my emotions well. I say, "Woman why are you talking out the side of your head? When do you plan to do this? You're really having him followed? Don't you think that's a little extreme?"

"No, I have the perfect time set up. John has a business meeting in Florida every month. I want to know why he is making these frequent visits down there, and I want to know the real reason. Candy, he better not be cheating on me, because if he is I am going to leave him — and drain him for everything he's got."

"The money. Is that what this is all about?"

"No, it's not about the money." Lisa snaps. Then her voice softens when she says, "Candy, of all people you should know me better than that. John loves his money and taking his money is the only way to get back at him. I don't need John's money even though I've earned it. I want my marriage back. I want the man I married to show up and tell me I've been having a nightmare."

"Lisa, come to church with me on Sunday. I don't think you should go about things this way. John will come after you if you take his money. Your life is worth more than money. I say let him keep it and move on with your life. You are young. You have your whole life ahead of you. Look at yourself. Do you have any idea how beautiful you are? God can deliver you from this. It grieves His heart to see you suffer like this."

Lisa narrows her eyes at me. "The same God you serve doesn't believe in divorce."

"Well, I think He understands when there is infidelity," I say and my voice hardens, "And physical violence."

Lisa immediately looks embarrassed. "The incident between John and me was an accident. I may have overreacted when I told you he hit me. He didn't mean to hit me."

Here we go. I am getting tired of hearing the excuses she makes for him.

I try to remain patient. I say, "Yes, you are right. God doesn't believe in divorce except in the case of sexual immorality, abuse, etc. Don't put yourself in any danger."

"I told you it was an accident."

"Is that what he told you? What is he going to tell you the next time it happens? You should leave him if he makes you so unhappy."

I've cornered her with my questions. Lisa shifts uncomfortably in her chair and sips on her watered down drink.

Staring straight ahead she says, "It's not that easy."

I challenge her. "Why? What's stopping you? You've been singing the blues to me about John for years. What stops you from walking out the door?"

Lisa's expression changes and she becomes defensive. "You think everything is black and white don't you? I am not running away just because things get hard, Candy. I am a fighter. It's in my blood. I want to fight for my marriage."

This is where I should be giving her advice about anything worth having is worth fighting for. John is not worth the hassle. Saving face is not worth the hassle. She has made John out to be her god and the more she worships him, the more he disrespects her.

"Do you know what you're fighting for? I think you're staying in this marriage for the wrong reasons."

She speaks with her hand. "Look, Candy, you don't understand."

"Well make me understand." I hate when she complains about her circumstances, but does nothing to correct the problem. "What's there to understand, Lisa? I've heard your case. John treats you badly and makes you unhappy. End of story."

"Things are complicated between us. I can't leave without giving my marriage one last try," Lisa insists. She crosses and uncrosses her legs, then she reverts to just folding her arms.

"I know you want your marriage to work, Lisa. Really, I do. Did John put his hands on you again?"

Lisa throws me an evil look. "Don't make me say something to you I'll regret. Why would you ask me that when I just told you the first time was an accident? No, he did not hit me. There... you satisfied?"

I let out a long sigh. It's hard to talk to a passive aggressive and I'm no Dr. Phil. Lisa doesn't need help. What she needs is someone to listen to her complaints. And I don't have all night for this back-and-forth husband-wife drama. God knows I want to help her, but I can only help those who are willing to accept help.

"I am not here to fight with you, Lisa. Remember I am on your side. I'm only trying to help."

"You're not helping. This is why I never tell you anything. You always assume things. I'm sorry I told you about the incident."

"Virgin daiquiri, can I get you anything else?" asks the bartender.

He has perfect timing. He frees me from having to go down this jagged road with Lisa, where we agree to disagree. After tonight, I'm washing my hands of this mess.

"Thank you," I reply staring at the gigantic glass holding my daiquiri. This should hold me all night.

"You have any nuts?" I ask, and I swear he has a glimpse of humor in his eyes, but it goes away so quickly I can't be sure of what I see.

"Yes, want me to get some for you?" he laughs.

"What's so funny?" I ask, uncertain of the joke.

"Nothing, ma'am. I'll go get your nuts."

"Is it because I said 'nuts'?" I ask and lick some whipped cream from the top of my daiquiri before taking a sip. I take another lick of my whipped cream.

He mumbles under his breath.

"Huh, what did you say?" I ask, looking up.

"How is your drink?"

Belatedly, I register what he mumbled seconds earlier: "What I wouldn't do to be that drink right now." Once the meaning behind his words catches up to me, I blush from my head right down to my Prada shoes. He is flirting with me and has been since he brought my drink out.

"It's good. I was thirsty."

He clears his throat. "I can only imagine."

I play innocent. "What do you mean?"

"You have no idea what you do to men? Or do you?"

"I have no idea of what you're talking about," I say sweetly.

"Right, go ahead and play innocent," he says with a twinkle in his eye. "You're not fooling me."

The sudden movement of his hand draws my attention to his watch. He's sporting a handmade watch worth five times what a bartender is paid.

That's odd.

Breguets aren't ordinary watches. The price tags on them are ridiculous and in most cases, the watches are custom made to the owner's specifications. I've been around enough wealthy men and their need for individuality to recognize tailor-made items. The engraved NL on his watch confirms it and there's no way a bartender's salary can afford him such luxury. Unless this is just a cover up job for what he does on the side. You hear about people living double lives on the news everyday.

"Is that a Breguet?"

He glances down at his wrist, and I can tell he is surprised I know what Breguet is. "Yes."

"Bartending must be a pretty lucrative business these days," I hint in a lighthearted tone.

He chuckles. "No, it's been slow this season."

Is that a joke? "Slow? Oh, I see."

His smile disappears, and a frown takes its place. "I am not into drugs, if that's what you are thinking."

Curiosity gets the best of me. "If you're not into drugs, then what are you into?"

"You ask a lot of questions. Who do you work for, the FBI?"

Ouch! That stings!

"Well how else am I going to get to know you? Before I form an opinion of you by assuming things, I wanted to give you an opportunity to fill in the blanks. Instead, you're being evasive," I respond as I run my hands across the counter.

"So you want to get to know me?" he asks.

"Yes, you seem interesting enough," I say. "Is that a crime?"

"No, I've always thought I was a pretty interesting fellow," he mocks.

I shoot him a reproving glare.

He leans in closer to me and says. "I'm only humoring you. I do a few things on the side here and there."

"Care to share?" I ask as I toy with the bottom of my glass and wait for a response that never comes. I look around the room and catch a group of brothers watching me with disapproving glares. I can only imagine what that's about.

I hear a sigh coming from Lisa's direction, but I don't pay any attention.

"Your glass is empty," he says. "Let me get you another daiquiri."

"Good save," I say with a knowing nod. "You must have something to hide."

"Your glass is empty and you look a little thirsty," he teases. "I'm a bartender. I'm supposed to notice these things. I'll be back."

"Uh-huh. You're leaving because you're avoiding the question."

His rich laughter fills our space. "Hold that thought."

He winks. "The name is Nick, by the way."

I smile slightly. "I'm Candy."

That sparkle I think I saw earlier returns. "Candy, huh?"

"Hey buddy, can I get another Mojito?" A guy on the other side of the bar yells. He's nice looking, short, brown skinned, and wears a tight fade. He winks at me. I smile and cast my eyes down to the counter.

"Sure thing, man." Nick assures the guy and hurries off.

Nick is as charming as he is creative. While making drinks he entertains us with his bartending tricks. His little bar antics attract the attentions of others, earning him applause. He eats it up. The ultimate crowd pleaser, he prolongs the show by flipping and tossing any and everything in his sight.

Lisa mumbles something, but I can't hear what she says over the cheers the crowd is sending Nick's way. I whisper to her, "Isn't he cute?" then turn back to see him toss a glass in the air and catch it behind his back.

Attraction to a white man is a first for me. Goodness! Forget about crossing the fence. Jumping over it is more like it. On Sunday pastor told us that God is doing a new thing and that we should get ready for it. Could this be what he meant?

"This one's on me, pretty lady."

"You look good out there. Where did you learn to do those tricks?" I ask.

"I picked them up here and there."

I have a desire to run my hand along his jawline. Hold his face in my hands and press my lips against his.

He asks, stealing me from my daze. "Are you sticking around for a while?"

"Yes."

"OK, then. Let me know if you need anything."

"Hey Nicky, come over here for a minute," a women in a red tight fitting dress purrs. She leans forward, exposing her cleavage.

He barely turns his head in her direction. "Be there in a minute, Nancy." He stops to usher one of the bartenders to her aid. "Tony, can you take care of them for me?"

"Nicky come on, we want you to make us a drink. No one can make them like you. Tony you're good, but we'll pass." She puts her hand in the air, stopping Tony in mid-stride. "Nicky I'm waiting," she sings.

The blonde-haired woman with the bodacious boobs stands on the barstool and yells his name again. This time he ignores her. She pouts, stares blue daggers at me then sits down. She whispers something to her friend and they both snicker. I laugh at their silly attempt to make me feel inferior. I throw them a look that lets them know I'm over that stage of immaturity and that they're not even in my league.

I can't resist the urge to mock his friends. "Nicky, come over here. Oh my gosh, my boobs. I'm falling over. Help me, help me Nicky."

He belts out a knee-slapping laugh and I join him. We both laugh until tears come to our eyes. Lisa shoots us odd looks and so do his friends. The appalled looks on their faces makes me laugh even harder.

"I've got to watch out for you woman. You're trouble, no more virgin daiquiris for you," he warns in a playful tone.

"Me trouble? No, I'm a good girl."

He doesn't buy it and tells me so indirectly when he places

two fingers under my chin and whispers in the softest voice yet, "I bet you are. I wonder what makes you tick?"

"Would you like to find out?" I smile warmly.

"I most definitely will." He says it with such assurance I believe it myself. "Well, I should let you get back to your company. Let me know if you ladies need anything else."

"Nice talking to you." I offer halfhearted. "Duty calls."

"Likewise, don't leave without saying goodbye," he says, pointedly.

"Is that your way of telling me you want to see more of me?"

His eyes dance with mischief. "Absolutely, sweetheart."

***

Lisa

Candy was always popular with men and tonight her show-stealing ways are in fine form. What is it about her that makes men lose their heads?

Apart from being a little more outgoing, she has nothing in the beauty department I lack. I have given her every hint to remind her that I didn't come out tonight to watch her hold a conversation with bartenders. Nicky whoever he is, needs to go back to tending the bar and stop running his mouth. I really have been trying not to watch them, or listen to their conversation as it floats over my head, but this has gone on for far too long.

Candy can run her mouth too, so I'm sure this conversation between them could've lasted all night. I'm glad to hear him tell her he's leaving.

She stops him. "Is it Nick or Nicky?"

"Nick," he corrects. "I hate Nicky." His mood darkens for a split second at the mention of his nickname.

"It didn't seem like you minded when your fans across the room called you Nicky," Candy says in a flirtatious tone.

Ugh. I thought this conversation was over. Yet, here Candy is, dragging it out. I invited her here to spend time with me, not some guy with two names.

The bartender takes her hand in his, letting it linger there before releasing it. Then he asks. "So, your name is Candy? Like Candy that melts in my mouth and not in my hand?"

"In your mouth mostly, sometimes in your hand," she replies, provocatively.

Humph! And she says she's a Christian. Please... the truth comes out.

"Is that right?" he asks with a broad smile.

"Jolly Ranchers have nothing on me." Candy says.

Her commentary brings a smile to my face and his too. I have to hand it to her; she is good at working her jelly. The poor saps fall for it every time. This Nick guy will be another collection to add to Candy's little black book. They will go out on a few dates. He will sleep with her and eventually find out that she is crazy, and then he will get tired of her crap and move on to the next person.

Candy has had a bad attitude toward men since college. She has no respect for them and talks to them however she pleases. I don't know of any men on this planet who would be willing to deal with her foolishness. I've known Candy for almost a decade now and I can't count any relationships of hers lasting past a year.

"Well Candy, again it was nice talking to you," Nick waves. "You ladies stick around."

"Same here Nick, it was nice talking to you, too," Candy says, and I see the hint of another flirtatious smirk on her lips. "I'll try to stick around. I won't make any promises."

"Let me know if you both need anything," Nick offers, finally including me in his glance. "I would love to sit here and chat with you, but I've got to go over here and serve these folks before they get out of hand."

"That is one fine looking man," Candy gloats as Nick goes to talk with other patrons.

"Wipe the drool off your mouth," I say dryly. "He is not all that, and it's about time he left."

"Why are you being rude?" Candy asks between gritted teeth. "Nick was a nice guy."

"To each his own, if that's what you're into," I say with a dismissive wave of my hand. I roll my eyes in Nick's direction.

Candy turns up her nose. "You know what? You're in

a funky mood tonight so I'm going to forgive your bad behavior."

"Gee, thanks," I retort sarcastically.

She bumps me playfully. "What happened to my nice, considerate friend?"

I smile reluctantly. "You know, you're wrong for leaving me to entertain myself, while you get your flirt on, right?"

"I didn't leave you. You could've chipped in at any time." Candy untwists the cap from her lip-gloss tube, spreads an ample amount on her lips then smoothes them together. "Want some?" she asks, handing it off to me. I shake my head in response and she recaps it and sticks it back into her purse.

"Now how would that look? I couldn't just jump into your conversation."

"Why you run the guy off who came up to ask you for a dance?" Candy asks, smiling in my face.

"Did you see what that guy looks like? His teeth were huge. I'm still trying to figure out how he shuts his mouth. Looks like a dang donkey."

"Lisa, you need to stop," Candy says with a laugh. "He probably was a nice guy."

"If you think he is nice then you go and find him. You're the single one."

Candy laughs, and I join in reluctantly. Laughing hurts nowadays, because I don't have much to laugh about. I delight in being John's wife, and now things are falling apart.

"Now what I can't get over is your crazy behind hiring a P.I. to follow your husband around," Candy says in a whisper. "I think you are crazy for wasting your money this way. Honey, I'll do it for you for a fraction of whatever it is you're paying this detective fellow."

I suck my teeth. "There you go. What do you know about being a private investigator?"

"How hard can detective work be?" Candy waves her hand in the same dismissive fashion I did when I was talking about Nick a moment ago. "Taking pictures and following people around looks pretty darn easy to me. You know how snoopy I am. I'm perfect for the job."

Appalled at the mockery she is making of my situation,

anger boils deep inside of me. I take in deep breaths of air to dissolve my anger. Don't go off on her, I say to myself. She's never been in a real relationship in her life, and that's just her ignorance talking. Composed and sure of myself, I put her in her place.

"Candy if you're not going to take this seriously, I don't want to have this conversation anymore," I say in a no nonsense tone. "You have never been here before, never had a liar for a husband or a cheater for that matter. Listen, if marriage was easy, everybody would be signing up in line to get married."

"No need for you to get mad," Candy says, holding up her hand to stop my words. "I am only making light of your situation because you are not giving me the impression to do otherwise. Everything you have said within the last hour has been contradictory. You want to leave John, but not really. You want to work things out. Make up your mind, and then maybe I will take you seriously."

Throwing my hands in the air, I confront her. "So now you don't think I know what I want?"

I want our conversation to end. Her truth about me being contradictory rings in my ears, and drags me down. I want to leave John, but I'm scared, scared of what people might say or won't say. I'm scared of making a mistake — what if I act too hastily and our marriage can be saved? What if I'm wrong in suspecting he is cheating?

Our marriage is supposed to last, not end up on the divorce casualty list. No one in my family has ever had a divorce. Getting married is a serious commitment in our family and once you get married, you're in it till death do you part.

"I'm not sure you understand the magnitude of what you're about to do," Candy cautions me.

"You think hiring a private investigator is going to be the answer, and it's not. We always say we want to know what the men in our lives are up to, but when we get the information we wish we would've left well enough alone. Once you open Pandora's box, you cannot close it. Some things are not visible to the naked eye, but when our gut feeling tells us, something is wrong we need to draw from that and make the right decisions based on those gut feelings."

Big lumps form in my throat and overdue tears sting the back of my eyes. I swallow hard to fight back the emotion. I refuse to make a spectacle of myself in front of all these strangers.

"Candy, I am tired of John mistreating me. I don't want to feel like his doormat anymore." All the anger I've held inside spins out of control like a runaway car ready to crash. "I deserve better, I do... but Candy, John has a hold on me and I can't let it go. I just can't, not without knowing."

Candy reaches for my hand, holds it in hers, and squeezes it reassuringly. The small gesture brings the suppressed tears to my eyes. John doesn't deserve any more tears shed over him tonight. I'm here to have a good time and a good time I'm going to have.

"Sweetie, I'm really sorry you have to go through this and if this is what you really want then I'm all for it. We will get through it together. I love you, girl," Candy's voice is soft.

A single teardrop trickles down my flushed cheeks.

"Thank you, Candy, I needed that. You are always here for me, and I appreciate you." I wipe the tear off my cheek and muster a shaky smile. "No offense, but I can't talk about John anymore. I want to forget about him and our problems if only for tonight, OK?"

I dab the rest of the tears from the corner of my eyes.

I sniffle away the last of the emotion as Candy nods in agreement. "OK, so what else have you been up to?"

"I really haven't been up to much, work been keeping me busy. What about you, what have you been doing? How is Mikhail? I haven't heard you say anything about him."

Candy's disposition changes with the mention of Mikhail. "Pretty much the same things you've been doing. Working... and um Mikhail. He's a... we're a... we're OK," she responds, tripping over her words.

I say, "Mmm."

She stares into her drink to avoid eye contact with me.

When she doesn't respond, I persist. "Just OK?"

"Yep, we're OK. Can I get one for next topic please?"

I paint a picture in my head of what I believe happened to Mikhail. If I can recall, they've only been dating for a year, if that. The scowl on Candy's face can't be a good sign.

I ask, "How's Ms. Norma?"

"She's doing fine. She got herself a new boyfriend. Correction. Fiancé, a young one at that." Her laugh is chirpy. It is the kind of laughter that shows approval.

"Get out! Really? Your mom's getting married?" I laugh, hardly containing myself. "Ms. Norma is getting her groove back, huh? I'm sensing that you're OK with this."

"Yeah, I'm OK with it. My mom is still fine, no point in her letting all that fineness go to waste."

"Where did they meet?"

"She met him at church. Mom's dreams are coming true. She makes me feel like I'm not even trying." I hear a touch of wistfulness in Candy's voice.

"Girl you are a nut. When is the wedding?"

"The end of January, they're trying to hurry up and get it over with. You know what that's about right?"

"Stella wants to get her swerve on," I say and we bubble over with laughter, not caring about the people watching us. "At least your mom has a life. Mine is still trying to live vicariously through mine."

I freeze mid-sentence. I don't know why I never thought of this. "Hey you know what we need to do? We need to get your mom and my mom to go out the way they used to before my dad passed away. Since Dad died she has been bugging the daylights out of me. I think she misses him and she is lonely, but she's driving me insane."

I recall a talk I had with my mom a few weeks back. My mom became extremely angry over my suggestion that she take up a hobby. Told me in all her fifty years of living she never had to take up a hobby other than bingo and she wasn't going to start now.

"She doesn't go anywhere?" Candy asked.

"Girl no, you know my mom's old-fashioned," I say with a sigh. "She stays in the house all day and constantly calls me for nothing. I finally had to put a stop to it a few weeks back. I told her to get a life — though I didn't use those words. She needs something to do. As it is right now, Wednesday night bingo is an adventure for mom."

Candy rolls her eyes and jerks her head. "Bingo? It's no

wonder she's always calling you. Mom is gone half the time. The woman takes off whenever the mood suits her; sometimes I can't find her. She did mention calling your mother a couple of times, but never got any calls back."

I sigh again. "That's what I'm saying, your mom and my mom were good friends when Dad was alive, but Mom just withdrew into herself. I have had a few of her closest friends call me at home trying to track her down. Her health is failing, and the doctors keep finding things wrong with her on every visit. I think she gave up on living. I am worried. Losing my dad was hard on me, I can't bear to lose mom too."

"You're not going to lose your mom. Your dad passed away a couple of years ago, give her a little more time. Everyone grieves differently. Whereas you were able to move on faster, she may not."

When did Candy become such an old soul with such amazing grace? Her seeking out Christian counseling really did make some improvements. Perhaps she does have a new lease on life.

"When did you become so wise?" I marvel.

Candy looks at me and shrugs.

"The caterpillar turned into a butterfly. I should start charging for my counseling services."

"You're too much," I say and look at the clock on my cell phone. "What time did Mona say she was going to be here?"

"She said she was coming by after work," Candy says. "You know Mona, she probably lost track of time. You know that woman is never on time. Don't worry, she'll be here."

"May I have this dance?" The invitation comes from a man who is old enough to be my daddy. I should say no, but I want to dance.

"Sure. Watch my drink for me, Candy."

Placing my hands in his, he leads me to the small dance floor in front of the dinner tables. It's been eons since I've set foot on a dance floor. I almost forgot how to dance. Lucky for me this old timer is a good leader. He moves effortlessly, smooth like liquid flowing.

He grunts and looks down at his feet. "You've got to watch my feet now, baby."

"Oops!" I laugh apologetically. "I'm sorry."

He chuckles. "It's OK, I don't mind getting trampled on by you." Well he is fresh with the compliments. He is old, but not bad looking. He probably was a rolling stone back in his heyday. I love that he is good on the dance floor.

"I give dancing lessons here on Tuesdays. It's free. Won't you come down and see me for some lessons."

"Oh, OK." I smile politely at his invitation. Dancing makes me feel empowered and free-spirited. This might be a good change from my everyday routine.

"I'm serious now, come down and see me," he persists.

"I'll see when I can fit it in my schedule. Sounds like fun."

I think I am imagining things when his hands touch my butt the first time. Then it happens again, and there is no mistaking it, he squeezes me again. I raise his hands to waist level and he casually lets them fall right back into place on my booty. The song ends, and I quickly step out of his arms. I could've and would've danced the entire night away, but Mr. Saturday Night Fever has problems keeping his paws off my booty. I don't walk. I run instead, back to where Candy sits waiting for me.

"Why did you stop dancing?" she asks. "You look like you were having a good time out there."

"Girl I would've, but have you ever had an old wrinkled up hand squeeze on your booty before?" I ask with a disgusted shudder.

Tossing her head back, she laughs so hard it rocks her entire body. "Is that what he was doing? He didn't look that old to me."

I shoot her a tiresome look. "Girl yes, you know these dim lights in here don't do any justice. Old pervert, someone needs to put a leash on that thing. Then he had the nerve to get aroused."

She gags and laughs again. "You should've slapped him."

"No, that man is old enough to be my daddy," I shake my head.

Candy's eyes dart to the front entrance of the club. She is looking for Mona to show up, no doubt. I'm beginning to wonder if she is coming at all. Considering we are not on good terms, I won't be surprised if she doesn't show her face.

Mona and I have never gotten along, because of John. Her paws are always all over him and she is always in his face. When he gets around Mona, something about him changes and he turns into a big flirt. It's harmless flirting John continues to defend and I want to believe him, but part of me can't shake this feeling of familiarity he has with her.

Candy is right. I am barking up a tree, but I have to know. I cannot live like this anymore. As the days go by, I find myself dying a little inside. I've run out of options. We tried marriage counseling and that was a disaster. John thinks psychologists are a bunch of quacks and refuses to go back to see one. Since I had the miscarriage, he's been acting strange. He told me it was not a big deal if I could not have children, and I foolishly believed him.

When I watch him play with his sister's children — children I wish were ours — it bothers me. I hate feeling like less of a woman in his eyes and adopting a child is out of the question. I ruined any chances of that when I brought up the subject of adoption to his mother. The woman is plain mean and hateful. I let her in on my most vulnerable concerns and she betrayed my trust by running back to tell John. He was furious with me for telling his mother our business. We got into a huge argument and he flat out told me he is not raising anyone's children but his own.

"Candy, would you adopt children if you couldn't have any of your own?" I turn to my friend.

Candy wasn't expecting that question. She raises her eyebrows as she stares pensively at me. She takes her time before answering me.

"I would if I had no choice and honestly I would even if I could have some of my own. I love children. Why do you think I'm always babysitting other people's kids? Why do you ask?"

"That might be my only option," I reveal. Sadness makes my voice come out as barely a whisper.

"Are you thinking about adopting?" she asks.

"Yes I want to but —"

She completes my sentence. "John doesn't want to. Do you think he wants children, Lisa? He doesn't seem to be in any rush to have any." She doesn't pause long enough for me to respond, and continues in one breath. "Are you still on those fertility drugs? Are they working? What's the latest update from your doctor?"

"Yes, but..." I start to answer all her crazy questions and stop in the midst of my response. Filling my lungs with air, I hold my breath, and then let it out slowly. "Candy, I can't have children."

There. I said it. What a relief to get it off my chest. She can judge me if she wants. I wait for her reaction. She is second to my doctor to know this deep, dark secret I've been carrying around.

"Does John know?"

Her response isn't quite what I expected. "No, he doesn't. I'm sure he has some idea, but I don't know how to come out and tell him. I wanted to tell him last night before we got into that big blowout. How could God do this to me? Why did He make me half of a woman? Candy, I can't tell my mother. I'm not ready to hear the criticisms."

"You are wonderfully made in the eyes of God, and He loves you," Candy says, touching my hand. "We may not understand why He does the things He do, but He doesn't make mistakes. What makes you think your mother is going to criticize you? She might be the best person to tell. Get her opinion on things. Our parents are wiser about these things than we give them credit." She stops in the middle of her speech. "I have been meaning to tell you something. I wasn't going to tell you, because I know your feelings are easily hurt." She stares out to the dance floor. People sway back and forth wrapped in each other's arms. The lights are dimmer and the floor is full to its capacity.

John enters my mind. I yearn for his touch. We used to have so much fun. I miss those times.

"Are you and your mother's family on good terms?" Candy asks, reclaiming my attention.

Clueless as to where this is going. I ask, "Why?"

"I ran into your cousin Angela at the gas station on Sunday and on my way out she stopped to ask me if you have AIDS."

"What? That no-good, trifling, hateful track-wearing-can't-keep-her-mind-on-her-own-business cow." I call Angela every name in the book except for the child of God. "I can't believe she would ask you such a thing. I lose a few pounds and now everybody thinks I have AIDS. I'm her cousin. She should've come to me."

"That's what I said. I told her no you didn't have AIDS. She was asking me all sorts of questions about you. She wanted to know why you lost so much weight and if I noticed how much weight you've lost. She wanted to know if you and John are having problems and all sorts of things. She went on and on until finally I told her to talk to you about her concerns, then she did a complete three sixty. The topic jumped from her concerns about you to some other woman in the store. Your cousin is messy."

"You think I'm too skinny? Tell the truth." Self-conscious-ly I jump to my feet. I'm five foot eight, but when I wear heels, I'm six feet tall.

"Yes, you've lost entirely too much weight, but I'm not con-cerned about that, Lisa," Candy says. "I liked the old you, the one who did not take bull from anyone, the one who took better care of herself. The one that did not let men beat her down. What happened to that woman?"

"I don't know." My voice is low and sad.

I don't take criticism well and hearing Candy say these things does nothing for my self-esteem. The truth hurts, and I know I need to hear it. I have become spineless, allowing a man to walk all over me. I prided myself on being a strong black woman and I am ashamed of who I've become. I strug-gle daily to get back that power, but life's pounding makes it seem unattainable.

I look down at my hands and say nothing.

CHAPTER SEVEN

Candy

Mona is not an overly attractive woman as far as I am concerned, but she has a certain aura about her that breathes sensuality. Her figure is all right, though it was better when she was in college. When she walks into a room, she commands attention. People have a hard time keeping their eyes off her. I guess it must be the long, black hair or those intense green eyes or maybe the honey-colored skin.

"Hey ya'll," Mona greets me with a hug and a kiss on the cheek, looking jazzy in a Dolce & Gabbana number. The shoes adorning her feet are Manolo Blahniks and matching her ensemble is a Dior tote bag. I have to hand it to her; from head to toe the girl looks fabulous.

"I was about to send a search party out to find you," I tease. Mona knows nothing about being on time, and I would have feared the worse if she had actually showed up on time tonight. "What took you so long?"

"We had a fashion show today that went over schedule," she says. "Then I had to rush home and change. I have been running around all day; my feet are killing me."

I look down at her heels. "I can see why."

She giggles. "You know I don't have one comfortable pair of shoes in my closet. Isn't that crazy?"

I laugh and nod. "You're a makeup artist; you need to invest in at least one pair."

She whines. "I know. I hate flats, though."

"You look nice," I say. "You also broke some necks coming up in here dressed like that. I hope these women brought handcuffs to put on their men."

"Girl, please," Mona flicks her hair over her shoulder. "I already checked out the competition as well as the tired looking men in here way before my Blahniks touched the stairway. Ain't nobody in here worth my time, and you know my time don't come with a budget."

Mona turns her attention to Lisa. "Hey Lisa, you cut your hair! Girl, I like it."

Lisa barely acknowledges her. "Mona, glad you could make it, as always I see you had to make a grand entrance."

Lisa's tone drips with sarcasm, her remark unnecessary and uncalled for. She is forever stirring up mess. Holding my breath and bracing on the back of a chair, I wait for Mona's response.

"I try," Mona, responds calmly. Her grip on her tote strap tightens, turning her knuckles white.

These two are at war over John. Lisa's jealousy of Mona and John's friendship is getting out of hand. The two women cannot be in the same room without being at each other's throat. Mona looks at her nails demurely. "You still tripping over the John and me nonsense you made up in your head."

Lisa's head whips around. "Mona I'm not tripping over you and John. The only thing I said to you was I am a little uncomfortable with the two of you being so close. I'm not tripping. You would be pissed off too if your husband spends more time in his female companion's company than he does in yours. You would be..."

Mona cut Lisa short. "Lisa, I wouldn't have those problems. I keep my men coming back for more. I serve them well, that way they never have to go out looking for it elsewhere."

Ouch! How is that last statement going to make things any better? From where I stand, a storm brews. Lisa stares Mona down with hateful eyes, while Mona looks at her cool, calm and at ease.

"So what you're saying is I don't know how to keep my husband happy at home and in bed?" Lisa's hands clench and unclench around her glass.

I mumble under my breath. "What you both really need to do is quit it with this high school mess."

"Look Lisa, we are tripping over some nonsense. There is nothing going on between John and me." Mona's reply stuns me. I have never seen her back down from anything.

"Well how do you explain the unanswered phone calls when he's with you?"

"What do I have to do with your husband picking up

his phone? Last I remember he's a grown man, I can't tell him to pick up his phone." Mona gets mad all over again, her voice loud and carries to the tables surrounding to us. People stare at us with their noses turned up.

"You two need to cut this foolishness out and keep your voices down!" I snap. "I didn't come out tonight to listen to you air your dirty laundry in public."

Mona tries to clear the air. "Look Lisa, I am not a bad person and I am not trying to steal your husband."

The tension is thick in our circle. Inviting Mona along was a bad idea. When I extended the invitation, I secretly hoped she'd decline. I should have known Lisa and she were going to bump heads before the night ended.

"Can I get a purple martini?" Mona asks the bartender, coming to rest her hand around my shoulder. "You mad? Sorry, I'm being a witch huh?"

I ignore her.

She begins to sing her apology. I'm so-rry, soooo so-rry." It's terrible. She hits a high note and I poke her in the ribs playfully. Mona is as irresistible as she is goofy. I can't stay mad at her for long. We've been friends for way too long.

"OK, OK. I am not mad anymore. Please don't sing. You can't carry a tune to save your life. You sound like a strangled cat," I beg.

Lisa pitches in. "And add another chocolate, apple, dirty martini to the tab."

Pulling Mona closer to me, I say, "Girl, look at him. Is he F.I.N.E or what?"

"Too late I've already scoped him out. Check out his butt."

"Close your mouth woman, you about to drip mouth water all over these folks' countertop and me."

We giggle like lovesick teenage girls.

A tray of glasses falls to the floor and the loud crashing noise, draws everyone's attention. "Everyone, sorry about that," Nick apologizes as he stoops down to scoop up the mess. Taut muscles ripple down his back, pressing against his shirt. The rugged blue jeans he wears hug his well-defined butt.

"Now that's what you call a tight end and he can tackle

me anytime. If he keeps up those moves I might have to take him home tonight."

Mona rolls her eyes in disbelief. "Yes miss holier-than-thou, as if that's gonna happen."

"Hey, I still got it," I protest.

"Mmm, sure you're right."

I'm not fooling anyone but me. I can't even remember what a naked man looks like. I probably wouldn't know what to do with one; it's been so long. Well not really but several months without having sex on the regular is like telling a fat kid he can't have any more sweets. Every time I come across a magazine, a TV commercial, or newsletter with a fine brother my body screams "deprived!"

"Do you think he has a big one?" Mona asks.

"Do I think who has a big one of what? I don't understand. I got on the short bus this morning, and I'm still trying to get off."

She elaborates further, "Candy, come on, you know what I'm trying to say... Have a big you know... ahhhh... You have become dense... Growing up I've always heard white men weren't packing."

Mona tires me, really she does. "That's the most ignorant thing I've ever heard you say. Girl it doesn't make a difference whether the man is black or white. I know plenty of black men who aren't packing as you so eloquently put it. Dated one who's Johnson was about as big as my pinky, but he was good at other things, if you catch my drift."

"Listen to you, you nasty." She shivers and wraps her arms around her bare shoulders. "It's cold in here. Are you cold?"

"Wear clothes and you wouldn't be cold," I say. "I miss being touched by a man."

From the corner of my eyes, I catch a glimpse of Lisa holding her own pity party to the side of us. She has grown quiet since Mona showed up. She plays with the straw in her almost empty chocolate apple martini and watches the jazz band recreate the 80's with their acoustic rendition of "Caught up in the Rapture."

"Hate to break it to you girlfriend, but you gave up that lifestyle. I guess I'll be the one going home with lover boy. I ain't never had no cream in my coffee before. Everybody trying it nowadays, maybe they know something I don't," says Mona, reclaiming my attention.

"Mona, you know good and well you're not having any cream in your coffee. The closest you have ever come to getting any cream in your coffee is from DiMaggio aka Mr. Maintenance man. And trust me, honey he's not white, he's high yellow."

She laughs. "Sho right, he was good, too. Did I tell you I had to cut him off? He was getting too greedy. Demanding too much of my time."

She cracks me up with her silliness. "What happened?"

Mona shrugs and reaches over to take the cherry from my almost empty drink. "Nothing major." She licks her fingers. "It's just that he was requiring a little more of my time than I was willing to give. I told him about it and he copped an attitude. I know my milkshake is good but the man was trying to box it all up for himself."

I laugh deliriously. "What do you expect the man to do? If you think about it, you're being selfish. He was good to you. The man bought you all that expensive jewelry you're sporting right now." I motion toward the 24-karat diamond earrings sparkling in her ears. Mona touches them self-consciously and smiles. "What? You didn't think he was going to want more from you? He's a man. There is always a hidden agenda. You can't always believe everything they tell you."

"I didn't ask him to buy these for me. He did this on his own.... Besides, I'm worth every penny he spent at the jewelry store. I'm not saying there is a price on me, but I'm nobody's fool."

"Well there's a price tag on me," I retort. "It's called marriage."

Mona frowns every time I mention marriage to her.

She says, "I'm not ready for all that marriage business, too much work. I don't see how anybody sleeps with the same man day in and day out."

"You can if you set your mind to it," I say. "God didn't put us here to run from one man to the next. You need to pick up your Bible and read about all the women before us. We are not a commodity."

Her frown deepens even more. "I'm not made for marriage. I think I'll take my chances with being single. Don't act like you weren't where I am."

"Oh I haven't forgotten. Been there, done that. I understand where you're coming from. Believe me, being celibate isn't easy. It's a struggle for me everyday, but I know who lives inside of me. I know which master I serve. This is why there is no one better than me to tell you what you're doing is wrong."

"Church never did anything for me," Mona says and shrugs. "Those people in church are worse than the folks out here."

"It's not about church, it's about fellowshipping with God... You know spending time in his word. 'For the word of God is quick and powerful, and sharper than any two-edged sword,'" I quote Hebrews 4:12. "Pick up your Bible. Get in the word. You'll be amazed at what God can deliver you from."

"You're not going to leave me alone with this God stuff until you convert me, are you?" she asks, and I can't tell if she is annoyed or resigned.

"I can't convert you," I say. "Only God can do that if you let Him. He loves you. He made you for his purpose, fashioned you into His image to do great things in His name and for His kingdom."

"I'll believe that when I see it." Mona's tone lets me know she is not convinced.

"Ask God to..." my voice trails as Nick walks by us and lust stirs up inside me.

The devil wants me to stumble and fall. He knows what to use to get me sidetracked. This is my weak area; this is the area I need God the most. Temptation is all around me. This is how the devil keeps me in bondage. Nick turns and smiles and I quiver inside. I press my legs together, and wish the longings away. This is my cross, my daily fight, the temptation of sexual desires.

"This man is really tempting. If I wasn't trying to live right and wait on a good man, I'd be all over him like white on rice," I confess to Mona. "Do you know how hard it is to see fine looking men like this and turn away? Mona, God is good. He has been better than good to me."

"You can borrow Mr. Lollipop if you get desperate," Mona jokes.

"Child please, nobody wants Mr. Lollipop. There's no telling how many times that thing has been around your block."

She purses her lips and snaps her fingers. "Too many to count, but at least I gets it on the regular. You won't ever hear me complaining. It's disease free, it answers to only me, and I can find it at night. You don't know what you're missing. Mr. Lollipop could be the best friend you never had."

"Yeah, I know your bus has been around the block more times than we can count on both of our fingers and toes," I say. "You're lucky the wheels haven't fallen off yet. I hope you have a warranty for the worn out parts."

"At least I'm having fun and getting some," Mona's tone is flippant. "I was made for sex and that's what I intend to have every time I can. Your prince charming — wherever he is — is going to have a hard time finding your buried treasure behind all the cobwebs."

"You need to slow your roll, honey. These men out here only want one thing and that's the thing between your legs. You give it away so freely. No one wants to buy the whole cow if the milk is free. You need to wise up. We're making it too easy for these men not to commit, and I'd rather have cobwebs than some unknown STD, or an unplanned pregnancy, resulting in trifling baby daddy drama."

Mona rolls her eyes and brushes me off. I watch sadly as my words fall on deaf ears. Mona always does what she wants anyway even when she sees the logic in what she's doing is wrong. It's one of the reasons we have always gotten along better with each other than we do with Lisa. We used to be one and the same.

It wasn't too long ago when Mona and I were running the streets that we created a motto. To do what we wanted, whenever we wanted, and with whomever, life's too short we'd say. We were going to enjoy the ride and get what we wanted from it now and worry about the consequences later.

Life was like a chess game for me. Making the next move

was all I lived for. That was until I woke up one morning and found a broken condom on my bedroom floor. It was a wake-up call. A face-to-face encounter with God about the wretched way I was living. It was an atypical day for me, and I spent countless hours at the doctor's office. The people around me treated me no better than a lab rat, poking and prodding me. The worst part of the experience was waiting for the lab results to come back. I was anxious for several days. I begged and pleaded with God to make everything turn out all right. I bargained. I promised I'd make changes, that I'd never put myself in that position again. When the test result came back clean, I knew I had avoided something dire only by the grace of God.

I should've learned then, but I didn't. I forgot my promises to God.

When I met Mikhail, I was at a pivotal time in my life. I thought he was God sent. I found out later how wrong I was when things turned sour between us. When he broke up with me, I was devastated and like a crack feign I relapsed into my old habits of promiscuity. I was out of control like a wild fire spreading throughout a dry forest igniting with everything in sight. Mona, bless her heart, was the one who stopped me from going completely over the edge. She helped talk some sense into me; helped me see I couldn't waste any more time chasing men who takes advantage of me. .

Now it is my turn to save her from herself. I don't know how I'm going to accomplish the impossible, but I know my God to be an overcomer. I will continue to edify her and feed her spirit with his words and he will do the rest.

"Chocolate, apple, dirty martini, sex on the beach, and a virgin daiquiri for the ladies, Do you want to put this on the same tab?"

"Nope, put it on this card." I hand Nick my American Express. He takes it over to the register, flips it over, scribbles something on a piece of paper then places it by the register. Nick is so intoxicating. He reminds me of Sunday mornings with the ease in which he moves, unhurried yet powerful.

"So what are you ladies' plans for the night?" He asks as he puts away liquor in a shelf above his head.

I tell him, "We're going to hang around here for a bit. And

then I don't know... head home I guess."

He chuckles. "You don't sound like you want to be here."

"You're probably right. I could find better things to do with my time."

"Like what?" He wants to know.

I smile into his smoky blue eyes. "Like getting some last minute work done. Catching up on some sleep... I don't know. You've put me in the spotlight, and now I can't think of anything in particular."

I lick my lips and his eyes dart to my mouth, linger there and then back up to my eyes. The desires I see in his echo mine. Goose bumps run up my arms, then down my legs and we become speechless as we stare at each other, undressing our souls.

"Nick, what do you want me to do with this crate?" One of the bartenders asks, interrupting our silent bonding session.

He makes a disgruntled sound. "I'll be back." He excuses himself.

On the sly, I check out the tautness of his rear, the strength in his thighs. I don't think the man has any idea what he does to a woman. I wonder what it would be like to wrap my legs around Nick, have his flesh caress my flesh, and be embraced in those strong, muscular arms. Brakes! Wow, now see I shouldn't even go there.

"Aww, this is so cute. Candy is lusting for the white man," Mona teases.

I swat her on the hips. "Shut your face. I'm not lusting for anybody."

"Yes you are. Look at your face. You're all blushing and stuff." She blinks and our conversation takes on another route. "Oh girls don't look now, but there are some fine looking men on the other side of the room checking us out. I think we should go over and introduce ourselves."

The men sitting at the other end of the bar are very attractive, but not my type. Too much on the metro-sexual side for me which means one thing. High Maintenance.

Men like that don't appeal to me. Shoot, I don't need to be with anyone who takes longer to get dressed than me.

"That's fine by me. You can't put your eggs in one basket you know, the bottom might fall out. Take it from me, look at my failing marriage." Lisa's comment is supposed to be funny, but no one laughs.

"At least you found out your marriage is failing before you got knocked up and end up having to stay home to raise children on your own. No man's worth all this trouble. Cut your losses, move on," Mona says and takes a sip from her drink.

Mona is such a cynic at times. I chuckle to myself. One minute they at each other's throat, then the next minute they're agreeing. "You two are crazy."

"You haven't seen anything." Lisa snaps her fingers and slides daintily off the barstool. "Wait 'til I have a few more of these." She takes a swig from a glass and finishes her drink in one gulp.

I don't want to be a party pooper, so I don't voice my concern on her last statement. Drinking brings out Lisa's alter ego, Desiree, who is not one of her better personalities. Desiree is the one who gets her in trouble most of the time. She is loud, obnoxious and very loose at the lips.

"You two can stay here and continue talking to each other if you want to, but I'm going over to where the men are," Mona sasses, then she makes a beeline in their direction. It never occurs to her that maybe she should let them come to us.

"She's crazy," I laugh as I grab my stuff to follow her.

Lisa pulls me aside and we stop to face each other. She asks, "Does Mona usually approach men like this?" Lisa asks turning her nose up at Mona.

"No, not really," I lie.

I don't like it when Mona puts me in a position to lie, but Lisa is judgmental, and I don't want to give her any more ammunition to use against Mona.

"Oh, because I don't remember her being that bold and aggressive," she continues in that condescending tone she uses when she's putting someone down.

"Girl a lot has changed," I say. "We can't stay the same forever."

"Whatever," Lisa sneers. "She's acting like a desperate

hussy if you ask me. I'm not judging her, you know."

"No one asked for your opinion and sure you're not judging her, hmmm," I stare at Lisa pointedly to let her know we're through with this conversation, then I walk off and leave her to stew in her messiness.

"Hey, ya'll what's going on? I'm Mona. I saw you guys appreciating the fine art and thought I'd come over to give you a better view up close and personal.

"Abracadabra!" It is like magic the way she wraps men around her finger.

They chuckle.

"That's cute, never had a female use a line on me before," one of the men says. "I'm Reggie. Nice to meet you."

He's handsome, tall, and athletic. He's cocky too, a little too much for me. You know the type of brother who thinks he's irresistible. Thinks he knows a whole lot, but doesn't really know much of anything.

Reggie says, "More honeys for the honey pot. What's your name, sweetheart?"

"I'm Mike and this is my brother Jack," one of his friends introduces, saving him from the lecture he was about to get from me.

"Candy," I offer, not feeling the change of scenery. I shake hands with Mike and Jack.

"I'm Curtis."

Curtis is a nice looking brother with a baby face. His unassuming appearance is what draws people. Lisa moves in closer to him.

"I'm Lisa, nice to meet you."

"You ladies come here often?" Curtis asks.

Lisa speaks up. "No, this is our first time. I heard about this place from a few of my co-workers. I like it here. Good music, nice setting, you can't ask for more. How about you? You come here often?"

He laughs. "Nah, this is our first time too. This is a nice place. We needed a place for the grown and sexy. I was getting tired of all these teenybopper hang spots."

He clears his throat.

"So, Lisa, what does a man have to do to get your attention? Beautiful women like yourself either have men beating down the door or have someone at home waiting up for you."

Lisa smiles then glances away shyly. "I don't know. I guess the man has to be himself, know how to hold a decent conversation. He has to know how to act around a woman, be a good listener and genuine... He has to be genuine. I can't stand phony men." She pauses to let him absorb her last statement then she continues. "He has to act like his mother gave him some manners, before she sent him out into the world. And if he has problems with independent women then he has problems with me."

"It's rare to find a straight forward woman," Curtis says. "I like that about you. A lot of the females nowadays are too fake, too aggressive, and all they want to know about a brother is how deep his pockets are."

Lisa takes a defensive stance. "What about men? Most men nowadays are cheaters, liars, and players."

Curtis tells her, "I'm not denying that fact, but I'm not trying to date dudes, so I don't care about them and their issues. I'm none of those things. I'm a simple man with simple needs. I want a good woman who cooks, because I like to eat and if she can't cook then I can only hope she'll let me have the remote control."

Lisa beams like a hundred watt bulb. "Well I hope you're not into men. It would be a total waste. Have you given thought to the reason you attract scandalous women?"

Chuckling, Curtis asks, "How am I doing that? And if I am, please tell me. How can I stop?"

I'm not one to be up in people's business, but did this brother take a good look in the mirror before he left the house? If he did, he wouldn't have asked Lisa that question. It's interesting the things you learn about people when you eavesdrop.

Lisa looks him over then she replies. "You really want to know?"

"Yeah, tell me."

If Lisa's not careful, she could end up breaking this one's heart. I'm willing to bet she doesn't notice the complimentary looks he throws her. Lisa isn't very sharp when it comes to the opposite sex.

Lisa pulls her lips; she does this when she thinks. "Well for one, the way you are dressed speaks volumes. Let's start with those expensive cuff links, your diamond encrusted ring, and, oh, the pristine tailor made suit down to your handmade shoes. You know what? I'm not even going to comment on the shoes, but if those things don't scream 'hey, look at me, I have money' then I don't know what does."

He lets out a big laugh. "So what you're saying is that I shouldn't wear nice things."

"No, that's not what I said. I only point out the obvious, and yes, maybe you should dress down a little and then maybe you wouldn't attract gold diggers. It will definitely open your eyes to the women who really want you for you, and not for what's in your wallet. It's good that you're successful and everything, but you don't have to be flashy."

"I get the feeling you don't like flashy men."

"You guess right. I like the simpler things, but your personal preference is your own. If that's what you're into then that's what you're into."

"Maybe you can help me tone it down a little," Curtis suggests and Lisa freezes in place.

"I... this," she stammers. "Wow!" Lisa blushes.

"I guess you two are going to stand over there and hold your own conversation," Mike intervenes. Mike's interruption is on point; it saves Lisa from having to answer the open invitation from Curtis.

Laughing at Mike, they go right back to talking and being in their own world. Lisa never answers Curtis's question. It's good to see Lisa having a good time. Despite not wanting to come over here to begin with, I'm actually having a good time myself. It turns out that Reggie did play professional basketball, which explains his attitude. He works as an accountant for Ford Motor Company now. His friends Jack and Mike are fraternal twins. I wouldn't have guessed that about them. Jack is the funnier of the two, but he needs to lose a couple of pounds around the stomach area. Both brothers own there own barbershop in Kansas City, Missouri, and are looking to open a few more in the surrounding areas.

"You look familiar. What high school you went to?" Jack

turns to ask me.

"Richard P Green," I reply.

Mike wags his finger in the air. "I knew it. This is such a small world. What class did you graduate?"

"It is a small world indeed." Reggie agrees.

"I graduated class of eighty eight."

Mike should've saved this useless piece of information, but he didn't.

"I try not to remember high school. I was a nerd back then and if you were a nerd, you were a loser. I was the dude who hung around the bleachers where the cheerleaders hung out and looked up their skirts. I was such an idiot back then. I remember drilling a hole in the girls' locker room. Hoping and praying that I would catch a glimpse of one of them naked. It never happened."

This man is insane. We laugh at Mike's honesty. He is something else, I muse to myself and if you ask me, he is still a dork and a pervert.

He continues, "My genius went kaput when I got caught by the janitor who reported me to the principal. When that principal called my parents, I was so shamed I didn't come out of my room for weeks. My old man still teases me about it now and then."

"Man, I didn't know you looked up women's skirts when we were in high school. You don't do that now, do you?" Reggie gives him flack.

Mike laughs it off, but he doesn't respond. "Did you play sports when you were in high school?"

"I did," I admit, pausing intentionally to gauge their reactions. None of them volunteers the information on how they know me so I continue. "I was the head cheerleader for the cheerleading squad."

Mike's face turns red, and his voice wavers. "Man ...this is some embarrassing situation right here. You can go ahead and strike it from the records about the looking up those cheerleaders' skirt. I never looked up your dress."

"You had better not. And if you did, you wouldn't tell me anyway."

We both chuckle.

Mike gazes down at his feet. I playfully shove him on

his shoulder. "Don't worry about it. You were a kid, doing kid stuff. Did you really look up girls' skirts? I'm kidding!" I laugh and shove him again.

"I would tell you. You were the hottest girl in high school. The cheerleader that every guy wanted to date, but were too scared to ask out for fear of rejection."

Mike's visible embarrassment makes it easy to pick on him. "That's OK. You don't have to be embarrassed. You can't help that you were a little pervert back in high school. Was I that unapproachable in high school? No wonder I didn't get asked out on many dates and when prom time came around I was the one who had to do the asking."

"No not unapproachable, more like intimidating. I remember you too. I had a real big crush on you." Jack nods his head.

"Really," I quip. "How come you never tried kicking it to a sister?" I meant it as a joke, but he took it seriously.

"I was real shy back then to ask you out. You're still smoking hot though. You look even hotter now that you're all grown up. We can give it the old college try now."

I smile, thinking he'd better back up off me. He wouldn't know what to do with all this if he had the opportunity.

"Look at you trying to get your mack on. But I must warn you, you will need a license to drive this car."

Mona chimes in. "Believe it or not guys, she's still pretty unapproachable."

"I'm not unapproachable," I defend. "I can't help it that men are intimidated by me."

"Woman calm down. I'm only messing with you."

I drink the last of my virgin daiquiri. I turn to head back to the bar for another round when Reggie offers to buy the next one.

"What are you drinking?" he asks.

"A virgin daiquiri." I reply in a nonchalant tone.

"Virgin daiquiri?" I swear Reggie's eyebrows shoot to his hairline with the question.

Amused I reply, "Yes a virgin daiquiri."

"Ooo-K."

I hope he doesn't think buying me something to drink will obligate me into sticking around. I have news for him if he does. I will drink what he buys and then drop him like hot cakes from a skillet.

One of the waiters passes by and he stops her. Hoochie describes the way she is dressed. This establishment has to change the dress code of its employees. For such a nice place, skintight pleather skirts look out of place. Are people wearing those anymore? Did she have to oil her body to get into it? Her skirt is too short and leaves nothing to the imagination. It hurts me to see young women inappropriately dressed.

Women like her make it easy for men to think less of us when they send out the wrong signal that they're cheap and easy with the things they wear. Reggie flirts with her, completely forgetting our drink order. Reggie leans closer to her and whispers in her ear and she giggles encouragingly.

Clearing a parched throat, I cut their convo short. I nudge Reggie's arm a little too hard to gain his attention and he turns to glare at me. I wave my empty glass in Reggie's face and he continues to glare, but hides his irritation from the server he's trying to impress.

He sighs. "Sorry, I forgot my manners. Candy, what do you want to drink?"

You're right about that. "Virgin daiquiri." The server looks at me funny. What, I can't have a virgin daiquiri? Everyone keeps looking at me as if I'm from Mars.

Reggie adds: "Get me a Jack Daniels with Coke to go with that too, sweetheart."

"One shot or two for the Jack Daniels?" she asks.

"Make it two." Reggie caresses the hand she writes with and she smiles.

"I'll have that out for you."

"And a daiquiri," I remind her. "Virgin."

"Oh... yeah I almost forgot," she licks the tip of her pen and writes it down.

Reggie smiles like an alley cat while staring at her butt as she walks away. "Now that's a walk behind. Dawg, did you see the melons on her chest?" He asks Jack and they chuckle. "I'm getting those digits tonight. I may even take her home. Baby girl was stacked! You think I might need help with those melons she got?"

"I'm still trying to figure out if she's wearing any underwear under that skirt," Jack adds. "Her skirt was short, real short."

Reggie chuckles again. "No, but I'll sure try to find out tonight. If she lets me take her home then maybe I'll get to tell you that in the morning after I put some mileage on that spoiler. "

"There's no way she could be wearing panties," Jack interjects. "Why take her home? The way she was grinning all up in your face. Looks like the backseat of your car would do just fine, but if you want to take her back to your place to stain up your sheets you go right ahead. Just make sure Ieisha don't catch you this time, because you know three strikes and you're out dude, and I'm not covering for you this time."

"Ieisha ain't going anywhere," Reggie shoots back. "I'm the only one who will put up with her bad attitude. Besides all I have to do is lay the pipe down on her one good time and we're cool again. Works every time."

Their vulgar talk rubs me the wrong way. It's one thing to do it behind our backs but doing it in our face is just plain rude. I say a silent prayer then flick Reggie on his ear and he jumps and turns around.

"What the heck is wrong with you, girl? You've been beating up on me since we met. Is that your way of flirting?" he rubs his ear. "Hey look I'm not into S and M."

"Oh please don't flatter yourself. I only want to remind you that I am still standing here. Or did you two forget? I cannot believe how disrespectful you men are. Where is your respect for women?" I ask. Reggie tries to say something and I raise my hand to silence him. "I'm appalled that you speak like that about us. I bet your girlfriend doesn't even know what a rotten soul you are."

In his defense, Reggie tells me, "My bad, I don't usually talk about women like that. I was just fooling around, doing the man thing, you know. I really did forget that you were standing there. I wasn't trying to be disrespectful."

I roll my eyes. "Whatever, go be a man somewhere else," I respond, shooing him away. Ignorance is bliss and this clown l has it bad.

"You're making too much out of this sweetheart, besides you can't tell me you women don't act the same way with your girlfriends when they come across a dude they find attractive," Reggie says, still defending himself.

He has a point, but I'm still short fused and if he thinks I'm going to allow him to use that double standard blackmail with me, he has another thing coming. This is the second time tonight he called me sweetheart and it irritates me.

"First of all, don't call me sweetheart. I'm not your sweetheart. Have some respect; that's all I'm asking."

"You know, you are right. I was out of line. I see that I offended you, and I apologize. We cool?" Reggie asks, cocking his head to one side like a child pleading to his parents for misbehaving.

"You have to forgive him. He is not accustomed to being around a real woman. It's one of the reasons we don't take him anywhere," Mike, says and laughs lightheartedly.

Mike's excuse doesn't make things any better and in making light of the situation he ticks me off even more. My expression darkens.

"Come on now, don't get upset. We're all just having a little fun. Look no harm was done," Reggie says with a smile, but I hear the irritation in his voice, even as he holds his hands up in surrender.

I'm still fuming, but decide to let it go. It isn't worth ruining my night over.

Meeting Reggie's stare and cold eyes, grudgingly I say, "Apology accepted, and yes we're cool."

Reggie's body language suggests he's still mad even though he shakes on it. A muscle in his jaw twitches. Respect is important to me, and if a man is going to be around me then he has to show me some. I hate strife; this is the reason I don't pursue the argument further. I'm over it. I only hope he understands where I'm coming from.

"Mona, what do you usually do when you are not using pickup lines on guys?" Mike quizzes, changing the subject.

"That wasn't a pickup line. That was an icebreaker. It generally works better than the usual 'Hi, hello. I'm so and so, nice to meet you,' etc., etc., blah, blah, blah."

"Well, it was a good icebreaker. I like a woman with a

sense of humor. We could have a lot of fun."

With sarcasm and a hint of seriousness, Mona replies, "You think? I work for a modeling agency. I'm a makeup artist for Vanity Inc. Model Agency."

"This means you get to hang around a lot of beautiful model chicks. What's that like?"

"Yes, unfortunately I do." While Mike isn't looking Mona turns to me and mouths: "I wish he would go away."

I laugh at her silliness. She had her eyes set on Reggie and got stuck with Mike.

"That would be the job," Mike says excitedly. "But I take it you don't care for your job from that comment."

"No don't get me wrong, I love my job; it's a lot of fun. It has its benefits, especially when I get to travel to different countries, but working with so many beautiful women can be a bit stressful. The constant gossiping, sabotaging, and frequent cat fights can wear you down."

"I didn't know all that drama goes on behind the scene. You work for a local company?" he gestures with his hands.

"It's all drama and more. We're a local and international agency."

"That's cool. Let's go to the bar. I can use another drink. Looks like you could do the same."

"Sure. Candy are you going to be all right by yourself?" Mona turns to ask me.

"I'll be fine," I reply reluctantly. Great, now I'm stuck with the knuckleheads.

The server brings our drinks and Reggie speaks to her briefly. He asks for her number and she gives it to him. Poor thing. I shake my head in pity. I'm half tempted to tell her what kind of man Reggie really is, but it's not my place, so I turn my attention back to the football game.

Texas Longhorns play the Oklahoma Sooners. The Sooners are getting their butts kicked. It's a good game; has everyone riled up. We all applaud at the touchdown the rookie scored. I wish I had known that Texas Longhorns were playing tonight, because I would've recorded it on my Tivo. I'm a huge fan of the Longhorns.

Charles & Riley's involvement in many college foundations led me to attend recruiting seminars all over the United States. The University of Texas is the only school I frequent twice a year and I fell in love with their campus. They have such an exhilarating passion for football. Their southern hospitality helped to win me over as a fan as well.

"Man. I can't wait till next week, when Missouri whoops up on Nebraska," Reggie interjects, looking braggadocios as a schoolboy with his tongue wagging out the side of his mouth.

I can't resist challenging him, so I ask. "How do you figure? Missouri really sucks this year. I wouldn't be surprised if Nebraska beat them this year from the way they're playing."

"Easy there killer, everybody knows that Nebraska is no competition for Missouri," he responds, looking smug. "I can tell you how the story ends on this one. Missouri is going to beat Nebraska next week. I'll call you up and we'll all go celebrate over beers and wings."

Yeah right. As if I'd go out with a sleaze ball like you.

"You mean the same way they beat KU," I say and cover my mouth in mock dismay. "Oh my bad, that was the other way around, wasn't it? Drinks and wings on you sure sound good and since you're buying won't you just throw in a couple of tickets to the next game."

Reggie gets hype. "That was a one-time event."

"We bring it to Missouri every time. Where have you been? KU always beats Missouri and last week was no exception. I know it is hard for you to claim defeat. What you really need is to accept that Missouri will never be a match for KU's football team."

"Yeah, whatever! They weren't always this good," Reggie leans against the pillar and watches me under hooded eyes. He smiles and nods suggestively. I paint a fake smile on my lips and ignore him.

"I'm not talking about the past. I'm all about the present and in the present your team is getting their face wiped on the field constantly."

He becomes defensive about the past games played between the two teams and as much as I'm always up for a heated debate about sports, he takes it to another level. His voice gets louder as he tries to dispute my statements.

"Whoa, it's not that serious. Calm down, brother." My attempt to calm him down only gets a rise out of him.

"Hey you started it. What?" Reggie flails his hands. "Don't tell me you backing down now."

"Look, no one's backing down. All I'm saying is that your team stinks. Just admit it, so we can move on to the next topic."

John Boutari walks right by me with a woman on his arm, and I don't notice until Reggie comments about the fine woman with some guy. I turn around to see what got Reggie in a frenzy again. I stare in dismay and disbelief at John and his Barbie doll look-alike woman friend as they swap saliva.

"What a dirty dog," I seethe through clenched teeth. "This two-faced Judas."

Reggie asks, "Hold up now woman, what dog you talking bout?"

"The guy with the woman hanging all over him is my friend's husband. If she finds him here with another woman, there's going to be trouble, and I really don't need the drama tonight. We need a fast exit out of this place before she finds him here with that toothpick."

Now that I am witnessing it for myself, I have no more reason to doubt Lisa's suspicions, and here I was giving him the benefit of the doubt. Lord, why can't men do right? Ungodly bouts of anger rise up in my spirit.

"What guy?" Jack asks looking around the room.

"The one with the woman the two of you were drooling over."

"What?" Reggie looks confused. "The guy that woman is with, is your friend's husband?"

"Busted, dang another brother caught. Little momma must not be taking care of home. That must be why homeboy is out here trying to get his life spiced up... Darn," Jack's laughing runs me hot. I blink once, twice and imagine having him in a chokehold, squeezing him until he has trouble breathing.

I inhale several times to dissolve my anger. "Is this funny to you?" I ask in the calmest voice I can muster.

"Naw, it's not that funny," he says, but continues to laugh. I itch to punch him straight between the eyes.

"You know what? You are dumber than I thought." I turn to Reggie. "Thanks again for the drink." I excuse myself and walk over to where Mona and her company sit in deep conversation.

I say, "Sorry to interrupt Mona, but I need to talk you." Mona's reaction is of relief, not annoyance, at the disturbance.

"Excuse me for a minute. What's wrong?" she asks, concerned.

Pulling her to the side, away from Mike's prying ears, I say, "You wouldn't believe who just walked up in here with some young Barbie on his arms."

"Who walked where? What are you talking about?" Mona asks impatiently.

"John is sitting in here somewhere with some woman he came in with and trust me this isn't one of his clients. Mona, she had her tongue down his throat."

"That no good, lowdown loser. I can't believe him, trifling, and sneaky."

Mona curses John. "I can't believe he would do this! Who does he think he is? He is just the worst example of a human being I have ever seen. To come parading in here with some other woman! See, that's why you can't trust a man! Always doing something dirty. That John is just no good at all. He's a piece of—"

"Hey!" I interrupt her. I expect some level of offense on Lisa's behave, but nothing like this. Especially since the two of them have such strong dislike for one another.

"You think Lisa saw him?" Mona asks, her voice still shaky, but trying to recover from her tantrum.

"No, but I'd like to get her out of here before she does."

I peer at Mona a bit more closely. "Why are you so angry?"

I see tears welling in Mona's eyes, and it hits me. Mona is having an affair with John. I've only seen Mona like this once before, and it involved a man she dated. The breakup almost killed her when he went back to his wife.

"I hate what he's doing to Lisa. You know we have all

been through similar situations and the memories still hurt," Mona says, but I can tell there is more.

I grab her arm. "What's going on between you and John?"

Her face crumbles and she opens her mouth to deny it, and I raise my hand. "And don't tell me 'nothing.' I've known you long enough to know when you're lying."

"And you have an over active imagination. Stop trying to find something that's not there. Nothing is going on between John and me."

We have been friends for a long time and I would hate to see our friendship crumble because of a man. I love Mona to death, and I wouldn't put certain things past her, but thinking she's sleeping with John is ludicrous.

"I'm sorry, Mona. It's just that... You have to admit that the two of you are a bit too chummy."

"You wouldn't feel that way if Lisa hadn't put the idea in your head," she waved her hand dismissively. "Forget all that. What the heck are we going to tell her to get her to leave?"

"I don't know, but we need to come up with something quick," I say and rub my throbbing temples. "I really don't want to..."

Lisa walks up before I could finish my sentence.

"Why are you two standing over here by yourselves? What happened to the men?" Lisa asks, looking around.

"Th— they're still around here somewhere," my words sound nervous, even to my own ears. "I had to leave them. They were getting a little too raunchy for my taste."

"You OK?" she asks, studying my face.

"Yeah, shouldn't I be?"

"You're acting strange," she says. "Did one of them try something? If someone messed with you, we can get that straightened out now."

"Calm down, Desiree," Mona tried to interject some humor. "Your alter ego is kicking in."

"No, I'm just saying," Lisa says, "if somebody tried to do something to Candy, we can handle that now."

"No, I'm fine," I say quickly.

Lisa seems satisfied with my response. "OK, cool. So are

we still on for the fiesta downtown?"

Mona and I exchange glances. The last thing the both of us want to do is go to the fiesta. I would prefer to go home and get in bed; it's empty but drama free.

"Don't tell me you're ready to go home," Lisa says, disappointed.

Her look of expectancy makes me glance away.

Pacifying her I say, "Let me go say my goodbyes to someone and then we can leave."

She says, "OK, I'll be right over here."

Lisa stops suddenly, frown on her face. Alarm bells go off in my head. Sweaty palms, brain malfunctioning, I take deep breaths and wait.

"Oh crud," she curses. "I didn't close my tab. I need to come with you to close my tab."

"Let Candy close your tab, Lisa, I need to talk to you about something," Mona jumps in hastily.

Mona's quick thinking saves me from having to explain why Lisa can't come to the bar with me.

Doubt still clouds Lisa's mind. She responds, "I don't think they'll let her do that, would they?"

"Yes, they will," Mona insists. "We do it all the time. Long as they're getting their money. I don't think they care who signs for the check. "

"Yeah, they're not going to give me any problems. Girl, stay here. I'll be back."

I walk off in a hurry, which leaves her no choice but to stay put to find out what Mona wants to talk to her about.

My hope of getting married diminishes everyday. Becoming a nun is starting to have its appeal. My mother once told me that marriage is an institution, and I'm starting to believe her. It's an institution, short of asylum.

I refuse to put up with the kind of disrespect Lisa puts up with from John. When God put two people together, He said and they become one. He didn't say they become two. We have let men trample on us for far too long and tolerate foolishness that the Lord didn't say we have to tolerate. The Lord doesn't believe in divorce and He has concerns about adultery, but still we live with these behaviors as if it's the norm, making excuses for unclean living.

LOVE IS ALL WE'RE AFTER

Proverbs 6:32 tells us that when we commit adultery, we destroy our lives. That's pretty serious, if you ask me. Adultery isn't just about a quick one night or an infatuation. It's about literally destroying your life. I didn't make it up. That's what the Word says. I know John is destroying lives with what he is doing.

↗ I almost made the same mistake Lisa made, by marrying the first man that asked me. Mikhail asked me to marry him when things were good between us, and I'm glad I told him to hold off until we were certain. I've seen too many broken homes, including my own, to know marriage takes two people to make it work. Mikhail wasn't responsible, and at the first signs of trouble, he would've been out the door.

I never knew my father. He left when I was too young to remember him. Mom told me he came home one day pissed off from the job and he told her he was going to one of the local bars to blow off steam, and he never came back. No phone calls, letters, nothing, he just vanished into thin air and when she told me, I was devastated. I felt betrayed, because the history I have of him was make-believe memories created by a mother who wanted to protect her child. I resented her for lying to me and it took me a long time to forgive her.

All those years I thought the birthday cards and gifts my mother signed his name to came from him. For years she told me he was in the Army. Her explanation was reasonable enough when I was a child, so I had no reason not to believe her.

I used to see other girls/women with their fathers and long for one, but I've come to a place of understanding that my father didn't want me. It's his loss. My father is not to blame for abandoning his family. No one taught him how to be a father. If his father had raised him better, I wouldn't have to find out about men the way I did at such a young age. I've been through so many chaotic circumstances with men while searching for my identity, because I was looking for a father figure to love me in men who were not worthy of the love I have to offer. Gone are the days when I look for men to validate me. I'm happy now, more so than I've ever been.

ANDREA' PORTER

Women need their fathers, but when you don't have one, a good mother can fill the gap. Knowing I have my mother in my life is the only comfort I need. She has made me into the person I am today, and I have no regrets of my upbringing. She worked two jobs to make sure I didn't lack anything, but we made it through and the quality times she spent with me made up for the times when she couldn't be there.

Yeah, I'm done grabbing for men who can't appreciate me. I just hope my friend can stop putting up with the lack of respect and appreciation her man shows her.

***

"What can I get you?" asks the bartender.

"I want to close the tab," I respond softly.

"What name is it under?"

"Lisa... Lisa Boutari and Candy Cameron. Is Nick still here?"

"Last time I checked, he was."

The bartender walks over to a register piled high with credit card slips and shuffles through them. The puzzled look on his face tells me he is having a hard time finding our tab and I get antsy. From the corner of my eyes, someone approaches.

Nick's mouth is close to my neck. "I thought you already left. Is someone helping you? Do you need anything?"

The clothes he has on are different from what he had on earlier.

"I'm closing our tabs. We have to leave; something came up."

"So um... when am I going to see you again? Can I call you sometime?" Nick moves in even closer to me.

"You can call me, but I'll have to be honest with you. Men ask for my number all the time, and they never call. If you're really interested in getting to know me then look me up in the phone book."

Surprised by my request, he chuckles.

"You're kidding right?"

"Nope, serious as a heart attack."

"Playing hard to get are we?"

I grin, mischievously. "No, I'm listed under Candace Cameron."

Since he blew me off for the plastic twins, I want him to work hard to convince me he's genuinely interested. I'm not making it easy for him, just because he is handsome. I'm sure women throw themselves at him all the time. He looks the type and flirting with him the way I did in the beginning may have given him the wrong impression. Now maybe he'll get the right one.

"Stay here, don't go anywhere," he cautions. "I'll be right back."

Where is he going? He disappears around the corner of the bar.

"OK, here is your card. Sign this for me. Top copies are mine, bottom copies are yours," the bartender points out, placing the credit card slip in front of me. I sign our names to the receipt. I hand him his copies and keep ours.

Unaware of Nick's presence, I turn around to leave and collide into him. He steadies me from tumbling over. The shock of his hands on my flesh sends my body into over-drive.

"You have a habit of sneaking up on people," I accuse jokingly.

"Only you."

I blush. "Is that so?"

He leans over as if he is going to kiss me, and I panic. I close my eyes and wait for his kiss. "What are you doing?" He asks and my eyes fly open.

"Ah nothing. Um nothing... Wow."

The faint scent of Burberry London slips into my space and my focus moves into another area filled with silk sheets, ribbons and body oils. Answering Nick's question is the fur-thest thing from my mind. Burberry is one of my favorite co-lognes on men. Mikhail wore the same cologne, but it didn't smell the same as it does on Nick.

"I wanted to know if the offer still stands."

Confused, I inquire. "What offer?"

"Earlier you asked if I wanted to go with you to the fiesta downtown. Does that offer still stand?"

Nick's fingers drum idly on the countertop.

"Yes. I would love to hang out with you tonight, but I can't. I'll have to take a rain check."

"Why? What's wrong?" Nick wants to know.

"I hope you don't think I'm blowing you off, really I'm not," I apologize. "I have to leave. Something came up with one of my friends."

"I'm starting to believe you are," Nick folds his arms and stares.

"No, I really am not. I really want to see you again. Look me up," I look him in the eyes boldly.

"I understand, but will I really ever see you again?"

"Call me and you'll find out."

"How am I going to do that? You won't even give me your number."

I stress. "Phone book remember?"

He chuckles. Seconds pass between us with me not budging.

He asks, "You can't be serious. Are you?"

Nick's stare wills me to budge. Once he realizes I'm not budging, and his competitiveness kicks in, he agrees to look for the number.

"OK I'll play your little game. You're something else, you know that?"

"I've been told. Call me," I say using an imaginary phone with my hand.

CHAPTER EIGHT

Mona

Relief washes over me when Lisa excuses herself to go back to her company. I sink down into the chair across from Mike and lean back into a comfortable position. He has been so patient with all this drama going on around him.

"Everything OK with your friends?" he asks.

"For the most part we are."

Mike nods and leans forward. "Do you want to dance?"

"Not right now."

I didn't realize that playing nice to Lisa would take all the energy out of me. My true intention was to break it down to her that John is here with another woman. To tell her I was late getting here to meet with her and Candy, because he was double dipping in my honey pot, to hurt her like I'm hurting. How could John do this to me?

I've been such a fool to believe I was the only one he was seeing behind his wife's back. Nausea washes over me, dizziness ensues, and the beat of my heart moves from my chest to the pinnacle of my head. It's sheer torture sitting here like nothing is wrong while anger grows in me by the minute. I nervously twist from side to side in my chair. Mike's continuous chatter turns into muffled sounds I don't comprehend. The voices in my head drown him out.

Mike's hand on my leg makes me jump. "Mona, you seem a bit distracted. Is everything OK?"

"I'm fine. I'm sorry if I seem a bit distracted. Trying to figure out what is taking my friend so long."

"I'm not boring you, am I?"

I smile and shake my head. "No, you're OK," I lie.

He is boring me, but I don't enjoy hurting people's feelings. Besides, after tonight I won't be seeing him again, and I hope he doesn't ask for my digits because he is not getting them. Mike seems decent enough. It's just that I'm not into him. Stealing another look over his shoulder, I spot Candy coming toward us.

I let out a long-winded sigh. "Here she comes." I thank

Mike for keeping me company and quickly move away before he can say anything.

"OK, Candy. What's the plan?" I ask as she walks up.

"I'm ready to call it a night," Candy says. "John is over there getting finger fed by this woman. Let's go before I do what I should've done when he first walked up in here with that cow. It must be a full moon tonight. These people are in rare form."

I glance over to Lisa and her company and see she is all over him. If I didn't know better I'd think these two were lovers and not two strangers who met a few hours ago. John needs to see her now, his perfect wife. I have a good mind to march right over there to drag that no good, two timing loser over here so he can see what his perfect wife is doing. She was the one he married. He didn't think I would make a good wife for him or a good mother to his children.

I'm not perfect. I don't know anyone who is perfect. I've made my share of mistakes, but the way John treats me is unreal. I'm good enough to share his bed, but not good enough to share his life. We have a good arrangement as long as I keep my mouth shut and my legs open so we can continue seeing each other. He hasn't said it in as much words, but that's the reality.

John and I started seeing each other secretly after he broke it off with Lisa back in college. He would still be mine if she hadn't shown back up in his life. Actually, he and I met before he and Lisa started dating, so if you want to be technical, I knew him first. He was mine before he was hers.

In our second year of college, Lisa moved off campus into a one-bedroom apartment. None of us knew she was looking for an apartment until the day she signed the lease. It came as a shock to us since the three of us always did things together, but that was John's plan all along to separate us, so he could continue seeing her behind my back. We never hung out at the same place together anymore and Lisa slowly withdrew from us. She was always too busy to hang out with us.

The night I found them together, I was out with some of my classmates. We had a change of plans and instead of staying on campus for the parties we ended up going into the city. I was expecting to have a blast, but got a broken heart when I saw Lisa and John strolling together locked in each other's arms by a waterfall. It crushed me. I should've confronted him, but I didn't. I was too humiliated. Later on back at the dorm when I was alone and had gathered my thoughts, I called to confront him only to hear an automated voice tell me the caller wasn't accepting any calls at this time.

Days went by before I heard from John. I confronted him and he made up some story about her needing to talk to him. Said he had to clear his head and begged me not leave him. I had an emotional week. I loved him, so like a fool I took him back believing all his lies. I knew he was lying to me but I kept up the charade. Every time he was missing in action, I made up excuses for him. I let myself believe his lies up until the day he got married. Then there was no more room to hide from the truth. The day before his wedding, we spent the night together and he gave me an option. Be his woman on the side or lose him forever. I choose him.

Now every time I see them together it makes my stomach churn with anger, jealousy, and envy for the things she has with him, things I'll never get to share with him. Candy is the only one stopping me from getting my revenge.

"Looks like Lisa is having fun to me. Maybe we should just leave her hot tail in here," I say sarcastically.

Candy stares daggers at me. "Mona, stop talking crazy."

She grabs me by the arm and pulls me alongside her as if I am a child. Mentally chastising Candy I fall into stride behind her.

"I was only kidding."

Only I'm not kidding. Left up to me, I'd leave Lisa here for John to bump into her, but Candy is always trying to play Captain Save the World. She is well intentioned, but sometimes it annoys me. The guy Lisa is paying all her attention to doesn't even hold a candle to John. He's handsome, but John looks a thousand times better.

John radiates an aura of magnetism that draws women to him. When we first met, I pretended not to notice him. I was in the school library studying for a final exam. I'm still not sure why he was there. He didn't have any books with him. I didn't see him doing any research. In fact, most of his time spent there was chatting up one of the younger librarians and of course, she was all giggles and laughs.

The constant laughter made it hard for me to concentrate and each time she giggled I found myself looking over to where they where. At the time, I wasn't sure if I was frustrated because I was finding it hard to focus or jealous that he was giving all his attention to her. Whatever the reasons, I snapped.

In a condescending voice, I asked, "Could you two take this elsewhere? There are people here to study. I'm not sure why you two are here. Obviously, it's not to do anything constructive. So please... Do us all a favor and take whatever you two got going on out to the parking lot."

He whispered something to her and she went away then he leaned against one of the bookshelves and watched me intently. I pretended not to care that he was watching me and brought my attention back to my book. When I looked up again he was standing at the other end of my table.

"What are you studying?" he drawled. For a young man he was brass.

Not that it was any of his business, but I told him anyway.

"Political Science."

John made himself comfortable and sat in the chair on the other end.

"Smart girl. I like that. What have you learned so far?"

"That you cannot study when you're being disturbed."

The corner of his mouth tightened. I watched him, thinking it was presumptuous of him to sit at my table without asking. He flipped through the pages of one of the books I had on the table.

Bored with it, he put it back down.

"She has a smart mouth also."

I rolled my eyes and looked down at my book not really concentrating with him being so close. A thousand things were running through my mind. None of which had a thing to do with the book I was concentrating on so fixedly.

"What are you doing after you finish studying?" he asked.

"I'll be studying all day," I said.

He smiled at my response. I never saw anyone smile quite like him. His smile captures and entangles one's soul.

"Do you ever take a break?" He wanted to know. "I mean you need brain food with all that studying you are doing. Let me take you out to grab a bite. It's only to grab a bite."

I put my hands under my chin, acting as though I was considering his invitation.

"Mmm... No."

"I find that hard to believe. Why are you being difficult? You don't even know me."

"Not only is it no, but it's heck no," I told him in sharp tone. "I know guys like you. It's never only a bite with you."

"Now I'm being categorized," he said, trying to sound innocent. "All a brother wants to do is get to know you. What's the harm in wanting to get to know a beautiful girl?"

His pager went off and he checked it.

"I don't have time to go out. Satisfied?"

"No, I don't believe you. When can I see you again? What are you doing the day after tomorrow? I was thinking we could go shoot the breeze or something."

"Look. Is there something else I can do for you?" I asked, exasperated by his persistence.

"Jeez! It's like an act of Congress to get next to you. Isn't it?"

"What? You didn't know."

I picked up my books and left him at the table.

In a loud voice targeted at my back, he yelled, "You're gonna go out with me."

"Dream on."

Those were my famous last words, but John had the last laugh. I went out with him two weeks later. Had I followed my head instead of the desires within, my soul wouldn't be under bondage. Have you ever been so in love with a man that the mere mention of his name makes your body burst into flames? Love scenes play out in your head? Well that's what John does to me. I'm in love with John, but my heart tells me he doesn't feel the same way.

I doubt if he really sees me. Majority of the times I feel like one of his possessions. What blows my mind is that it matters little to me whether he really sees me for me or not; truth be told I can't break free anyway. I've reached a point of no return.

When I can't be with him and I'm lonely, I call up my maintenance man. I don't get serious with anyone, because John is my only interest. The last guy I had on reserve forced me to put him out of commission because of his neediness. This is no walk in the park, but I've made up my mind to be with John.

Candy hits my arm. "Is that her leg on him?"

"Mmm... What?"

Lisa's legs rest casually across this brother's leg and his hand rests possessively on her thigh. They smile adoringly into each other's eyes.

I say, "You reap what you sow. A few more drinks in her and she will be laying flat on her back."

***

Candy

"You might be right about leaving Lisa here for John to find her acting like a fool with another man," I say.

"'Bout time you listened to me," Mona agrees.

"But that wouldn't solve anything would it?"

Mona's reaction is intense. "Yes, it would."

"Somehow I doubt that."

I beckon to Mona. "Now, let's go grab this girl and get out of here before it gets ugly."

I have no idea what I would do if my husband were two-timing me. John deserves everything coming to him. I can imagine how Lisa feels, and I know she is hurting, but this is not the way to handle the situation. I know this first-hand, because I've been there before, throwing myself at men, seeking them out for comfort and attention. All I ever got in return for my troubles were bruised egos that left me shackled with low self-esteem.

I hold Lisa in high regard. She is better than this, smarter than this. Lisa is acting like a two-dollar common street-walker, when she's a queen. The closer I get to her friend and her, the more I envision slapping her across her head.

Mona's approach is beyond tacky. "Sorry to break up your little party. Lisa, you ready to go?"

Lisa struggles to stand straight on her feet and she reeks of alcohol. She reaches for the rest of her drink and Curtis moves it out of her reach. He should've done that way before this.

"Candy, are we still on for the fiesta?" Lisa asks, steadying herself. "Curtis said he and his friends might stop by and have a couple of drinks with us."

I don't answer her. I ask, "How much did you have to drink?"

"Not much." Lisa shrugs as if it's no big deal. "We're still going to the fiesta, right?"

I stall and Mona saves me. "Yes, we're still going to the fiesta, now get your stuff, and tell your little friend goodbye."

Mona's tone offends Lisa. It offends me too since the man is sitting within hearing distance.

"Hey wait a darn minute! You don't have to be so rude about it, OK?" Lisa snarls.

I bite my fingernails one by one, a nervous habit. I say, "Mona meant nothing by what she just said. Please can we go?"

Lisa leans over and whispers into Curtis's ear. He smiles, reaches into his back pocket and pulls out his billfold. He hands Lisa a card, which she drops into her purse. Embracing, they kiss each other full on the lips then pull away.

Mona and I stare at our friend with disgust.

Mona huffs and asks, "Did you just stick your tongue down that guy's throat?"

Lisa giggles as if it's funny. "Oh that? Please, I was only playing around. It meant nothing. Why are you tripping? Besides it's none of your business, Mona."

I butt into the conversation as we walk toward the door. "Yes it is our business. We came out to cheer you up. I don't want to be a part of this, Lisa. I didn't sign up to help you destroy your marriage."

"Earth to Candy — it is already messed up," Lisa says. "John's married too. You don't see that stopping him."

I could kill her and would if they wouldn't put me in jail. "Do I look like I care about John? Why are you acting cheap?"

My outburst catches her by surprise. She is angry and I am, too. I've had enough. Lisa has pushed me to my limit.

Lisa points her finger in my face and verbally attacks me. "What I do in my marriage is my business, not yours. You've never been married, so you have no right to give me advice on how I should or shouldn't be acting. You can't even keep a man past a year. So how are you going to give me advice?"

It doesn't stop there, like a derailed train spiraling out of control Lisa continues to tell me exactly what she thinks of me. Things I'm sure she has wanted to say to me for a while come pouring out of her. This is my friend, the person I gave one of my kidneys, shared my fears, and deep, dark secrets. I let her talk, what else can I do?

"It's not like I pulled one of your stunts and took him home on the first night to screw him. I enjoyed an innocent kiss from a man who made me feel special. I don't know why you're starting to act all self-righteous with me. We all know you ain't a saint."

She would've continued, but Mona doesn't give her the opportunity to finish her onslaught. Mona slaps her so hard, the loud smacking sound catches the attention of a few bystanders. Lisa rubs her bruised cheek then launches at Mona like a hellcat. I try to intervene and they push me to the side. We're causing a scene, something we're getting good at doing.

"Stop it!" I cry out, glaring at the both of them. "You two are acting like idiots. Mona, what is wrong with you?"

"Me? Why are you getting mad at me? She's the one talking all this bull to you!" Mona defends.

"Let her talk, we're all friends here. At least now, I know how she really feels about me." I'm shouting and people are really staring.

"Lisa and I have never been friends and this makes it

worse. This is why I didn't want to come here, but you insisted," Mona's accusation stings.

"I could say the same, and I didn't want you here. Thanks a lot, Candy," Lisa slings back in her defense.

"All I want is for us to go back to being friends, but we can't go back into the past, we can only move forward and accept things for what they are," I say, chastising them both. "Until the bitterness between you subsides, it seems to me the two of you will never be friends."

Mona turns and leaves. She exits the restaurant without as much as a second glance. Lisa's anger dissolves some, but her breathing is still heavy. She turns from the door and reaches out to touch my shoulder.

"Candy, I'm really sorry for my outburst. I don't know what came over me."

"You know, Lisa, if you don't value your marriage then who am I to tell you to value it?" I ask.

"I'm really sorry." Lisa is full of remorse.

"I know you are, but I also know you meant what you said about me. If you felt that way about me, why didn't you tell me?" Lisa doesn't respond. "You know what? Let's drop it. Let's go."

We step outside and the night air cools my face. Mona moves ahead of us stewing in her anger. Lisa had a little bit too much to drink, but regardless of how much she had to drink, she struck a cord in me tonight when she brought up my past sexual lifestyle. This sure is something. We come out to make her feel good tonight and now we're the ones going home to lick our wounds. Misery loves company and the devil plays dirty.

Out of nowhere, Lisa yells, "Hey girl you, you lost my earring."

Frustration coats my voice. I say, "Let it go, Lisa. How much did you have to drink? The alcohol is making you talk crazy. Can you drive yourself home? Do you need me to take you home?"

"I'm not talking crazy. I am going to teach her a lesson. You hear me, Mona, I'm going to press charges on you for assault."

Her voice echoes into the night. Lisa is acting straight ghetto by bringing our troubles to the streets. Teenage boys going by turn around to laugh and yell obscenity. Lisa takes off her shoe and throws it at the boys and they run. I watch her hop over to where her shoe lands and she slips it on.

"You think I'm kidding don't you, Mona?" Lisa continues to yell.

I answer for Mona. "Lisa, go right ahead. Do whatever you want, because nobody cares... Do me a favor. Don't call me when things aren't working out in your marriage. I am not your counselor. I don't want to hear it anymore and I don't want to be around to help you clean it up when it falls apart."

"I don't need you or anybody else," she brushes angrily past me.

Mona and I fix our eyes on Lisa as she gets into her car, slams the car door and pulls out of the parking lot. I cringe when she almost runs into the back of a parked car. The woman drives off so fast her tires screech.

"Talk about a freakin' drama queen," Mona comments.

I glance over at Mona. "What just happened?"

"Beats me, I think she's psycho if you ask me. Don't ever invite me anywhere she's going to be."

The beeping of car horns, noisy chatter and laughter blows in the wind from a group of people across the street waiting in line to get into a nightclub. Those same people would've been us a few years back. I don't miss the nightlife and I should have listened to my first thought and stayed home tonight. I should be relieved, but I feel like crud.

"Mona, I'm going to head on home. Get home safe."

"You too, I'll talk to you tomorrow."

The night was full of way too much drama and hostility, and as I climb into my car, I wonder: What is happening to us?

***

The next morning my growling stomach wakes me. This happens every time I stay out late. Light from outside illuminates my bedroom, casting a peaceful glow. Morning comes too quickly. Sinking back into a comfortable position I pull the covers over my head and try to go back to sleep.

Saturday is my lazy day, and it wouldn't take much for me to sleep the day away, except the strange sounds vibrating in my stomach make it impossible. Flinging the covers aside, I throw my legs over the sides of the bed and stretch the sleep from my body.

The cold floor sends goose bumps up my legs the moment they hit the ground, which reminds me to call Lowe's to have them install a heating system for the floors. Winter is coming and the floor will be colder than it is now.

Last night's events play in my head. Lisa's words were cruel and they cut like a knife. She had me checking myself for physical damage. Lisa took me back to a place of bondage I didn't want to be. The devil is forever bringing up my past, but God told me He has redeemed me from my past and that I'm not the person Lisa claims I am anymore. I'm the head and not the tail. I kneel and pray for strength and God's blessing. When I finish, the peace I had before Lisa's little drama quickly takes root into my spirit. Then hunger pangs take its place and gnaw at my stomach. Fried eggs and bacon, with toast beckon me to the refrigerator.

I open the refrigerator ready to prepare the breakfast I conjure up in my head only to be let down. With the exception of a couple of speckled bananas, store-bought baked chicken, and a half-empty carton of milk with some kid wearing a milk mustache, an empty refrigerator greets me. Slamming the door shut, I pick up the phone and dial Mikhail's number.

"Hello." Sleep laces his voice.

"Mikhail?"

"Huh-huh?"

"Did I wake you?"

"You went out last night, didn't you? And now you're hungry."

It still surprises me at how well he knows me. Chuckling in response I say, "Go back to sleep, I didn't mean to wake you."

He grunts. "OK. I had to stay on the job late last night, and I'm tired. I'll call you when I wake up."

I don't believe him; still I play along. "OK then. I'll talk to you later."

Mona is next on the list so I dial her number. The phone doesn't ring, but she picks up.

"You're up pretty early this morning. You must be hungry and looking for someone to go have breakfast with you."

Am I that obvious?

"Can't a friend call anymore?"

"No," Mona says. "Where do you want to meet for breakfast?"

"Meet me at the Denny's off Metcalf in thirty minutes. I'm starving."

"Who you telling! I'll see you in a minute." She clicks off on me.

I don an old pair of beat up Robert Cavalli jeans I picked up from a flea market years before with a plain T-shirt and sweep my hair into a ponytail, and I am ready to tackle the morning. I stop by the mailbox to send a birthday card to my Aunt Becky. Morning dew glistens like silver beads across my lawn. The grass needs cutting, but the lawn man I usually use hurt himself on another job.

I look across the road and notice Mr. Henley's night lamps are still burning. Which means he hasn't taken his morning walk yet. The only sound for miles comes from an old grandfather clock that chimes on the hour. The neighborhood I live in is quiet and aside from the occasionally child's play, I hardly ever see my neighbors. People around here are like CIA agents. They hit a button, garage door comes up, cars go in, and you don't see them again until the next day when they repeat the whole process. I live in a beautiful modernized early 20th century house. It's one of the best-kept houses in this cul-de-sac and it should be — because I pay a small fortune for the upkeep.

Nestled in a prominent part of the city this fully updated home with its three-car garage, five bedrooms, four and a half baths, living room, dining room, den, and huge kitchen built for raising a large family is my pride and joy. Owning a home of this magnitude is such an achievement for a single black female from the ghetto. My family doesn't own anything. I'm the first in my family to go to college and the first to own anything of real value.

All those late nights at work are paying off. Maybe one day I'll be able to complete the picture, with a family filling this space.

CHAPTER NINE

Mikhail

Sleep eludes me after Candy's phone call. I'm still shocked that she returned my call. Why did she call back? Does she miss me, the way I miss her? Should I ask her out to dinner? Thoughts of her rush through my mind like a whirlwind. I roll onto my back and stare up at the ceiling.

Candy was the woman of my dreams, until she began to smother me. I've never met a more beautiful woman than her. She is breathtaking, perfectly shaped, great smile, and has a love for people. Her only turnoff is her insecurities.

Last night I made a call to her, and I'm still not sure why I did. Maybe it was because of the old photograph of her that fell from my glove compartment. Seeing Candy's picture brought back so many memories I thought I'd forgotten, memories that unlocked doors to suppressed longings for her.

My most memorable day of Candy is February 14, St. Valentine's Day, a day for lovers. The day was foggy and overcast and big droplets of rain rolled down the windowpane. We stayed in my one-bedroom apartment all afternoon making love.

Looking at me dreamily, Candy voiced, "Baby, I got you something."

She captivated me with her smile. In my mind, I knew it couldn't top what she had already given me. She was scantily dressed in a red teddy I bought her from Victoria's Secret, bouncing up and down on my bed. Her beautiful curls on top of her head were a wild mess from our lovemaking, looking sexy.

Getting on her stomach, she reached under the bed and pulled out a big box in white wrapping paper with a big, red bow on top. She placed it between us and told me to open it. I've never seen her so excited, and I didn't know what to expect.

"Go ahead. Open it," she coaxed.

Sitting back on her heels, she watched me read the card

attached to the box, watched me rip the beautiful decorative paper from it. She snickered when I opened the box only to find a smaller box inside wrapped just as decoratively as the first. The second box was the same, nothing and the third, still nothing. The last box was tiny and had no wrapping.

I shook it then asked, "Is there anything in this box?"

She giggled. She acted indifferent and insisted I open the box.

"There had better be something in this box. Or I'm going to show you how bad girls get punished when they're being naughty."

She made goofy faces and ignored my threats. "There's something in the box. Open it and stop nursing the thing," she said.

"All right jokester, I'm going to open this box now. Something better be in here." I shook the box again, nodded my head and opened the box.

The blue box I held in my hand had my best friend Clare's class ring I thought I had lost during my last move here. I would've cried, but I didn't want Candy to think I was soft. The ring meant a lot to me. When I lost it I ripped this entire apartment apart looking for the darn thing. That day I fell in love with Candy.

"Is something wrong?" she asked.

"Nah baby, everything is right. How did you find this? When? Did my momma give this to you?"

Candy smiled as she explained. "Your mother mentioned in passing that you lost the class ring of a close friend who died. I know a few people so I made some phone calls. The ring is a replica of the ring from a picture your mother gave me. Do you like it?"

"What? Yeah, I like it. I love it. Come here, baby." I threw my arms around her, kissed her, and held her tight. "I don't deserve you, and I don't want to lose you, Candy."

I used that statement then ... thinking back now I didn't realize how true of a statement it was. I don't deserve Candy. She is a good woman and I am a scoundrel looking only for what I can get. I let her slip through my hands with the foolishness I continued to bring to her doorsteps. I've wasted all this time chasing behind skirts and didn't recognize I had the best thing all along.

Next to me, my company stirs, jarring me back to the present. I glance over at the woman lying next to me, her name I can't remember. I feast my eyes over her naked silhouette under the covers. Remembered the pleasure it gave me last night, she's what we fellows call a dime piece. She curbed my sexual appetite last night, but I still feel empty inside. Emptiness I've been carrying around my entire life. Lately I've been more worrisome about where my life is going. What is my purpose for existing?

I picked her up at Stanton's, a little hole-in-the-wall club down on the Boulevard. If the wind blows too hard at this joint, it would lay flat on the ground. Over time, I have developed a pattern of bringing females home with me from the club. It's nothing I learned growing up, because my parents raised me better than this. My mom and pops are still together living a happy and fulfilling married life. If they knew the lifestyle I've grown accustomed to, they'd have a fit. I doubt if my pops ever cheated on my mother. Between work, being a good husband, father and philosopher, I don't know where he'd find the time.

Pops is always preaching to me about how to be a man. "Mikhail, a virtuous woman is hard to find, so when you find one son, you better hold on to her," he likes to say. Somewhere along the line, I got off the beaten path and haven't gotten back on. It's like my mind has a life of its own. When I meet a good-looking woman, all I think up are ways to get her back to my pad. I don't make it a practice to sleep with women I hardly know, but there are the occasional one-night stands. Majority of the women I get with are women I keep around to feed my sexual appetite. You know friends with benefits, no pressure of commitment.

The ultimate thrill of the chase is reliving the conquest with my boys and the newness of a female. The feeling I get when I sleep with a woman for the first time is incredible. The new scent, taste, touch, and the way the buried treasure feels when I devour the conquest for the first time... It's like warm apple pie.

My companion moans little orgasmic sounds to come alive. "Good morning," she purrs.

I turn my head to meet her gaze. "She's alive."

She squints. "I'm barely living."

She lets out a long drawn out yawn, followed by those same sounds.

"What time is it?"

The clock on the dresser reads 9:30. "Nine thirty."

An alarmed look taints her beautiful face. "Why didn't you wake me up?"

"You looked comfortable, and I didn't want to disturb you."

She props herself up onto her elbow. Her subtle movement glides the sheet down to her hips, exposing her torso. I reach out to touch her, but she slides out of my bed, taking the covers with her.

"Where are you off to, girl?" I ask, disappointed.

She takes in her surroundings, studies a photo on the dresser of Candy and me on a skiing trip in Colorado. Candy has her arms wrapped around my neck from behind in the picture and she smiles up at me like a woman in love. I took it from its hiding place yesterday when I was going down memory lane yesterday and forgot to put it away. I wait expectantly for the questions, because women are always questioning things.

She grips the sheet firmly. "I've got to use your the bathroom. Where is it?" she asks in a blank tone.

"Go straight through the door to your left."

"OK."

She lets the sheet fall to the floor and cascade in a pile around her ankles. She looks back over her shoulders and smiles seductively.

I ask, "How you goin' get me worked up and then just leave?"

She licks her lips. "I'll be back."

I lean back on the headboard with my fingers entwined behind my head and marvel at her slow come hither walk to the bathroom until the door separates us.

My cell phone vibrates, but I don't get it. It beeps to let me know the caller left a message. Images of Candy invade my mind again. The picture of her on my dresser watches me and guilt takes the place of lust. I decide to remove it. I know that I have to make a decision on what steps to take next with this revelation about her and me, but not today.

The toilet flushes, scurrying sounds follow then old girl emerges from the bathroom. She is a very attractive woman and it takes all of my will power not to spring up from the bed to jump her. I admire her beautiful anatomy and her flat stomach with a silver ring dangling from her navel. She saunters to the edge of the bed and stops. We hold each other's gaze, her mouth curls into a sensual smile then she crawls slowly and seductively onto the bed. She never takes her eyes of mine and I pull her to me.

Afterward, we lie in bed to catch our breaths and come down off cloud nine. Half hour later old girl hasn't moved from under me and panic sets in. I want her gone, wish I knew what to say to get her to leave — without coming off like a total jerk.

Why can't women have sex like men? They make things so complicated when they linger. This part of casual sex ruins it for me. I close my eyes and inhale deeply.

"Are you asleep?" she interrupts my thoughts.

Ah shucks, she wants to have a conversation. Eyes still closed, I say, "No, just resting my eyes."

"I need to go. I have a couple things to attend to this afternoon. I hope you won't feel cheap with me rushing off on you like this."

"Nah, you OK," I reply relieved she gave me an out.

Sitting up in bed I admire her while she gets dressed, taking in her every movement. From the rise and fall of her chest, to the seductive way she moves when she bends over to pick up her top. She slips it on and I want to take it off her again. Her shoulder length hair is in a ponytail, held in place by a rubber band. Her makeup left black smudges under her eyes, made her look like she was going for tryouts for a football team. I scoot off the bed and come to stand facing her.

She places perfectly manicured hands on my chest. "Thanks for last night and a triple thank you for this morning. I had a really good time."

I hook my fingers in the loops of her jeans. "Your pleasure, and I had a good time too."

She leans in for a kiss, her lips linger above mine, and she probes. "Maybe we could do it again?"

"Absolutely, I'll give you a call." I'm glad I didn't have to make up an excuse to get you to leave. I'm not calling you. You'll be waiting for a long time. When a girl gives it up on the first night, the challenge is gone. There is no more mystery, because the competitiveness to disrobe her is no longer there.

I nod toward the door. "I'll walk you out."

I throw on something decent to walk her to the door. The last thing I need is for one of my nosy neighbors passing by to see me in my birthday suit. They already labeled me as the neighborhood dog, so I don't need to give them more room to talk. She turns to face me at the door. She folds a white piece of paper in half and shoves it in my hand.

Melody

Oh, so her name is Melody. OK. Under the name, I see a phone number.

"Call me," she gives me a kiss on the cheek.

"When is a good time?"

"You can reach me anytime."

CHAPTER TEN

Lisa

John is sound asleep and snoring loudly. He didn't come home until after five this morning smelling like some fragrance I don't even wear, and I'm cross with him. I'm so tempted to hit him while he sleeps. I should have killed him this morning when he came through the door, but I pretended to be asleep. I didn't move even when he called out my name.

He is up to his old tricks again. I can feel it in my bones, but knowing him, asking will only give him permission to deny it and tell me that I am being paranoid. All John has to do is admit that things aren't working out between us and we can cut our ties. He goes his way and I go mine, but no that's too easy. He'd rather fool around on me. I am starting to think he enjoys making me look like a crazy person or maybe he just likes to have his cake and eat it too.

I was certain he was seeing Mona behind my back. Now I'm not so sure since she was with us last night. I'm getting sick and tired of sleepless nights and of putting up with his nonsense. My head pounds; from the alcohol the night before or thinking about this mess with John, I don't know.

The coffee machine gurgles and chokes before spitting out the first drip of coffee. The thing is old and I need a new one, but I'm too frugal to buy one. It will have to break before I invest in another.

The little fiasco between Mona and me last night broke my nails. I called the nail shop and made an appointment. I should call Candy and apologize for my ugly behavior, but I'm too shame to it. This time I don't think a simple "I'm sorry" is going to fix things between us. Candy has always been a good friend to me, and she didn't deserve the treatment I gave her last night. She pointed out my sin, and I hated her for it. I didn't want to hear anymore of her criticism of me for loosening up for once in my life.

I've been hurting for far too long in this marriage and

having Curtis cater to me the way he did last night brought something out in me I've been missing in my marriage. He gave me back my raw animalistic passion. I wanted him, and I wanted him desperately. I already knew my behavior was inappropriate, didn't need to hear it from someone else. Candy made it seem dirty because I took pleasure in another man's company. No, I'm not calling her. I'll give it a few days before approaching her. I scroll down to my mom's number and hit the speed dial button.

"Hello," she bellows as if she's deaf. Her voice makes my headache pound even harder.

"Hi, Mom. It's Lisa," I announce as if she can't recognize her own daughter's voice. She doesn't sound quite like herself this morning. Her coughs sound angrier. She has had this chest cold for almost a month now and has been in and out of the doctor's office with the same result. They don't know what's wrong with her.

"Hi, sweetheart. How's my baby doing?"

"I'm doing fine, Mom. How are? Your cough sounds like it's gotten worse."

"Not good, sweetheart," she says in a raspy voice. "This week has been hard on me. I went to the doctor on Monday and he told me I have high blood pressure. He prescribed some medicine for me to take, but it makes me sleepy. I haven't been able to do anything all week."

"Why didn't you call to tell me this?"

Hearing about this now upsets me. Then I remember telling her not to call me for every little thing, and I could kick myself for my insensitivity. The woman carried me for nine months, the least I can do is be bothered by her.

She sighs heavily. "I didn't want to worry you unnecessarily anymore... you have a lot going on in your life right now and I didn't want to add more to your plate."

"Mom, I'm sorry for what I said the other day. You can call me anytime. I was having a bad day and took it out on you. Can you forgive an insensitive daughter?"

"It's OK, baby. I know you didn't mean any harm. I'm getting old, nothing to worry about. Nobody can stop the will of God when it's their turn," she says with resignation.

Before I can say anything more, she changes the subject. "How is that handsome husband of yours doing? The last time I spoke to you, you told me he was cheating on you. Accusation of infidelity is a serious charge, you know. Has he straightened out your suspicions?"

She had to go there. My mom has a way of making me feel stupid and inadequate. We constantly butt heads when John is the topic of discussion.

"Straighten out my suspicions? Mom, I know he is cheating on me. Doesn't that bother you?"

"Lisa, honey you need to give it a rest. You don't have any evidence the man is cheating on you. All you have are your suspicions, baby. I'm sure it's that girlfriend of yours who John don't want you hanging around that's filling your head up with these lies about him. You ever wonder why she can't keep a man around? It's because she is her mother's child."

"Who, Candy? She never badmouths John and this isn't about Candy. This is about John and his doggish ways."

The grip I have on the phone tightens and rage fills my lungs. Chanting "she's your mother" repeatedly in my head clears the rage rising to consume me.

"You haven't been able to prove that he's doing anything wrong. Just let the man be a man," my mom says.

She tsks. The lecture continues. It goes in one ear and comes out the other. I don't have to commit myself to listening to her nonsense way of thinking. Tapping the receiver, I wait for my moment of escape.

She is like Duracell batteries; she keeps going and going. "You have a husband that most women would kill for and you want to throw it away, because you think he's had a few indiscretions. Listen to me, Lisa, a good man is hard to find. Take my advice and let it go."

I want to say: "The same way you allowed Daddy to be a man when he ran around town on you." I keep my mouth shut, because I'm not crazy. I may be grown, but my mom will still come through this phone after me.

"Mom I—"

"No, let me finish. You think there is anything better out

there? You think because things get a little hard sometimes in a marriage that you can just turn tail and run. You have to fight for your marriage. I didn't stay married to your father for fifty-three years because I quit when things got rough. I stayed and fought for what was mine. Listen child, our marriage was built on truth and all the women after me were built on a lie, that's why they never lasted. What God joins together let no man put asunder. When I married your father I took my vows seriously and the only thing that could pull us apart was death."

She is preaching high upon her pulpit this morning. She is on a roll. I'm quiet now. I have nothing to say. It wouldn't matter anyway; when my mom gets this way, the best thing to do is let her have the floor.

"What you need to do is go out and buy some lingerie, cook your husband a good meal and seduce him back into your own bed instead of the bed you think he's frequenting. While you busy nagging him, you're just making it easy for Ms. Fix-it to show up and take your man."

"Mom—"

She ignores me. I rest my head on the table with the phone lying next to me. Francine Ann Billings is a beautiful biracial woman, born in Ardmore, Oklahoma to Scott and Darlene Brooks. She is one of five children. She grew up extremely poor and spent most of her life struggling to survive until she met my dad. Ernest G. Billings was a man of stature and wealth. He promised her the world and she gave him the chance to live up to that promise. He did, but he was a very unfaithful man.

Growing up I watched my mom let my daddy walk all over her. She allowed him to do what he wanted, when he wanted, and with whom he wanted. She turned a blind eye every time he did her wrong. Her silent cries pierced at my young heart. The burden of shouldering her hurt was too much for a child. I grew older and angrier with my dad for making my mom's life miserable. I hated him for his womanizing ways and for a while we weren't on speaking terms. The two of us didn't speak to each other until I was away at college and even then, our relationship was strained. Many of the trust issues I have now come from watching him. I was determine not to allow any man to have so much control over me and my emotions that I didn't have a say in what goes on under my own roof.

My mom thinks the world of John and he does no wrong in her eyes. He is good at camouflaging. John is a very educated man. He is handsome, charismatic, and a good provider, along with manipulative, selfish, and unfaithful. It bothers me the only concern mom has, is what he gives me. "He gives you everything any woman would want," she often says. What about my needs? I am not my mom, and try as she might I'll never be her. Materialistic things don't impress me. I want his heart, not his wallet.

I felt lucky when I met John. Convinced I had found a man unlike my dad, I married him in haste. My father never laid a hand on my mother. He wasn't that kind of man. John, on the other hand, hits women. It happened once, but I fear it won't be the last.

Mom stops her podium speech and I switch subjects on her. "So what else did the doctor say?" Old age on my side, she doesn't notice what I have done.

"He didn't say anything new; just that I need to keep taking these medications, follow a good diet and to keep my stress level down. But how can I when my only—"

Oh no you don't, I'm not giving you another chance to start in on me. Taking control of the direction in which our conversation should flow, I ask, "Is there anything you need me to do? Do you need me to come by there?"

"No, sweetheart, I'll be fine. Don't worry yourself. I'm going back in to see him in a couple of weeks. I should be OK as long as I follow his instructions. Everything should turn out fine."

I won't call my mom a liar to her face, but she is lying to me. She is hiding something. I will call Dr. Neil. He has been our family physician for years, and I keep tabs on her health through him.

"OK, well if you need anything will you call me?" I say, hardly keeping the worry from my voice.

"I'll be fine, don't worry about me. If I need you, I will call you. And don't you worry too much about John. That man loves you." I desperately want to believe my mother.

"I love you, Mom." She tells me she loves me and then we disconnect.

John is awake. He moves around in the bedroom, opening and slamming draws, then the rummaging stops. I pour two cups of coffee, stir sugar and cream into John's and hurry back into our bedroom, only to find it empty. The patio doors leading to the indoor pool stand ajar, and I walk through them. At the end of the pool, John stands half-naked in all his glory fixing his goggles.

I clear my throat. "Good morning."

"Hey baby, are you coming in with me?"

"No, I don't have anything under this T-shirt."

"Since when did that stop you?" he asks.

Since you've been coming home late in the morning.

"Come on in, the water is perfect." He splatters water at me to get me to come in. I back up from the edge. He's in a playful mood this morning, and it ticks me off. The water looks good. I'm tempted to get in with him even though I'm angry. I can't explain that, maybe the Pheromones he produces have my name on them.

"You standing there with nothing under that T-shirt gives me dirty thoughts," John says in a suggestive voice. "You really should come in so I can take it off."

John's good at convincing people when he wants something. He splashes water at me again and this time the water lands right on my bosom. He laughs, and I smile at his childish antics.

The first time I heard that laugh I fell in love with him. This morning his laugh annoys me. It has too much cheeriness in it, and I'm far from being cheery. Taking him up on his offer, I scoot to the edge of the pool and sit. The water warms my legs.

"I thought you might like a cup of coffee."

He wades to the edge of the pool. "Thanks, baby."

I clear the imaginary lump from my throat and ask, "How was your business meeting last night?"

"It went well. We closed the deal early then we went out

to celebrate with the new clients," he says.

Fiddling with the mug, I persist. "Is that the reason you didn't come home until five o'clock this morning? Can't see why anyone who works all day would want to stay out till five the next morning."

I'm fishing for answers and he knows. "Lisa, please don't start on me this morning."

"Start on you what? What? I can't ask you why you didn't get home until the crack of dawn," I ask, the pitch of my voice going up.

"That's not what I meant and you know it. I work hard so we.... No so you can have a roof over your head, money in your pocket, buy the finer things in life, and have a few nice cars to drive around in," he rubs his temple, then his head.

He rattles off all the things that mean nothing to me. I hear him talking and I let him, hoping he will hang himself by saying something stupid.

"I'm a businessman, Lisa. If a client wants me to stay with them until five o'clock the next day, then five o'clock it will be."

Uncomfortable silence passes between us. I'm still not saying much. He's lying. I see it in his eyes. We face-off then he flips the script. John's good at placing blame on anyone except himself.

"I thought you were asleep when I got home last night. Why didn't you answer me when I called out your name? Yeah, see you like playing games. Are there any women out there who don't play games?" he asks sarcastically.

I get to my feet and ask. "Are there any men out there who know how to keep it at home?"

"I don't have time for this. You're looking for a fight, but I'm not giving you one today."

"John, I'm not trying to start a fight," I soften my tone. "Baby, all I'm saying is that I don't like it when you stay out late. You could have at least given me a call to let me know what your plans were. I'm your wife and I think I deserve a phone call. You could've been laid up in a ditch somewhere for all I know. Why didn't you answer your cell phone when I called you?"

John dives back into the water. He does a few more laps in the pool and then gets out. As angry as I am with him, I still can't ignore his well-sculpted body glistening with water. John comes to sit by me on the diving board, our body inches apart.

John puts his arms around me and draws me near. "Baby look, I didn't mean to make you worry and if I did, I'm sorry. I know I should've called." He runs an unsteady hand along the side of my face. "I forgot my phone in the car. You know how I am with these gadgets. Let's not start the morning fighting." John sweeps his thumb against my lips, then he kisses me, and all the fight vanishes.

In one swift movement, he pulls me to my feet and swings me across his arms. Placing me on a nearby table, he plays sweet symphony on my body. He traces small kisses down my earlobe, makes his way down to my neck. John whispers sweet words into my ear that cause my insides to tingle with joy. My headache has dissipated and I refuse to let bad thoughts distract me. I surrender.

Somewhere in the house, his cell phone rings, interrupting the one moment we've had with each other all week. The fear of another woman is back to haunt me. Every time his phone rings, my stomach turns. The demons in my mind take me there.

"Let it ring, baby. I need you to hold me a little longer," I plead.

He loosens our embrace, sighs deeply and backs away from me.

"Honey you know I can't do that. I have a company to run, people depend on me."

That is not what I want to hear.

"It's Saturday," I remind him. "Let the voicemail get it. What about me? Don't you think I need you too? I depend on you as much as they do."

"Look... How many times have I got to explain this to you? What do you want from me?" he yells.

"Nothing, go and answer your phone," I snap and turn away.

Tears of disappointment mist my eyes, a knot forms in

the back of my throat big enough to choke me. John deserts me on the patio table like a rag doll without so much as a second glance. The tears trickle down my face and disappear into my hair.

After composing myself, I go in after John and find him yelling at someone on the phone. He becomes aware of me and resigns himself to the study. John is taking this privacy thing a little too far. Swinging into full gear, I head to his office then the house phone rings.

Shoot! "Hello." No one answer.

Frustrated, I say: "I'm getting tired of these hang-up calls. Stop calling here."

I slam the phone down in its cradle. This is the fifth phone call this week with no one on the other end. Whoever this person is, they have a lot of time on their hands.

John's voice isn't audible anymore, which is strange. Curious, I tiptoe up to his study door and place my ear against it, still no sounds from inside. Then without warning, his study door opens, and I stumble forward. Too embarrassed for words I turn tail and walk away with him right on my trail.

"What are you doing spying on me now?" John yells at my back.

"Who keeps calling here and hanging up?" I stop to face him.

"How would I know?"

I'm mad, all rationality put aside. "You know darn well who is calling here and you better tell them to stop. I'm going to subpoena our phone records. See if I don't stop this nonsense."

He starts in on the criticism, finding fault with me. "Do you listen to yourself? You're crazy, too friggin' insecure, and I'm not going to stand here and hold this conversation with you."

"Walk away, you're good at that!" I snap, flailing my hands in the air.

"Whatever, Lisa! I'm going to the office," John throws over his shoulder and continues to walk away.

My mom's words come back to haunt me. "What you

need to do is go out and buy some lingerie, cook your husband a good meal and seduce him back into your own bed instead of the bed you think he's frequenting. While you busy nagging him, you're just making it easy for Ms. Fix-it to show up and take your man."

Maybe my mom is right. Maybe I should seduce my husband back into my bed. But then I wonder if it's already too late to salvage my marriage. What should I do?

CHAPTER ELEVEN

Candy

A mob of people waiting in line for a table blocks my entry to Denny's at the front door. I move through clouds of smoke coming from a cancer stick dangling from the hand of a still-wet-behind-the-ears girl. I sneeze, cough and nearly choke. I shoot the offender a less than pleasant glare.

America has gone mad; everywhere you go you see little children puffing on cigarettes now. It's like a freaking epidemic.

Sweatshops in Chinatown aren't this packed. It's a good thing Mona got here before me. My cell phone goes off. It's Mona. I swear that women must be a physic.

"Yes, ma'am."

"Candy, are you on your way yet? These people are gonna kick me out of here if you don't hurry up and get down here."

"Girl, I'm right outside the door."

"Oh, well good luck getting through the mob squad outside. I've never seen Denny's this pack. This place is packed tighter than the food stamp office on Cranbury Street."

I laugh. "I'll see you inside."

"OK. I'll see you when you get in here... Come to the back."

It's nine o'clock in the morning and she looks fresh in a black and white Versace ensemble. Mona's head rolls as she gives someone lip service over the phone.

"Hey girl, you weren't joking when you said this place was full," I say sneaking up beside her.

Mona swats at me, for creeping up on her. "Oh my goodness! You scared the devil out of me."

"That'll be hard to do," I tease and she hits me.

"Listen, I'll catch up with you later. My friend is here." She told the person on the receiving end of her anger and hangs up.

"Last week was bad, but this week is worse," I say, glancing around. "Mona, I couldn't find a parking spot to save my life. I had to park across the street."

"We can go some place else if you want," Mona says. "I haven't seen our server since I sat down. Breakfast might be awhile."

"I hope not, I'm starving. Somebody better come over here and feed me. They better not make me go back there to help myself." I turn to see if I can find a server anywhere.

The aroma from the kitchen floats up to my nostrils and it stirs up hunger in my stomach. I pick up the menu and skim through it, from among a range of options I choose the same thing I always get when I come here. Mona peeks over her menu at me and pouts.

Finally, I ask. "What?"

"Why did you invite me out with you and Lisa last night? You of all people should know not to put us in the same room. She was drunk and mad at the same time. Lisa doesn't like me and she was acting like a blooming lunatic."

"I wanted to see if you two could work out your differences. I was wrong," I admit.

"I know you want to help Candy, but it's best if you leave it alone."

"You two waste too much energy being at each other's throat," I say and place my elbows on the table. I rearrange the sugar container, by putting the Splenda with the Splenda and NutraSweet with NutraSweet. "Forgiveness is free. It doesn't cost anything."

"I'm not the one who has the problem." Mona's defense is reasonable, but futile.

"What's the real reason behind this feud between you and Lisa? We've been friends for a long time, you, her, and me. I remember when we were inseparable in college then something changed. What changed? Why don't you two get along?"

Mona doesn't make eye contact. "I don't have a clue why Lisa dislikes me. Did you see the look on her face last night when I slapped her?" she says, and I smile regrettably.

"I'm glad you found that entertaining."

"I'm sorry, girl," Mona says with a bit of glee. "I don't know about you, but that was funny. She deserves to be put in her place. Why did you take that from her?"

"It wasn't funny to me, she didn't deserve public humilia-tion," I say. "On the flip side, she needs to know about John's dirty lifestyle, and I don't know how to tell her, Mona."

"You are the only one that can tell her something like this and she doesn't come unglued." She sucks her gums and continues. "Men are jerks. I'm tired of them always wanting to have their cake and eat it too."

"I know, right? Did you see how bold he was about it? He wasn't even hiding this woman."

"I'm sorry for Lisa," Mona says. "I know for a fact that John is one certifiable dog. For her sake I hope she finds this out before they start on a family."

"How is it you know so much about John?" I'm so hunger I open one of the saltine crackers and eat it.

"I work with him, remember? And it's not that I know so much about him. Remember that party Lisa threw at her house some months ago?"

"Vaguely," I reply as I look at Mona, intrigued.

"Well, while Lisa was busy entertaining her guests, John was busy entertaining me. He told me how stunning I was and how he always had a thing for me. I asked him about Lisa and the serpent told me she didn't have to know."

"Why would you even entertain a conversation with him knowing what he was doing was wrong?" I ask, appalled.

"I wanted to hear what he had to say. I noticed him star-ing at me when we worked alone together and I wanted to make sure I wouldn't be in a situation where our environ-ment could become hostile. When he realized his mistake, he apologized and asked me not to mention it to Lisa. So I didn't."

My gut feeling tells me Mona is selling me a lie. I can't put my finger on it and don't understand why she would make up such an elaborate story, but she is telling me stories.

"You should've said something to Lisa. What did you say to him? How is it you're sharing this with me now?"

"I told you he asked me not to say anything," she rests back in the booth and pins me with a nasty glare.

"What did you say to him?" I ask not in the least moved by her obvious irritation.

"I told him to jump in a lake."

"Unbelievable. You two work together, doesn't that make you feel uncomfortable?"

"No, he never brought it up again. We have a professional relationship and he understands that business is the only thing we have between us."

"That's crazy."

A petite young woman holding a pen and pad in her hand walks up to our table, immaculately dressed in a Denny's uniform, hair pulled back in a tight bun and ready to take our orders.

She speaks with a thick Spanish accent. "Hello, my name is Rosa and I'm your server today. Are you ready to order?" She clicks her pen and waits expectantly.

"It's pretty busy today huh?" Mona asks as she fiddles with the menu.

Rosa doesn't smile. "Yes, ma'am. It's like this on the weekends. I'm sorry if you had to wait long. Can I start you off with something to drink?"

"Yes um... Well, we'll take a large carafe of orange juice and we're ready to order. Is that OK, Mona?" I ask.

Mona confirms with a nod.

"Then I'm going to have your breakfast platter, bacon in place of the sausage, and wheat bread instead of white." I order and point to the picture.

"She's difficult ma'am," Mona says. "I'll have the Tex-Mex Scrambler as it comes."

Rosa scribbles down our request on her pad and nods in response. She's not a bad looking woman. Without the dark circles under her eyes and stress lines on her face and some makeup she could be very pretty.

She repeats, "OK. I have a breakfast platter with bacon and wheat bread and a Tex-Mex scrambler?"

"Sound right to me. Oh, and can you leave the butter off my toast please," I ask and Mona rolls her eyes and laughs.

"Will do ma'am, anything else?" Rosa asks, trying to hide her annoyance.

"No." I turn to Mona. "What about you, Mona?"

"I'm good," she laughs and kicks me under the table.

I shake my head and laugh.

Two tables up from us a couple of unruly children scream at their mother and she doesn't reprimand them. Now someone needs to pop those children behind the head. The mother is a skinny white woman with blonde hair, and desperately in need of a tan. She seems a bit timid and afraid of her own children. The oldest child hits his little brother on the head and back talks her every time she asks him to stop.

White people discipline their children way different from black folks. If this were my mother, she would take me in the restroom and beat the black off my butt. The makeshift parents we have in this 21st century are a trip and this saving the rod and spoiling the child cliché is killing off our children and sending them to jail.

A few more minutes of watching and listening to this madness goes on until the restaurant manager pays a visit to their table. He murmurs something to them and the noise dies down, but it doesn't last for very long. As soon as he leaves their table they are at it again. The younger child sticks his tongue out at his older brother and he pops him in the mouth.

I turn my attention back to Mona who is deep in thought. Her face is downcast by whatever thoughts she has rolling around inside her head.

"What's wrong with you?" I quiz.

"Nothing, I'm tired. You may not know this, but someone woke me up early this morning to come out of a warm bed to have breakfast with them," she shoots of at the mouth.

"What is wrong with people?" I laugh. "Were you ever intimate with him?"

"Have I been intimate? What are you referring to?"

"John."

She glares at me. "You and I both know that if I was sleeping with John you'd be the first to know... Why are you going there? I already told you nothing happened between us."

"I know... I know I had to ask anyway. I can't believe John is such a dog."

"He's an alpha dog." She pauses. "While we're on the subject of men, haven't heard you say anything about Mikhail...What's up with you and him?"

I could have gone all day without hearing his name. Calling him this morning was a bad idea.

I play with my fingernails. "Heck if I know, girl. That thing between us is dead. Sometimes it's best not to resurrect the dead. He called me last night and against my better judgment I called him back this morning only for him to tell me he couldn't talk, because he was tired."

She rolls her eyes. "Code word for out picking up women and didn't get back in the house until the crack of dawn. You sure you wanna let all that man go?"

"Girl yes, if sex was the only thing keeping us together then it's not worth saving."

"You've changed." Mona analyzes me, picks me apart and I'm sure she came up with her own conclusion.

"Well, you know I gave up sex after Mikhail, and it's just as well," I say. "I want a relationship built on the right things. And so far, the men I meet keep showing me the wrong thing. They all hit the road as soon as I let them know they're not climbing into my bed, not without giving me a ring first."

"Girl, are you trying to bribe some man into marrying you?"

"Bribe?" I am offended. "I don't have to bribe anyone to be with me."

"Well, some women act all holy and try to hold out on the sex thinking they can push a man down the aisle that way," Mona says.

"Well, for me, it's about the Lord," I huff. "And I have decided to show my commitment to him by trying to live right. That means no drinking. No sexing. No—"

"Oh, so you just like to flaunt sex, but not have it?"

"What do you mean?"

"You know what I mean," Mona says. "Wearing all those tight dresses and low-cut tops."

"Girl, the Lord didn't say we have to dress like nuns," I say. I can't help it if I am sexy.

Mona looks like she wants to say more, but she just rolls her eyes instead.

I ignore her. That's what's wrong with people today. They always think a Christian woman has to walk around wearing a paper bag. God doesn't mind if we look good. I don't think anything is wrong with the way I dress. So what if I show a little skin, it's not like I'm letting anyone touch it.

And maybe it would do Mona some good if she did more showing and less doing. I've lost count of the number of men who have been in her bed. Maybe she should try to live her life like mine, then maybe she could actually get a man, and not just a one-night stand. I can't remember the last time she had a man of her own. At least I can get one, even if I can't seem to keep him.

"Anyway, my celibacy has nothing to do with luring a man into my bed," I say. "I think if a man wants to be with me, he'll want to have a relationship that isn't built on sex. Sex doesn't have to be a part of a real relationship."

"Yeah, OK," Mona says. "Just be careful. If a man wants it, if he's not getting it from you, he'll get it from somewhere else."

We fall silent, each in our own thoughts. I've not had much success with any relationships since deciding to follow the Lord, so maybe Mona is right. Maybe I'm asking too much to have a relationship that doesn't include the physical. You can't think like that. You have to trust in the Lord and his word, I chide myself. I have to believe the man God has for me is out there.

But a little bit of doubt pricks me.

"We sure know how to pick 'em, don't we?" Mona breaks our silence, a rueful smile on her face.

"Ain't that the truth? I'm tired of these biodegradable men."

"What happened to the bartender from last night? Did you really give him your number?"

I ask, "And what if I did?"

"Here goes another sistah crossing the fence. Do your thing, girlfriend."

"These brothers can't give me what I want, maybe it's time for me to start taking applications elsewhere. I didn't give him my number, but I sent him on a scavenger hunt instead."

Mona looks at me as though I'm off my rocker. "Scavenger hunt? What the devil is a scavenger hunt?"

"I told him to look me up in the phone book."

Her eyes narrow on me. She says, "There goes a fine man out the window. Girl you crazy if you think that man is gonna go through a phone book to look for your number. What if he thinks you gave him the brush off?"

"Oh well, he knows the ball is in his court."

She leans back, crosses her arms over her chest and stares me down. "Wanna know my opinion on that?"

I don't, but she is going to give it to me anyway. Mona is also the kind of person who says what's on her mind even when what she's about to say isn't good. This means I can always count on her honesty and straight-to-the-point attitude.

"You spend all this time wondering where is your prince charming and when he shows up, maybe it's this guy. You put him through obstacles. Why you got to be so difficult?"

"Thanks, Dr. Phil, but when I need your opinion I'll give it to you," I say and look around for our food.

"You know I'm right. I'm just saying--"

I give her a penetrating stare. "What? What are you saying?"

"Nothing, it's not like what I say to you will make a difference."

Mona plays with her earlobe. Fourteen karat half cut diamond gold studs glistening in her ear. I want to hear what she has to say, but at the same time I don't.

I humor her. "Probably not, try me anyway."

"Are you afraid of commitment, afraid of failing? I mean what is the deal with you?"

I fiddle with my purse straps, and I don't respond. I look everywhere else but at her. Mona thinks she has me figured out and maybe she does. Rosa walks out with a tray of food and sets it down at the table behind Mona.

The aroma from the food waters my mouth, and my stomach does flip-flops. She catches me looking at their food and smile. Wow! She can smile. I didn't think she had it in her since she's been giving us the stiff treatment.

Satisfied that she has taken care of her patrons' needs,

she moves to our table.

She says, placing a carafe on our table, "Here is your orange juice and I will bring out your food when it's finished."

I pour a cup. "What did you serve those people over there?"

She glances over to their table. "Which one you talking about, ma'am?"

"I'm talking about the lady."

"Oh, she had the new Spanish platter."

"It looks good."

One more smile. "It's very good, ma'am. I'll go check on your food."

"Mona, are you going to Shelly's bachelorette party with me tonight?"

"No... I don't know... I'll let you know later. You still have not answered my question."

Pretending not to hear what she said I say, "I don't want to go, but I don't want to offend Shelly. There will be many naked men running around in G-string bikinis. I will show my face then leave."

"You need to stop people pleasing and tell her you can't go to those places anymore. I'll have to think about this one. I'm not sure I want to be in a room full of frowzy men walking around."

I snicker and admit to myself that Mona is right about people pleasing, but I didn't want to hurt Shelly's feelings by turning her down.

"I'm sure the men won't be frowzy — I know Shelly has better taste than that — but all the same, I truly don't want to go, but I probably will," I say. "You are crazy, though. If you change your mind, call me."

"I'm serious about the people pleasing part. I see where your life was before and I'm real proud of where you are now. Don't let anybody take that away from you."

"I'm working on that part and you need to commit to coming to church with me at least once a month."

"OK," Mona says grudgingly. Her answer surprises me and I smile, glad that I won the battle to get her to church.

She adds, "Bet you'll never guess who I bumped into the other day on my lunch break?"

"Sylvester."

Surprised I guessed it right, she inquires, "How did you know?"

"He told me he saw you. You know we still stay in touch."

"Yes, but I didn't think he'd run back and tell you so fast."

"He called me right after he bumped into you. You know that man still loooves you. He was begging for your phone number. I almost gave it me, because he was holding me hostage on the phone."

The look she gives me is far from pleasant. "You better not. You give him my number and I will put your name and number in every public male restroom. In big caption I'll write 'Call me for a good time, Candy.'"

"I wish you would. I would beat you like you stole somethin' from me. "

"Give Sylvester my number and you'll find out," she threatens.

"I'm only playing. You know I'm not going to give Sylvester your number."

Rosa brings us our meal and we eat in silence. The American Association research says you're supposed to get thirty-two chews in before you swallow. I barely got ten in.

Mona looks at me and shakes her head. "You ate that food like it was going to sprout legs and run off your plate."

"I didn't eat anything last night before meeting Lisa and you. I was so hungry my side was starting to ache."

I rub my satisfied tummy. I had too much to eat and I can't move, don't want to move. "Somebody's gonna have to roll me ought this place."

"You might get your wish. Don't think these people won't kick you out their restaurant. You see the line outside. I can't believe these people standing up outside waiting for seats. They act like this is the only restaurant in town."

I reach for my wallet. "If you're finished we can take care of the bill and leave. I need to pick up a few things from the mall. Do you have any plans after this? If you don't have any, you should come with me."

"I don't have any plans. Put your money away, breakfast is on me this morning."

"No complaints here," I put my wallet away as suggest. "Thanks for breakfast this morning."

"Oh you're welcome."

Mona parked closer to Denny's so we take her car. I kick the McDonald's bags covering the passenger floor to the side.

"Have you ever heard of trash cans?"

Mona laughs. "You can throw those out on the side of the car."

"No, I will not."

"Oh my goodness, you are so anal. Give me the darn bags."

I hand them to her and she stuffs them in the back of the passenger seat. There's no telling how long she will leave them in that spot. The car starts and the music comes on blasting through the speakers so loud, I jump and hit my head.

I rub the bruised spot on my head. "Why the heck do you have to listen to the music so loud?" I yell. "You're gonna go deaf one of these days."

I turn down her stereo. Then "Whatever" by Jill Scott comes on and I turn it right back up. We sing along with the very talented Ms. Scott not caring that we are singing off key messing up the girl's song.

We are fancy-free and not worried about anything. Life feels pretty good.

CHAPTER TWELVE

Mikhail

Momma hugs me. "Sorry I'm late. I just couldn't get it together this morning," I say and plant a kiss on her warm cheek.

"That's all right baby. I knew you were coming." She squeezes me. "How is my baby doing today?"

For such a small woman she has the presence of someone who stands ten feet tall. She once had jet-black hair, but now sprinkles of gray cover her head. She couldn't be more beautiful. Lily Mae Robinson is one of the sweetest, gentlest people I know and the only woman to hold the key to my heart and the secrets to what makes me tick.

I scratch my arm. "Tired, I had a rough day on the job yesterday."

"I wish you didn't have to work so hard ... I worry about you all the time, especially with all those accidents that place been having lately."

I squeeze her shoulder reassuringly. "You don't have to worry about me Momma. I'm always careful when I'm out there on the job. Where's Pops?"

"He's inside the house. You spoke to your brother lately?"

"I spoke to him the other day. I'm hanging out with him tonight. Something wrong?" I ask. Momma's concerned look bothers me.

"Nothing, I was only wondering. You know him and that wife of his moving to Detroit right?" she admits half-heartedly.

"He mentioned it," I answer vaguely. I don't want Momma to know I know more about this moving thing than she does are she'll be pumping me for information.

"I'm going to miss them grandkids of mine. Michael probably wouldn't be moving to Detroit if his wife didn't put him up to it. She's been trying to get him to move for years and I guess she finally got her way. They my only grandchildren Mikhail, what am I suppose to do when they're gone? I quit working those crazy hours at the hospital so I could spend more time with them and now they leaving."

"I know, but it's not like you can't go visit them. We'll have to make a big trip up to Detroit once they settle in."

"You know I can't stand being around that woman. Lord, help me if her scrawny behind say anything upsetting to me. I'm tired of treading softly around her and having to watch everything I say," she sucks her teeth.

"You're always telling me about forgiving and forgetting. You preach that stuff to me day in and day out, I guess the same rules don't apply to you."

"Boy, are you smelling yourself? Don't get fresh with me. I'm only saying I don't want to go up to see them and she shows me bad face. Talk to Michael for me, see if you can change his mind about leaving."

I should have known she had ulterior motives when she told me to come over. Momma does this to me every time. Manipulates me into doing something for her, and then she springs the real reason for her sudden need of help. This has to stop.

"Momma, Michael is not going to listen to a word I have to say. You know Kelsey runs that household. I'm not trying to cause no problems between married folks. No ma'am, I'm leaving that one alone."

"It figures you'd be on their side."

"I'm not on anybody's side."

She shushes me. "Help me finish up this place."

She turns around and goes back to packing boxes. I bow my head to the ground. I don't like to see my momma sad. Still I can't ask Michael to stay here just to appease her. For Michael taking this job in Detroit is a big career move and this may even be a once-in-a-lifetime opportunity. Momma needs realize that we are not her little boys anymore.

Dismissing it from my mind, I rifle through the garage and come across some things I thought she sold or gave away. It's been a few years since I've been in this part of the house. The garage is chock-full with a majority of our childhood memories. An old red bicycle of mine, still in mint condition is propped up against the wall. I remember the first time my pops tried teaching me to ride that thing. I must have fallen off a thousand times, before finally getting the hang of it.

I chuckle.

My breath kicks up dust from one of the shelves holding memorabilia from my dad's many fishing and hunting trips. There is also an old black and white photograph propped up on a stuffed catfish. It's of Michael and me rocking afros and holding our first kill. I chuckle some more, remembering how much fun we had that day.

I threw my first house party in this garage. It was my parents' ten-year anniversary and they went out of town, but before Momma and Pops could turn the corner, the neighborhood kids were filling the house. Boy, I had some good times in this house. I stand still and marvel at the vast amount of stuff my mom kept.

Michael's old high school football jacket rests on a hook. It still is in the same spot he hung it after school. I try it on. Michael and I got into many fights over this jacket. I can still hear him yelling, "Take it off!" It fit, except for the snugness around my arms.

There are other things she kept that shock me. Some of them I have good memories of and others not so good. Like this trophy. I won it the same day my best friend Clare died in a car wreck. I will never forget that day. Time stood still.

God cheated me of someone who deserved to live and I have been mad at him since. That's why I don't go to church. I don't understand what kind of God takes innocent people and no amount of anything can make me understand.

I have so many regrets. Clare and I never developed a romance between us. The timing was never right. She was always with someone when I was single and me with someone when she was single. It just never happened. Her face haunted my dreams months after the accident. Eventually I had to make peace with her death, because the torments grew too much for me to carry.

This place has too many memories; being in here is not such a good idea.

"Hey Momma, I'm going to head inside and holla at Pops for a minute. I'll be back out to help you," I yell outside to her.

"He's down in the basement. Don't be surprise if he doesn't roll out the welcome carpet."

"Great."

We're not on speaking terms, my dad and I. Correction. He's not on speaking terms with me. The last time I called the house for him he didn't come to the phone and Momma, the peacemaker, made up some sob story for him. Pops is mad because of the decision I made not to take over the family business to run the auto shop. At the end of the day, I have to be my own man and Pops is always trying to run my life. We are always falling out and now I have to be the bigger man to go and patch things up. If it's up to him, he'd carry a grudge to his grave.

My parents own a two-story brick house built back in the early seventies. It was a beautiful home at one time. Their place is not in ruins, it's just not up-to-date like the rest of the homes in this neighborhood. Some cosmetic work would do the trick in the living room. The ceiling is the most noticeable with the water circles left there from a leak in the roof. It smells musty and old side paneling paves the walls, which darkens the room.

Now that Pops' business is doing well and Momma changed the amount of hours she works at the hospital, they decided to remodel the house. There's even a new addition in the works.

Lots of childhood memories in this house and I was not sold on the idea of a new addition, but I quickly was outvoted when Momma and Pops reminded me that I don't live there anymore.

There is a big hole in the middle of the dining room and kitchen wall, where the demolition crews began to knock it down. Having an open space was my dad's idea, talking 'bout he always had to yell at Momma through a solid wall when he wanted something. If the wall came down, he wouldn't have to yell anymore. Momma is not too thrilled about the idea, because now she can't ignore him when he thinks she's not inside the kitchen.

Family photos once displayed on the wall sit in boxes tucked away to the side. Unsightly beige and brown nineteen seventies wallpaper strips cover part of the wall and floor. I stick my head through the basement door and yell out to Pops. I hear the television playing, but he doesn't answer. I call out to him again, still no answer.

A little on the frustrated side I yell again, "Hey Pops, you down there?"

"Yeah I'm down here and you don't have to yell. I'm not deaf you know," he retorts with a hint of sarcasm.

Sure acting like it. The old stairs to the basement squeak under me and they have me worrying about falling. I get down there and he's sitting at the end of the stairway in close proximity of the basement door where he can hear me. I look over at him and shake my head as I take the seat opposite him.

Trying to strike up a conversation I ask, "Hey, Pops, how is it going?"

His eyes never leaving the tube, he gives me a weak response: "It's going."

Too uncomfortable to say anything else I reply, "Good... good."

While I sit here struggling to think of what to say next, he watches the fishing channel, chewed on cheap tobacco and sipping on a Budweiser. It's not even twelve o'clock in the afternoon and this man is already sipping on booze. Pops took another sip of his Budweiser. I watch as moisture drips from the bottle and he wipes it on his pants.

"Looks like they doing some good fishing, huh Pops?"

He spits tobacco into a can. "Yep."

Aw man! How can he chew on that nasty stuff?

I look around the basement and cringe. Down here needs remodeling and some Febreze, because it smells like one of my old pairs of basketball shoes. I look my dad's way and wonder if he smells the stench in this raggedy basement.

The first vacuum cleaner Momma ever owned is leaning against an old Zenith radio as if it's a prized trophy. They look out of place down here with all of my dad's fishing and hunting items.

"Pops, I think it'll be a good idea to go out fishing before Michael leaves town."

"Mmmm."

Yeah, this is really going great. Tired of his one-liners, I shut up and let the noise from the TV fill the room. He can't ignore me forever.

Thirty minutes go by like a breeze and still no words pass between us. The only thing left for me to do is leave. I get to my feet and I'm hesitant to walk out. I don't want to leave without saying what I came to say. I feel like a six-teen-year-old in my dad's presence. We've had our share of disagreements over the years, and I thought we were past the hold-a-grudge stage after a disagreement.

I can recall the first falling-out Pops and I had. I was only sixteen and he wanted me to play football like him, and all the other Robinson men in the family did before me, includ-ing Michael. However, I had other plans for my life. I knew I'd fare better at playing basketball because of my height so when draft season came around for football, I didn't go to the tryout. Pops was furious. He practically disowned me until he realized how good I was when Momma forced him to come to one of my games. I was good enough to go all the way to the pros, but got injured fooling around.

I scratch my head again and look at Pops. The man is stubborn. I rub my temple and decide that he'll come around when he's ready or when Momma makes him.

"Well Pops, I'm heading back upstairs to finish helping Momma. I just wanted to come down to holla at you for a minute."

I turn to head back upstairs when he calls out to me. "Mikhail."

"Yes sir?"

"Sit down, there is something I need to say to you," he motions for me sit back down.

"Yes sir."

In his way of an apologizing, he says, "The last time we were in the same room we said some things that we're both probably regretting now that they've been said. Well at least that I'm regretting. I was a bit disappointed and hurt when you shot my offer down of partnership at the auto shop."

"I know, but..." He holds up his palm.

"Let me finish or I'll never get this out... I don't under-stand your decision, but I also realize I cannot make deci-sions for you anymore. You're a grown man now — one that can make his own decisions. Son, what I'm trying to say is I respect your decision even if I don't agree with it and I want you to know that if things don't work out at your job, you'll always have a place at the shop."

I grin, thinking it must be hard for him to express regret, because he's not a regretful man. Momma must have put him up to it or he's getting the cold shoulder from her.

"Thanks Pops. That makes me feel a whole lot better," I express, sticking my hand out to shake his. He brushes my hand away, and hugs me instead. His action removes the burden from my shoulders. I can live my life and not feel like I've let him down.

"Well with that being said don't wait so long to come back over here. You know how worried your momma gets when you boys don't come to visit and it puts me in the doghouse especially when I'm the reason," he chuckles then coughs from choking on his own spit.

Pops is a burly man, but today he looks heavier and tired. All those crazy hours he's working at the shop are catching up to him. The doctor warns him about overworking and from the looks of things, he's not taking the doctor's advice seriously. Earlier this year he had open-heart surgery and he needs to take it slow. I should say something and I will when the timing is right, but for now I want to savor this new comradeship we have.

Momma is still busy packing and putting away boxes when I walk back into the garage. The sun is up now and it burns hot inside there. A rinky-dink fan she has blowing air only makes the place hotter.

"Looks like you got a lot done since I've been down-stairs."

"I sure have, and now I'm tired," she admits, popping a squat on the chest in the middle of the garage.

"What you need me to do?"

She hands me the tape. "See those boxes over there. Tape them up and put them with the rest of the boxes in the corner of the garage. What did that old goat have to say for himself?"

"We talked. Momma is Pops doing OK?"

"Yeah he's doing better." She wipes her brow. "Why? What's wrong?" I notice her voice breaks and that concerns me.

"Nothing really. He just seems a little tired... you know what, don't mind me."

Momma doesn't press and I'm glad, because I don't want to get her worked up over nothing.

I lift up the first box to put it away and put it back down it's so heavy. What did she put in this box? Leaving it for last, I put away the rest, and then haul the pile of trash out to the curb. I'm almost through doing her manual labor and she blindsides me by bringing up Candy.

"Honey, what happened to Candy?" Momma wants to know. "Notice you don't bring her around anymore."

I pretend not to hear her and continue to put the trash out.

"I take it from your silence that the two of you aren't on good terms. Are you still together?"

"Momma, I don't want to talk about this right now. Do you have anything else you want me to do?" I ask and look over her shoulders into the garage.

She scolds me. "Boy, I'm still your Momma and when I ask you a question I expect an answer. Now tell your momma what's going on."

Wishing she wouldn't pry any further, I grunt my reply. "Don't know."

"What do you mean you don't know?" she asks and her face takes on a serious expression.

"I don't know, we had an argument and we haven't spoken since. As I said, I don't know. Are we done here?" I demand sternly, letting her know our discussing is over.

She says, "There's no need for you to take that tone with me, young man. I suppose we're finished with the conversation for now. If you need to talk about it let me know. I may be an old woman, but I still know a thing or two about relationships. You're never too old to learn something from your mother."

Her words soften my heart and make me feel awful for talking rough to her. I don't want to talk about Candy and Momma doesn't know when to stay out of people's business. It's the main reason why she and Michael's wife don't get along. Kelsey is not bad. She's just not momma's choice for Michael. Kelsey doesn't let Momma run her the way she ran some of the other women Michael dated in the past. Momma wanted Michael to marry a good church- going women and not some girl who stripped to put herself through college.

Candy is her favorite, smart, articulate, and pretty. Momma told me I made an excellent choice. She even said we'd give her some more grandkids before long. She was wrong.

I nod and shove my hands into my pockets. "So I've been told. I got to get going."

"OK baby, come over here and give your momma a hug."

"Don't worry bout Michael, he's going to be fine." I say as I pat her back.

She holds my face between her hands as if I'm still five. "Promise me, you'll come over for dinner tomorrow night."

"We'll see."

CHAPTER THIRTEEN

Lisa

I decided to take my mother's advice and tried to put my suspicions out of my mind, and cajoled John back into a good mood sometime after our fight about the phone call. We made love. It was good, but it certainly wasn't John's best, at least not Grade A quality. The tension still hung between us, and my mind kept replaying the week's arguments. I had to fake it again, and it's getting to the point where it's not worth it to me to keep giving in to pleasuring him and receiving none of my own. But I was determined to give this seduction a shot. If my mom could make her marriage work all those years, I could try a little harder on my own.

Now, as I stand looking in the mirror after taking a shower, the reflection staring back at me shows signs of a woman filled with bitterness, defeat, and sadness. Nowhere is the warm, loving, and trusting woman I was before John came into my life.

Mediocrity is setting in, and I'm tired of living in it. I run unsteady fingers across the fine lines under my eyes, paying close attention to the dullness in those eyes. The curviness I once had and loved to show off is now skin-and-bones. It's no wonder my cousin suggested I have AIDS. I'm not sure how I got here. I had envisioned so much for my life. I work hard to stand out from everyone else in my family. I made partner at my firm and that went unnoticed. I've been so busy trying to keep this marriage together that I forgot about me.

"When was the last time your husband asked about your needs?" I inquire of the mirror softly. "When was the last time he took you out and made you feel special? Better yet when was the last time he made love to you in a real way?" Sex to shut you up doesn't count. My wounded pride shoots back.

I've been staring at myself for entirely too long and too

deep in thought to notice that John has wandered back in the room and is now leaning against the bedpost watching me.

"Is something wrong, baby?" he probes and I jump.

How much did he witness of me evaluating myself? I hate it when he sneaks up on me like this. "No, I'm fine... I'm... I'm just tired." I retort, running the rake comb hastily through my hair.

"Are you sure? You seem a bit tense," he hints and comes to stand behind me.

Pushing up against me, John begins to rub my shoulders and my insides flinch. I want him to stop. I turn to face him and rest my butt against the dresser. We are close, but we're not touching. His eyes search mine, probing me. I don't want his kindness; don't want him to love me right now. I feel repulsive and worn to shreds.

"John, I need some sleep. Maybe I'll get some today."

"OK... well I'm going to head off to the office. I have some unfinished business from last night I need to take care of... I hope you don't mind." He kisses my forehead.

"No. Go ahead and take care of your business."

If I mind that wouldn't stop him from leaving. I'm not sure why he's developing a conscience all of a sudden. I thought he had left hours ago anyway.

"I'm not convinced you're OK. Look, I'm not mad you were spying on me, if that's what this is all about."

"I know."

He grunts and draws me close. He smells good and looks good; the man could put a dish towel on and he'd still be the hottest man alive to me. I want to be indifferent, but I can't, not when he's this close.

"You know?"

"Yes."

"Lisa, I love you and I hate it when we fight. Let me make it up to you by taking you out tonight. I know we haven't been out for a minute, because it's been crazy at the office. I want you to feel appreciated and special. We can celebrate my success in getting that new contract. How does that sound?" he beams.

"That's fine," I answer dryly.

"That's it, fine?" he asks, flabbergasted.

I can only assume my answer falls short of the applause he expected. He thinks he's doing me a favor by asking me to dinner. Shucks, that's not a treat. Taking me on that vacation he promised me would've gotten him a better response.

Here I am still upset with him and he is acting as if nothing's wrong. I swear for an educated man, he is dumb when it comes to women. I want to yell at him and the words I want to say are at the back of my throat. I try to hide my anger behind a forced smile and acquiesce to his request.

"Yes, John, that would be nice. What time should I expect you?" I ask with as much sweetness as I can muster.

He hesitates and closes our space. "Are you sure you're OK?"

His sudden niceness is annoying.

Pushing him toward the door, I reassure. "I'm fine, baby. Go on and stop worrying about me."

"OK then I'll see you around seven thirty. Lisa, I'm going to make this a special night for you."

"Sure, baby," I reply automatically as he leaves, not giving what he said much thought.

Investing in anything John says to me is a complete waste of my time, because I can usually guarantee he will break his promises. I've had many cancelled dinner engagements because of work or whatever else excuses he can pull out of his sleeve. We have become experts at pretending to have a good marriage, but it's nothing but a farce. I don't think I can follow my mom's advice anymore. My anger won't let me keep excusing John's behavior. I wish I hadn't let him touch me.

Uneasiness settles over me, and I run trembling hands through my new funky hairdo. This cut is cute, but I miss my long hair, especially now that I want to put it in a ponytail and go.

John was very upset that I had it cut and his response to me cutting my hair was tacky and cruel. He told me he likes his woman with long hair and added that if he wanted to be with someone who looks like a man, he would've married one. He was the only one with something negative to say, but then again his opinion of me is the only one that matters.

"This place is a pigsty," I mutter.

Thursday is the earliest the cleaning crew can make it out to our house and dirty clothes are in piles on the floor of my walk-in closet. Kicking the door shut with disgust, I sit on the edge of the bed and dial the detective's number.

"This is Seymour Private Eye." Ray's voice, a deep rich baritone, resonates through the phone.

The phone wheezes and crackles, because of the bad connection on this wireless phone. The signal in this house is low and I use my cell, because there is no telling what John has hooked up to the house phone.

Ray has been in the business for thirty-nine years. He's discreet and detailed. This is why I'm hiring him. If anybody can get the job done, he can.

"Ray, it's Lisa Boutari. How are you doing today?" my voice is shaky and hoarse.

Ray sighs very loudly into the receiver as if he leaned back into a chair or something.

"Doing good, wasn't expecting to hear from you today. Is everything OK with the documents I left at your office?"

"Yes, yes... um look Ray. I'm calling you on some personal business. What I'm proposing to you must remain confidential."

"Mrs. Boutari, everything I do is confidential. You have my word. What can I do for you?"

"I want you to follow my husband around for a few weeks. I have reasons to believe he's having an affair," I tell him as I play in the carpet with my toes.

I knew that would get his full attention and he asks, "What gave you that idea?"

"Let's just say it's woman's intuition." I'm so nervous my stomach cramps. I keep looking at the room door, half expecting John to jump out and ask me what I'm doing.

Ray gets political. "You've got to give me something more than that. I'll do the work, but I need more to go on than just your intuition. I don't normally say this to my clients, but I'm saying it to you because I like you, Mrs. Boutari, and don't want to take your money unnecessarily."

He catches me off guard with this one, because people with principals in this business are rare. I cannot see him, but I know he's being genuine.

"I have a lot of unexplained out-of-town trips, hang-up calls, and the other day someone sent him a postcard in the mail, only it was addressed to me with no return address or signatures. They sealed the envelope with a red lipstick and the essence of a woman was all over the card."

"There could be something there. Tell you what. I'll give you some time to think about it and if you still want me to..." I cut him short.

"No, I need to meet you at a remote location where we can discuss the details. I've already made up my mind."

"OK ... then I'll have to make some arrangements and get back to you, say middle of the week."

"Sounds great. I'll talk to you then." I smile sweetly.

I have something for you, John Boutari, and I bet you won't look so smug the next time I confront you. I don't know how long you thought I was going to bend over back-wards and continue to let you take advantage of me.

John, you won't have a pot to piss in after I'm through with you.

CHAPTER FOURTEEN

Candy

Nordstrom's annual shoe sale completely slipped my mind and all the shoe addicts are up in here trying to find a bargain. It's ridiculous to see grown women fight over shoes. Mona and I scuttle out of the two women's way when they begin to squabble over the only pair of Coach shoes left in their size. They are like wild animals sizing up the prey. To avoid being stampeded by the rest of the herd Mona and I quickly navigate our way over to the makeup counter.

Shelly's bachelorette party is tonight and I'm in desperate need of a makeover. The tired, bland look is out. Glimmer and glamour is the new thing and I need to shine tonight big time, because everyone from the office will be there.

The makeup counter is full with women busying themselves, arranging cosmetic gift baskets and stocking makeup in the display case. There is one of the women in particular who has my attention and not in a good way. This woman's face looks stiffer than plywood board from doing too much Botox and her makeup is all wrong; it scares me that she is behind the makeup counter.

"Look, Mona. It's Mimi from the Drew Carey Show," I snicker and jerk my head to the left.

Mona looks then chuckles. "Candy, you know you wrong for that."

"Hello, can I help you?" Mimi asks, not really paying attention to us.

Stuck up and obviously prejudiced. She licks her finger and turns the page of the book she is leafing through, probably looking up the latest Botox trend for her body to match the rest of her face.

I step closer to the counter and put my purse down. "Yes. I need someone to help me with a makeover."

"Have you been here before?" she asks with her nose turned up.

This stiff-faced hussy had better not tick me off this morning, because I'm not the one. I would tell her I pay her salary, but I don't go there with her.

"Yes, I have been here before. Half my paycheck goes here on occasion... I have a question... don't you people work off commission?"

She closes her book and puts it away. "I'm not sure what relevance that has to the question I asked you."

"You wouldn't... What you can do for me is find someone else to help me. I don't care for your attitude. You might mess up my makeup, seeing as it's obvious to me you have a problem with serving our kind and I sure don't want my face coming out looking like yours."

Our confrontation has Mona in stitches and I want to laugh too, but this is not funny anymore. The color of my skin shouldn't mean lesser respect. Our money is good as anybody else's, and I'm not having it.

She patronizes me. "Ma'am I was only asking you a question. I'm sorry if you took offense."

"Whatever you say lady, either get me someone else or we can continue this discussion with your boss." I open my mouth to say more, but clamp my lips together. God has brought me too far, for me to start acting the way I used to again.

Mona murmurs, "This one has some nerve."

Mimi walks briskly away with mouth turned up and nose in the air. She has words with one of the women at the end of the counter, a pretty brunette.

Mona teases. "They are really going to mess up your make-up now. Don't they have any black people back there?"

"Please. I'm not worried about these folks. Someone's going to do my makeup today and it will be done right. Trust me."

"Hi, I'm Kelly. How can I help?" Kelly is chipper and a pleasant encounter.

"Yes, Kelly, I need a makeover. I'm going to a party tonight, and I want to try something to spice up my look. On the other hand, I also want something that is low maintenance for work during the week."

"Sure we can do that. You have beautiful cheekbones. Have you ever tried Max Factor products before?" Kelly asks as she pulls out a clipboard.

"Thanks and no, I only use lip gloss and foundation and that's about the extent of my makeup collection."

"OK. I need you to fill out a questionnaire chart before we get started. This will fill me in on any allergies you may have as well as give me some ideas of what kind of products would work best on your skin type."

"Sure."

She hands me the clipboard with a pen attached and I read the questionnaire and proceed to fill it out as she requested.

"How about you ma'am, can I find you something too?" Kelly asks Mona.

"I actually know what I want."

Mona keeps Kelly busy while I complete the long questionnaire. Kelly places a few items on the counter for Mona and tallies it up on the register.

"Your total is one hundred fifty five dollars and forty five cents." My head snaps in their direction at the price she rattles off to Mona, who pulls out her wallet.

I ask, "Those five things cost a hundred and fifty five dollars? .... What's in them — gold?"

Mona laughs and takes the receipt from Kelly and puts it in her bag.

Mona says, "I had to get some things for my skin and my face. Girl I'm starting to break out now that the weather has changed."

Kelly adds, "Mona, I placed a few samples in your bag as well. You may find some to your liking." She smiles and turns to me. "Are you through filling out the information?"

"Yeah, here you go." I hand her the clipboard.

She takes it and scans through it. Mumbles a few incoherent words then tells me she'll be back. To pass the time I browse through some of the products they have for display. One cream guarantees younger looking skin and improved collagen in less than two weeks.

"Do women really use all these products to look good? What happened to the era of aging naturally?" I turn to ask Mona.

"Everybody wants to look like Demi Moore so they can snag them an Ashton Kutcher."

"That's insane and somebody will buy it nonetheless. The people who invented this foolishness are no doubt laughing all the way to the bank."

Kelly reappears with a handful of products and her color selection has me worried. This woman is about to have me looking like Bozo the clown with all this makeup in her hand.

"OK. I have a few things I think will work for you. When I get through with you I'll have you looking like you've just stepped off Glamour magazine," She convinces me.

"This reminds me of when I was a teenager getting all glammed up for the prom. I had younger skin then; now I don't know what I have. I break out if I sneeze too hard."

She smiles. "You may need to wash your face more often. You just missed the prom crowd we had a few teenagers here not too long ago. It was a mad house. I almost quit this morning. One of the girls didn't show up for work today and if you've ever worked retail you'd know that every hand counts."

"I don't understand how anyone works in retail."

A woman accompanied by her family interrupts our conversation, asking for directions to the women's department. Kelly gives them directions. They thank her and shuffle away in that direction.

Kelly motions me to sit in the seat. "Like I was saying, it's not easy. I'll tell you that. Tilt your face to the left."

I do as she asks. Kelly wipes foundation from my face. My skin tingles, fresh scents of orange fill my nostrils. Great. I smell like a fruit cocktail.

"I'm going with the Max Factor line for you today; it's low maintenance. Max Factor came out with new lip products. Color perfection is a gel-based lipstick. It lasts awhile on your lips. It also helps moisturize. The foundation I'm applying to your face is good all day to evening. The eye shadow makeup does the same. We're going to have some fun with this stuff. Relax. I'm going to take care of you."

"That sounds good. I'm putting my trust in you. My face better come out looking good," I threaten, and wink so she knows I'm joking.

"Too late now, she already started on your face. I can't

believe this is the first time you're getting a makeover done since you were a teenager," Mona comments, coming to stand closer to me. "You should do a makeup makeover at least once a year."

A dose of cockiness takes over and I reply with my head rolling, and finger snapping. "I never really needed it until now, besides I've always relied on my natural beauty."

She returns the favor, mimicking my exact attitude. "Well excuse me."

Kelly's eyebrows rise at my last statement. "Why now?" She asks, curiously.

I tease, "Well aren't you a nosy-parker."

Her face turns pink. "No I'm not trying to be nosy. I just thought you were doing this for a man. I don't know, I guess I am being kind of nosy huh?" she admits.

"No, you're OK. I'm only giving you a hard time. I'm getting a makeover because my style has gone flat overall and I'm starting to find things on my face as I get older."

Kelly is not convinced. She replies, "Oh, OK."

"Why do you say it like that?" I lean back to look up at her.

"No reason. I think you have beautiful skin, but I really thought this was for a guy."

"I have to find the guy first. Maybe with this transformation I can attract better quality men. All I've been running into is dead beats."

We all laugh.

"I doubt you have that problem," Kelly says.

Kelly is fun to be around. We all joke with each other as she works on my new look. She shares her marriage plans with us and talks non-stop about the baby she's expecting. What was supposed to be a joyful event for both her fiancé and her has turned into a family feud between the parents because they don't approve of the pregnancy or the wedding plans.

All this fussing, because the daddy is a black man.

Neither of their parents is speaking to them. They'd rather cut off their noses to spite their faces than to come together and make the best of the situation. As Kelly describes the nightmare she's going through I pray silently for her, but something tells me I need to do more than just say a prayer.

Sharing my beliefs with strangers doesn't come easy for me, but I know that's what I have to do with Kelly.

"Kelly, do you believe that Jesus died on the cross for our sins?" I ask and Mona shifts uncomfortably.

"I have controversy with it sometimes, but for the most part, yes I believe."

"Do you want to get into a better relationship with him?"

"Yes."

"Good, please repeat after me." I motion for her to close her eyes and we do. "Lord I believe your son Jesus died on the cross for me in Calvary and I know I don't deserve it because I am a sinner, but I'm asking for your forgiveness and for you to come into my heart Lord Jesus and set me free. Amen."

I open my eyes and Kelly is crying and nodding her head, then she throws her arms around me. I get excited when I win someone to Christ, but this one is more so because of our diversity. I really admire Kelly's strength and believe she will overcome her struggles.

"You know... I haven't told Gavin this yet, but my mom tried to push me down the stairs in my first trimester."

My mouth drops and I say, "The Lord is going to handle that. Evil can only last for a moment. Weapons may form against us, but they never prosper. Find a good church for you and Gavin to attend and let God direct your life. Trust me you won't regret following him."

"You came here for me. I've been praying to God for some miracle that He was listening and He sent you here to reassure me. Thank you." She puts her arms around me again. We get mushy and tears flow.

"I think I ruined my makeup," I sniffle and wipe under my eyes.

"No, you're fine. I'll just add some loose powder to your face... OK there, we're done. Take a look and see for yourself." She hands me a mirror.

I gasp.

Mona gasps too.

I take her speechlessness as a good sign. I am thrilled, can hardly contain my excitement. This is truly an Oscar moment!

I touch my face. "Oh my goodness Kelly this looks... I have no words."

I hardly recognize the person staring back at me. She played up my eyelids and eyelashes making them appear fuller, sultrier, and sexier. Even the foundation is a perfect match to my skin tone. The result of my makeover is flawless and she made all this possible in less than ten minutes.

"I'm going to take that as you're happy with the results."

"She better be, her makeup looks good. You did a great job," Mona nudges me in the side. "Why didn't you ever let me do your makeup? It's not like I don't do this stuff every day."

"I don't know," I say, still admiring my new look. "I guess I had no idea just how big of an impact it would make. Plus I didn't want to bug you about my makeup when that's your job."

"Well, it's OK," Mona said. "Now that you've been broken in, you can let me try some looks on you sometime."

I turn back to Kelly. "I love it... absolutely love it. I had no idea that my face could look like this... thank you, thank you Kelly."

"You're welcome, it was my pleasure. Come back to see me again."

"You did an awesome job. I'm pleased with the outcome."

Kelly explains quick tips on how to achieve the look. I walk out of Nordstrom's feeling like Julia Roberts in Pretty Woman. And I would've gone home, but Mona's bright idea after we leave Nordstrom is to walk the mall. I'm not in the mood, because there are too many people in one place, bustling about aimlessly.

Interesting characters roam the place, lurking around are the I'm-just-here-to-pick-up-women brothers yelling "Shorty" to every woman with a big rear-end who passes by them. Then we have the I-know-next-week-I-won't-be-able-to-pay-my-rent sisters buying up folks' things knowing full well they can't afford it. Old men walk the mall with girls young enough to be their daughters. You name it, and it is in this mall today.

Mona talks me into stopping in one of the trendier stores to try on a few things. The prices are outrageous, the clothes K-mart quality. What person in their right is going to pay one hundred and nineteen dollars for no-name jeans?

Mona elbows me. "Girl you see what she got on?"

I laugh, more like a cackle. "Child, yes."

"Maybe she got dressed in the dark today."

"You think?... What I want to know is, where are the parents for these kids?" I marvel.

"Some people let their children out of the house looking all kinds of way."

This child has red hair, spiked with blue. Rock star T-shirt, mini skirt, orange combat booths adorn her feet. People passing her mirror our reaction. They laugh and point. She's listening to music, bopping her head and doesn't notice. The headphones in her ears deafen her to the world. She catches me staring and dares me to continue. Mona nudges me again and we lose eye contact.

"Let's stop in here." The neon lights flickering like a disco club in Guess do not look inviting and my head hurts.

"OK. You go in and I'll stay out here."

Mona goes inside Guess and leaves me to sit and wait, but staying out here was a bad idea. When will men learn that using lines like "Can a brother holla at you for a minute'" or "Baby, no wonder you tired, you've been running through my mind all day" don't work on real women?

Thirty minutes pass and Mona is still in the Guess store shopping. I'm tired and on the cranky side. The little food I ate at Denny's this morning is gone. Waking up early this morning and getting in late last night ruined my regular eating schedule.

Inside the music blares and the Guess feels more like a nightclub than a store. Add a bar, a few booty shakers dressed half-naked, strobe lights and it would be on and popping in here. People throw odd looks my way for looking under every stall door. I stop when I come across Mona's tattooed ankle of Betty Boop.

"Mona, I can't believe you're still in here."

"I'll be out in a minute," she yells and throws a pink and white flowery shirt over the door.

"OK then, are you ready to leave?"

"I'm almost ready, Ms. Impatient."

"I got things to do. I haven't found anything to wear for tonight."

"You can't find anything to wear in this big mall? You too picky," she hisses.

"Well, believe it. I'm going back outside... and hurry up."

I'm getting a headache from being hungry, so now I'm full of attitude. It's not Mona's fault, but she's adding to it.

"There is an outfit in the front entrance of the store I thought would look good on you," Mona suggests.

I gape at the stall door, but Mona can't see me. "Are you talking about the two-piece set with the back out?" I ask with feigned interest.

"Yep, that's the one. Won't you try it on and see how it looks on you."

"Are you in your right mind? I don't wear that stuff anymore."

"Suit yourself," she says and dismisses the idea.

In a huff I walk back outside to take up residence on the bench and resume my people watch.

***

Lisa

Dark clouds settle over the sky, threatening rain. The Weather Channel forecasts a seventy-five percent chance of rain today. The weather people seem to always be wrong, but I bring an umbrella with me just in case.

Curtis is fresh on my mind and has been on it all morning. I would call and take him up on his offer from last night, but I have cold feet. The business card he gave me is still in my purse, which I hid under my car seat for fear that John would go snooping around.

I've never done this before and I wrestle with my conscience for another ten minutes, then I dial. Curtis' phone does a short ring on my side, but I hang up before the call registers. I do this several times before I allow it to ring completely.

"Mason here, speak to me."

I had prepared what I wanted to say, but I'm stumped. "Hi... um... I'm calling for Curtis. Is this the right number?"

"This is Curtis, can I help you?"

"Ah it's Lisa from the um... from the other night, do you remember me?"

"Hey! I thought I'd never hear from you again."

Sighs of relief leave my body. I smile, pleased he remembers me. "What gave you that idea?"

"Well, let's see. After we left Zane's last night we went by that spot you and your girlfriends told us you'd be, but you weren't there."

"Yeah, well I'm sorry. Last night turned out to be a total bust. One of my girlfriends and I got into it and we ended up not going anywhere."

"What happened?"

Curtis sneezes.

"Bless you... I'm not sure," I reply and laugh. "That being said I really didn't call to talk about them."

"True, true, so what you want to talk about?" he asks and his voice takes on a sultrier tone.

"I don't know; let's talk about you. And who is Mason?"

"Mason is a pet name and what about me? Where are you? Sounds like you're driving."

"I want to know everything there is to know about you, and yes I'm driving. I was on my way to the mall, but changed my mind. I'm really not in the mood to shop."

"What kind of mood are you in?"

"Nothing comes to mind. I needed to get out of the house, and taking a long drive sounded good to me," I reply as I veer to my right onto Nall Street.

I bite down on my bottom lip and wait for his response. I hope he takes the hint and asks me out. I don't want to make the first move, don't want to seem desperate.

Finally, he catches on. "Then meet me for lunch."

I do a victory cheer, silently — of course — and say: "That sounds good."

"If you like seafood we could meet at Joe's Crab Shack off College Boulevard... say in a about an hour?"

"I love seafood. Heard it's an aphrodisiac," I say, then quickly add: "I'm kidding. Can we do Italian instead?"

"Sure, whatever works for you. I'm not picky." He mentions the name of another restaurant and I agree.

"See you in about an hour? I'm in that area already."

He chuckles. "You'll have to tell me more about seafood being an aphrodisiac when I see you."

I'm nervous with anticipation and giddy enough to do cartwheels. Our conversation from last night drifts into my head. Then I remember that I'm married and a twinge of guilt puts a damper on my excitement. Here I am thrilled about going to lunch with another man, when not too long ago I was making love on the patio table with my husband. The guilt is short-lived, though, because after all, I'm only doing what John did to me first.

CHAPTER FIFTEEN

Mikhail

"Hey Mikhail, thought you weren't coming in today." Jaime greets me with a dazzling smile.

I've known Jaime since the gym opened its doors to the public. Jaime was one of the first people hired on here, and now she is the manager. I scan my card and grab a towel from the neat stack laid out for members.

"Yeah, I'm running a little behind today," I say and rub my eye.

"You look tired. What have you been doing to yourself? I guess all the partying you're doing on the weekends is catching up to you." Jaime walks out from behind the desk and leads me to the center of the gym.

Her sexy laughter caresses my ears.

"You know me, haven't seen you out in a minute though. Who's the new guy?"

"What makes you think it's a new guy?" she challenges and smiles mockingly.

I shrug and throw the towel over my shoulder. "OK then who is the old guy?"

She humors me. "I don't like them old and it's not a guy."

"Tell the truth. It's always a guy with you when you're no longer hanging out at your favorite pastime."

She cast her eyes down to the floor. "All right, you got me. I am seeing someone."

"Where'd you meet him this time?"

"The Spot. He's really nice. I think this one's a winner."

"Yeah so were the others before him. Won't you let a brother like me take you out for a spin? I promise you'll like the ride. You won't wanna come down afterward."

"Oh ah-hah you are so not right." She swats me playfully on the shoulders.

"I'm only offering you an opportunity here baby."

She swings at me again and I sidestep her. "An opportunity of chaos. You're too much for me."

I smile and say, "See you later, precious."

"Have a good workout." Jaime giggles and sashays back to the desk.

The flirting we do with each other is harmless, because we both know nothing will come of it. Jaime gorgeous, but she's nothing to play with. She will chew you up and then spit you out after she's through with you.

The gym is in full swing today, quite a few half-naked honeys in here and as I pass by a group of them, they smile and watch me. Too bad this is the gym, because a few of them could definitely be on my hit list. The problem with dating people where you work out is that if things go sour, you can't avoid running into each other. The inviting looks thrown my way are just that, inviting. I keep moving. These females tend to get too crazy sometimes and I don't need anyone stalking me or spreading vicious rumors about me in this place.

I change out of my street clothes, throw my duffel bag in the locker and head back out to the zoo. I stop to holler at a couple of dudes in what we call the pit. This side of the gym is for men only. Vince, one of the body builders prepping for a fitness show, occupies the bench I need for chest press. The man lifts two hundred and eight pounds of iron like it's nothing. This is where we come to get serious about getting and staying in shape without all the female distraction.

"Ace, I thought that was you." Someone shouts my old college nickname from behind.

I turn around to see Derrick walking toward me. "What's up big D? Where you been bro?"

"I've been around. How's it going?"

The man is always out of town. I can never get a hold of him. We used to be close, but we lost contact. Derrick is always on one of his moneymaking schemes to take over Corporate America. He made a smart move when he opened this club after he got injured playing professional football. He was good at playing ball and he would've been great, but the girl he was engaged to talked him out of going back.

That's when he decided to come up with the concept of Build a Better Body. A renowned gym, it's one of the most sought after gyms in the country. It is stocked with state-of-the-art equipment used for rehabilitation of professional athletes. Derrick is at the top of his game with this career move.

He offered me partnership before he opened this gym, but I was young, faithless and doubtful of his idea going anywhere, so I turned him down. I regret not making the investment when I could have, and now my boy is rolling in the dough.

I slap my hands together and take a stance. "I'm just trying to get my workout in for the day. I got to keep my body tight you know, got to look right for the ladies."

"Man, what ladies? Weren't you the one who told me a couple of months back that you found the lady of your dreams? What happened?" Derrick asks and rests his elbows on one of the machines.

"You got me there. These women are a trip. Some days you think everything is nice and crisp and then other days..." I let my voice trail and throw my hands up. "It's like being in hell. These females are crazy."

"Man, that bad huh?" Derrick nods. "So um what? Ya'll not together no more?"

"I'm not so sure I'm feeling her anymore and I'm starting to feel like she's not feeling me either. Know what I mean?"

"I feel you, dawg. These females are like that sometimes, bloodhounds. This is why I do, what I do. Hit and run bro, hit and run, forget all that emotional jazz. I ain't giving my heart to a female that ain't happening, for real."

I smile. Some things never change. Derrick has his reasons for cynicism. I'm not there yet.

"You talk all that trash now, trust me you haven't met the right female to turn the tables around on you. When that day comes — and believe me, it will — I want to be the first in line to witness the downfall of Mr. Derrick Washington."

He chuckles. "You got me messed up, that'll never happen. Be forewarned... never happen and I know you ain't talking smack. Always wanting something on the side in case things don't work out with the main chick."

"Man please, don't even start on me, you've got no room to talk. You got more drama than the dude on Beebe's kids with that psycho baby mama you have."

Derrick's face looks like he doesn't know whether to laugh or cry.

"Man, you had to go there."

"You ain't smiling now huh?... How is Shawna doing these days?" I ask, ragging on him some more.

"Man that woman is gonna make me kill her. Did you know she took me to court again for more child support and alimony? Talking 'bout now that I'm opening up a new gym I should be able to afford to give her more money. You hear this mess, more of my hard earned money. Now ain't that something!" He pushes up from the machine and paces then stops in front of me. "I'm gonna kill her."

I snicker, then full-blown laughter follows. Derrick is not finding it funny and he remains serious. His seriousness makes me laugh even harder.

I laugh so hard it turns into a cough. "I told you about that girl. Remember when I told you she was a gold-digger and you got mad at me for talking bad about your girl? Man you should have listened to me when I told you not to marry her. It would have saved you a lot of grief and of course money, but that's jacked up she's swindling you like that. On a different tip though, I didn't know you were planning on opening another gym."

Derrick scratches his neck and pops it. "Yeah, things have been going pretty good at this gym and it's really getting a little too crowded. My partner and I thought it would be a good idea for us to branch out."

"What, like starting up a franchise?"

"Nothing elaborate as that. It's gonna be a smaller version to this one. You should come run it for me. I can always use a friend who will hold down the fort for me when I'm gone."

"That's a generous offer partner, but I'm trying to make my own moves," I say.

"Oh yeah, what you have in mind?" Derrick asks with curiosity.

"I'm planning on opening up a restaurant, dance club, or a combination of both. I need the funds, though. Since I can't work for you maybe you can loan me the funds when

I come up with a good business plan."

"When you're ready, holla at me," Derrick says and nods. "I'll take a look at it. You know me. I'm always down for making an investment. A brother got mouths to feed."

"I'll let you know."

"All right man, I'm a holla at you later. I'm meeting up with some people across town," he says as he slaps my hand and pulls me into a brotherly hug.

"OK, take it easy man."

Derrick reassures. "I'm for real Mikhail, holla at me when you ready, a'ight."

"I hear you."

Derrick's agreement to back my idea sounds good. He makes good on his promises. There's only one thing holding me back. I'm not convinced I want to get financially involved with a friend. I walk to the back of the gym to start on my regular routine for legs. Dumbbell squats, leg extensions, leg curls, and traveling lunges. I work them for an hour and then start on my upper body. Every muscle in my body cries out in pain, good pain.

The stretch I put in after following my workout has me feeling like an old man with all the snap, crackle, and popping my muscles are doing and my legs burn from the intense workout they just endured. Sure would be nice if Candy were waiting at home for me. I could use one of those massages she usually gives me after I've had an intense workout. I twist the knob on the showerhead and the flow of warm liquid caresses my chest and works its way down to my torso.

Memories of Candy touching my body cloud my mind. Her scent, the way she tastes, the sexy sounds she makes when she is excited, all come back to me like she's next to me. The worst place to get aroused is in a male public restroom, because anyone can walk in, but this is what Candy does to me.

***

Stan's barbershop stays packed with people, today being no different. He is always two or three people behind, regardless if you make an appointment. Two major factors stop me from looking for another barber. One, he's my close friend; the other, he's crafty.

"Stan, how long you think this goin' take today man? I don't plan on being here all day."

Mr. Harper who is in his prime put his newspaper down to watch the showdown between us. This is an every Saturday occurrence for Stan and me to go back and forth with one another.

"Man, sit your black tail down."

"You better be glad I know your momma boy. You must be out your mind talking to me like that," I joke.

"So what's up, playa?"

Stan trims a young boy's hair who giggles and moves away every time he runs the blades near his nape. Stan is mad, but he hides it well.

"You've got to keep your head still, Kenny. You know your momma will trip if I don't get your hair looking right," Stan warns and continues to move the clippers toward the little boy's nape.

"But it tickles." He whines, sniffles and repeats the same thing when Stan puts the shears next to his nape.

Stan spins his chair around to face him. "Kenny look, you wanna go back to school with a jacked up fade?"

The boy's voice soft and complaisant, he replies. "No."

"Then keep your head still." And that was the end of that. "So what's happening man?"

"Aw man I ain't up to nothin' much, just came from working out," I respond as I flip through one of the magazines on the table.

Eye candy flaunts their stuff like choice beef on every page. Thick sistahs are taking over the video vixen business. Ki Toy Johnson is one chocolate covered bar I'd like to have melting in my mouth. The girl is bad. Maybe she can make me forget Candy and all my worries.

"Man I can't tell the last time I've set foot inside a gym. How much the boy Derrick charging for memberships over there?"

I shrug. "Shoot, I don't know," I answer and jump to my feet to stand next to him. "Look at all this chocolate?... Now you know this doesn't make any sense."

"What you mean you don't know?" He quizzes, stopping in the middle of what he's doing. He pauses to look at the magazine. "What she goin' do with all that back? I think I've just sinned by looking at this magazine with you."

"She has a phat back. I don't know how much Derrick charges for a membership. He gave me a discounted rate."

"Watch your mouth man there's a child in here. Think if I call him, he'll hook me up."

"He might. When was the last time the two of you talked?"

"It's been awhile. To tell you the truth with me being so busy here at the shop, I haven't been keeping in touch with him."

"Me neither. He's opening up another gym."

"He's doing that for real?" Stan asks, looking sideways at me. "When he plan on doing that?"

"He was talking about doing it some time next year."

"Looks like I might be in the wrong business. Derrick's doing it big, huh?"

"That's what I said when he told me. Hey, you remember when Derrick first came to me with that idea and I turned him down. Man I was talking to him today and wish I didn't."

"Yeah, but you know…. You didn't know his business idea would blow up. What happened to your dream of opening up your own club? It's not as if you have to look far for collateral. Your old man would be the perfect investor."

I look at him crazy, thinking he forgot who my old man is.

"You know he wants me to run his shop, not open some booty shaking club. You know how he acted when I turned him down."

"So what, you just goin' continue to deliver people's packages for the rest of your life?"

I ignore his last statement. "What I need to do is apply for a grant."

"That's not a bad idea. I know a dude who writes business plans. I could get in touch with him for you, if you're serious."

"Yeah I'm serious."

"A'right then, I'll let you know in a few days."

I make waves with my hands. "Nah for real, get at your boy."

"All right, I got you," Stan replies.

We both turn our heads to the jingle of the chimes from the door. Ms. Emma is at it again. Rain, snow, or sunshine this woman is out selling her food. Her meals on wheels business has been around since I was knee high. Ms. Emma's food is famous in every shop on this block. When Stan's father was alive, he allowed her to come in and sell to his patrons, so naturally Stan continues the tradition.

Ms. Emma stops to catch her breath and wipe perspiration from her brow with the back of her hand then she pushes her cart to the middle of the shop.

She cools her face with a makeshift fan. "Whew, I'm tired. How are my babies doing today?... Ya'll hungry? I have a variety of soul food dishes with me today."

Stan laughs quietly. "What you got for us today Ms. Emma?"

"I've got some collard greens, some slap yo momma fried chicken, cornbread, and some macaroni and cheese."

"I want me a plate, Ms. Emma. It sure smells good from where I'm sitting," Mr. Lennox put his bid in and stands to his feet. He limps toward her cart. "I've been waiting all day for you to pass through here," he says and flashes a toothless grin.

It doesn't take long for the food in the cart to give off the scent to what she already told us. Everyone inside the barbershop hovers around Ms. Emma's food cart to place an order. The full cart of food she brought in emptied in no time. I want a plate so badly my stomach hurts, but I can't eat that kind of food, not after working out as hard as I did at the gym.

Ms. Emma tallies up her money and walks right back out the door leaving the aroma of soul food in the shop to torment me. I watch with regret as the men greedily scarf down their food and yearn for a plate. The bottle of water I took from Stan's icebox to quiet my stomach's rumblings lost it appeal. The cold water coats my insides, but the hunger is still eminent.

"You ready, Mikhail?" asks Stan.

I settle in the empty chair in front of him and he throws a cape around my neck then elevates the chair to his height. What I'm about to ask him will shock him.

I say, "I want it shaved off."

"What?"

"Shave it off."

"Man, you joking."

"No, I'm being serious. I've been thinking about this for awhile. Time for a change, my man. Shave it off."

"Cold as this weather gets, you want me to shave your head. Man you out your mind?" Stan scolds as he squeezes shaving cream on my head.

Stan shaves my hair off row-by-row, clumps of hair fall to the floor until I'm completely bald. He dusts talc on a brush then distributes it over my head. I run my hands over my head. It's smooth.

"You're good to go, head shaved and smooth as a baby's butt. I hope you brought a hat because your head's probably gonna feel different when you go back outside."

"Nah, I'll be a'right. How much I owe you?"

"It's cool, this one's on me."

"Man, are you sure 'bout that?"

"Sure I'm sure. What you got going on tonight?"

"I'm meeting up with Michael downtown. Won't you come down after you lock up the shop and let me buy you a drink?"

Stan acts as though he's giving it some thought. Stan cleans his shears and preps them for his next client then he hangs them on a hook.

"All right, I'll let you know man."

"Why are you faking the funk? You know you ain't coming to the club."

"It made you stop asking though, right?"

"You got a point. Well, I'll see you later bro." We swap handshakes and pats on the back.

Stan gave his life to God two years ago after losing his twin brother to drugs. It was hard for him to deal with at first and he was going down the wrong path, until he met

Kendra who turned things around for him. Life was beating him up. Kendra is the best thing to happen to him. They have two beautiful baby girls together and I've never seen him happier.

"I'll holla at you later. Say hello to Kendra and the kids for me."

"All right, man."

The autumn air hits my head, sending tremors through me. Zipping up my bomber jacket, I sprint to my car. I would've made it too, but someone stops me.

"Mikhail?" The female voice shakes with uncertainty.

I turn around. "Who's asking?"

"Monique... Monique Taylor I went to high school with you," she offers and looks at me expectantly.

The face is familiar; still I don't make the connection. I figure she has to be one of my casualties. She still carries a smile on her face, so the parting between us couldn't have been all that bad.

The smile she wears on her face wavers slightly. She asks, "You don't remember me, do you?"

"Sorry... can't say I do, sweetheart. I'm bad with both faces and names."

"I figured you'd remember me since you played football with my older brother Tobey."

"Yeah I know you. You're Tobey's little sister?" I ask, brows raised. Tobey's sister or not, she is wearing those jeans. I ease back to admire the way she fills them out.

Sensual lips part showing off her pretty smile. "Yes. I grew up."

I like what I see, and let her know. "That's for sure. Do you need some help getting out of those later?"

She laughs and looks away. "No, think I can manage getting out of them myself."

"If you change your mind, let me know. What's Tobey been up to these days?"

Her face stiffens and all signs of life disappear from her eyes.

"Tobey died a few years ago," her voice cracks.

I'm speechless. Her words echo in my head. This can't be. Not Tobey, he's too young. I heard wrong. I must have.

"Died? You're not serious?... Of course, you're serious... you have to be serious... I mean... I'm so sorry."

I've known Tobey for half my lifetime; it's devastating to find out about his death this way. I can't find the right words to comfort her.

Trying to be strong, a faint smile plays at her lips. "Thank you...." This is not a comfortable subject for either one of us. I want to know more, but she doesn't seem to be in the mood to continue. "Well I'm not going to keep you. I thought it was you and wanted to stop to say hello." She makes for her escape, merely a few feet away.

I ask, "How did he die?"

She stops and turns to face me.

"He got shot for being in the wrong place at the wrong time."

"Man, was this by cops? Street thugs?"

"Street thugs. How are your parents?" she asks, reaching for a better topic.

"Good. They're good."

"Tell them hello for me."

"I will. Say Monique can I call you sometimes?"

"Sure." We exchange numbers. "See you around Mikhail."

"Yeah, see you around."

It's a small world. I slip the paper with her number in my pocket. I'm not sure if I'll ever call her, but it still doesn't hurt to keep the number.

CHAPTER SIXTEEN

Lisa

Getting a table at Carrabba's is nerve-racking; too many patrons. A few shots of something strong would do me good right now.

"Welcome to Carrabba's. Dining for one?" The greeter asks with a smile.

"No. Um, I need a table for two," I say, glancing around the room. "Something by the window please."

"OK. Right this way."

I follow her. The other patrons look up briefly from their meals to feed the human nature to be nosy. Others do not notice the mild interruption as the hostess seats me. The window table she seats me is prefect to watch for Curtis's arrival. I'm fifteen minutes early. I'm always early, work habit. I touch my nape, rubbing my newly shortened mane. I catch myself displaying this nervous habit, so I stop. I place my hands in my lap, but end up playing with my fingernails.

I'm having second thoughts about being here. Every time someone pulls into a parking space, my eyes snap in their direction only to discover it's not him.

Our waiter checks up on me. "Are you still doing OK ma'am?"

"Still doing OK," I pipe up.

"OK then I'll just check back on you in a few minutes."

I nod and stare into the drink I've been nursing since I got here. It's almost finished and I don't want to order anything else. Last night's drama is proof I should drink slowly and stick with the light stuff.

Curtis shows up looking sexy. He strolls up to the host and she points him to my table. He comes over. We size each other up the way lovers do when passion boils through their veins. I'm transfixed. I don't remember him being this tall and built. He wears a white canvas shirt that compliments his dark skin and shows off his broad shoulders. We hug. He's strong and warm, not to mention smells good. I like. It takes everything in me to let him go.

He speaks my mind. "Hmm, you smell good." His lips are close to my ear. His breath warms my skin.

I smile shyly. "Thank you."

"I see you already got started without me." He nods toward my half empty glass of daiquiri.

"I couldn't resist the drink special."

He chuckles. "Ah."

Curtis sits across from me and I try not to stare, but it's difficult. He's an extremely attractive man, one who fascinates me. I want him and the knowledge of this scares me. I would rather skip lunch and go some place where he can have me for lunch instead.

"I'm glad you called." He rests his elbows on the table and leans forward. "You're probably not going to believe this, but I was thinking of you minutes before you called."

"Oh yeah? What were you thinking?"

"I was remembering you, the mystery lady from last night and hoping that you would put my card to use."

"Mystery lady, why do you think I'm mysterious?"

"Last night you got to know me better than I got to know you. Not that I'm prying, it's just you didn't tell me much about yourself."

"Oh."

He has a valid argument. I deliberately left out a few details last night. Getting to know him was the easy part. He was candid. He had nothing to hide — or did he?

These days you can never tell with men, they are so deceiving. There's no telling what his agenda is. Every man does and if his agenda is the same as mine then I've hit the jackpot. I'm not looking for a commitment and I hope he isn't looking for one either. I want him to put the F in fun.

"There you go again, avoiding giving up information about yourself. If I didn't know better I'd say you are hiding something." Curtis reaches for my hand. He studies my palm and runs imaginary lines over it. It feels good, much better than I expected.

More than you know. I laugh to cover my nervousness. "I don't have anything to hide. I really don't like talking about myself. People often learn things about me when it comes out naturally."

"You mean when you don't have to volunteer information."

Smart guy. I smile. "That's one way of putting it."

He removes his hand and I feel deserted. "What do you do?" he asks, clasping long fingers, thick, clean and well manicured together. A man who takes cares of himself, hmm.

"I'm an attorney."

He chuckles. "That's why you're evasive with info, an attorney huh? What kind?"

"I'm a divorce attorney."

"A divorce attorney, that's interesting. Wow. So you're the one helping out with the divorce rate rising in the world."

"I wouldn't put it quite that way," I say quietly

"Have you ever lost a case?"

Our meal comes, and we pause. The server exits and I answer his question.

"Yes, once. It never happened again. I don't like losing. I get my clients the results they want."

"What inspired you to become a divorce attorney?"

"Growing up I watched my mom and dad stay with each other for all the wrong reasons and in them staying together it caused a lot of problems for me."

"I'm sorry," he says and sounds like he means it.

"Oh don't be," I say and brush off the moment.

"It looks like you turned out OK."

"Yes indeed, the money is good as well as the thrill of the win. When I'm in a courtroom, I'm powerful. The debate between my opponents and me is electrifying. I love the win."

"You're powerful outside of the courtroom also." I like the way he slips that in. "Do you get a lot of hard cases?"

"It depends on the case. Some cases are easy, others are tougher."

He takes a bite of his meal. Stuffed lobster tails, shrimp with bourbon sauce. I ordered the house special, shrimp primavera. We eat in comfortable silence for a few moments.

"Lisa, I'm curious. What made you decide to call me?"

"I don't know. I... um... I didn't feel like being alone, and I wanted to see you again."

He chuckles. "Well whatever the reason, I'm glad you called. You are a very beautiful woman. I want to get to know you a little better."

I blush. Hope he's not a mind reader, because what I'm thinking about doing to him has to be illegal in all fifty states.

"Thank you, flattery will get you everywhere." I smile when I say the words.

"I hope it will take me many places with you."

Our eyes lock across the table. His eyes mirror the same ache as mine. Fiery sensations spread throughout my body. I desire his soft lips on mine. It's been a while since a man has looked at me the way Curtis looks at me.

"I want to do something that will put us both in a relaxing mood. Come let's go for a ride."

"OK, I can go for that."

He motions the waiter and pays the bill. I collect my things and he escorts me to his Mercedes Benz. He unlocks the car door, steps aside and holds it open for me to get in. I watch him in the side mirror as he walks back to his side and gets in beside me.

"So where are we going?" I probe and reach for my seat belt. It clicks into place and Curtis pulls out of the parking lot.

"It's a surprise."

"You're not trying to kidnap me are you?"

He grins showing off perfect white teeth. "No ma'am. I'm not going to kidnap you. Shouldn't you be concerned about that before you get into the car?" Curtis asks, still chuckling at my expense. "What do you like to do in your idle time?"

"What idle time? I can't remember the last time I had idle time. I use it to do a lot of charity work... and if I'm lucky, I might get to jot down a little poetry. Life has gotten so busy for me. I haven't had the time to sit down and pen my thoughts down on paper."

Excitement sparkles in his eyes. "You write poetry? What kind?"

"Erotic poems and some ballads."

He takes his eyes off the road to glance over at me. "Do you know any of them from memory?"

"Some."

"Would you mind reciting one for me?" He smiles coyly. "Would it be in bad taste if I asked you to read one of your erotic poems?"

With boldness I don't possess, I say, "It's never in bad taste to ask for what you want."

"I'm glad you see things my way. I knew there was something special about you."

I smile, catch my breath then exhale and recite the poem.

Silence is his reaction. This is my first time reciting a poem aloud to someone other than John. Goose bumps cover my skin. His silence is killing me. We pull into the parking lot of Dream Angels Day Spa.

He sits in awe for a moment then asks, "You wrote that?"

Overwhelmed by his admiration, I nod. "Yes."

"Wow. I don't know what to say. That was incredible."

"You really like it?"

Curtis's gaze explores my lips then my eyes. No longer ashamed of the desires there, I don't hide them from him. He wants to kiss me. I eagerly wait for his lips to become acquainted with mine. I bring my eyes down to his lips letting him know I want to taste him too.

He reaches out to caress my face then leans over to ravish my lips. I moan with pleasure, his lips sweet. I lose control and there's no room for holding back. I'm deep in our realm of passion then he breaks our kiss. We stare at each; his eyes burn with raw lust.

"I want you Lisa, but not like this. I'm not the kind of man who sleeps around for fun. I like to get to know the women I take to my bed."

I'm disappointed and relieved all in one. Curtis seems to be one of the good ones. I don't know if I want to drag him into my dirt.

"That's good, Curtis. I'm not in a rush either."

He clears his throat. "Good. Now that we've straightened that up let's go inside."

"Why are we sitting in front of a day spa?"

"We're here to pamper and put you in a relaxing mood. You look like you could use a massage to ease that busy mind of yours."

"Do you always take women to day spas on the first date?"

Curtis slides from the car, and comes around to open my door. He extends his hand to help me from my seat and without notice he pulls me into an embrace and kisses me.

His nearness speeds up my heart rate. "No. Only you."

Feeling a bit mischievous, I ask: "What if I didn't like massages?"

"Guess we'd be doing something else then, but in the back of mind I'd think you're weird. Most of the women I know — my mother, my sisters, and aunties — they all like getting their body massaged with hot oil and all the other concoctions you women like to use on yourselves."

I laugh and he joins in. Laughter rumbles from his chest. Curiosity compels me to touch his chest. I love the way he feels under my hands, solid, fit, and powerful. I visualize what would happen if I undo the buttons on his shirt. Run my hands over his naked chest and encourage him to do the same to me. Our eyes collide. I swallow nervously and look away.

"I love massages. It was thoughtful of you to take me here," I express, filling the silence.

"Good then let's go in before I renege on my previous statement, you temptress."

The lady at the counter greets us. "Hi Curtis, it's nice to see you back."

She's friendly, a little too friendly. I want to snatch the silly smile from her face. This is what I hate about females in this day and age they're so desperate for a little male attention they don't even care if the man is spoken for.

She hits on him, gets outright bold in my face and touches his arm. He doesn't say anything; I'm uncomfortable, shifting from side to side. Curtis looks over his shoulder and ushers me closer to him. I smile and step into his arms.

"Jen are we going to be in the same room?"

"Yes, unless you want separate rooms."

Curtis answers. "Nope room for two is perfect."

"Ooh, you two are together, together."

This heifer has lost her mind, she must have. Why does she think I'm in his arms? She glances briefly in my direction and offers a phony smile. If looks could kill, she'd be dead. What should've taken only a few minutes lasts well over thirty minutes. She deliberately makes Curtis fill out additional paperwork.

"Are any of you allergic to anything?" She asks.

"Didn't I fill out one of these before?" Curtis asks.

"It's for your company."

"I'm not allergic to anything. What about you, Lisa?"

"No allergies I can get rid of fast enough."

She catches my underlining meaning and rolls her eyes. The questions continue. I'm fuming inside, but I have to contain myself in front of Curtis. Boy, if he weren't here, I'd sure give this little girl a piece of my mind. Four pages later and we're still answering questions.

I lose my composure and forget about Curtis. "Is this really necessary?"

"Actually I'm done," she says smoothly and hands the pen to Curtis. "I need you to sign this for me."

The lawyer in me asks. "What is it?"

"It's a waiver, stating we're not liable for any allergic reaction you may have from using our products which could result in hospitalization, surgery, etc. It's not a big deal. I've been here for five years and no one's had any problems. We need it in order to give you a massage."

Curtis doesn't read the thing. He just takes her word for it and signs. This is how these people get you when you want to file a lawsuit against them. If they were sure about their products, a waiver agreement wouldn't be necessary.

"Aren't you going to read it before you sign? You could be signing your life away," I press against his back.

"At a day spa? Relax counselor, I've been here many times. I think we'll be OK."

He shoves the paper in my hands. "Sign, don't read it, just sign it right there." He taps his finger on the dotted line, without another word, I sign the paper. She takes it, and tucks it in with the other files.

The narrow hallway leading to the massage room grows dim. I adjust my eyes. The set up of the room is inviting and tastefully arranged. Soft relaxing sounds of ocean waves play on a stereo nearby and the smell of lavender and Jasmine lingers in the air. The atmosphere causes my body to relax involuntarily. In my mind I'm already sprawled out on the bed getting my body rubbed.

"Curtis, it's good to see you again. I wasn't expecting you until next week. I see you brought a friend. Hi, I'm Melissa and this is my husband Gary," she introduces, gripping my hand.

Melissa shows us two stalls on the far left of the room to use. I undress, drape my clothes on the rack, and wrap myself in the pink and brown towel lying on the stool. Did they give Curtis a pink and brown towel too? I am holding on to the towel with a vice grip so tight, not even the Jaws of Life could pry it open.

Curtis already has Melissa massaging him. He moans and groans his satisfaction. I'm amused at his almost incoherent mumblings of gratitude to Melissa. She's amused as well and laughs at his reaction.

"He does this every time," says Melissa.

The corners of Gary's mouth spread into a smile. "Are you ready to get started? Have you had a massage before?"

I nod. "I mean yes, I have but it's been some time."

"Sounds like we have quite a few kinks to work out," he jokes.

I smile. "I guess we do."

"Then let's begin. I need you to lay on the table face down, arms straight by your side. Make yourself very comfortable because you are going to be in that position for an hour."

I climb onto the table, securing the towel around me. Little good it did me. Gary pulls it down to expose my full back. The oil he pours on me is warm, and laced with the scent of jasmine. Strong arms, slow, and firm, meticulously knead massage oil into my skin. Sleep overtakes me, my eyes droop, my body becomes limber, and my mind is at peace as I drift off to sleep.

I'm dreaming. The dream is so real, someone whispers my name, plays with my hair, and shakes me tenderly. In a voice unrecognizable to me, I shoo them away. The voice grows loud.

"Lisa... Lisa you got to wake up now baby."

My eyes flutter open. I wipe sleep from my eyes I wink, and it takes me a moment to figure out where I am. Curtis stands over me; concern clouds his face.

I moan and stretch real big, arms above my head. Curtis looks at me big-eyed. He grins. He has dimples on one side of his face. I'm a big fan of dimples. I touch his face.

"How long have I been out?"

"Ah." He chuckle. "For a little bit."

"I haven't felt this relaxed in years. Mmm... what time is it?"

"Six thirty. You slept through the whole thing."

"Holy cow!"

Springing from the massage table, I run into the stall completely forgetting my nudeness under the towel. John will kill me if I'm not at the house dressed and ready to go with him.

Scatterbrained I drag my clothes on, check my cell and text log for missed calls or messages. I see none. I take a deep breath, before rejoining Curtis. He's still rooted in the same spot. He's silent. I'm not sure if that's good; I don't know his moods yet.

"What was that all about?" He asks, watching me under hooded eyes. "You dashed out of here like the devil was after you."

"I'm sorry. I have company coming over to the house this evening and here I am sleeping in a day spa." I giggle nervously. Lying is not natural for me.

Curtis continues to look at me strangely, then shrugs and grins sheepishly. "Is that my cue that our time together has come to an end?"

"No, it means we'll have to set up another time when we

can spend more time together. This was good. Thanks for taking me here. I feel relaxed."

"OK, when can we do this again?"

Curtis cups my face, runs his thumbs across my cheeks then he brings his mouth down to mesh with mine. My lips part to receive him. Curtis drinks greedily from them, my body melts into him, and our kiss heightens. Curtis caresses the small of my back. This is getting deep. I crave his hands and his tongue, anything of his on me. This is wrong, my head reminds me, but I'm burning with desire for him. Like a moth to a flame, I curl my body into him. Tremors run through my secret place, a dull achy feeling settles there. Nervous hands unbutton his shirt. Curtis hikes up my skirt and draws me closer into him. Things are about to get out of hand when someone knocks on the door. I jump to my feet.

The person on the other side of the door, asks, "Are you two OK in there?"

Smiling at me Curtis clears his throat then replies, "Yes. We'll be out in a few minutes." He whispers loudly enough for my ears only. "I think we better leave before we start something we can't stop."

Giggling like a ridiculous schoolgirl who almost got caught with her pants down, I nod in agreement. "I'm ready."

The drive back to the restaurant ends much too quickly. I love his company, the way he makes me feel, and the ease in which we communicate with each other. It's easy to sit here and listen to his deep Bahamian voice.

"Where did you park?" he asks, reclaiming my attention.

"Over there," I point to my silver Jaguar parked between two SUVs. Curtis pulls up in front of it and parks.

"When will I see you again?" Curtis asks, turning in his seat to look at me.

"I don't know. When do you want to see me again?"

"How does tomorrow night sound?"

"Tomorrow sounds fine," I agree. Giving him another kiss on the lips, I get out of his car.

"See you tomorrow."

Out of Curtis' immediate view, I whip out my cell to dial John's number again. This time it goes straight to his voice mail. That's strange. It rang earlier. Hmm. I hang up and try the office number; no answer there either. I doubt he'll pick up the house phone. Nevertheless, I dial our home and still no answer.

Where could he be?

CHAPTER SEVENTEEN

Candy

It's a quarter to seven and I still haven't found any-thing to wear tonight. Mona bailed on me two hours ago to go out with a new man she met. I exhaust my options in Town Center Plaza, swapping out dress after dress in Black Market-White House and still manage to turn up empty handed with nothing to wear.

"Ma'am, I have one last dress for you to try."

Great! She hands me a plain Jane dress. "I don't like this."

"Try it on. You might be surprised. A lot of women are buying this one."

I don't ask what kind of women. I don't want to offend her. "OK I'll try it. I'm already naked anyway."

Still reluctant to put it on, I just look at it from its hanger. Two minutes later, I'm singing a different tune. This dress clings to my body like a second skin, detailing every curve and the light jacket that comes with tones it down a bit. The sales clerk gives me two thumbs up when I walk out of the dressing room to check out the dress on me in the four-way mirror. This is the best hundred dollars I've ever spent.

The moment I walk through the door, the telephone begins to ring. The machine picks up, and then Mikhail's voice comes over the speaker.

"Hey this is Mikhail, where are you? ...I'm calling to see what you're up to tonight. Call me when you get this mes-sage." Click, he hangs up.

I throw my shopping bags down on the sofa, kick my shoes off, and stretch my feet. These are some of the pret-tiest shoes, but they hurt like something else. I press the button on the answering machine.

The first caller is my crazy cousin Janie on my father's side. The next few are bill collectors for the person who owned the telephone number before me. Then I hear Nick's message. Stunned, I hit the rewind button. "Hi this message

160

is for Candy... this is Nick from last night ah... I really hope this is the right number and if it is um... give me a call at 444-5042 when you get this message. Oh area code 816. Look forward to hearing from you."

Undecided about whether I should call him back right now, I fiddle with the phone. I decide to let him wait, and I get undressed instead. In the middle of undressing my house phone rings. Shoot! This line is busier than the psychic hotline tonight! This better not be Mikhail. Caller ID tells me it is Lisa.

"Hey, Lisa."

"Candy... did I disturb you?"

"No, girl what's up?" I pause, almost missing the sadness in her voice. "What's wrong?"

She sniffles. "I know you told me not to call you with my mess but," she stops to take a deep breath, "I didn't have anyone else to call." Soft sobs come across the phone line. "I'm truly sorry about the way I treated you last night, but I need to talk to you."

Her sobs tug at my heart. I know why she's calling. I expected it. The first thing I want to do is save her, but I know I can't. This is out of my hands; this is between her and God. God is dealing with her and she has to come to terms with it. I've tried to show her. Now all I can do is listen.

"Girl, don't worry about last night. We've both said and done some things in the past that meant nothing. Just tell me what's wrong.... Is everything OK?"

Curling up on my chaise lounge, I wait for her to speak. Lisa blows air into the phone. She struggles to keep it together, and fails. She cries some more, blows her nose, and stammers out a few words. "Yes... no... I mean, I'm OK physically. Mentally I'm a mess right now."

"Tell me what's wrong," I coax again.

"I am so frustrated with John. He made plans with me tonight. Told me to dress up and be ready, because he was going to take me out on the town. You know... to make up for neglecting me. Candy, I haven't heard from him since he left this morning. He's not answering his phone."

The moment the words leave her mouth my conscience

goes into full gear. It messes with me. I have an idea where John is, but I don't tell her. How can I tell her? This will crush Lisa. She might even turn on me for telling her. Therefore, I don't say what I should.

"Maybe he got tied up at the office and he's not answering because he's in the middle of something. Hasn't he been busy at work lately? I remember you saying so yourself."

"He's not busy because of work! I called him two hours ago at his office, and on his cell phone and he's not answering any if them. John's in the middle of something, all right. I'm going to kill him."

"Lisa—"

"He's probably out with some home-wrecker while.... while I am sitting here all dressed up waiting for him with nowhere to go. I'm getting tired of this."

Why does she do this to herself? Lisa's cry of anguish is hard to bear. Tears of my own trickle down my face. Her pain is my pain. I had torments like this of my own. She pours her heart out to me. Lisa confesses going out with the man from last night to a day spa today. I listen to her tell me how close she came to making a mistake by sleeping with him.

"The devil is a liar, Lisa, don't fall for his tricks. If you do that, it will only put you in more bondage. Come to this bachelorette party with me. I need to be there for Shelly."

She declines. "No, I'm going to stay here and have another glass of wine then go to bed."

"Are you positive? I'll come get you."

"No, I don't really feel like being around people right now."

"OK… well, call me if you need me."

"Have fun, Candy. Talk to you tomorrow."

"All right, don't drink too much." As I hang up the phone, my spirit feels so unsettled.

Something wrestles within me: Should I go to Lisa's or maintain my plans and go to the bachelorette party? I know the answer. I grab my Bible from the side of my bed. I head straight for the door on a mission. We are going to get this thing right with God tonight. I don't know what God is using me to do, but I trust Him and when He says move, I move.

***

"Lisa, I want to pray for you. Will you let me?" I ask Lisa. She steps aside, and I enter her foyer.

"Candy, I don't believe in prayer. That stuff doesn't work." Lisa follows me into the living room. She plops down on the love seat. I sit next to her.

"Do you believe Jesus died for our sins, is risen from the dead and is coming back to pass judgment and take home his saints?" I ask, holding the Bible on my lap.

"No... Yes, I'm not sure what to believe," Lisa waves her hand in frustration. "If there is a God, why won't He fix my marriage?"

"I don't know why," I touch her arm. "Maybe He's trying to tell you something and maybe He already told you what to do. You can't hear from God when you're not in His presence."

"What does that mean?" she asks. It's a genuine question. She's not trying to be flippant or dismissive.

"Seek God, Lisa. That's the only way you will find the answer."

She seems puzzled, and I kneel and grab her by the hand, gently pulling her down beside me. She follows, and we pray for Jesus to come into our hearts. She is a bit hesitant at first, but I can tell she is willing to give even this a try. She is stressed and is just looking for answers, and if God can help her, she is open. She tells God she accepts Him as Lord and savior of her life. Her voice is full of pain and when she squeezes my hand, my bones seem to get crushed. The emotion coming from her is almost palpable. Something unexplainable happens in the room and the presence of the Lord governs the space.

CHAPTER EIGHTEEN

Mikhail

I'm at one of the city's hottest nightspots. Some of the finest ladies come here to play. Women dominate the place, baring stomachs, legs, and whatever else they can use to distract us. Still I can't enjoy myself, because Candy overshadows my mind. She doesn't return my calls, and I'm going crazy with wondering.

I press the send button on my phone. This is the third text message I've sent to her. Minutes go by, and still no response. Darn woman has me checking my phone for malfunction. Michael looks at me funny. He chuckles at my predicament.

"Man why you keep looking at your phone. Are you still waiting for Candy to call you back?"

I play it off, don't want to be labeled as soft. "Nah, I'm expecting an important phone call."

He laughs harder. "Man, why you lying?... You know you waiting for that girl to call you."

I hiss through my teeth. "Whatever, think what you like. I'm not sweating her right now. Look at all these fine honeys walking around here."

"You tell yourself whatever you need to in order to feel better, but I know you. That girl got your head all screwed up. You just don't want to admit it. If you still care for her, why you out here trying to get with all these other females?"

Frustration gets the best of me. He is saying all the things I don't want to hear right now, especially since he is right. I haven't been able to get her out of my head since I heard her voice this morning.

"What you need to do is drop it." Taking the focus off me and placing it on someone else, I bring up what I learned about Tobey. "Man, you will never believe who I ran into today."

"Besides Derrick? What is this, reunion day?" Michael jokes.

"Tobey's little sister Monique and she looks good. She is

built like a brick house."

"Yeah, how's Tobey doing?"

"Man, that's the messed up part. He's dead."

His face turns from excitement to shock. "What you mean dead? When did this?.... How did this happen?"

"His sister said he was in the wrong place at the wrong time," I explain.

"That's foul."

"My sentiments exactly. On a different topic though, when are you guys moving to Detroit?"

Michael belches before replying. "To tell you truth I don't even know. I'm still waiting for this cat to call me back about the job offer he put on the table last week. I still think I can get more money out of the deal and now I'm just waiting to see what kind of offer he's gonna come to me with."

"You know Momma tripping about you leaving and moving so far away from family. Do you have to take a job that moves you to another state?"

"I have a family to feed and as the man of the house I have to make sacrifices I don't want to make."

"I have to agree with Momma, you are moving too far away from family. What does the wife think about all this?"

"Shoot you know Kelsey is down for whatever is gonna make us more bank."

He chuckles. I chuckle too.

Michael is right about his wife Kelsey (a.k.a gold digger). Kelsey is no joke, stripping for a living before she met Michael has made her hard, taught her only to look out for numero uno, herself. If Michael decides he wants a divorce, she will take him to the cleaners and take both their children. Michael will not admit it, but he's also whipped from that voodoo she throws on him.

My eyes connect with a sensational looking sister with skin the color of butter pecan and curves in all the right places. She gives me a once over. I hope she likes what she sees, because I definitely dig her style. I salute her with my beer, she smiles and raises her wine glass. Michael is still talking, but I'm not paying attention. He's jabbering about something to do with women and settling down.

"When are you going to stop chasing behind these women and settle down?.... You know you ain't getting any younger little brother."

I'm not in the mood for this pep talk and Michael needs to shut up about this settling down business. I'm still young. There's still plenty of room to sow my wild oats.

"I'll settle down when I find Ms. Right, but tonight I'm just looking for Ms. Right Now and she might be right over there. You'll have to excuse me big brother but I see someone I need to holla at. I feel bad about leaving you here on your own bro but I got to go."

The flock of women I approach, hollering and hooting stop in their tracks once I get in the midst of them. The alcohol has them lit, and acting loose and bubbly just the way I like them. Tipsy and scandalous, these females begin to fix themselves up, re-applying lipsticks, pushing up their breast in their tops to show more cleavage. While the honey I'm interested in remains calm and unaffected.

This is humorous. There's a shortage of men but these females act as if I am the only male up in here. Hunger shows in their eyes. I could bring any one of them back to my crib to get it on, no strings attached and they'd be OK with it.

"Good evening ladies."

A sea of smiles and group hellos greets me. I feel like Howard Stern at a bikini talent show, watching these females trip over each other to get closer to me.

I ask, "Can we talk for a minute?"

She hesitates. I'm thinking she's going to turn me down in front of all these females.

A friend of hers intervenes. "Claire you better go on and talk to that man before I do."

We laugh and it eases the tension.

"You'll have to excuse her."

"Claire is it?"

"Yes. You know my name, but I don't know yours." She's soft-spoken, barely audible.

"Mikhail. You had me worried there for a minute. Thought you were gonna shoot a brother down."

Her friend interrupts again. "Who's the guy you were

standing with earlier?"

"What guy?" I had forgotten about Michael. "Oh my bad, that's brother."

"Why didn't he come over with you?" she quizzes. "Is he shy, scared of women, gay, or what?"

I feign a laugh to cover up my irritation with her friend. I'm trying to get my mack on and she's here holding us up with her twenty questions. Then she ruins the impression I had of her by calling my brother gay. We don't roll like that in this family.

"Married and definitely not gay. The Robinson boys love females only. We don't get down like that."

She frowns. "I ask because there are too many down low brothers playing straight nowadays. You never know who you're getting involved with, you know what I mean?" She pauses to gain my approval. I remain silent, when I don't reply she persists. "So is he happily married?"

What kind of question is that? These girls sure don't waste time. Claire gets involved.

"Ingrid, what's wrong with you? I think he already told you the man is married. Leave it alone, girl."

Ingrid shrugs her shoulder. "Well I'm curious. He's out here in the club without his wife. I just wanted to know if he's happy," she concedes. "Plus he looks like he could use some company since his brother left him all alone and I'm not about to stand here and watch you two hold a conversion."

"It's not like you're standing here by yourself," Claire retorts. "I'm sorry she's acting this way."

I hold up my hand to stop her from apologizing. "Don't even worry about it. I'll have to agree with Ingrid I did leave him hanging out by himself. Ingrid you can go over and talk him? He won't bite."

"Well you're right no sense in me standing here wondering. You kids have fun," she says and sashays over to where Michael is standing.

"Now where were we?" I ask focusing all my attention on her and the dress she's wearing. Low cut with her breasts hoisted up to the forefront.

"You were telling me about yourself."

"I think you were the one on trial. We're not gonna have any unexpected visitors popping up are we?"

"Is that your way of asking me if I have a boyfriend?" she relaxes her stance. "No I don't have a boyfriend. It's just you and me."

"Fine as you are, men should be waiting in line just to get next to you."

Claire laughs. "So what you do?"

She wastes no time getting into a man's pocket. I should've known she was a moneygrubber from the way she acted all stuck up when I approached her.

"I have my own business," I lie, knowing exactly what to say to get this chick out of them draws. And Bingo! The moment I say those five words, her eyes light up like a Christmas tree.

"What kind a business?" she fishes.

"I own a wholesale business downtown."

"Really? That's nice." She coos and leans in a little closer.

"It's no easy task, trust me. What do you do?"

"I am an executive administrative assistant for a law firm in Midtown."

What you need to say is that you are just someone's secretary. "So you get to work with a lot of big shot attorneys."

"You could say that. So where is your girlfriend?"

"I don't have a girlfriend."

Claire analyzes me. "Why not, what's wrong with you?" Claire's expression and assumption don't surprise me. I get that from women a lot. "No disrespect but from what you've told me you're a very handsome and successful man, a woman would be out of her mind not to find you a catch."

"Compliments. I like those. Keep them coming." This isn't where I want the conversation to lead, so I ignore her question. "I'm sorry, but we've been talking for a minute now and I haven't even offered to buy you drink. Would you like something to drink?"

"Yes, I'll take a glass of White Zin."

At least she didn't order the most expensive drink on the menu like most women do when they think a man can afford it. I wave a server over, another fine looking sister.

"I need a Remy Martin on ice and a glass of white wine for the lady." I turn to Claire after the server leaves. "Claire what are your plans after you leave here tonight?"

"I'm not sure; going home I suppose."

"What, no after parties?"

I'm a lip man and Claire's unconscious wetting of her lips every five seconds has parts of me boiling in curious anticipation of what she can do with them.

"What do you have in mind?" she asks with a slight smile. She licks her lips again and my imagination goes wild.

"Well I was hoping after we leave here we could go somewhere quiet to talk and get to know each other better."

"Well the night is young. We could chill and see what it brings."

"That's cool with me."

We find a booth and sit down. Claire is easy going, unlike some of the other women I had conversations with earlier. She is animated, attentive, and she laughs at my jokes. After exchanging meaningless conversation, we ease our way to the dance floor. Claire rubs her rear all up on me. It's soft, and tempting to touch. This girl is wild and she has me riled up. We're dancing so hard, sweat runs down my back. I'm getting in the groove of things when the DJ announces last call for alcohol.

"Would you like another drink for the road?" I ask.

"Um... No, I'm fine. I think I had a little bit too much to drink."

I laugh and circle my hands around her tiny waist. "Well I hope I didn't get you too lit where you can't drive home."

"No I'm good," she says and presses up against me.

"It's a shame the party has to end," I hint, hoping she'll catch the drift and invite me back to her place.

"Tonight doesn't have to be the last time I see you," Claire says and pulls out a pen and scrap of paper. "Let me give you my number."

Tapping Claire's spine tonight is out of the question. I watch with disappointment as she scribbles down her number, and I punch it into my cell phone's memory. We say our goodbyes. I scroll through my phone book and dial a few of my F.W.B's (friends with benefits). I listen to excuses, voicemails, and not in the mood for company replies and get even more sexually frustrated.

From the way things look, I'll be going home alone tonight. My cell goes off. Claire's number appears on the caller ID.

"Hey baby girl," I say with a smile.

"I'm in the parking lot," Claire says. Her voice drops to a sexy tone. "Do you still want to have that after party?"

"I'll be outside."

CHAPTER NINETEEN

Lisa

I pour two Tylenols into my hand, fill the glass with water, and wash them down. John is asleep and snoring like a horse as always. I guess he must be tired after his late night. I waited on him for hours. When he showed up, I pretended to be asleep, but my racing emotions wouldn't let me rest. All the stress has given me a headache. Now I'm pacing around in the bathroom in the wee hours, plotting. I refill the glass with cold water. Glass in my hand, fierce vindictiveness courses through my being as I tiptoe back into the bedroom.

John is on his side of the bed, and that's good because I don't want to wet my side. The more I look at him, the angrier I get. So many disappointments, so many tears shed, so many sleepless nights I had to endure at his mercy. His verbal put-downs, betrayals, and sorry excuses. The prayers I had with Candy helped at the moment, but I still feel as if I hate and resent him for treating me so badly. I made up my mind last night I'm not dealing with this anymore.

John is either going to shape up or ship out! Slowly and meticulously, I pour the water over his face, startling him from his sleep.

John jumps from the bed sputtering and spurting. "What the heck!" Confusion darkens his face then realization sinks in and his brows furrow into a scowl. The change in his temperament is laughable and a deep laugh rumbles up from my gut. I laugh and laugh, and laugh until my sides ache. John's scowl deepens. I'm not fazed by him. The lack of respect I have for my husband produces my uncaring attitude.

"Woman, what is wrong with you?" he asks, angrily wiping water from his face.

Hands on my hips, I retaliate. "What's wrong with me? You want to know what's wrong me? You! That's what's wrong with me. You have some nerve asking me that question. Where were you? I waited for you. I got dressed up for you to take me out. The problem with that is I couldn't find you. You had me looking like a flipping fool. What's your excuse now John, huh? That... That you were at the office or maybe you're going to tell me you were with a client. Come on, enlighten me."

"For your information... I was at the office. I had to catch up on some work I had missed the night before, as I told you. I don't know why you're acting crazy." His calmness enrages me. Anger rises and falls inside of me like a heat wave, ready to consume all in its path.

I poke him in the forehead and he boxes my hand away. "You're a liar and a deceiver. You're going to get what's coming to you, John. You can count on it."

"Whatever. I don't expect you to believe me. You're losing your mind."

"You're right. I lost my mind when I married you, lost more of it having to put up with your nonsense," I say in a loud voice. "John, I called your office several times and you never answered. Why is that?" I move closer to him. "Before you start out with some sorry explanation, stop. I drove by your office and your car wasn't there. John, be a man and tell the truth for once. Then at least I can respect you, instead of coming up with these weak explanations. What do you take me for?"

"I'm tired of your nagging, woman," John says, eying the empty glass in my hand. "If you don't have anything else to do other than to nag me then get out of my face, because I'm tired. I can't believe you threw water on me in my sleep. That's messed up. You crazy and you need to seek professional help."

John snatches the wet cover off the bed and gets back in it. He rolls over onto his side and turns his back to me. His action is answer enough for me. I have come to a dead end. It's decision-making time. Earlier tonight I prayed and cried, prayed and cried and the answer remained the same. Candy stopped by and the prayer she led me in truly touched my soul. She talked with me for a while before leaving. She would have stayed longer, but I told her I needed some time alone. I've not been a big believer in prayer but for some reason, pray is exactly what I did. I poured out my heart to the God Candy told me about, and I told Him my hurt and asked for strength.

I knew I had come to a time of decision. Choose life or death. John is killing me emotionally. We are no good for each other, and I want to live. So I can't remain here.

"You know I used to think there was something wrong with me, that I lacked in something, but I've come to realize it's not me," I say, walking around to his side of the bed and standing in front of him. "It's you. You're the one who lacks in something. I remember a time when I was deeply in love with you, John, and I would've moved mountains to make you happy. Now... now I feel like I'm going through the motions just holding onto something that's no longer there. I'm sick of all the arguments, all the fighting, all of your lies. I just can't take it anymore."

A long pause ensues. John doesn't move. He doesn't speak. He just lies there. I want to wrap my hands around his neck and squeeze. It would be worth it just to hear him beg for his life.

"Is that it? Because I'm going back to sleep."

Help me, Jesus! "You keep saying that there isn't another woman in your life, but if it's not another woman, John, then it must be another man. Which is it?"

I wait for some kind of reaction out of him, because I'm not done. I need an answer and he is going to give me one willingly or unwillingly. John leaps from the bed and gets in my face before I know what is happening.

"You know the reason why you're so insecure, Lisa? Don't answer that." He pushes me up against the wall so hard the bones in my back feel crushed. He adds, "I'll answer for you. You're not good at taking care of home. If you were then you wouldn't have to worry about someone else doing what you should be doing."

"I can't believe this is coming from you, you disrespectful, no good lowdown dirty dog," I say in a low, calm voice.

With all the force I possess, I push myself from the wall to slap John's face. The contact of my hand to his face stings, and the resounding noise rings in my ears.

John chuckles and it sends uneasy shivers down my spine. In one quick movement, he pins me against the wall again, his face mere inches away from mine. John rests his hands on each side of my face.

"That, I am, but I'm not gay. You think you're so smart don't you?" he asks condescendingly. "Tell me something Lisa, if you're so smart, what am I going to do next?"

My chin juts out and my tone is defiant. "Go ahead, John, hit me. You've done it before. How soon we forget what happened the last time you laid hands on me. Believe me when I say it, this time I won't be sympathetic. If you hit me again, you will pay."

We stare each other down for a beat before I speak. "If it's not another man then who is she, John?"

He laughs nervously and steps away from me. He points knowingly and says, "I see what you're trying to do. I'm not falling for it and you know the last time was an accident. I wasn't going to hit you, only wanted to scare you. I already paid the price for my mistake. I'm not a punk, and you know it. I don't know why you are trying to anger me, Lisa. I'm going to suggest you stop right now."

"Then answer the question: If it's not a man, who is she?"

"You better stop fooling around and quit asking me all this nonsense. There is no other woman or man. I was at work. I didn't know you were calling me because our phone lines were down."

"It's funny how things around your office conveniently break when you're missing in action. Why are you lying? Where was your car? Why didn't you answer your cell phone? ...Why didn't you call me to let me know you were going to be late? John, you can't get yourself out of this one."

"You're paranoid. Maybe you should call the office if you don't believe me."

"Get real. What do I look like calling your office to ask them about your whereabouts? I'm asking you and that still doesn't explain what happened to your car."

"In the secured parking garage. Lisa you know how I get sometimes when I'm working on something important. I lost track of time baby, I'm sorry. Let me make it up to you."

John starts in on his smooth talk, but I'm not trying to

hear it this time.

"The heck you will."

John's brow furrows. "What do you mean?"

"It means... that... you can't... charm me... anymore. There is no... making it up to me," I say, dragging my sentence out to get my point across.

"Lisa, I know you're upset. Honey, please let's not make any hasty decisions."

"This is not hasty. I had all of tonight and a few lonely nights before this to think about it. John I want you to leave. I don't trust you, and I want you to pack your things and get out." The words come out calmer than I'm feeling.

"Now you've definitely lost it, woman. I'm not going anywhere."

"You can leave of your own free will or I can have the police help you. The choice is yours."

"You conniving little bi—."

"Oh so now you want to call me out my name," I interrupt his outburst. "Pack your things, John, pack them and vacate the premises. Don't make me call the police." I walk across the room before I break down and change my mind.

"Get back here! I'm not through talking to you." John hits the bedroom wall. "Come here!"

I spin around, thinking he is coming after me. He hasn't moved. John stares daggers at me as he nurses his hand. It will serve him right if he broke it.

"I'm done talking to you." I toss the words over my shoulder and step into the bathroom. I splash water on my face. Outside, I hear John moving around. He is ripping drawers open and banging them shut. I hear the clank of perfume bottles on the dresser and hope he doesn't knock my favorite fragrance to the floor.

John does not take long to pack. I'm scared of being by myself. I made the decision to stop being his doormat and that meant asking him to leave. I don't see any other way. But I wish we could just have everything turn out all right.

"I hope you can live with your decision. If I leave here today I won't be coming back," he threatens, through the door. He is trying to scare me into changing my mind, the old mind trick.

I take a deep breath, then step back into the bedroom and watch him pull on khakis and shoes. Eying the single overnight bag at his side, I dig into the wound. "Is that all the clothes you're carrying? You're going to need more than that."

"I'll get the rest of my things tomorrow. Then again, it might be sometime later in the week if that's OK with you," he says and pauses for a beat. "Are you sure you want me to leave?"

I huff. "John, I have never been as sure of anything as I am sure of this. I need some time and space to figure some things out."

"Then I guess you'll be getting all the time in the world. I didn't do anything wrong, Lisa. You're making a big mistake."

I ponder what he said. "Am I? John, you have forgotten our wedding vows. You don't appreciate me, and you don't respect me. I've talked to you about this time and time again and you haven't done a thing to show me. Frankly, I'm sick of it! I'm tired of feeling like a warm body for you to come home to at night. I feel like I'm alone in this marriage, and since I'm feeling that way then I might as well be alone."

"What are you talking about?" he asks as if he has no idea what I've been saying or why I'm upset. "I'm always here for you, Lisa. Don't throw away our marriage. I want to secure a better future for us and you want to leave me, just because I stay late at the office a few times."

"That's not the reason and you know it, John," I say in a tone that lets him know I'm not buying his sudden act. "You're never here and when you are, it's as if you're off somewhere else. I'm sick and tired of being sick and tired. We need a break. I need a break!"

"You know what? Do whatever you want!" he says in exasperation. "I'm getting off this roller coaster ride. Call me when you get some sense into that head of yours."

The slamming of the garage door seems so final against the silence of the night. I stare down at the departing car from my bedroom window. John speeds out of our darkened driveway and drives away without looking back. The tears I've held back roll down my cheeks and the more I wipe them away the more they pour out, each drop like a cleansing of my soul. We keep doing the same things, we women, living for men who don't live for us.

I sit on the floor, the tears finally dry and my chest feeling heavy. Two hours go by and I'm in the same position replaying the scene between John and me in my head. I realize he isn't coming back and that the pain is greater than I imagine. I want to call him and tell him to come back but I stifle the urge. I manage to scramble to my feet, feeling as if all of my energy left with the tears that flowed from my eyes. I slowly prowl the house, worrying about John's whereabouts and with whom. I sent him away, but I still want to know where he is. I decide on a warm bath to relax and clear my mind. Lavender always does the trick, so I pour a half-cup in the bath, switch on some easy listening music, discard my clothes and get in the tub. The water is just right. After my bath, I curl up on the love seat with a book. I read the first paragraph then read it again. The words don't make sense to me. Somehow the words on the page do not register in my mind. I finally give up and lay the book to the side.

I walk to John's closet. The space is immaculate, a place for everything and everything in its place. I didn't realize it before, but that's how he feels about me too. I have a place and that was to be his wife and his footstool, nothing more. As long as I let him run me and say nothing about the way I'm treated I'm perfect.

Impulsively I pack up his clothes and drag them out to the garage next to the trash cans. I leave them there and tomorrow when I wake up, they are going out with the trash. I laugh, satisfied with my handiwork because I know John will be ticked off when he realizes his collection of Brooks Brothers, Donna Karan, Kenneth Cole, and many other designer labels he wears are sitting in trash bags in our garage, wrinkled and funky.

"Brring-brring." My cell phone startles me from the dazed state I've been in ever since John's departure. I didn't really expect him to leave. Funny thing is, he did it so easily.

"Hello." I answer, knowing I sound like an Amtrak hit me, but I don't care.

"Hey, beautiful." Curtis' voice trails off. "Um... you OK?"

Trying to divert his attention away from me, I ask, "I'm fine and you?"

"You sure you're OK? You sound sad." Curtis sounds so concerned, I almost want to break down and cry.

Instead I say, "I'm OK, honestly." I pump as much sunshine into my voice as I can muster.

"Were you sleeping? I know it's early in the morning, but I just wanted to hear your voice. Do you want me to call you back another time?"

"No. I'm not sleeping," I glance at the time on the cell phone screen. It's just shy of five in the morning. "And it's not too early. Your timing is perfect." I flop back down on the love seat and curl up next to the pillows.

"I'm an early riser," Curtis says. "You were the first thing I thought of when I woke up. I know I should have waited a few hours to call you, but I just wanted to say good morning."

"OK," I say. I don't mind the early call. All of my energy has been spent, and I have none left to protest much of anything else right now.

"You sure you're OK?" Curtis asks again.

My world has turned upside down. "I'm as fine as I'll ever be." I change subjects. "What are you doing?"

"Missing you. I've thought of nothing else since our time together yesterday afternoon."

I smile. "I'm amazed at how you know exactly what to say to me."

"I was hoping I could treat you to an early breakfast."

My stomach rumbles before he can get the question out and I hope he doesn't hear it. I've not eaten since Curtis and I went to lunch at the Italian restaurant yesterday. It feels like years ago. "I don't feel like eating anything."

"You have to eat something. Come have breakfast with me."

I hesitate. "I'm in bed, and I don't want to mingle with people."

"Then come by here and I'll cook you a meal. Didn't I tell you I'm an excellent chef?"

"Once or twice," I reply mechanically. Curtis' offer is

tempting and it would cheer me up. Throwing caution to the wind, I take my wedding ring off and lay it on the edge of the table. What use do I have for it now?

"Then I'll see you in an about an hour," he says, and I hear the excitement in his voice. "That way you can judge for yourself."

"OK, I'll see you in an hour." I write down the directions to his home.

CHAPTER TWENTY

Mona

"John what ... what are you doing here?" I ask with my heart in my mouth. I immediately forget my slumber as I wonder why John has shown up on my doorstep.

He brushes past me. "Nice to see you, too. Lisa kicked me out, and I needed some place to stay. I hope you don't mind me coming here."

"Well I.... Do you think she followed you?" I peek out of the window.

"She didn't, so stop worrying." John drops his keys on a table. He walks around as if he owns the place.

"How can you be sure? Why did she kick you out in the first place? Please tell me she didn't find out about us."

"No she doesn't know about us. She kicked me out because she suspects that I'm seeing someone. I'm sure she doesn't know who I'm seeing. She's just blowing off some steam right now."

"I'm not taking any chances. Where did you park your car?"

"Out back. Come here," John assures and grabs for me.

"I'm not feeling right about this, John. A woman doesn't kick her man out of the house without evidence of infidelity. She must know something."

"Stop worrying. You're starting to sound like her. I'm only staying here for tonight. I'll find a hotel to check into first thing in the morning. If it makes you feel any better, I didn't come here right after she threw me out. I went to the office for a couple of hours. Come here, I need to hold you."

John's arms are strong and inviting. They put the worry right out of me. His kiss forces my breath out me, dulling my senses; makes me forget all the reasons why I should be worried about him being in my house.

I forget the feelings of hurt and anger I had seeing him out with another woman the other night.

For the moment, I'm wrapped up in the thought that he

is now here with me.

John has always known where I live, but I have never invited him to my home. Our meetings have always been in a discreet place. The details of his newfound freedom pique my interest. I want to ask him for all the particulars, but his hands are roaming all over my body. Under his spell, my body trembles uncontrollably and moans of pleasure escape my lips. The soft glow of the rising sun illuminates us, and I can see from John's face he is enjoying our time as much as I am.

John and I are in the midst of things when my house phone rings. The answering machine clicks on and Candy's voice fills the room.

"Mona, where are you?" Dead air lingers. "I've been trying to get a hold of you since yesterday. I'm beginning to get worried about you." More dead air fills the space, then she lets out a heavy breath. "Call me when you get this message. I just spoke to Lisa and she had another fight with that jerk husband of hers and this time she kicked him out.... Umm, just call me when you get this." She disconnects.

"What are we going to do? I think she knows about us." I chew on my bottom lip. "John, you said you were going to ask Lisa for a divorce. Now would be a good time to do it; she already told you to leave. That to me is an indication that she doesn't need you."

John watches me and chooses his words carefully. He says, "This is not a good time, Mona." He disengages himself from me. "If I ask her for a divorce now she's going to be more suspicious. Kicking me out doesn't mean she doesn't need me. Do you think I'm a jerk too?"

"No, I don't think you are a jerk. Lisa is already suspicious, John. How much more suspicious can she get? You need to tell her it's over instead of playing these hide-and-seek games." I eye him. "I have a feeling you have no intention of leaving her."

"Why? Because I'm not doing it when you say I should?" John pushes off the sofa, gathers his things, and moves to the door. "I came here for comfort and now you are giving me grief."

"I'm sorry," I say, quickly following him to the door. "I didn't mean to get you upset. John, I want you to myself. I'm getting tired of sharing you and waiting for the next time when I can see you. You should be with me and we both know this."

"Convince me."

John lifts me off the floor and runs with me to my room. He lays me out on my king sized bed and I show him how much I love and care for him. We steam up the room as our bodies writhe together and I give him my all. My goal is to erase his wife and the female from the other night. Two is company and three is a crowd. I sold my soul to the devil awhile back and there's no turning back. I've gone too far to come back from this.

"I'll tell her soon, I promise," John assures me and cups my face in his hands. "I love you. You know that don't you?"

That's the first time I can recall him saying those words to me. My heart fills.

"I love you too."

John squeezes me tight, kisses my lips and we wrap ourselves in a cocoon.

It's nice lying in my own bed with John, instead of one of those sleazy motels he takes me to across town. John sleeps peacefully, his breathing moves in pace with mine. I'm living my dream right now, but Candy's phone call from earlier still has me worried. I don't want her popping up over here so I decide to call her. Prevention is better than cure, better to deal with her over the phone than here.

***

"I'm glad you called me back. You just saved me from making a trip to your house. I was just about to drive by there to check on you. Where have you been and why haven't you been answering your phone, girl?" Candy demands.

"I was catching up on some much-needed rest. I've been tired lately and I didn't feel good after I dropped you off yesterday... An awful wave of nausea came over me, and I went to bed when I got home; been there ever since."

Half-truth, half-lies.

"You couldn't call and tell me? I hope you are not pregnant?"

"Not likely. Puh-lease, I'm still going through a dry spell. Drought season is still not over for me." I let out a little chuckle, to ease her mind.

"You ain't even right. Did you listen to my message?" Candy asks.

"What message? The one you left on my answering machine with you acting like a mother hen missing one of her chicks?" I say.

"Well if you'd pick up the phone when I call, I wouldn't have to behave that way..." Candy's voice trails off for a second. Then she gets to the purpose of her call. "I'm talking about John and Lisa's situation."

"I can't believe she would throw him out because she suspects him of cheating," I say, frowning, though I realize she can't see it. "Don't you think it's a bad idea to kick him out so he can spend even more time with the other woman?"

"I don't blame her. She is tired of the way he treats her under her own roof and I can understand where she's coming from. I wouldn't want to be in a marriage with a man who disrespects me."

"What do you mean, her house? It's his house, too," I shoot back.

"John didn't pay for that house. Lisa did, and why in the world are you defending him?"

"I'm not defending him," I say quickly, trying to distract Candy from that line of questioning. " I know she and John were having problems but I didn't think it was this serious. I still wouldn't kick my man out for some other woman to sink her claws into him."

"I hear you, but another woman can't have your man if he doesn't want to be had," Candy says. "If it's that easy for him to walk away then the other woman can have him. What makes her so special that he won't do the same thing to her? Hmm... A leopard never changes his spots, honey."

I block out all that mess she says about John. I don't like this conversation. "OK, well, let me know the scoop when you talk to her again."

"I will."

"How was the party last night?" I change the subject.

"I didn't go. I was over by Lisa's last night, helping her to put the pieces back together. That's why she put John out. He was missing last night, too. When I left Lisa's, he still hadn't shown up."

"Really, what time was it?" I ask.

"Oh, I don't know," Candy says. "I think I left around nine-thirty or so. I don't know what time he finally dragged in last night. When I talked to her this morning, she didn't really say anything about the time, but I know it was late."

That is not good news, since John wasn't with me at that time. My stomach cramps and releases, then cramps again. I think I'm going to be sick.

I let out a weak, "Really, where was he?"

"She doesn't know. He told her he was at the office, but that's a lie. That man is going to get his, and it's coming sooner than he thinks."

"What do you mean by that?"

"Hold on, you'll see."

Her last statement can't be good, but I don't push the issue. The one thing I've learned with Candy is not to push her into revealing things; it makes her even more suspicious. Our conversation dissolves into meaningless chatter and time passes. We must have been on the phone a little too long. John drags into the room, blood-red eyes, welt marks on his right cheek. He taps the watch on his wrist, signaling it's time to get off.

I yawn. "Girl I need to go and get back in the bed. I'm all talked out. I'll talk to you later."

"You should've come to church with me this morning," Candy says.

"I know, I was really tired," I say, then add quickly, "Maybe next time."

"Oh. OK. Well, I need to go call Lisa."

"Well you go do that," I say. "Talk to you later."

LOVE IS ALL WE'RE AFTER

Lisa is going to find out John is cheating on her without implicating me. I love John and it's high time I get my turn with him, and if he won't tell her then I'll have to do it for him. I'm tired of him dragging his feet. I need to move this situation along. It's time John finally belonged to me.

CHAPTER TWENTY-ONE

Candy

I dial Lisa's number when I get off with Mona. I'm concerned. Last time I talked to her, a few hours ago, it was really early, before I went to church. She was having breakfast with somebody, and she said she was doing all right. I didn't press because I know she is going through some things. But I do want to see her.

Maybe she'll go with me to my church's revival tomorrow night. I know it will do her some good. God laid it on my heart to minister to her last night, and she was receptive, not like so many times when she has brushed me off. Lisa doesn't really want to hear too much about things she can't see, like prayer and faith. But yesterday evening, her soul was ready for a word.

I know she has to be hurting after the split with John. A good church service always makes me feel better. I have a feeling it will help her, too. My pastor is a teacher. He puts the Bible in plain language and really brings the scriptures home so you see how they relate to you. And our choir is jamming! I can get full just listening to those singers.

Her voice mail picks up, so I hang up. I'll try her later. The afternoon stretches ahead of me and I get in some quiet time. I watch a movie and paint my nails, then organize my closet. I work on the files I brought home from the office on Friday. I try Lisa again.

Her voice mail picks up again, so I leave a message. "Hey, Lisa, I just wanted to see how you're doing," I say. "I won't be heading to bed until late, so you can call me back when you get this message."

The shrill sound of the house telephone startles me. It must be Mona. I quickly hang up the cell and answer, not looking at the caller ID.

"Girl I'm glad you called back. There's something I forgot to tell you."

"What is that?" asks a male voice I don't recognize.

"Who's this?"

"Nick."

Playing it cool, I ask. "Nick who?"

"Huh?... I'm sorry... um. I'm sorry I must have dialed the wrong number. Sorry to bother," he apologizes, stumbling over his every word.

"Oh no you're not, Nick from the bar."

He chuckles. "That was a dirty trick you played."

"I'm sorry, I couldn't help it," I say, grinning.

I fumble with the phone, twisting the cord in knots and fix my hair as if he can see me.

"That was just wrong, especially since I had to call all over town trying to find you. It's not like you're the only Candace Cameron in this city."

"Did you really?" I flirt.

"No, I'm pulling your leg. You had me going there for a minute."

"What if this was really the wrong number? What would you do?" I lean against the cold wall and listen to his voice.

"I knew it was the right number. You had me thinking you didn't want to be bothered, having me jumping through hoops to find you. Lucky for you I like a good challenge."

"Is that so? How did you know this was the right number?"

"Your voice on your answering machine. Your voice is undeniably sexy. I could pick it up out of a room full of people. I left you a message last night. Did you get it?"

"I did," I say. "Last night was a busy night for me. I had a party to attend, but I didn't make it and everything turned into fast forward for me."

"That's OK. You don't have to explain."

"Perfect. I was just about to ramble on and on if that would've gotten me off the hook," I joke and he laughs.

He has a sexy laugh, resonant, and bold. It travels to your spirit.

"Well you can make it up to me by allowing me to take you out to dinner."

"Dinner sounds good," I say. "You were so evasive the last time I spoke to you. Can I trust you not to try any funny business?"

He belts out another laugh. I think up things to say to

him just so I can hear him laugh again. Nick is white, but with a black voice. Someone has a little bit of soul.

Nick asks, "When are we going out?"

"When do you want to take me out? I'm warning you, I like to eat. I'm no soup and salad girl."

"I don't like those types anyway. What are you doing on Thursday night?"

"Nothing sticks out in my mind," I say, knowing my after-work calendar is clear.

"Let me take you out then," he says. "I'll pick you up around 7 o'clock. How does that sound?"

"I'll be ready."

"Oh and dress casual."

"OK."

***

Monday mornings at the office are a struggle and it takes every ounce of my energy to get back into the swing of things after a long weekend of drama. I look at my desk and sigh loudly. I swear it doesn't do any good for me to clean off my desk on Fridays. I clean it up only for Miranda to pile it high with junk again for Monday. The intercom on my desk goes off and my secretary's voice comes through.

"Ms. Cameron. Ms. Bradshaw would like to see you in her office."

I depress the button on my intercom. "Did she say why?"

"She didn't say."

The devil wants to dance early. What she wants this early in the morning, God only knows. The woman is a piranha!

I hesitate long enough to hear Miranda buzz Kerrey again to summon me.

"Let her know I'll be there."

The minute Miranda's office door closes behind me I'm behind enemy lines, ducking bullets. She is angry with me for not meeting the deadline for a project she assigned me last week. Its 6 o'clock in the morning and this witch is screaming at me in her thousand-dollar pinstripe suit.

Miranda adds insult to injury. Good thing I'm not thinned skin. She tells me my complete work is being handle by someone else. Her words replay in my cranium "Quite frankly Ms. Cameron I don't think you can pull your weight around here, so I gave the work to someone who can."

I take what she says in stride. I'm hot, but I won't let her get the best of me. Miranda always looks for flaws in my work. I'm the only black female at this level. I know my stuff, I could have her job and she knows it. I have her running scared; this is why she harps on me. I wait patiently for her to finish belittling me, while in my mind I am giving her a piece of my mind. Forget just a piece of my mind; I am letting her have it, I would say what I'm thinking, but I'll settle for making her look foolish.

Miranda shuts up long enough for me to get a word in.

I tell her, "Miranda, I met your deadline. I handed your secretary the documents on my way out on Friday."

It's her turn to look like an idiot. Miranda's flabbergasted look confirms what I already knew; her secretary didn't give her the documents. If she could keep a secretary and stop firing them for every mistake then she would have one trained to perfection by now.

"You did? I was beginning to worry about you slacking off. Candy you're such a good worker, why did I doubt you? Forgive me. I'll get on my secretary about this."

Miranda is such an award winning diva, just like that she apologizes and praises me then quickly dismisses me as promptly as she summoned me. The buzzer on the secretary's desk beeps on my way out, and Miranda bark orders for the woman to get in there.

Shannon her secretary is this tiny little white girl that reminds me of a porcelain doll. She peers at me with a frightened expression. Her face devoid of makeup, wire rim glasses frame her oval shape face. It's a dog eat dog world and she is just a pup.

I say, "Her bark is worse than her bite."

The girl's face pales even more. She won't last a month.

"What did I do now?" she asks in a timid voice.

"You forgot to give her the file I gave you Friday."

"Oh no! I forgot." The girl's eyes are terrified.

"The faster you go in, the faster you'll get out. Your warden awaits. Miranda doesn't like to wait."

This girl had better grow a spine and put that cold-hearted scrawny she devil in her place.

CHAPTER TWENTY-TWO

Mona

I feel like I've won the lotto.

Lovemaking earlier in the morning with John reaffirms my intentions to keep him in my life forever. Scheming is not one of my strong points, but I always get what I want and I want John. I nuzzle my head beside his and breathe in his scent.

I've waited a lifetime for this moment. It is almost surreal. I blow gently into his ear, intent on waking John from his slumber. He brushes at his ear. I giggle. I do it again, this time he rolls onto his back and takes me with him.

"You're being a naughty girl." John swats my rear, it stings, and I rub the spot.

"I thought you like me that way."

"This is true," he confesses and cups my rear.

"How long have you been awake?"

"If I tell you, will that stop the face tickling or the funny smiling faces?"

Guilty as charged, I blush crimson. "That long, huh?"

"Yes," John gives a kiss to my forehead. "I'm hungry."

"I'll make us something to eat."

John likes this rear-swatting thing, because he does it again when I bend over to pick up my robe.

He whistles and says, "Nice."

"Did you enjoy yourself?"

"Won't you come back to bed and let me show you just how much I enjoyed myself."

He can't be serious? He is. Desire burns in his eyes. I'm hungry and worn out from this morning's sex feast. We stayed in bed pretty much all day Sunday, and then were at it again this morning. John is truly a sex maniac. I'm no match for him. His stamina is immeasurable. I get tired thinking about doing it again.

"Hmm, that sounds good, but you better stop or we'll never get out of bed," I say. "Plus, I've got to get to work. Save it for later."

John stretches out in my bed and I marvel at how good he looks in it. "That's fine with me."

"You can stay here, but I'm going to go in the kitchen to find something to eat. I'm starving."

"You should be full from having some of me."

"You're too much. I love waking up next to you." I climb back in the bed and get on top of him. John doesn't give up, and he tries to seduce me again. I fight off his wayward hands, touching me in places he knows will get me started.

"No, baby let me go make us something to eat."

More kissing and I'm on the verge of giving in, but I scramble up and head to the kitchen.

John being here with me feels natural. It's hard to imagine him being anywhere else. I knew if I waited long enough, I would win him. I let him get away from me way back in college. John and I met long before he and Lisa, and we used to fool around. We had an on-again, off-again thing and were off when I found out he had hooked up with Lisa.

I'm not sure what made her so special, but he actually got serious about her. Even married her. To this day, I don't know what she had that I didn't have way back then, but it doesn't matter. John has finally chosen me.

Lisa doesn't know what she had. I pour the premixed batter and it sizzles as it hits the stainless steel. The scrambled eggs are done and covered up to keep warm.

Ninety-two point five plays in the background and the bulletin news broadcasts the latest death poll, something about a man found dead last night in his house. The police are still investigating the murder and they will offer up a $1,500 reward to anyone who has witnessed the shady events surrounding the crime. I switch to some easy listening music.

Breakfast is ready in less than ten minutes. Scrambled eggs, bacon, sausage and pancakes with fresh strawberries on a breakfast tray for two.

John clears a spot for me on the bed.

"That smells good. What all you got on that tray?" he asks sitting up in the bed.

Proud of myself I set the tray down on the empty spot beside John. "Breakfast for my baby. Let's see we have pancakes, sausages, eggs, oh yeah and strawberries."

John pops a strawberry into his mouth. "Mmm this looks delicious. You're so good to me."

"Am I?"

John stops to stare. "Yes you are very good to me," he says it in such a serious tone that I have to believe him. "I don't know what I'd do if you weren't in my life. You're the greatest."

"I love you, John. Now eat up before your food gets cold."

"Yes, ma'am!"

He takes a mouthful of his breakfast. "This is really good! If you keep this up, I may never want to leave."

"I don't want you to leave anyway. I'll just have to keep cooking you breakfast in bed."

"And don't forget that good loving too." John feeds me strawberries, some of the juices run down my chin and he licks them from my lips.

"If you keep this up you're gonna be my breakfast."

"Is that right?"

"Yes that's right."

"Bring that body to me, woman."

I love it when he wraps his arms around me. I feel safe and secure in them. They even make me feel like I'm the only one, but that's just foolish thinking. One day my demons will catch up with me. I hope it's not today.

CHAPTER TWENTY-THREE

Mikhail

"Mikhail, your truck is loaded and ready to go." Ron's voice thunders over the loud clanking noise and people bustling about in the warehouse.

The inventory manager Ron is a stout fellow, thick-necked, and average in height. He's one of the suits, strict, but fair. He was a courier like me, and then they promoted him to management. Once in awhile he comes out of his office to help us out with a load.

"Cool. I'll roll out of here in a minute. I need to holla at you before I leave out. Let me finish up this paperwork."

"The keys are in the ignition."

"All right man, thanks."

Finishing my paper work is my immediate goal. Day isn't turning out the way I anticipated. I'm behind schedule which means I'll be here all day. The truck broke down and I had to have it towed back to the warehouse. Had to move all the packages to another truck. With Ron's help I was able to get the work done in record time.

Ron clues me in on the position I interviewed for a few weeks ago. Some new dude off the street filled it. I'm livid and I want an explanation as to why I didn't get the position. Ron is about to tell me what happened when one of the big bosses shows up.

Hard as I work for the company I feel like they stab me in the back by giving an outsider a position I know like the back of my hands. Paperwork finalized, I make waves to Ron's office.

"Ron, are you in here?"

He yells, "Yeah, come on back here."

"Man I need to ask you something. Can they just hire someone off the street like that?" I ask, patting my legs with the paperwork.

"It's their company they can do whatever they want. Man I know you wanted this gig, but let it ride. Something else will show up."

"Easy for you to say, you're not the one driving everyday in this heat and cold."

"Mikhail, I know where you're coming from and believe me I've been where you are. You wouldn't believe how many times they passed me up for a few positions in this company and look at me now. I'm a manager doing what I love. Hang in there Mikhail. There will be other openings. I'll keep my eyes peeled for you. Don't let this get you down."

Ron rolls up a piece of paper and throws it in the waste-basket. I hear him, but I don't like what he's saying. Maybe this cat doesn't want me to succeed. I'm tripping. Ron's the only one in management I trust in this place. He has saved me from self-destructing too many times to start being un-grateful.

I sigh heavily. "I know, but I'm still ticked off. Here is the paperwork."

Stubby hands latch onto the edge of the papers. Ron scans them and tells me, "Everything looks good. Here is your new delivery log. I made some changes, look it over."

I take the new log and scan it over, everything looks good, and I tuck it under my arm.

"Thanks Ron I'll see you later," I say and push up off the doorsill.

"We have a meeting tonight. Think you can make it?"

"I don't see why not."

"Keep your head up man." He frowns and asks. "Did you really look at the log I handed you?"

I frown too. "Yeah, it looks good."

"No you didn't, look again."

I skim over it again. First stop today is at Candy's office, Charles and Riley Investment Firm. Can the day get any worse? Stunned, I shake my head.

"Thanks Ron."

"I know Mikhail, it couldn't be helped."

I have been trying to reach this woman all week and now I have the opportunity to see her face to face without even going out of my way. I haven't seen Candy in a long time and I'm nervous of her reaction to seeing me. She can be a little hot tempered. I hope she doesn't act all ugly with me.

***

Candy

It's lunchtime and everybody vacates the building except me. I'm playing catch up, because I didn't get a darn thing done this weekend. Lisa consumed it with the marital issues. My phone lights up and a text message flashes across the screen. It's Shelly telling me to meet her in her office.

I wait five minutes for my laptop to go on standby before closing it. The darn thing is running slow again, which means it's time to defrag, to take some things off I don't use anymore. Shelly's office is next to mine. I get to Shelly's office and she's on the phone with her back turned to me. I tap her door to get her attention. She swivels around in her chair, smiles and waves me in. I don't sit down as she instructs.

I mouth. "Let's go."

Shelly pretends she doesn't hear me, and keeps on yakking. I roll my eyes, hit my watch vigorously, and mouth off at her some more. She grabs her purse, swings it over her shoulder and tells her caller goodbye.

"My, we're touchy."

"I'm hungry and you're sitting there holding lovemaking conversations." I squint and brush the hair off her white blouse. "Something's different about you today."

We stop in front of the elevator and Shelly hits the down button. The elevator squeaks into motion and we wait for it to stop on our floor.

"I had an amazing weekend. Thanks for showing up at the bachelorette party. I hope you had fun." Shelly's sarcasm is understandable, and I deserve it.

"Shelly you know I wouldn't have missed it for the world. I had a crisis I had to deal with." After the emotional time with Lisa, I didn't feel up to partying, so I drove back home when I left my friend's house.

"OK you're forgiven. I didn't leave until five o'clock in the morning. I don't remember. I can only remember bits and pieces... I left before it ended. Oh my gosh! Candy I have a confession to make."

I wait for Shelly to let me in on the secret. My stomach growls again. What is taking this elevator so long?

"I took one of the dancers back to my hotel room. Candy, I had sex with him."

My mouth opens, shuts, and then opens again. Frozen in place, I wait for the other shoe to drop. Shelly never struck me as the kind of woman who has casual sex. At least that's the impression she gives. Yeah we joke around as women do, but half the time we don't mean anything by it. All those stories men tell about women being the real players is mumbo jumbo, real women don't trick. I know I'm a serial monogamist, proud, respectable, and uncompromising.

The elevator saves her from hearing my opinion on her confession. The door opens and Mikhail is standing in the elevator, and that shocks me even more. I've been doing a good job avoiding him, now he stands right in my face. It's easy to ignore someone's text and phone calls, but when you come face to face, things aren't as easy. Eternity goes by before he speaks.

"Aren't you going to say something?"

The sound of his voice makes my back arch in response to him. He has no idea what he does to me. I've already undressed him with my eyes and made love to him a thousand times.

"Mikhail," is all I can squeeze from my constricted lungs. Of all the heroic things, he turns up when I least expect it, to pursue me. It's a romantic notion, until I notice the packages in his hand as well as his uniform. I'm such a fool.

Mikhail looks fine, really fine, even smells fine. His shaved his head is something I begged him to do while we were together. His new girl must be running things now. I notice Mikhail's buff body. It looks like he's been working out. Mikhail looks at me with expectation.

Inside I struggle to remain calm and unmoved. I could use Shelly's help, but she just stands there staring at the two of us. I can't talk. My thoughts go on a rampage in my head. It would be easy to say let's forget our past and start fresh. Then a play-by-play of how our relationship ended paints our reality. We were never right for each other. Our love-hate relationship and breakup to make up love disaster has ended. I press rewind and I don't like our history. Fast-forward is what God has for me and I'm content with that knowledge. I drink in as much of Mikhail as I can then I look away. I need to look at something, anything, but at him. The little sparkles on my shoes seem like the best place and I count the different colors they radiate, blue, green, red, and purple.

"How have you been? It's real good to see you Candy," he says it so softly, I almost give in to the temptation of desires I'm feeling.

Regaining composure I say, "I've been great. It's good to see you too. We are on our way to lunch, are you getting off?"

Mikhail ignores my hint and question. "Can I speak to you for a minute?"

Once again, I look at Shelly for help and she looks up at the ceiling. Traitor. "This is not a good time, Mikhail. Can I call you later?"

"I tried to return your phone call from the other day, but you haven't been answering my calls. What, your phone doesn't work?"

"It works. I've been really busy."

Mikhail looks at Shelly, then back at me. The elevator gets ready to move again and he hits the button to keep it from closing. Someone downstairs or upstairs is mad at him for holding up the elevator. He fidgets with the packages and stares me down as he tries to read me and tries to hint at me to tell Shelly to leave. Mikhail's mind ticks like a time-piece, spinning as he looks for a way to get me alone. I'm not telling Shelly to leave. I'm afraid of what will happen if she leaves me with him.

"Busy?" he looks indignant.

"Yes, busy."

"Too busy to call an old friend?"

"Yes."

He repeats every answer with a question. "Yes?"

Mikhail's lips move to say something, but nothing comes out. Instead, he simply steps out of the opened elevator doors, leaving Shelly and me to stare at the back of his head. I have words too inappropriate to hurl at him in Charles and Riley.

Shelly gets on the elevator with me and we ride it to the first floor. "Did I miss something?" She asks.

I wish she had. Mikhail embarrassed me in front of a colleague and I'm mad as all get out. Shelly is my friend, but he doesn't know that.

"Shelly, every dog has its day. Sorry you had to be here for that."

"Don't worry about it girl, he's the one that should be apologizing, not you."

"I know. I just felt like I had to, you know." I sigh. My heart is heavy, and my thoughts jumbled. "What are you going to do about your current situation?"

Shelly shrugs. "I don't know. What do you think I should do?"

"Me? You can't ask me. This is your life, your circumstance. Do you still want to go through with the wedding?"

"No, I'm confused... er... maybe it's not a good idea to get married. I mean, I've been having second thoughts about this whole thing since Tom asked me to marry him. What if he's not the right one?"

I turn to her and say, "You kids have been together since the stone ages. Just be honest with him. He won't like hearing what you did, but he will forgive you. And if he doesn't, then it's better to get this out of the way now. You can't enter marriage with a lie between you. So just confess, and then maybe you two can go to premarital counseling and work on your issues. What you did was a big mistake, but don't make it worse by trying to deceive Tom."

"I'm not sure about telling him the truth," Shelly wrestles with her emotions then she smiles. "The sex was good. The man turned me out, made me feel and do things I didn't think I was capable of doing or feeling. I want more, and I can't have more if I'm getting married."

"Now see, that's lust talking. Girl, you are supposed to control the thing between your legs, not let it be in control of you. So what? This guy did some things to you that blew your mind and now you want to throw away a five-year relationship? Tom is one of the kindest, sweetest men I've had the privilege to know. Trust me when I say you don't want to throw away what you have for a roll in the sack."

"That's not what I'm saying. What I'm trying to say is that maybe I haven't sowed all my wild oats yet and if I haven't I don't want to make the same mistakes my sister made and become the wife that sleeps around on her husband."

"You are not your sister. Your sister is a she-dog. No pun intended."

"None taken."

"Just think of it as your last fling as a single woman. Put it behind you and go on about your business. This guy you were with does this for a living. What makes you think you're the first bachelorette he seduced? He's a stripper for crying out loud... A trained seducer, that's his profession, which by the way is what he did to you," I pause. "But if you truly don't think Tom is the man God has for you, then you owe it to yourself and to him to call it off. But be very sure."

"I love Tom," Shelly says. "He is truly my soul mate. But the sex is nothing like it was with this other man."

"Look, girl, if sex is getting boring, then you can spice it up," I tell her. "Share with him what you are telling me. Get some books. Do something! Better yet, cut out the sex until your wedding night. And you'll see a newness and special feel to your love making as a result."

"Stop having sex?" She asks incredulously.

"Yes," I say. "Maybe part of the problem is the fact that you are having sex at a time when you shouldn't be. Focus on your relationship and preparing for marriage. Pray about it."

I wonder if I would be able to just stop having sex if I had a man. It's difficult for me to be celibate now, and I'm not even dating anyone. I couldn't imagine if I was in a good relationship and then decided to stop all of a sudden. Maybe I'm giving Shelly unrealistic advice. Judging by the way she is looking at me, it looks like I am. But then I give myself a mental shake. Of course I'm not giving bad advice. I am giving spirit-led advice. A couple can have a relationship without sex. I'm counting on that. Because one day, I want to be in Shelly's position — engaged, not having slept with a stripper — and I want to be able to honor this commitment I've made to God.

So I reiterate what I've just said. As much for her as for me. "Yes, take the sex out of the equation right now and spend more time on your relationship," I say. "God will honor your choice."

Shelly does not look convinced. "I don't know," she says slowly. "I'm not sure about just cutting out sex altogether. That seems a bit drastic. But maybe you are right. Maybe I will try to have a conversation with Tom and tell him what happened. And then I'll tell him we need to spice up our sex life."

The elevator stops, the doors open, people trample us to get on before letting us off. The Christianity in me won't make me bring shame to God, by speaking what I'm thinking. I smile and say excuse, when I'm the victim.

"Where do want to go eat? I don't want to hear anymore about your sexcapade."

"What sounds good to you?"

"Rosario's pizzeria."

Rosario's is this little Italian pizzeria across the street from our office and one of my favorite places to dine. They serve the best calzones, lasagna, and New York-style pizza.

"What was all of that back there with you and Mikhail?"

Bringing up Mikhail's and my past is hard for me. Shelly is a good friend and not acknowledging her question would be an insult to her. Shelly is not like most people — she is easily offended.

"Mikhail is into playing games and I don't have time for games. He wants to be serious then he doesn't. He disappears and reappears at a drop of a hat and expects us to pick up where we left off. To put it simply, I'm tired. I need a man who knows what he wants in a woman, someone who knows my worth and knows how to please me."

"Amen. Well I'm sorry it didn't work out. It all seemed so promising."

It hurts. I cover up the pain with a fake smile. Mikhail and I have reached our final destination, chapter closed.

"Girl please, there's no reason for you to be sorry. It's nobody's fault but mine. I'm the one who continues to fall for the wrong men. You know how we are sometimes. Thinking we can change men. We ignore the warning signs until it's too late."

"I think it's the mother in us. He's a fool. Any man who lets a woman like you get away is a fool. Don't worry about him Candy, you got it going on and sooner or later he will realize his mistake."

"Trust me he will. I met someone. Maybe he'll help me get over Mikhail once and for all."

"Well, that's great," Shelly says. "You deserve to be happy. Tell me about this new man."

"He's white," I blurt.

Her step falters. Shelly isn't prejudiced, so I know that's not the reason for the shock.

She smiles and asks, "You've come across the fence?"

"Nick is a bartender. I met him at Zane's when I went out Friday night."

We stand in front of the restaurant and watch people go in and out of Rosario's restaurant. The food beckons me to come in. I want to go inside, but Shelly wants to be nosy.

"Really, what's he like?" she asks oblivious to the hunger pangs gnawing at my sides.

"He's like a man."

"You're hungry. Tell me more about this man, greedy. We're not going in until you give me all the juicy details."

I sigh and throw my head back. "All right. He's sweet, funny, smart and articulate. He's simply refreshing. We have a date this Thursday and I can't wait."

"Look at you. I've never seen you this excited about a man. He must be something."

"It seems like he is. I feel things for him no man has ever made me feel. I don't even know him. How can this be?"

"Love at first sight is unexpected."

"There is no truth in that theory, lust at first sight maybe."

We're next in line when my phone rings in my suit pocket. Miranda's office number sings, "Highway to Hell."

"What does she want now?" I huff and hit the talk button.

"Who are you talking about?"

"Miranda," I mouth and answer the call. "Yes, Miranda."

"Candace I need you back at the office," Miranda snaps through the phone.

Last time I checked, slavery was abolished years ago. Does a sister get to eat anymore?

"Miranda, do I have to do this right now? Can it wait 'til after lunch?"

"No it can't. I just got you a new client and I don't think you want to miss out on this opportunity. Trust me. Come back to the office, lunch can wait. I need you back here ASAP!"

"OK, I'll be there in a few minutes." Whatever is up her sleeve, it had better be good enough for me to miss lunch.

"Looks like you're having lunch by yourself today. I have to go back to the office."

Shelly frowns. "Why?"

"Apparently Miranda assigned me to a new client and she wants me to come back to the office. Do you mind ordering me a calzone?"

"Honey, of course not."

"Dang gummit, I don't have any cash on me."

"I got it, go," she shoos.

"Thanks. I'll see you back at the office."

I quickly weave my way through the maze of tables and dart across the street. Minutes later, I step into Miranda's office, and I get the third shock of the day. Following Shelly's news and bumping into Mikhail, this was the most surprising. Nick sits in a chair across from Miranda dressed in an Armani tailored suit, talking to her as if they're old friends. The two of them are too deep in their conversation to notice my presence.

What is he doing here? How did he know where I work? I

scan the room for my new client and find none. A thousands questions form in my head and my hands spring sweat like a sprinkler. I try to move my legs, but they've lost mechanics.

"Candace, there you are. Close the door and come on in and have a seat honey." Miranda waves me over to come and join to them. "This is Nick Lancaster of Lancaster's Enterprises. Nick, this is Candace Cameron, the investment banker I told you about earlier."

"It's nice to make your acquaintance, Mr. Lancaster." We exchange handshakes.

Humor only I understand crazes the corner of his eyes. "It's a pleasure making yours, Ms. Cameron."

Miranda cuts in; she likes to take center stage. "Now that we've gotten the introductions out of the way, let's get down to business."

"Yes, let's. What do you know about Zionics?" Nick directs his question to me.

I clear my throat. "Zionics Inc. has been in the software industry for quite some time, but as you may know it was the new software they came out with last fall that put them on the map. Excuse me," I say and pour water from the pitcher they have on the table into a Styrofoam cup. I take a sip and continue. "As I was saying, their stock is still at a comparable bargain compared to where I expect it will go. If you want to invest in them, now would be a good time."

Nick asks, "What about this merger with Valco? How does that affect anything?"

"I see we've been doing our homework. Not a lot of people know about the possible merger." Nick raises his eyebrows at my remark. "Valco is a smaller software company Zionics wants to acquire. Valco is going in the same direction Zionics is. If these two companies merge this would create more wealth for the company."

"Do you have any information about when these two companies will merge? Would it be better to wait until they merge before I invest?"

"I recommend investing because these stocks are going to climb. Even if the merger does not go through, Zionics will show tremendous growth. And if the merger does go through, well, you could have an extremely profitable opportunity here. When would you like me to start the paperwork?"

"She doesn't waste time now, does she?" he asks, glancing over at Miranda. "You weren't exaggerating when you told me she's a shark."

I'm in the room! "Time is money, Mr. Lancaster. We are in the business to make our clients money," I reply, a little too testily. Being in the room with him flusters me. What troubles me the most is the relationship he has with Miranda. Their comfort level with each other borders on intimacy. Most of the men Miranda knows personally, she has bedded and the thought of Nick and her in bed together perturbs me.

"I have no doubt that you're good at what you do, Ms. Cameron," his response is coy. "Can you have the paperwork ready for me tomorrow?"

"I'll have them send it over to your office first thing in the morning. Please sign it and I'll handle the rest. It was a pleasure doing business with you." I get to my feet and extend my hand. Nick grasps firmly at first then loosens his grip.

Nick still holds my hand as he tells me. "I look forward to doing business with you."

"And I you," I reply, wriggling my hand away. "Well if you'll excuse me I need to get back to my office. I need to get started on your paperwork."

"What's the hurry? Come have lunch with Miranda and me. It is the least we can do."

"Mr. Lancaster, as tempting as it sounds I'll have to decline. I have lunch waiting in my office, but thanks for the invitation. You two go on and enjoy your lunch."

"Now what kind of guy would I be to let the person who's going to take care of my finances go back to their office to feast on a cold lunch? Come have lunch with us. I won't take no for an answer."

The temperature goes up fifty degrees in the boardroom. "Um, I ah..."

"Nick, sweetheart, stop badgering Candace. Besides I

have something I need to run by you over lunch in private," Miranda cuts in, silencing any response I have.

"Is it possible for us to have lunch some other time, Candace?" he asks looking at me expectantly.

I sidestep his question. "If you two will excuse me I really do have to go back to my office."

In my office, I close the door, plop down in my chair and try to come to terms with the fact that I cannot pursue any romantic involvement with Nick. He is one of my clients now and Miranda's love interest. It now makes sense why he looked so familiar to me the other night. I've seen him in the newspaper. He is an active businessman in our community. I think he is an owner of that bar, that's why he was working there. No wonder he was wearing that expensive watch. I had entertained visions of Nick and me, but now that can't be. I can't date a client.

The lunch Shelly bought me looks unappealing, and I push it to the side.

CHAPTER TWENTY-FOUR

Lisa

Strange not hearing from John today, I think as I answer the phone.

It is Curtis.

Normally John calls a couple times a day to check on me then it hits me that this might be the end of the road for us. We've been separated for days now, and I miss him, but I'm not calling him. If he wants our marriage to work, he will have to make the effort this time. I have somebody keeping me company now. If John isn't careful this man might capture my heart.

I try to put John out of my mind and tune back in to the conversation, listening to the sweet way Curtis talks to me.

"I haven't been able to stop thinking about you," Curtis says.

"Mmm, what were you thinking?" I ask. He is so open with his feelings, and I like that.

"Hearing the sound of your laughter, the smell of your sweet perfume, and the way your eyes twinkle when you get excited," Curtis says. "I could go on forever about my thoughts of you, but I really called to see if you'd come out and have dinner with me?"

"I'd love to. Let me get some clothes on. Where do you want to meet?"

"Michael's Steakhouse downtown. Do you need me to come pick you up?"

I haven't told Curtis my situation yet and I need to tell him, but I haven't found the time. I'm enjoying his companionship. I don't want anything to sabotage it, and telling him would do just that. We've seen each other every day since meeting, and I welcome his attention. He doesn't pressure me and that puts me at ease with him.

I say, "No that's OK. I'll just meet you there."

"OK... um say in about one hour?"

"Can't wait to see you," I whisper breathlessly.
"Can't wait to see you too, baby."

CHAPTER TWENTY-FIVE

Mikhail

It's been days since I bumped into Candy and her foul attitude, and she's been on my mind more so today than any other day. It's my birthday and I miss her something terrible. Candy was the only woman I've ever dated that made a special day out of my birthday.

Last party she threw me is still table talk. All my friends from college I hadn't seen in years were invited. Candy even had the food catered by my favorite restaurant. The Rolex watch on my wrist was what sealed the deal for me.

How did I manage to screw this one up? I let the one thing that meant the most to me slip through my hands. I've done everything to get over Candy, but I can't and I know she doesn't want me back, judging from her reaction.

I called her moments ago and all I got was her voicemail on both phones. I don't want to end up on Jerry Springer as the stalker ex-boyfriend so I've got to find a way to stop these impulses to call her.

Today Momma is throwing a little shindig for me at the house. I'm not supposed to know about it, but Michael can't keep a secret. To get me over there she asks me to come over to help her and Pops move some furniture.

Maxine my nosy next-door neighbor sits on the porch with her nosy friends. I'm halfway down the stairs before she busts me.

"Well hello neighbor. You can't speak today?" she purrs.

Without glancing up I say, "Hey. Hi Maxine, how is it going?"

"I'm fine and you?"

"I'm good Maxine."

"You look good. I haven't seen you with that little girlfriend of yours lately?"

This is my cue to leave. "Nice talking to you Maxine."

"Where are you running off to? Need any company later?"

"See you later, Maxine."

***

Where are all the people for this thing?

There are no cars in front of my parents' house or on the side streets and I'm starting to wonder if I got the days mixed up. It would be the first. I walk to the front porch, knock on the door, and then look through the peephole. Can't see a thing; seconds tick away before the doorknob turns and the door screeches open.

Family and friends greet me. "Surprise! Happy birthday." Cousins, aunts, uncles, and old friends I haven't seen in years come up to hug me.

Momma knows how to throw a party. She has a DJ booth set up, liquor bar, and of course, black folks can't have a gathering without food.

"Happy birthday, sweetheart." Momma shoos everyone off so she can hug me.

"What's up little brother, it's about time you showed up. I thought you were gonna miss your own birthday bash." Michael bellows coming from behind me. He slaps me on the back, and hands me a Heineken.

I take it and sip. "Never that, what did I miss?"

"Nothin'. I'm just glad you showed up. Uncle Lionel was starting to get on my nerves. You know how many times that man approached me with the same questions. 'When are you moving?' 'Don't forget us when you move to that big city.' 'Remember family comes first.' I think the man has Alzheimer's."

I chuckle. "Man, I know what you mean. At least he didn't start telling you his war stories."

"Don't remind me of those."

Barbeque on the grill stirs my stomach. "Man, let me go in the back and get something to eat. I'm hungry."

"Who you telling! If we didn't have to wait on you to get here playboy we wouldn't be starving."

"Man move out my way so I can go get me some grub."

Kinfolk crowd Momma's backyard. I hug and kiss my grandmamma. She scolds me for not visiting her and reminds me of my absence at church. Going to church is a major thing in my household. Growing up I had to go to church every Sunday, whether I was sick, tired, hungry, or had a hangover. Momma didn't care what we were going through on that day. The only thing she cared about was that our tails were in church on Sundays praising the Lord. Sometimes I'd be so doggone tired from partying the night before I'd sleep through the whole service and snore like I was at my house.

Pops is cooking up some tasty looking barbeque ribs, chicken, and sausage. He looks better today, all decked out in a chef hat and apron, the black Chef Boyardee.

"Pops, how's it going?"

"Doing a' right, I can't complain. Happy birthday son, you're getting up there in age."

We slap each other on the backs.

"I'm good. Pops it's hot in here. If this is what it feels like now, how does hell feel? I'm a start living right from now on," I say as I rub my overnight beard.

We both chuckle. The twinkle is back in his eyes too. "What do you think of Michael getting that job?"

"Michael didn't tell me anything."

Pops frowns. "Boy you didn't tell your brother?"

Michael shrugs and sits on a one of the kegs. "I didn't get a chance to tell him."

Ignoring the two of them, I ask, "What you fixing back here Pops? I'm hungry."

Pops rearranges the meats on the grill, flips a couple of burgers, and adds some buns to the bottom grill. "You can have this here burger when it's done. You want cheese on it?"

"Yeah, load me up and don't be cheap with the food, Pops. Make sure I get my share before Benny and his greedy family come over here and eat up all the food," I joke.

Pops lets out a roar of laughter. "You missed it. The whole lot of them already been up here several times."

Uncle Lionel is the laughing stock for the young kids. Dancing to TI's "What you know about that." I chuckle to myself. I love our family gatherings, because someone is always acting the fool after too much alcohol consumption.

Been awhile since we've had a family get-together.

Things won't be the same after Michael leaves. I'm happy for him, still twinges of jealousy stab at my gut. When I look at my life, I see a black man, single, childless, and no real sense of direction. Even though I have a college degree, and on the job experience, I get passed up for good positions.

I haven't told my parents about what went down and I don't think I'll be telling them. Stan's suggestion about asking Pops for a loan to open up my own business crossed my mind several times, but the Johnson pride in me won't let me ask for help.

Pops regains my attention. "Son your plate is ready. Michael, what you want on your plate?"

"Gimme everything. It'll be a while before I get some of your cooking again. I'm gonna miss your cooking more than anything."

My stomach does jumping jacks at the sight of my plate. "Let me take this off your hand. Thanks. This looks good Pops."

Juices run down the sides of my mouth from the big bite I take out of my burger and I wipe it away with the back of my hand. Pops makes the best burgers this side of town. I missed lunch deliberately so I could put away some of his burgers. The man needs to open his own burger joint.

I tell him, "Pops, you know I still think you should open up a restaurant."

"Boy, you still talking about that foolishness."

Michael and I chuckle.

"Yes, Pops if you had opened up a restaurant you'd be making a killing right now. It's not too late to open one." I bite into my burger.

"What, with you as my only customer?" He shoots back. "Boy you better not start bringing up that nonsense again."

I shrug. "At least I believe in you. I'm not the only one who thinks your burgers are the best. Why you think all these people here? They not just here for my birthday. Knowing our family, if the food ain't good, you won't see them."

Michael helps me out. "Pops, Mikhail's right, you can burn."

Pops scratches his head and scrapes the grill. "You really

think my burgers are good?"

"Yeah Pops, they the shi... um... I mean they're pretty good, sir." I forgot my manners for a hot minute, but Pops doesn't notice the near slip-up.

"Well when I find someone to help out at the auto shop, I'll think about opening up a restaurant."

Aw-shucks, same sob story about being short staffed at the auto shop. I stuff the last bite of my burger into my mouth and wash it down with the rest of my beer.

"Thanks for the food Pops. I'm going to mingle with the rest of the family." I make a hasty retreat before we open up another can of worms with this auto shop business.

Pops says, "Mikhail, come back by here before you disappear for the rest of the day. OK?"

"I'll do that."

"Mikhail wait up, I got something to tell you." Michael falls in step with me. "Do you have to work Friday night?"

"Nah, I'm off this weekend."

"A few of us are meeting up at the Platinum club the night before I leave out."

My eyes light up. "I'll be there. It's been awhile since I've seen my favorite stripper Chocolate."

"Man where'd you find those fast girls from the other night? That Ingrid girl is a freak. She was saying some interesting things, but I had to send her on her way."

"It was too much for you, huh?" A football comes flying in our direction. It lands just to my left.

"Yeah, man," Michael says. "I like to go hang out at the club every now and then, but I can't take it beyond that. As it was, Kelsey gave me the third degree for coming in late. Imagine if I had actually done something with that Ingrid. No, man, that's not how I get down."

"Your crazy wife left me a message on my phone that night too," I say and kick the football back over to my little nephew.

I think when a man ties the knot, all extracurricular activities with other women should cease.

I don't always act right, especially now when I've been having these one-night stands, but our parents gave us a good example. Michael may talk noise sometimes, but he believes in his vows — even though that Kelsey can be worrisome. Those vows mean something.

If you can't honor that commitment then it's pointless to get married. I look at my mom and pops and I commend them for their loyalty to each other. Some day I'll have that, some day the right woman will come along. Until some day, I'll fantasize about the possibilities of Candy and me.

CHAPTER TWENTY-SIX

Candy

People who once filled the foyer of the art gallery are now inside. I don't want to miss Mona so I stand near the entrance. I pull the shawl up around my neck to protect myself from the AC vent shooting cold air down my back.

The door swings open and I move toward it, but stop in my tracks when two young couples stroll in instead of Mona, laughing and flirting with each other. Startled by my presence, they stop and wave hello as they go by. The door opens again and a smooth looking brother walks in dressed in a black and white tailor made suit.

He raises his eyebrows at the sight of me and slows his pace.

Singleness is like a virus, once you catch it, you'll do anything to get rid of it. I've been by myself for way too long and saving myself for the right man is getting old.

Sometimes I wonder if God forgot about me... if He forgot that my biological clock is ticking.

When will my man show up? Nick tried to hook up with me right after our meeting in Miranda's office, but I blew him off.

I told him I was busy. He called me another time, and I did the same thing. The last time I heard from him was a couple of weeks ago. I've had nothing else going on, on the man front since then. Maybe this man standing in front of me now could be a potential date. I am about to smile at him when Mona shows up and interrupts the moment.

"I thought you were gonna wait inside the gallery." Mona says. Her timing is imperfect. My potential mate walks on into the gallery, leaving Mona and me to fuss at each other.

Annoyed I ask, "What took you so long?"

She acts indifferent. "I couldn't find a spot to park."

"Come on let's go inside."

"Where did all these people come from? I guess wherever

there is free alcohol and food black folks are going to show up, huh? I always thought art shows were supposed to be boring."

"This isn't just any art show. Sometimes it's hard to believe that you're black."

"What's your problem tonight?" Mona asks, raising a brow. "You've been acting like a witch for a while now. Did I do something to offend you?"

I'm angry, but not at her. Mikhail's nasty message about forgetting his birthday has put me in a foul mood, and I'm having a tough time letting it go.

"Hellooo. Earth to Candy." Mona snaps her fingers in my face. That ticks me off too, but I let it slide.

"I'm sorry, Mona. It's not you and I feel bad for taking it out on you."

"I give up. When you're ready to talk let me know. I need to use the ladies room."

Mona walks off in the direction of the restroom, leaving me to my own devices. This is the first time I've had the pleasure of viewing an art exhibition that features artwork from the Jean Pigozzi Collection and I'm thrilled. His collection of contemporary arts consists of masks, game skin products, woods and stone handmade artifacts.

The love I have for art has developed over the years and it has taken me to different countries all over the world. It is a very expensive hobby, but one I enjoy very much. When I was a little girl, Mom took me to my first art museum. The affair started there.

"See something you like?"

Mr. Potential and I meet again. I turn to face him, smile on my face. "No I haven't worked the room yet, but I'm sure I'll find something to my liking."

"Darnell. You are?"

"Candace."

He brings my hand to his lips.

I blush, feeling a little shy all of a sudden. "Did you find anything you like?"

"I like everything in here and I should since I own the

gallery. But none of it compares to your beauty."

Oh God let this be the one. My knees wobble. "Oh."

"Does that surprise you?" he asks, amused.

"Somewhat and not because you don't look the part. It's just that I thought you were more of a model than a business owner."

Darnell is still amused. "I'm not talking about owning the gallery. I'm referring to your beauty."

I smile in response to his compliments. "I'm sure you've been told this a thousand times or more but you're a very beautiful man as well, and I mean that in the most masculine way."

He chuckles. "May I have the pleasure of showing you around?" he asks extending his hand. Mona's narrow behind is man blocking tonight, if her silly self didn't have to use the bathroom I'd be all over this brother like white on rice.

He follows my stare to the restroom and he says, "Don't worry about your friend. She's currently being accompanied by my partner."

"I see," I smile then frown. "How did you know who my friend was?"

"I noticed the two of you when you entered the room and I wanted to get to know you. Mona was kind enough to give me the goods on you but only if I found someone to entertain her while I pursue you."

Mona will die a slow death when I see her if this brother turns out to be a knucklehead. He seems astute, like he's on my level and strikes me as the kind of guy who can be businesslike or a little thuggish when he needs to be, which is very sexy to me.

"Well since you've got Mona covered then I wouldn't mind you showing me around."

Darnell grins, obviously pleased with my answer. Placing his hand in the small of my back he escorts me around the gallery. He is knowledgeable about each and every piece we come across.

After Darnell's art 101, he suggests we join Mona and his

partner Fred in his private suite. We get to his loft and I'm impressed once again with the décor.

"You have a very beautiful home."

"Thank you. Would you like something to drink?"

"I'll take some water."

Darnell's mini bar is stocked to serve a group of alcohol anonymously. His place is clean. I like a tidy man. Darnell's cell phone rings. He looks at it, hits a button then puts it down. Probably one of his female companions trying to get a hold of him and he doesn't want her to know he's trying to replace her. Mona's laughter echoes from one of the other rooms, and I go in search of her.

"Oh Fred stop!" she yells.

The noise stops then a male voice responds. "Do you really want me to stop?"

Mona giggles. "Yes."

"OK but only because I'm such a nice guy."

"No, that's not why. You're cheating."

Hunkered over Motownopoly Fred and Mona are at each other's throats. Mona's shoes are off, so are Fred's.

Mona looks up and sees me. She says, "Hey, Candy. You should come play this game. It's pretty neat."

I smile. "No, I'll pass. Looks like you guys are having a good time."

"Yeah he's cheating. He tickled me and took one of my game pieces."

Fred chuckles. "No, that's not true. She cheated first."

"I know. She does that all the time. Sorry you had to find out the hard way."

I ask, "So who's winning Fred?"

"Your cheating friend. Would you like something to drink Candy?"

"Thank you, but Darnell is already getting me something."

"OK. Sure you don't want to join the game?" Fred asks again.

"No, you guys go ahead. I'll just stay here and watch."

Fred asks, "How is it looking downstairs?"

"It looks—"

"—Pretty good," Darnell answers, coming up behind me. "We have a nice crowd down there. Antoine just texted me with the updates. More people showed up after we left."

Darnell reminds me of Mikhail. In some ways I miss Mikhail, because I keep comparing him to every man I meet, except for one. Nick.

***

Mona

Candy unsnaps her seat belt, looks out the window to her house, and hugs her purse to her bosom. She hasn't spoken to me since we left the art gallery.

She says, "Home sweet home. I'll be cozying up to an empty bed with cold sheets."

I can tell she is feeling lonely. She probably could have brought that Darnell home tonight, but since she is on this celibacy trip, she'll go to bed all by herself. I offer my suggestion.

"You need to buy one of those plastic men they are selling down at the adult store. Because that's the closest you're gonna get to a man who doesn't want to see what you are working with."

"The right man will come," Candy says and I wonder if even she believes that. "I'm trusting God. And in the meantime, I have some work to do on my own. Night."

"Goodnight."

Candy's home is a beautiful early 20th century house she purchased and remodeled a couple of years ago. Even in the dark, you can see enough of its beauty to appreciate it. Her home is perfect to raise a big family. The thought of family causes me to subconsciously touch the bump starting to form around my midsection. I'm not a hundred percent sure, but I think I'm pregnant. When I realize what I'm doing, I quickly move my hand away, afraid Candy might see me. She taps on the window. I hit the automatic button, and it rolls down.

"I'm glad we're friends, Mona."

"Me too, Candy, you're the greatest friend I've ever known."

"Gimme a call to let me know you got home safely."

"OK."

I watch her go inside then I drive off. It's been days since I've called and pestered Lisa at home. I hit the speed dial button to her house. Whoever created star sixty-seven is a genius.

"Hello?" she says. And I am silent. She repeats, "Hello?" Followed by more silence. "Hello? Who is this? If you're not going to say anything when you call, then stop calling me. If you're looking for John he doesn't live here anymore." She slams the phone down.

He sure doesn't.

I smile and redial her number. This time instead of waiting for her to pick up I hang up after the first ring. This continues until I get home.

CHAPTER TWENTY-SEVEN

Lisa

I am pulling into my garage when my cell phone rings. I glance down at the caller ID. "Hi, girl," I say with a smile.

"Hey, how are you?" Candy asks.

"Oh, I'm doing all right," I say, parking the car.

"OK," she says. "I just wanted to check on you. I've been so worried about you, with so much drama going on."

"Well, it's hard on some days, but thanks for touching base," I say, climbing out of the car. I step into the house and silence greets me.

"Why don't you come to Bible study with me tonight?" Candy asks, and I groan. I let her pray with me that night I decided to kick John out a few weeks ago, and I've listened to some of the pep talks she has given me since then, but I'm not so sure about going to church with her.

"I don't know..." I say and my voice trails off.

"Come on," Candy pleads. "It'll be good."

"Good is pretty subjective," I say. "I don't want a bunch of holy rollers hounding me."

"Nobody is going to hound you," Candy says. "I promise."

As I walk through the house, my heart aches for all that has been lost. I'm glad to have my new friend in Curtis, but I am filled with sadness at the failure of my marriage.

"Just come with me. Tonight," Candy presses. "I'm headed over there now. I can come by and get you."

My eyes fall on a wedding picture. At least going to church with Candy would get me out of this house for a few hours. "OK," I say and I can almost see the smile on her face. "I'll meet you there. You're still at the same church, huh?"

"Yeah, you know where it is," Candy says. "I'm so happy you'll come! It'll be good. You'll see."

"Yeah, we will see, all right," I say.

"OK, bye," Candy says. "See you in a bit."

***

Candy

I stand around outside waiting for Lisa, and a huge smile splits my face the second I see her car turn into the parking lot. I've been asking her to come to church with me for ages. I wasn't sure she would accept my invitation tonight, but God placed on my heart to invite her, all the same.

I wasn't even planning to come to midweek Bible study, but something just pushed me to do so. Work was kind of stressful today, and all I wanted to do when I got off was head home and relax. But I knew Lisa could use some ministering to, and I could be the instrument to help her find her way to church, somebody's church. Lord knows she has been going through it lately. I recall the hateful words she said to me when we went out that night all those weeks ago. And now she's thrown her husband out. Yes, the Lord sure does need to come into that heart.

"Hey," Lisa says, walking toward me. She reaches out her arms and hugs me.

"Good to see you," I say. That girl really is too skinny.

"Hi, Sister Cameron," someone says and I turn to see Sister Turner coming toward me.

"Hi, Sister Turner," I say and nudge Lisa, whispering, "Hurry, let's get inside."

"Huh?"

"She talks too much," I say in a low voice, but it's too late. Sister Turner is upon us now.

"Hey, baby!" She pulls me into a tight hug, suffocating me in her bosom. I manage to wrestle free, and I point to Lisa.

"This is my friend, Lisa, Sister Turner."

Sister Turner's smile grows wider. "Oh, Lisa, what a pretty little thing you are!" Sister Turner hugs Lisa as tightly as she hugged me. "How are you doing today?"

Lisa smiles. "Oh, I'm doing well, thank you."

"Well, the Lord has a blessing in store for you, tonight," Sister Turner says. "Your healing is at hand. The Lord has heard your cry. There is a balm in Gilead."

Sister Turner is ready to kick it into high gear; I see it in her face. I grab Lisa's arm. "Sister Turner, we're going to head on inside so we can get a seat. I'm looking forward to the study."

"Yes, Lord!" Sister Turner says. "Tonight, a mighty word will come from on high, I tell you."

She turns to Lisa. "Your eyes tell your story," she says, peering into Lisa's face.

Oh Jesus. I roll my eyes behind Sister Turner's back. This is the last thing Lisa needs, somebody in her face with all this talk. This is a big turnoff for Lisa. Sister Turner is always witnessing. Every word out of her mouth will be something related to a scripture or she'll be quoting from some old song like those are her original words. "Sister Turner, we've got to go," I insist.

"Oh, OK, baby," Sister Turner says, and rummages through her purse. She presses something into Lisa's hand. "Here is a little devotional for women. It's my favorite. Take it."

Lisa raises her hand. "Oh, no. I couldn't take your book —"

"Nonsense!" Sister Turner says, and the piano begins to play inside the church. "You take it. It spoke to my heart. I have a feeling it'll speak to yours. The Lord says when you call, he will answer."

Lisa glances at me, and then takes the devotional, shoving it into her own purse. "Thank you," she says to Sister Turner.

Sister Turner squeezes Lisa into another hug. "You'll be all right, baby. Just trust in the Lord."

As soon as Sister Turner steps away, I laugh. "See, I told you, she talks too much. You don't have to read that devotional. Don't feel any pressure. She's just an old lady who loves to push her religion on everybody else."

Lisa shakes her head. "It's OK," she says, surprising me. "It's weird, but it was nice hearing her talk. Her voice is so comforting. And her words didn't bother me."

The music grew louder, and the choir sings to the rafters. "I guess we should go in," I say, still marveling that Lisa would be receptive to Sister Turner.

I forget Sister Turner, though, when I step into the sanctuary and my eyes meet those of a brother I've not seen before. He is clean-shaven with strong features. Maybe I can chat him up after service to see what his story is.

I sashay on to my seat, confident that he is watching me walk past.

I am conscious of Lisa sitting next to me. Whenever the pastor says something, I glance at her out of the corner of my eye. I want her to get a word out of today's service. She needs it.

And she seems to really be into it. I even find her nodding in agreement at one point. "Pay attention!" she hisses to me and catches me off guard.

"Huh?"

"Listen," she says. "And stop looking at me."

"I am listening," I hiss back.

How is it that she is telling me to listen? I already know this stuff. But I put my reaction in check and focus on my pastor.

"The devil is full of deceit!" he says. "Whenever we are going through hard times, he tries to convince us that there is no way out. That sin is the only answer. He tries to make us believe that our way is too far strayed off the path; that we can never come back to God. But that's not true. God loves us. And he is always ready to welcome us into his arms."

"Amen!" Sister Turner says.

The pastor goes on with another point. "And we who call ourselves Christians must let our lives bear witness. It's not enough to just call yourself a Christian. You must act the part."

Again, amens.

"Are we so full of judgment for others that we can't see

our own lives?" the pastor asks. "Sometimes we look at the infractions of others, but fail to see where we can grow. Jesus said take care of the plank in your own eye before you talk about the speck in mine. That's what many of us sitting right here need to do. We're so busy talking about people that we can't see the dirt we do ourselves. We see the wrong everyone else is doing, but not what we're doing."

The pastor is really onto something today.

He goes on. "And then we're so busy chasing men that we don't have any time to spend with the Lord."

That last statement pricked me a little. Had I become so wrapped up in my desire for a man that I was neglecting my spiritual life? And what about the other stuff the preacher said? Maybe I was too busy focusing on Lisa's shortcomings that I couldn't see my own. Maybe God didn't just bring me to church tonight to prick Lisa's heart. Maybe he wanted mine to be pricked, too.

CHAPTER TWENTY-EIGHT

Mikhail

I'm not opposed to hard work, but today was a killer. They had me working like a Hebrew slave on the job today. I'm so tired I can hardly stand.

I pop one of those little precooked meals in the microwave, wash my hands and am about to sit down and wait for the food to warm when the doorbell rings. Uninvited guests aren't welcome at this house so I ignore whoever it is, hoping they will go away. No such luck, the ring turns into an insistent knock.

"This is one persistent mother lover," I mumble aloud. "This better be Publishers Clearing House with a million dollar check in their hands."

I look through the peephole to see some dude with a baseball hat on, standing at my door holding a clipboard in his hand. I open the door, rest against it, and fold my arms across my chest.

"Can I help you?" I ask, perplexed.

The man adjusts the clipboard in his hand, pulls out an envelope, and signs something on the clipboard. He asks, "Are you Mikhail Robinson?"

When someone asks you to identify yourself it's bound to be bad. Feelings of dread cover my neck down to my gut. I look at him, and then back at the envelope he holds in his hand.

I sigh. "Yes, I'm him."

He tells me. "I need you to sign for this."

He extends the clipboard and pen to me. The envelope is addressed to me, but the addresser is what has me worried, Kansas City Municipal Court.

"What... What is this?"

"You've been served, Mr. Robinson. Have a good evening." He leaves as quickly as he came.

"What do you mean served?"

He is down the stairs and in his vehicle before I can ask more questions. Frantic I rip the envelope open and my knees buckle beneath me.

I'm a father!

Maria Lopez is suing for child support. The name is familiar, but the face is hard to frame. I didn't even know I had a child. How can she do this?

Jack Daniels settles the tremors in my gut. Drinking something stiff usually does the trick, but not this time. I look at the bottle and frown. What is in here, water? I pour another glass. I leave it there and take the bottle with me into the living room where I plop down on the couch. Evil you do in your past has a way of catching up to you.

I should call Momma, but she'd trip. This is something I have to handle on my own. I don't know the first place to locate this woman. I start with the phone book. I go through every Lopez in the listing and come up empty handed.

A man ain't supposed to cry, but weeping would make me feel so much better right now. In a few short weeks I've managed to lose out on a job, lose all hopes of getting back with my lady, and now I have a child I don't know.

Momma's voice rings clear in my ears. "If you'd just leave these women alone and settle down with one like your brother Michael you wouldn't be in this mess." Then I recall the other point she likes to bring up. "Why didn't you use a condom? You better go and check yourself out to make sure you didn't pick up anything from these loose females you lay up with."

If only I'd listened to her wisdom. Whatever chance I had with Candy is definitely gone.

CHAPTER TWENTY-NINE

Lisa

Curtis' and my lips make sweet melody. He has me feeling like the first day of spring. My lips scream with joy and pure bliss. I don't want it to end. His kiss drowns my senses, makes me weak with an insatiable longings. We pull away long enough to take in some air. Deep dark eyes, dilated with desire stare back at me.

"Lisa, I know I've only known you for a few weeks now, but I think I've fallen in love with you."

I don't know how to respond. I stumble over my words. "I... I... that's... Curtis...."

"You don't have to say anything now. I wanted and needed you to know how I feel."

Curtis' grip loosens around my waist. When had this happened? How is he going to react when I tell him I'm married? Funny thing is, I've fallen for him too. We haven't slept together, but this thing between us has grown strong. Curtis hasn't forced the issue and I really can't say I have either.

My conscience stings and I recall something I read in a women's devotional I got from a lady at Candy's church. Trust in the Lord to guide you. Maybe I should trust that if I do the right thing by coming clean, it will all work out.

Curtis reclaims my attention. "I hope I haven't scared you away by sharing this with you?"

"Oh no, no. But I have to admit I am a little speechless and flattered by your candidness. You are such a sweet and gentle man. Words cannot express what these past few weeks have meant to me. When I'm with you, I feel like a queen." Tears sting the back of my eyes.

Curtis kisses them away, pulls me close and rubs my back in circular motion. For a moment, my imagination runs wild. Curtis and I love on each other; the loving is good, our spiritual connection ascends into heaven.

I want to be free of John; marriage to him has become a burden. With Curtis, I'm free to love, free to be me. These chains of bondage keeping me attached to John are psychological. I don't need the cars. I don't need the house. And it shouldn't matter what people think. This is my life. Who can live it better than me? If I want this to work, I'll have to tell Curtis everything.

Family is important to Curtis and I've already met his. We drove up to the country last weekend to attend a fall festival and meet his family. All his relatives were there waiting for us when we arrived. They are some of the nicest people I've had the pleasure of meeting, unlike John's family. The first time I met John's people, they were standoffish. It's rare to find a family that welcomes a stranger into their home with open arms but that's just what Curtis's family did. His mother and I have become great friends.

Curtis' silence worries me.

"What's on your mind?" I inquire.

"You." He answers readily.

"What about me?"

"You're remarkable. I can't get enough of you, my beautiful Cleopatra." His voice is full of warmth.

"Am I?" I ask, because it still touches my soul that he speaks to me with such affection. I didn't have that with John.

Guilt tells me to spill my story now. The real story about me isn't going to be so attractive once we journey down that road. I can bet my bottom dollar Curtis will be saying something different.

Worry lines crease Curtis's brow. He asks, "You asked as if you don't believe me. Has no one ever told you that before?"

Afraid of what he may see — guilt — I look the other way. "No, can't say anyone has."

"I find that hard to believe because you are such a beautiful person inside and out."

"Curtis, I hope you realize that all these compliments you're paying me are going straight to my head, and if you keep it up my head's going to explode."

He laughs, and rubs the back of my neck. It feels good. He makes me feel good. One hand becomes two, rubbing the tension from my neck.

Curtis captures my mouth, lip covering lip, doubts, insecurities, and worries disappear. He has me wide open, loose, and ready. If he doesn't make the first move, I will.

***

"Ahem. Aren't you home a bit late? It's 4:30 in the morning. Did you have fun?"

John's voice out of the darkness scares me. My keys fall to the floor.

"What are you doing here?" I ask, regaining my composure. Irritated, I bend over to pick up the keys.

"I live here, remember."

I raise an eyebrow. "Funny I don't remember telling you to move back in. Did you come back to get the rest of your things?"

The corners of his mouth tighten. He is trying to control his emotions and I'm trying to unravel them.

"How long is this going to go on?" he says. "I'm tired of playing this game with you. I want to come back home."

I walk into the next room with John in hot pursuit behind me. "What I need to do is change the locks."

"I think you're forgetting I pay the bills here too."

"How can I? There wasn't a day that went by that you didn't remind me of this, but what you fail to realize is that I make my own money too. John, if there is nothing else I can do for you, please leave and make sure you leave the keys... You know what, keep them. I'll call the locksmith in the morning and have the locks changed."

"So it's like that now, huh?"

"You made your bed, John, now lie in it."

John scratches the back of his head and looks at me with sorrow. "Was I that horrible of a husband to you?"

"You weren't horrible John. Disconnected, selfish, and two-timing. That about covers it."

He makes himself comfortable on one of the kitchen chairs. Tired as I am, I want him to leave. I don't want to discuss our marital affairs, don't want to face the disappointments there.

Out of politeness, I offer him a drink. Coke is all I have; we're not drinkers John and I. Until recently, anyway. I started back drinking toward the end of our stressful time together. He takes a sip of the soda. He fumbles through some papers on the table. Bills he and I have accumulated over the years. Separating this stuff is going to be nightmarish. He mirrors my thoughts; I see the grimace on his face.

For such a big strong man right now he looks broken down and beaten up. His face is thin.

"You've lost weight." The words flow from me before I'm able to stop them.

"Yeah well not eating will do that to you. Baby, please let me come home. I miss you. I need you in my life, can't you see that?"

"John was there something you needed? It's a little late and I want to go to bed so if there isn't anything else then I must insist that you leave."

"Who is he?" I've never seen John jealous, and I like it.

I laugh nervously "Who is who?"

"Well it's almost five o'clock in the morning and you're just waltzing in. You weren't out with your friends, and you weren't at your mother's. The only other explanation is a man. Who is he?"

I bite my bottom lip and draw blood from it. "What a tangled web we weave when at first we plan to deceive. You think because you are an alpha dog that everyone follows into your footstep?"

"You're avoiding the question. Go ahead rack your brain and try to come up with a convincing lie."

"How does it feel to have the shoe on the other foot?" I say with narrowed eyes. "All this time I was being a perfect wife, doing my wifely duties as promised. Putting up with your antics all this time and now all of a sudden, I'm doing what I want, when I want. You're interested in my affairs."

"Is this what it's all about? Revenge."

"Revenge is such an ugly word."

"But it is an accurate one."

"What John? You woke up and finally realized that I'm an important asset in your life?"

My words sting. He flinches.

"You've always been an important asset in my life," he says. "Things got complicated in my head and now I've straighten them out. Now I can see past myself and live for you."

My laughter bounces off the walls and echoes through the house. "What a crock. It's too late."

"Do you love him?" He studies my face.

"John, stop. I'm not seeing anyone. I went out for a few drinks alone, didn't think I needed your permission."

"No you don't, but I'm still your husband," he says, gathering his keys. "I think I've over stayed my welcome. I'll be on my way."

This is how he gets me to feel sorry for him. He manipulates. I've learned his trade, and I'm not fazed. Used to be I'd say, "baby please don't go, stay and let's talk it out." Sad thing is, I want him gone.

He tries one more tactic. He says, "You look good, baby. It was nice seeing you."

"Since when have you noticed?" I mumble under my breath.

"What was that?"

He heard me; he's just looking for something to keep him here longer. He's probably going to sit outside in his car and watch the house, as if I'm stupid enough to bring a man here.

"I said it was nice seeing you too."

"Oh," he says, and then he is gone.

First thing in the morning, I'm going to get the locks changed. I can't have John popping up whenever it suits him.

CHAPTER THIRTY

Candy

Nick has impeccable taste for the finer things in life. Lunch today is at a beautiful art deco style Japanese restaurant downtown. We've been here for at least thirty minutes and work hasn't come up in our conversation once. I'm beginning to think he got me here under false pretenses just like he did on the two dinners before this.

"I'm glad you accepted my invitation to lunch today. I was beginning to feel ignored."

Mouth full of prawn, I could do no more than look at him. So this was a set up; I should've known. His secretary was too evasive with information.

Once two people agree on their attraction for one another, they have to see where it takes them. I'm trying to avoid the client/agent affair, and he's trying to pursue it. And aside from the professional situation, I truly am trying to live better. I've made a vow to be celibate, but it's so hard. Maybe I don't trust myself to be alone with Nick. Maybe all of this avoidance has something to do with that. The more you avoid a man, the more he's determined to win you over, though.

"Why would I avoid you?"

"Cut the games, Candy. You know what I'm talking about."

"I don't know what you mean."

"You know exactly what I mean. Ever since you found out who I am, you've been avoiding me like the plague. If I hadn't told you something was wrong with the documents you sent to my office you wouldn't be here today."

"Something has been wrong with your documents two dinners before. So yes, I have been avoiding you a little."

His lips curl into a smile. "Just a little?"

"OK a lot, but speaking from one professional to another. I'm sure you can clearly see that pursuing anything other than a business relationship with each other could lead to catastrophic results in the future."

"Who said I wanted anything more than a business relationship?"

This throws me. Deeply embarrassed, I grab for words. I sputter like a blooming fool.

"You're... You're not interested in me?"

Nick's chuckle is a cross between devilishness and mischief. "No. Maybe I should be asking you if you're interested in me."

Lesson learned; ask the right questions before assuming.

"If you're not interested in me then why go through all the trouble?" I ask.

"OK, I lied, sue me. I wanted to see your reaction when a man tells you that you do not captivate him. I would be a fool to not be fascinated by you. I've wanted you since the moment I laid eyes on you and I'm willing to do whatever it takes to win you over. So what are you going to do, Candace Cameron, because I'm not going anywhere?"

I avert my eyes. Nick's intense stare warms my skin. This man has a way of getting inside my head, something not a lot of people are able to do. This is way beyond the physical, two kindred souls. It's why I'm keeping him at bay. I felt it the very first night we met, felt it back at the office, and I'm definitely feeling it now.

Nick covers my hand. His fingers caress every detail of the finest lines. He interlocks our hands, brings them to his lips and kisses them. His lips are soft, breath warm, unexpected tongue touches my skin. Desire ripples through my body. Completely caught up in a daze forgetting where we are, Nick slips one of my fingers between his lips and suckles on it. He then leans in and kisses me. My mouth opens slightly and my tongue searches for his. I breathe in his scent and give myself to the moment.

"Tell me you're not attracted to me. I could have you, right here and right now," Nick professes, snapping me back into reality.

Snatching myself away, I get righteously indignant, cursing myself for allowing him to get this close. I never go against my rules and there are three.

Rule No 1. Never get personal with the client.

Rule No 2. Never show any signs of interest beyond business.

Rule No 3. Never, ever, ever, ever discuss business over lunch without the documents in question.

I have broken all three rules.

When Nick told me he left the documents back at the office I should've rescheduled our meeting.

Jackson, my previous boss, led me to create these rules. Jackson and I met when I was fresh out of college. I deemed him a god among men. Sophisticated, well educate, distinguished, and rich beyond his years. It was my first time being exposed to anyone of his stature and I guess he knew it; after all, I was only a little country girl trying to survive in a big city.

He hired me, gave me one of the highest paying positions in the company. I passed up people who'd been there for years. People who had a lot more experience than I had and deserved the chance to shine, but I was too young and full of myself to worry about anyone other than myself. Little did I know I was being set up for a fall.

The first big project I was assigned to, had us working together late at night. We spent a lot of our time together and before long, we were sleeping with each other secretly. I was starting to fall for him big time and told him so. It didn't take long for his true shades to come out; he became distant with me and almost irritated by my presence, dodging me when he saw me in the hallway. This went on for days until I confronted him. Jackson was a player of the worst kind. I came into the office the next day after the confrontation and all my things were neatly packed in boxes waiting for my exit. Attached to the box was a note of recommendation and a security guard standing in my office ready to escort me out of the building. Just like that I was fired and wasn't even notified or given a reason.

Humiliation wouldn't allow me to ask for an explanation or to even put up a fight, so I left with my tail tucked between my legs. I had gotten off with only a broken heart, and I was thankful that I was able to find a job after that ordeal. That's when I made up these rules and I need to reinforce them before things get out of hand with Nick. The chair scraping on the floor draws a few heads our way as I stand to my feet.

"Nick that should not have happened. You tricked me into coming here and I don't like that. Don't think that I have changed my mind simply because you had your tongue down my throat."

Nick corrects. "Your tongue down my throat. If you're going to reprimand me at least get it right." He can't be serious.

He makes me feel like a child. "Well, whatever."

Nick is slow to his feet. The table between us is not enough protection. If he kisses me again, I won't be able to stop him and he knows this.

"When two people have this much chemistry between them it's a waste to deny ourselves the pleasure," he says. "Why won't you give me a chance to get close to you? Being your client can't be the only reason and if that's it then I'll find someone else to take over my account."

"Nick I don't deny the chemistry we have, but I don't mix business with pleasure. If you take the account and give it to someone else I still won't get involved with you. My ethics won't allow it, and besides what would Miranda think if you were to do such a thing?"

"I'm not worried about what Miranda thinks. I'm going to let you go for now but I mean to have you, Candy, one way or another." Nick's sureness goes beyond cockiness. I could say something scathing to cut him down to size and would if he wasn't so right. Nick blocks the way to my purse. He doesn't move and I'm forced to come in contact with his body.

"I'll have to consent to it first. Surely you wouldn't force a girl to make love with you, would you?"

Nick is close now; his breath is on my ear. "I can assure you, Candy, when I make love to you, and I will, it won't be because I forced you, but because you want me to."

Nick places his hands below my chin, tilts my head backward and then he subdues my mouth. He releases me. Too astonished to say anything, I grab my purse off the table and storm out of the restaurant. Nick's stare burns a hole in my back. I refuse to turn around and give him the pleasure of knowing he has rattled me. My legs carry me quickly to my car.

In there I brush distressed hair from my face, reapply my lipstick, and adjust my bra strap. I repeat the 23rd Psalm three times and then drive off looking over my shoulder to make sure Nick hasn't followed me. I have to execute a plan to assign Nick to another agent while keeping Miranda happy, and my job intact. First thing on my list to do right now is to wash away any desires of Nick and me becoming one before marriage. Lord, help me.

***

I have been in the office for hours and have accomplished nothing. I can't concentrate on a darn thing. Vivid images of Nick and me wrapped in a lovers cocoon creep into my head. I still remember the heat of his mouth when our lips connected, the softness of it, the taste, the urgency in which he kissed me. I remember the manliness of him when he brought me close to him. Sexually frustrated and distracted I give up on working. I toss the pen on the desk. It bounces back and rolls to the floor. Lord, I want to do your will, but sometimes I feel so weak.

I could use some fresh air, but the windows up here are designed to keep sun out and us in. This place is bulletproof, soundproof and suicide-proof. Personally, I hate high-rise buildings. I worry about terrorist situations, fire breaking out, or just some disgruntled employee fired from the job coming up in here spraying us with bullets. These people walk around in here as if being up this high is as natural as breathing.

I look below at the people going about their every day life. They look like tiny dots, a colony of ants. Downtown Kansas City doesn't have many of these tall buildings, but that's what sets this city apart from most major metropolitan cities. There isn't a lot of hustle and bustle, definitely a laid back city. When I graduated college this wasn't the city I had planned on settling down in, but circumstances prevented me from moving.

Mom needed me here. We're meeting for lunch today and

I'm not looking forward to the third degree I know she's going to give me. Like when will it be her turn to watch me walk down the aisle or hold her first grandchild? The woman is always trying to marry me off to the first man that shows some interest in me. When I broke the news to her about Mikhail and me parting ways, I think she was more devastated than I was. She never said anything about Mikhail's and me breaking it off, but the questions were there. I see the questions form on her lips every time we visit. I usually tell her everything. I think my reason for not telling her about the real deal between Mikhail and me was because I thought we'd eventually get back together and I didn't want her knowing certain things about him if we did. A sharp knock on my door claims my attention.

"Come in!" I yell through the 3-inch thick door.

Miranda walks in. "Hope I'm not interrupting anything," she surveys my office. Sits in my chair as if she owns it, crosses her legs and black eyes penetrates brown.

What did she expect to interrupt? "No, not at all, what can I do for you?"

She hesitates, thinks on what to say. Then she speaks, "How was lunch with Nick yesterday?"

That is the last thing I expect her to ask.

"I... It uh, it went well... I think. Is there something wrong?

"He's pulling out from under you. Did you two become intimate?" she asks in an accusatory voice.

Her question knocks the wind from me. I hyperventilate; Miranda's face goes in and out of focus. She waits for me to speak. I feel like I'm locked in an interrogation room.

"What? Just what are you suggesting, Miranda?"

"If you didn't sleep with him then how do you explain why he would take an account worth millions from under you and ask that I assign him to someone else?"

Boss or not she has crossed the line. This rivalry thing is getting old. Somewhere in the back of my mind, I remember the devotional I read today. "Follow peace with all men, and holiness, without which no man shall see the Lord. (Hebrews 12:14)

"Miranda, I value my job enough to know not to mix

238

business with pleasure," I say. "Thank you for the vote of confidence."

"Candy, I'm sorry. I was out of line. It's just that I know how Nick is around beautiful women."

Miranda walks to the window, checks out the depth and height. She fiddles with the fake flowers on the table and admires the picture I took with Mona on an Aspen trip. There is more. She is struggling to tell me, but I know it's coming.

Miranda holds nothing back. She says, "Nick and I have been friends since childhood Candy and he has a way with women. He's a love 'em and leave 'em kind of guy. You are a very impressionable young lady, and I would hate to see you get hurt. I've seen many women come in and out of his life. Take this advise, stay away from him and if you haven't slept with him yet then count your blessings."

I laugh not quite hysterically, but on the verge of cynicism.

"Why are you telling me this?"

"I believe I just did. Consider yourself warned."

Miranda speaks like a woman who has something to lose. She mashes pause at the door. She opens her mouth to add more to her words of wisdom, but I stop her.

"Miranda, it's best if you don't say anything else."

"Candy I know you don't think much of me, but I'm only looking out for your best interest."

"Mine or yours, Miranda?"

I struck a nerve, for a brief moment Miranda shows me her weakness. Her comeback stings. That was the intent.

"Don't fool yourself into thinking a man like Nick wants you for anything more than his new black Barbie doll. You're something new, something he has never had."

Miranda's words burn, the residue of her words goes deep. She has earned herself an enemy, played her cards way too early in the game. She slams the door; suddenly my chair loses its comfort. She struck a nerve in me too, a racist nerve. She reveals to me the reasons for her instant dislike of me when I first started here. This country we live in has us in constant bondage, fighting for our rights, freedom and liberty. The national anthem proudly declares it, but no one really upholds it. If any man does, it's on convenience because as soon as people are offended, we're back to the race card.

My eyes narrow. Miranda does not want to play games with me. Because she will lose.

CHAPTER THIRTY-ONE

Mikhail

Ever since I received that letter, I've been rethinking my life and where it's going.

I broke it off with old girl Claire, because the relationship we have is purely about sex, the quintessential relationship one would think. Well, not for me anymore. I track down the woman who says I'm the father of her child. I'm having a hard time confronting her. I go to her home to ask for a paternity test, but I punk when I see her outside bringing in groceries.

Maria Lopez is a waitress I met at a pub I used to frequent in downtown Westport. Our illicit affair was so short it's hard to believe she conceived from one night. I was drunk as a skunk the night we slept together, but I usually suit up before taking a ride, so her coming up pregnant is a mystery to me.

This happened two years ago and she waited this long to tell me. I'm scared of being a father, especially to a child I hardly know. I turned thirty this year, live in an apartment, my car is my prized possession, and I'm still lost. Most of the guys I know my age own their homes and are married with children. How did I get here? I need to speak with Candy.

She gets off from work in less than an hour. If I leave now I could beat rush hour traffic. What do I say when I get there or what if she rejects me? That thought is enough to stop me in my tracks. We will have to cross that bridge when I get there. I've got to win her back before some other man takes my place.

***

Behind the wheel, I zip in and out of traffic like a NASCAR driver. I make it to Candy's building in record time. I even have minutes to spare. I park two cars over from hers between a Beemer and a Jaguar. I recline back in my car and listen to "Shine" by Luther Vandross. I wait for Candy to exit the building.

I exhale deeply. My stomach tightens. My heart rises to meet my throat when she exits the building wearing a pin-stripe business skirt suit that shows off her slender legs and accentuates her curves. I imagine removing her clothes layer by layer to reveal her honey drenched skin. Skin as soft as rose petals and silky as cashmere. The cherry Coke I've been sipping on spills on the front of my pants. I look down to brush it off and when I look up again the scene in front of me doesn't impress me. A brother parks his Mercedes Benz possessively beside Candy, gets out and escorts her to the passenger side of the car. He gets in beside her and kisses her on the mouth. Candy doesn't pull away.

I close my eyes and will my heart to stop beating. I commit a felony in mind. Some two, three hours later I'm still sitting in Candy's parking lot with her car two rows over from mine.

Streetlights come on. I put my car in drive, switch on my own lights and head for the freeway. It troubles me that I'm hurting and the world still turns. I need an ego boost.

Connie's outside lights come on the moment I pull into her driveway and she is by my side greeting me in a football jersey and socks before I can get out the car. Connie is petite and the jersey fits more like a dress than a shirt. We've known each other for some years; we have an on again off again thing. She knows about Candy and I know about the dude she lives with. We don't pry into each other's lives; we provide comfort to each other, no strings.

As I walk toward Connie, my step falters a little. I don't want this, not another empty romp with some woman. But force of habit keeps me moving forward. I've been so quick to fall into bed with various women lately, but I'm starting to realize that's not the person I want to be. My irresponsibility has possibly produced a child I had no idea was around, un-til recently. My mom's word about God and the old sermons I used to hear when I attended church regularly have been playing in my head lately. "Fornication is the weapon of the enemy." Another fire and brimstone message starts to play in my head, but I cut it off.

Connie stretches out her arms to me.

"Hey you," she welcomes me with a kiss.

I hold on tight and squeeze. "Hey baby girl, you doing OK?" I try to sound enthusiastic, but fail. Connie's smile turns into a frown.

She feigns another smile. "You sounded strange on the phone when you called earlier, is everything all right?"

"Everything is fine," I lie. "Nah everything is not all right. I almost made a fool of myself today at Candy's job."

"Why? What happen?"

I run tired hands roughly over my head.

"I went by her job today to talk to her. I wanted to tell her how I've been feeling without her in my life. I thought I would surprise her but I'm the one who got the surprised. She's seeing someone new." I choke on the last sentence.

"Oh, Mikhail." Connie sympathizes. "I'm real sorry you had to witness that, because I know just how much you care for her. Did she see you?"

I shake my head in denial. "No or at least I don't think she did. I can't understand how it's so easy for her to start seeing someone else when just a few months ago she was professing her undying love for me."

Anger in a man's heart can erupt into uncontrolled rage when he feels betrayed and Candy has my insides raging; the veins in my arms swell to twice their normal size.

"Just because Candy is seeing someone new doesn't mean she is over you. She might still love you. Maybe she's seeing this new guy to get over you. Sometimes we do that to fill the emptiness we feel when we break it off with some-one we care for deeply. You think it's still too late to talk to her?"

"I don't want her if she's been with someone else."

Connie's tolerance turns into intolerance. "Aren't you being a little selfish? You haven't been Mr. Goody Two-shoes yourself. I hate to kick you while you're down buddy, but it's your fault she's not with you and she's with someone else."

"Thanks."

"You want a beer?"

"Got anything stronger?"

"No."

"I'll take the beer."

Refrigerator door slams, bottles clink together then she walks out with two beers in her hand.

"I only have Heinekens left."

"It'll do. So where is Leroy tonight?"

Connie looks away and sits on the arm of the sofa.

I ask, "What's wrong?"

"Leroy and I broke up again." She is vague. It's not like her to be vague.

"What!... Why you upset?... You should be happy. The Negro wasn't good for you anyway."

Tears roll down her cheeks. "He hit me. We got into a real big argument and he put his hands on me, so I kicked him out."

The protective side of me wants to rip Leroy's head off. I will never understand what drives a man to raise his hands to a woman. I hold her in my arms. Connie fits right, the scent of her perfume hits my nostrils, reminds me that I'm a man.

I kiss her and she doesn't pull away, a kiss intensified by vulnerability, she's hurting, and I'm hurting. From the depth of despair, my inner voice screams. Save me from myself Lord.

"I think you should leave, Mikhail, before we both do something that we'll regret," Connie's voice is a little raspy, yet she doesn't move.

Just like that, God put the brakes on things. Something has to give; I can't keep living my life in fear. I need help and no one is going to help me, but God. I need a touch from him. I can no longer deal with my problems by having sex.

I step away from her. She makes a step toward me.

"Connie please don't come any closer. You're right. We said we weren't going to do this anymore. I violated that promise."

LOVE IS ALL WE'RE AFTER

I set the half-empty bottle of beer on the table next to her pink iPod. We picked that out together at Best Buy. She was so excited to own one. She couldn't wait to get the software uploaded to her computer. Memories don't live as people do. This is goodbye for us; I can't continue to see her while I go through this healing process. There is a time when a man comes to the end of himself and I'm at my end.

CHAPTER THIRTY-TWO

Candy

Darnell holds the door for me as we enter the restaurant. I wink at him, as I breeze past. We've been on a few dates, and I like him. We get to talk art, which I absolutely love. It's not often you meet a man who has a bit of culture about him.

The host shows us to our table and a server comes to take our orders. Darnell takes charge and orders for me. I don't feel put upon by that, as if he is trying to run my life. Instead, I feel somewhat protected, as if he is looking out for me. And since he is paying anyway for this meal at this very expensive restaurant, I sit back and bask in the luxury of the moment.

We flirt a bit while we eat our appetizers, escargot baked in puffed pastry and shrimp cocktail. He dips a shrimp into the cocktail sauce and brings the fork to my mouth. I giggle and take it in, my eyes never leaving Darnell's face.

When the meal comes, it looks absolutely delicious. He has the porterhouse steak and I get the filet mignon with asparagus and roasted garlic risotto.

"So, we're flying off to South Africa next month," he says when the server leaves.

"Really? That must be exciting," I say.

"I was thinking you could come with me," Darnell says, and I gasp.

"You want me to come with you to South Africa?" I've never been to the African continent. I've been to Europe and to Asia, but never to Africa. I'd love to see the history and heritage, all rolled into one. Maybe I can even do some missionary work while I'm there. Maybe I can visit some of the AIDS orphans or bring books or something. And then, of course, I can get my shopping on.

"Sure," Darnell says and reaches across the table for my hand. "I'm really feeling a connection to you. We've been out a few times, and each time, I sense the electricity flying between us."

He's right. There is chemistry. I like the way he smells. He wears a musky cologne that screams sexuality, and he always has a way of brushing my arm or my back or even my neck in a fashion that lets me know the touch is not quite an accident. Even now, as our fingers play, I can feel those fingers want to do more.

"Well, we do get along well," I say, hedging.

"And I think we'll do some other things well, too," he says and smiles in that sexy way.

I've been putting off this conversation, but I know now is probably a good time to have it. I clear my throat and take a sip of water. "Well, I'm sure we will do some other things well, too, but sleeping together won't be one of them."

He laughs and rubs one hand down his chin. "You are funny!"

"No, I'm serious, actually," I say. "But there are a lot of other things we can do. We like the same types of music, the same types of —"

"What do you mean exactly?"

"You know, I'm celibate." There. The words are out. "I've been born again and part of my spiritual commitment is to save myself for marriage."

"Save yourself?" he says, a bemused expression on his face. "Isn't it a little late to talk about saving yourself?"

I snatch my hand back from his. "A little late? What does that mean?"

He raises his hand to stop my words. "Hey, no offense, but this fake virginity thing is a bit tired. The last girl I dated tried that mess. Talking about she was having a second virginity. Once it's gone, it's gone."

"Well, I'm sorry you feel that way," I say in clipped tones. "The Bible tells us that we can be born again, and we can start over in life. And while I may have had sexual relationships before, I can choose now not to do those things."

Darnell's entire demeanor changes. "Well, that's interesting," he says. "You never said anything about this before."

"I know, and I'm sorry," I say. "I just wanted to see how things went before I got into all of that. That is personal information."

"You wanted to see how things went?" he repeats my words. "What, don't you mean you wanted to see how much I could wine and dine you first, before you broke the news?"

"No, that's not what I meant!" I'm offended at his words. "Do you think I can't pay for my own food or whatever else I want? I don't need you to pay for me, if that's what you're thinking."

"Well, it's funny that, not once have you raised a hand to so much as offer to buy a bottle of water," he says. "You told me from the start that you like to eat. I've taken you out to eat several times, and never to anywhere cheap. And I've sent you flowers to work — twice — and I've bought you those shoes you were hinting about last week."

He is right. He has spent some money on me, but that was all on him. I didn't ask him to do it. I might have mentioned those shoes, but I didn't ask him for them. "I think you've gotten your facts mixed up. I didn't ask you to bring me to this restaurant. And I didn't ask for the flowers. And I didn't ask for the shoes."

"Yeah, well—"

I interrupt. "So you're saying all of this money means I'm supposed to repay you with me, is that what you're saying?"

"Look, Candy, you're no child," Darnell says. "I'm not saying it's a tit for tat, but a man has a certain expectation when he is doing things. And I've been taking you out and trying to get to know you because I wanted to have a relationship with you."

"Well, who is saying we can't have a relationship?"

He is incredulous. "Well, you just said you don't have sex."

"Well, that doesn't mean we can't have a relationship," I say.

"What kind of relationship would we have, without sex?" he asks, and the words sting. I'm trying to live right, and this is what happens. Whenever I meet a guy I even half-way like, once I tell him I'm living for the Lord, he's not even trying to hear that. Seems that I have to choose either Jesus or a man. What a choice.

"Well, we can have a very fulfilling relationship without —"

"I'm going to tell you this because I like you," he says, and dots the corner of his mouth with his napkin. "No man in his right mind is going to go for the bull you are pulling. So you need to get that fairy tale out of your head. A mature, adult relationship includes sex."

"So are you saying it's all about the sex?"

"No, I'm not saying it's all about the sex, but I am saying sex is a part of it," he says, and he holds up his hand as I open my mouth to interrupt. "Let me finish. I know it's easy for you ladies to say, 'oh, he's just after me for sex,' and you'll paint me as the bad guy. Well, I'm not just after sex, but I do expect sex to be part of the equation. I'm not going to lie."

The line was drawn. I could either step over it and give in and enjoy a life of expensive restaurants and exotic trips, or I could stand true on God's promises to me. Darnell is generous and sexy. And up until tonight, he has been very agreeable. But I know I'm after something else.

I nod. "Well, thanks for breaking it down for me."

***

Lisa

Curtis and I have sipped on good wine, eaten good food, and held great conversation almost every night this week. This is the fourth night this week alone he has cooked me dinner and he is a darn good chef. Tonight his eyes dance with excitement. Knowing I've put it there makes me happy. The past two months have been so good for me.

"Baby you're so beautiful, sometimes I have to pinch myself to make sure I'm not dreaming you."

He gives me butterflies every time I see, hear, or think about him.

"You say the sweetest things to me."

"Saying them is easy, because it's true. Lisa, I'll be leaving on a business trip in a few days."

"How long will you be gone?" I move to my feet, taking my wine with me.

The outdoor fireplace pops and hisses, its glow casting shadows on the canopy surrounding us. My shadow moves with me to the edge of the balcony.

Curtis joins me. "It'll only be for a few days."

"I'm going to miss you." I run my hands along chiseled cheekbones.

I have waited a long time to give myself to him and tonight is as good a night as any. Overly excited and in heat I tear and remove Curtis clothes. He's glorious in the nude. I come alive before him.

"Wait. I want to see you." Curtis slows me down.

"I don't…"

"Sh-sh-sh. You are breathtaking, such a wonderful gift."

I hold my breath afraid to breathe, watching him stare at my body with hungry eyes. I'm a nervous wreck. One touch from him, and I fall under his sorcery. If I intend to tell him to stop, this is the time to do it, a small voice in my head counsels. In one slow movement, Curtis bends his head and plants kisses across my body.

"You're so beautiful," he moans as he nibbles his way back up to my shoulder. "Perfect."

"Um… Curtis… I ah I don't know how to say this." I heave a sigh; take as much oxygen as I can. "Baby there is something I need to tell you, and it's not good."

I move from the security of his arms. I become cold and in need of his body warmth again but I can't confess my deception wrapped up in his arms. Curtis' facial expression expects the worse; his smile turns into a grimace.

"What do you have to tell me?" he asks as he braces himself against the wall.

"I wanted to tell you, but I couldn't. I didn't know how you would take it...."

"Lisa, come on and spit out what you have to tell me and stop stalling."

"I'm married." The hurt on his face grieves my spirit. I would given anything to take my words back. The damage is done and the price too much.

Curtis' face darkens with anger. He springs to his feet and marches inside the house. Reluctant to follow him I linger outside. Seconds go by and he doesn't rejoin me so I join him.

The clanking of dishes thrown in the dishwasher greets me. I watch Curtis clean up all evidence of the night. He picks up things around me. He doesn't bother to look at me. Clenching and unclenching my hands, I plead with my eyes for him to say something.

Curtis demands. "How long?"

Confused I ask, "How long what?"

"How long were you going to drag this out? How long have you been married?"

"Four years." I want to run and hide.

"Four years, hmm, four years," he tosses around the words.

"And when in your four years of marriage did you think it was OK to cheat on your husband?" he asks with disdain.

I turn cold from his question. "It's not what you think."

"Well help me to understand. You must have thought me a fool watching me fall for you and your innocent act of being a good girl, but you're just like all the other women that have passed through my hands. I've had to deal with compulsive liars, gold diggers, and now you."

His eyes drill into me.

"You have every right to be angry with me, and I'll understand if you never want to see me again, but I'm not leaving until you hear me out." I pause long enough for him to say something.

With coldness he says, "What makes you think I want to

hear anything you have to say? Thanks for the moments; nonetheless I need you to leave."

"I am married to a man who cheats on me and verbally abuses me. I'm in an unhappy marriage that I was too scared to end, because I didn't want to be by myself. For the past two years I've contemplated suicide just so I wouldn't hear my mother's voice telling me what a failure I was and that it was my fault my marriage wasn't working. Our marriage wasn't supposed to end up this way. Our wedding was a fairy tale; the whole thing was perfect. I pictured forever with him until recently when we separated. I didn't mean to drag you into my mess, but I enjoyed being around you. You make me feel special and worthwhile. I wanted to tell you, but by that time I had fallen in love with you and I didn't want to say or do anything that would make you look at me any different."

He shakes his head, laughs with bitterness and says, "You're good."

With hurried steps Curtis, advances toward the balcony and when he re-enters the room, it's with my clothes. Unspoken words, followed up with action, and he shoves them into my bosom.

"Curtis, baby, please," I plead, touching his arm. He jerks away from my touch as if I have some deadly disease he doesn't want to catch.

"I want you to leave. Don't call. Don't write. I don't want to remember you."

The impact of his words rips my heart from my chest. All hopes of having a future with him after my divorce disintegrate into thin air. Picking up what's left of my heart, I dress in silence. I don't shed a tear. The pain is too great. Pride won't let me.

Leaving Curtis' home is hard. Closed door behind me, I let the first drop of tears fall. I bellow in anguish. All the hurt I've endured at the hands of men comes crashing down on my head. Another lesson learned. The scripture I read in the Bible devotional a woman at Candy's church gave me weeks ago finally makes sense.

"'Neither cast ye your pearls before swine, lest they trample them under their feet.' "

I've been doing this all wrong. I've become exactly like John, except worse. I've been going to Bible study with Candy. The elders have prayed over me for deliverance of unforgiveness, strife, and bitterness of soul. I reassured them of my healing, but the truth is my demons haven't gone anywhere. Bitterness still consumes me like a flesh-eating virus.

CHAPTER THIRTY-THREE

Mona

This is the second morning in a row I've sprinted to the ladies restroom. I make it to the toilet this time, crouched over the seat gripping onto the edge of it for dear life while I puke my guts. Too weak to stand, I sit down on the cold floor, twist my hand back and turn on the faucet.

Pulling myself together, I climb to my feet. The splash of cool water soothes my hot face. I run wet hands over my hair and readjust my makeup cape. I run water over my hands again, lather up with soap. I wipe my hands on a paper towel then toss the used cotton in the bin next to the door.

Everyone in the makeup studio looks at me strangely upon my return. I ignore their prying stares. It's business as usual, everyone wants to know, but no one really cares. I don't know how long I can keep telling them it's food poisoning. Sooner or later they're going to catch on. No one has food poisoning this long.

One of the girls whose face I'm working on ogles me from the corner of her eye. Her eyes dart from my face to my stomach every five minutes as if doing so she would some how learn the truth.

I ask, "You OK, Gia?"

Amber's nickname in the studio. She has a slight resemblance to the model Gia Carangi of the late 1970's. Most of the girls here hate her because of her beauty. The camera loves her and she loves the camera, but she's trouble.

"I was just wondering if you went to see the doctor for your food poisoning. You know two days is a long time for someone to have food poisoning."

"Is that right," I reply, leaving it at that.

"Yes. Maybe you're pregnant," she continues. "Is it John's?"

Unsure of where she is going with this. I ask, "Excuse me?"

She smiles smartly. "Oh come on Mona everyone here

knows about you and John, leaving together for long lunches, closing the office door and drawing the blinds when the two of you are in there alone. The way he constantly stares at you when he thinks no one is looking. We're not dummies."

"I don't know what you're talking about, the man's married for Pete's sake."

"OK if you say so, maybe I read too much into it. Now that I know, he's fair play I can make my move. It doesn't make a difference to me he's married, I like them that way. No commitment means no demands of my time."

Slapping her would be sweet, but I have to remain professional and ignore her scrawny behind. John wouldn't want her anyway, she's too bony and he likes his women with a little meat.

"Your face looks great. You're gonna knock 'em dead."

"I will," she says with conceit and stands to her feet. "Aren't you friends with his wife?"

"Amber whatever obsession you have with my personal life, I suggest you drop it because I'm someone you don't want to fool with and that's not a threat, it's a promise from me to you."

John and I have been discreet with our affair. Gia said everyone knew. Could she be telling the truth? Caught up in a daze I knock one of the models over.

"Excuse me Monica."

"Look where you're going," she barks. When they were giving away manners, she jumped the line.

The hair shows we put on are chaotic. Women prance around half dressed, some with rollers in their hair, and some fully dressed waiting for their piece of the limelight. That queasy feeling was coming back again; the aroma from the food laid out on a table for the models to snack on isn't helping one bit.

"Oh there you are," Cleo clucks. Her voice gets on my nerves. I've been hiding from her all day. She likes to talk, and mostly about nothing of interest.

"Yes here I am."

"I heard you've been sick today, something about you eating bad food."

"Late night food and margaritas. I went out with a couple of the models a few nights ago."

"You better leave the drinking to those skinny little toothpicks parading around here, we getting too old for this line of work."

"Speak for yourself. I may be in my thirties but I'm like age-old wine. I get better with the years."

"Like they say black don't crack?"

"Got that right, let me pack up and get out of here. I'm done for the day, right?"

"Yeah you can leave."

Cleo is also the boss. I may not care for her, but I know how to work her. My job ended hours ago, but I usually stick around and wait until everyone has graced the runway. On my way to the parking lot, I glimpse a car driving off with a brunette in it. The car is identical to John's. Another vehicle blocks my view making it impossible to read the license plate. I speed dial John's office number.

"Boutari Advertising Agency, this is Helen. How may I direct your call?"

"Helen, is John available?"

"I'm sorry, Mona, he's in an all-day meeting. Would you like to leave him a message?"

"No, no that's OK. I'll try him again later."

Strange. John didn't mention anything to me about him being in meetings all day today.

I head on over to Country Club Plaza, Kansas City's Premier entertainment district.

Five quarters buys you two hours of parking on the meter. Pennsylvania Street isn't the best street to park; its steepness makes it impossible to walk down in heels. Blahniks are for showing, not walking.

Pottery Barn Kids is a baby heaven, they thought of everything. Baby cribs, engraved blankets, mobiles, rattlers, and lighting. Nanny services are the only thing they don't offer.

"How far along are you?" asks the young sales girl who greeted me at the front door.

"I don't know."

"Well congratulations. Is this your first?"

"Yes."

"You must be very excited."

"I am. I would start buying up everything in here if I knew the sex."

"Well, you can always go neutral. We're having a store-wide sale of forty percent off today."

"Thanks, but I'm really just looking."

"Oops I almost forgot we also have a baby registry."

"OK, thanks."

Walking around the store touching and gushing over an array of baby items builds my appetite. Starbucks isn't too far from here, just over on Nichols Street. I cut cross 47th street to Broadway.

Starbucks has its cliques: computer techs, college football groupies, and the business professionals. They all have one connection, a good cup of Starbucks coffee.

I walk up to the counter. "Dulce de Leche, Oreo brownie, raspberry muffin and a bottled water please."

"Will that be all?"

The young girl's question is innocent enough, but I can't help to think she has a hidden meaning behind it. My order is a lot for one person, but I lost both breakfast and lunch down the toilet this morning. I should be eating something of some nutritional value and I will, just not right this minute.

Munching on my Oreo brownie, I watch a little girl with a head full of light brown curls stop to stare inside. Big, brown eyes of innocence smile and she waves to me. I wave back. Her mom, curious to what holds her child's interest, peers inside only to find me grinning like a mascot. I love children. Their innocence draws the best from me, makes me forget my grown up world. For a moment, I picture myself as a child again, until memories carry me off to the abuse I suffered. Broken bones now healed, aches from the knowledge of a child's helplessness.

The little girl radiates happiness, happiness I desire for my child. I touch my stomach, something I find myself doing lately. Thanksgiving will be different this year; John and I have the perfect reasons to be thankful.

"Excuse me ma'am, you occupying this table?" The

disturbance comes from a fair-haired handsome young boy, his jacket proudly displaying his captain of the football team logo.

"No."

"Do you mind if we crash here?"

His teammates stand off to the side looking like "American Idol" hopefuls. I don't care much for jocks, young jocks at that. I came in here for some quiet time and I doubt I will have peace sitting next to these younglings.

"No not at all, I was just leaving."

I don't wait for his response. Half eaten muffin and half cup of Dulce de Leche to go. I scoop up my portion and grab a to-go bag from the clerk. I barely make it through the door before the uproar from the football group begins. I look back at the clerks behind the counter and almost felt sorry for them. They get to deal with the public, so many different people, with different personalities and attitude. I worked retail once. It took me a day to find out it wasn't a fit for me.

Nibbling on the remainder of my muffin, I window-shop BCBG fall fashion. With a baby on the way, this time of year is perfect. When I pack on the pounds, it will be easy to hide. Stretch marks are something I'm worried about though, which means I'll have to keep my eating down to a minimum. I want to have a healthy baby, but I don't want to blow up like an elephant.

John loves me curvy, but he doesn't care for chunky. Things are going smoothly between us now that he is living with me. No more sneaking around and broken engagements. He is mine, all mine.

CHAPTER THIRTY-FOUR

Candy

Nothing is better for curing you of lustful intentions like a nice cold shower and a few Bible verses to correct you on why celibacy is the right way to go.

God is so good. He always brings me to the right scriptures every time. It doesn't matter what I'm going through, He's always on top of it.

I recite Corinthians 6:18: "'Flee fornication. Every sin that a man doeth is without the body; but he that committeth fornication sinneth against his own body.'" The passage goes on to remind me that my body is a temple and that I am not my own. I have been bought with a price. I am precious, and so is my body. The enemy wants me to believe I can't find a man who will marry me without sampling the merchandise first, but I believe God and the promise He made to me, when I made a covenant with Him.

Darnell was a waste of my time. After I told him about my celibacy, he told me he wasn't down for that. We finished the meal, with cordial conversation, but the ride back to my place was quiet. When he got out of the car to open the door for me, I knew I wouldn't be seeing him anymore. I thanked him for a lovely evening, and he nodded and even kissed me on the cheek.

He couldn't have a relationship without sex. And I couldn't have one with it.

The red light on my phone blinks, but the phone doesn't ring. Nick's number is getting popular on my caller ID. The man is incorrigible. He has been chasing me for about two months now. He lured me to those so-called business dinners, and then of course to that lunch where he kissed me. After I gave him a piece of my mind, he still had the nerve to ask me to dinner. He has been calling and even dropped by the office one day, supposedly because he was "in the neighborhood." I even came home one night to find a garment bag with another little bag sitting on my porch with a note: Meet me for dinner at 8 p.m.

Nick.

Nick took the liberty of picking me out a stunning red dress, Badgley Mischka, red pumps to match. Once again, he demonstrated his superb taste. He surprised me with his knowledge of my dress size, my favorite color, and what size shoe I wear. He had to have gotten the information from Shelly, but as impressed as I was, I still stood him up for dinner.

Charlton, his chauffeur, showed up promptly at eight that evening and I sent him away. This is the first time I've heard from him since then.

I should've known Nick wouldn't take no for an answer. Nick is the last person I want to think about right now. Opening the freezer door, I vow not to waste any more energy thinking about that man. Ice cream is just what I need after a day like today. Scooping a heaping amount of Ben & Jerry's Phish Food in a bowl, I place the tub back in the freezer, then shut the door.

Buying a house with stairs was a great idea, until I realized just how many times I have to go up and down in a day and the doorbell always rings when I'm at the top of them. Darnell wouldn't be crazy to show his face here again, but I wouldn't put it past him to come back begging. I open the door without looking and almost slam the door shut again, but Nick is too quick for me.

"Now that wasn't very nice, was it?" he drawls.

"I wasn't trying to be nice, Nick. What are you doing here?"

Nick doesn't wait for an invitation. He slips by me and starts toward the living room, turning only to see if I am following him. I'm thinking about the many conversations I've had with my mom about dressing for unexpected guests. My mom has an open door policy; I have a call before you come policy. Nick must share the same policy with her.

Mud cream on my face, terry towel wrap around my hair, and a bathrobe on, I cannot imagine the sight I must be. I'm being less than hospitable standing here looking a mess, holding the front door open, hoping Nick will take the hint and go.

"May I have a seat?"

Has he gone mad? "No." I growl, still holding the door open.

Nick sits anyway.

"These are nice sofas."

I almost tell him where I bought them. Wait a minute. I'm mad he's here or am I?

"Are you going to stand there all night?" he asks looking smug.

"I'll sit when you leave."

"Ah. You have a beautiful home." Nick uncrosses his legs and reclines against the sofa with his hands supporting his head. A clear indication he isn't going anywhere soon.

"Thanks, one that you weren't invited to." Nick leaves me no choice but to close the darn door.

"Well since I can't get you to meet me anywhere, I figured I'd meet you instead."

"You figured wrong."

He chuckles. "You're certainly the ice queen this evening. Won't you have a seat and relax. You look like you are about to crack."

Easy for you to say. You're not the one standing up in a housecoat and a towel wrapped around your head.

Anxiety outweighs patience. I ask, "Enough of this cat-and-mouse game, what do you want?"

"You," he confesses, taking an account of the visible and hidden parts of me under this terry cloth robe.

"Well you can't have me so you can leave."

"Why did you stand me up for dinner?"

"I'm sure your chauffeur gave you my explanation."

"He did, but I want to hear it from you."

What is with this guy?

"What difference does it make?"

Nick leaps to his feet and closes in on my space in a matter of seconds. Before I realize what is happening, he unwraps the towel around my head. He pauses to play with my rebellious curls then he lets my hair fall to my shoulders.

"You're going to be mine, Candy. Don't fight it. Just accept it. You knew it the moment we met at Zane's. Why are you fighting this?"

He's too close. I can't breathe. My vocal cords aren't working. Nick's hand lightly brushes against my cheeks and I lose all senses. I try to speak again but manage a moan, which he takes as an invitation. Nick kisses render me speechless, when his tongue licks the top of mine electric waves run through me. I clutch onto his shirt, forcing my breasts to press against his chest. As thick as this garment is, it feels like I'm naked up against Nick's body.

He breaks away from me proving his theory. Nick's declaration that he can have me when he wants me is on point, but he will have to torture me first to get me to admit it. There's a part of me that wants him to continue is torture. The naughty side, the side I've been suppressing all these months.

"See Candy I can have you right here, right now and you wouldn't even put up a fight to stop me. And that flimsy little terry robe you're clutching on to won't save you from me."

Nick is 5 inches taller than I am, which puts me at a disadvantage, because I have to bend my neck to look into his face.

Putting a safe distance between us as I move around the sofa, I say, "Who says I need saving? You will never have me, Nick. I know about your womanizing ways. I refuse to become one of your collections and I know you won't force yourself on me. You want to win, you like the surrender, the admittance of need from a woman."

"Someone has been busy."

He doesn't deny the accusations. Miranda was telling the truth. I'm only a new conquest for him. It hurts. I force myself not to crumble before him, show no weakness.

"Do you really think that sofa can save you from me?"

LOVE IS ALL WE'RE AFTER

Nick doesn't move, but I know he can make it around this sofa before I have to time to think up an escape route. He laughs at the betrayal of panic registered in my eyes. His confidence irritates me. His arrogance infuriates me.

"But not to worry, Candy. I won't be cashing in tonight. There will be other nights such as this one. And I won't have to stop. You won't want me to."

I should be frightened, but Nick's threat turns me on.

CHAPTER THIRTY-FIVE

Mikhail

I have been cruising along Westport aimlessly since I got off work a couple of hours ago. I must be out of my mind. Gas prices are at an all time high, $4.45 per gallon. The war with Saddam Hussein's country isn't about weapons of mass destruction. That's an on-the-surface-excuse. Dig a little deeper and what this really boils down to is the oil.

Candy got me driving around out here obsessed with the knowledge of the love I lost. Seeing her with another man drove a stake through my heart. I've been able to think of nothing else since then. I replay in my mind that day, and I replay scenes from the time we spent together, all the great memories. It's pretty messed up the way she just moved on like that. All the things we shared weren't easy for me to put behind me, but apparently she has managed to push them from her mind.

The next street I turn onto is Baltimore. I breeze down the historical district, pass by some dead guy's museum. Harry Kearney House Public Museum. I continue to drive down to the end of the street, turn right on 36th Street, and about half a mile down 36th, I bust a left on Kenwood Avenue, down a one-way street. Thank God, there isn't any oncoming traffic.

I have no idea where I am. Next time I'll stick to major roads. I park my car, cut the engine, kill the stereo, and rest my head against the car seat. I need to go home, want to go home, but don't want to face my demons there. Every time I try to do something good, something bad happens.

It's quite peaceful, but the words in my head echo above the quietness. Laughter from children playing on the leaf-strewn playground steals my attention. Cast a light on the fact that I'm a father now. Emotions of shame and pride bounce about in my head like tidal waves. I'm twisted inside; I'm not sure I want to know this child. Then again, I'm not sure I don't. I get out of the car and walk over to the bridge.

"If I didn't know better I'd say you were stalking me," a familiar female voice accuses.

Puzzled, I turn to find Monique watching me.

"You might be the stalker. I was here first," I reply and turn to face her.

"We've got to stop meeting in the streets like this, Mikhail."

I chuckle. "What are you doing here?"

"I live over there." She points to cobblestone steps leading to a brown and white two-story house. A naked tree next to it reminds us it's November and the seasons have changed.

"Oh." I say, taking in the residence.

"So where are you off to, looking like you just lost your best friend?" she asks.

I groan. "Nowhere, anywhere, and everywhere. I'm just out for a walk really."

"Out for a walk?" she asks, and one brow is raised.

My answer sounds odd even to me. I am counting on Monique's good manners not to pry further.

"What, you don't think I go for walks?" I ask her with a slight smile.

"Well yeah, it's just that I've never seen you in my neighborhood before. What, you just moved in or something?"

"Or something."

Her cute little facial expressions are fun to watch. Her innocence fascinates me.

She says, "You're not going to tell me are you?"

"How long have you lived here?"

"Six years."

"Alone?"

My question throws her off. She gives my question careful thought before answering.

"Alone. Why? Does that surprise you?"

"Yes, I figure you'd have all the boys beating down your door."

She laughs. "You're still hilarious Mikhail. You haven't changed one bit. Are you still chasing girls?"

"Women, I don't chase girls." I correct her.

"Ah, right. Is it one of them that has you out here looking like a lost puppy?" She searches my face.

"How can I be lost when I'm standing here with you?" I try to keep the conversation light.

"Well it's a good thing I'm here. Isn't it? I'm glad we met. I sure needed some company." For the first time, I hear the sadness in her voice.

"Why is that?" I ask.

Monique moans, then heaves a sigh. "Tobey died three years ago today. I visited his grave site this morning. Why is it when people pass away we have so much more to tell them than when they were alive? I wasted so much time putting off all the things I wanted to tell Tobey. I never thanked him for taking care of me. When Momma died, I was just a child so I don't remember her. Auntie Lorna took us in, but Tobey was the one who raised me. He was the daddy I never had, Mikhail, and when he passed, he took a big chunk of my heart. There are days when I don't want to get up from being so depressed."

Monique's sadness tugs at my heartstrings.

"Is there anything I can do for you?" I'm avoiding any contact between her and me, because the last time I felt sorry for a woman I wound up doing the wrong thing.

"You taking the time to listen to me is more than enough," Monique sniffles. "I'm sorry to fall apart on you."

"No, it's OK. I can't pretend to understand what you're going through but I feel your pain. When you told me Tobey was gone, I was shocked beyond belief. That cat was like family to me. It's a shame our paths got crossed up and we lost touch with each other."

My regrets are deeper than that of a friend.

"I know. He always talked about you."

"Did he tell you how we became friends?" I laugh at the memory. Monique cracks a smile, a surface one.

"Yes, getting beat up by a school bully."

"Jackson was big for his age and he took pride in throwing his weight around and I was a little skinny dude in junior high," I say, remembering that time. "Your brother Tobey wasn't any bigger than I was, but that day he decided he was going to stand up to Jackson. He was getting his tail whipped by Jackson and no one dared intervene, except me. We took our beating that day though, but Jackson never messed with us again."

"That's why out of all the friends Tobey had, I liked you the best. You were a good friend to him and he always said that he was sorry he lost touch with you."

Talking to Monique shed some light on my situation. I'm being foolish; this may be the only chance I get to be a father. God brings situations in our lives for reasons beyond our understanding, and I'm getting a revelation of that reason daily.

"Monique, you ever feel like you're alone in this world?"

"Yes." Her voice was soft.

"No I mean really lonely, take me for instance. I have great family, good friends, and yet I feel like the loneliest person in the world. I'm in love with a woman I let get away because of my foolish pride and selfishness and now I may have lost her forever. To put the icing on top, the other day I was sitting at home and my doorbell rang. I opened the door and got served with child support papers from a woman who wants financial support for a child I never knew I had. I've been holding onto this little piece of information for weeks now and I haven't told anyone, heck I'm not sure why I'm telling you." I scratch my head and look toward heaven.

"It's easier to speak to someone who won't judge you. What are you going to do?"

"I don't know. I want to do the right thing by this woman, but I don't know where to begin or even how to approach her. We had a one-night stand with each other. It wasn't as if we even knew each other very well. We knew each other in passing, but I didn't really know her know her."

"Are you scared about what your family will say or are you afraid of taking on responsibility for someone other than yourself?"

"Both," I admit.

Monique's scrutiny of me gives away nothing. She moves along the sidewalk to sit on a bench nearby. Monique lays her head on the bench sideways and peers up at me. She has a very exquisite face, peaceful and inviting, an extraordinary young woman with wisdom beyond her years.

"Why did you break up?" Monique puts her hand up to block the sunlight from her face. I sit down to keep her from doing that.

"Selfishness."

Monique sits straight up. "What do you mean?"

"I was too busy proving to other women I was a man, instead of being the man she needed me to be. I was so wrapped up in myself thinking I was God's gift to women, I didn't recognize the love she had for me."

"That's how it works. We never know the value of something until we lose it."

"Do you think it's too late to make amends?" I want to know.

"It's never too late to try," she shrugs. "We all have weaknesses, Mikhail. It's what makes us human and determines our strength."

"I'm sure you're right, but where do I start?"

"You start with the truth."

CHAPTER THIRTY-SIX

Candy

"Ms. Cameron, there is someone here to see you." The voice comes over my speaker.

"Who is...?" Before I could get the question out of my mouth, Nick barges through my door, with my secretary nipping at his heels.

"It's OK," I reassure her. She throws Nick's back an irritated glare.

Heat waves cover my body when he walks into a room. His threat from the other day still burns in my mind. I dreamt about him. Did things in my dreams, I'll never get the chance to experience with him.

"Happy to see me?" He stares pointedly at the white semi see-through top I am wearing with my black high waist, hip hugging skirt.

I look down, outraged and embarrassed, because my nipples betray me. In remembrance of my dream, they harden. Self-conscious of my glasscutters I fold my arms over my bosom and grunt my disapproval of Nick's behavior.

"Ah, now why did you ruin the one thing I had pleasure in today?"

"I am not here for your pleasure. Cut to the chase. Why have you bullied your way into my office?"

Considering he is still my client that was a dumb question, but I can almost bet my lunch on this, Nick's not here for business. The look in his eyes is of pure pleasure and I'm the target.

"Have lunch with me."

"No."

"I'm not leaving until you say yes."

Nick's gaze travels to the roundness of my breasts then to the curve of where my waist meets my backside. He admires the fuchsia on my toes. He pretends to be interested in the things on my desk.

I fidget in place and hope he leaves.

"I like it when you get mad. You pout. It's the cutest thing ever, but I'm not leaving until you say yes."

I moan in resignation. I ask, "Where are we going for lunch?"

Nick looks surprised that I agreed. "Your choice."

I grab my purse. Hit the intercom. "Kerrey hold all my calls. I'm going to lunch."

"Yes, Ms. Cameron." Nick smiles happily.

We bump into Miranda going to the elevator. She is on her way out, too. Versace bag under her arm, last year's model. We were never on good speaking terms before and since that last confrontation in my office, she has completely ignored me, which is fine by me. I have no malice toward her and I have forgiven her, but I don't go out of my way to seek her out either.

Miranda smiles up at Nick. "Hi, Nick, how are you today?"

"Doing great," Nick says. "I wanted to discuss some things with Candy, and fortunately, she is free for a quick lunch."

Miranda cuts her eyes at me, but says only, "Well, I'm sure she will handle all of your concerns properly. And if not, you can always come see me."

The elevator doors open.

"See you later, Nick," Miranda steps off.

"Take care," he says to her and turns to me, stepping aside to let me exit the elevator before him. "Let's go handle a few matters."

I send up a quick prayer. I have only so much strength.

***

"Why aren't you married, Candy?"

"I thought we came out here to talk business?" I ask as I feed the doves in the pond.

"I want to know you on a personal level."

"Nick, what do you want?"

"Why won't you give me a chance? Are you scared that

I'll be exactly what you desire in your life?"

"I can't be with you, Nick. You are one of my clients, and I don't mix busi—"

Nick cuts me off. "Don't give me that story. Who was he?"

I sigh and rub my hands across my thighs. "It's in the past."

"But you still hurt."

"A little. I'm learning to live for me and God right now."

"So you're a Christian?"

I nod. "Yes, got saved and freed from the shackles that were holding me down."

"I'm not much of a Christian. I go to church now and then, but I want to get to know you better. All I'm asking you for is a chance to prove myself. I'm not asking you to go to bed with me, even though I want to."

I search Nick's eyes and for the first time I recognize something there that I may have missed, because I was looking at what he isn't, instead of what he could become. Honesty, it was right there in his eyes.

"How do you feel about dating someone who is celibate?" I ask and still nothing changes in his expression.

"I want to know you, Candy. That will come later. I want to respect you and your body and if this is how I have to prove it then I'm OK."

Could it really be that I've met a man who won't make me choose between faith and freakiness? "Are you sure? Most men don't want to deal with a woman who is celibate."

"I'm not most men," Nick says. "All I can do is speak for me. And I just want to be with you. In whatever way you allow."

Thank you, God. I want to get on my feet at that moment and sing praises, but I keep my composure. "Then I'll give you a chance."

"Are you dating anyone right now?"

"I've gone out on a few dates."

"Is any of them serious?"

"Not sure right now."

"Fair enough, but I'm going to change that," he said. "Come let me take you back to work."

CHAPTER THIRTY-SEVEN

Lisa

Curtis has become a thorn in my flesh. After constantly tossing and turning from thinking about him for the umpteenth time tonight, I drag my depressed, lovesick fanny out of bed and onto the balcony. The night air feels great on my skin.

Two in the morning, and I'm wide awake — listening to the sounds of the night. The sky is as dark as my mood. I haven't been able to eat, sleep, or focus on anything. My work is suffering, and to put it mildly, I am falling apart.

Curtis and my love affair is a secret I kept from everyone including Candy. I'm a married woman. It's not like I can broadcast my indiscretions.

Mom is not even on the radar to discuss this with. She will disown me, but not before badgering me about what a bad wife I am. God knows what else she will throw at me. I couldn't stand to see the look of disappointment in her eyes anyway.

Detective Ray Seymour dropped by the office today. The unopened envelope along with the rest of my unopened mail holds our future. I'm afraid of what I will find inside. I toy with the idea of opening it, but I toss it aside and walk back into the bedroom.

***

"Good morning, Boutari and Powell," Leslie answers crisply.

"Morning Leslie, listen it's Lisa. I was supposed to come into the office today for a one thirty appointment, but I need to reschedule."

"OK, Mrs. Boutari. What day do you want me to reschedule Mrs. Clark?"

"I'm not sure, Leslie. Let me call you back on that one. Thank you," I disconnect the connection.

Brent Powell won't be happy about the reschedule. I have rescheduled this client twice. Breakfast was in the making when the phone rings. "Restricted" flashes across the caller ID.

"Ya'll are starting early today," I yell into the phone, ready to give whoever it is a piece of my mind.

"This is Geico Insurance calling to let you know you can save hundreds of dollars on your car insurance a year. Press 1. To get more information. Press 2. For more options. Press 3. To place you on the do not call list." These companies have gotten so big, they get the machines to call and do the harassing for them.

I laugh hysterically which turns into uncontrollable sobbing. I sob for the love I lost with John, for the love I discovered with Curtis and lost, for having a mother who was never there for me, for things that I can't change in my life. I cry so hard God feels my pain and begins to cry with me. Big drops of rain shower down on the lawn.

John has been gone for weeks, and I'm still getting harassing phone calls. I could change my number, but I refuse to go through the hassle. I decide to open the envelope after all.

"Oh my God!" My hand flies to my mouth as I stare at the first photo. "Oh, Lord, please no... this is a sick joke."

Just when I thought things could not get any worse, they do. The pictures of John and his cousin kissing baffle me. We met at the family reunion last year and she was unfriendly, but I thought that was because she wasn't used to me.

It all comes together when I read Ray's handwritten note. The alleged cousin in the picture swapping spit with my husband is John's high school sweetheart. His family knew and no one said a word to me. They have a little girl together. I re-read that last line.

The realization makes my heart pound hard in my chest.

LOVE IS ALL WE'RE AFTER

My husband had a baby with another woman.
   I slide to the floor.

CHAPTER THIRTY-EIGHT

Candy

Nick pulls into the parking lot of a skating rink. I give him a sidelong glance. "What are we doing here?"

"We're going to skate," he says, and climbs out of the car. He rounds the front to come to my side, but I hop out.

"Skating?" This man has lost his mind.

"Yeah."

"Nick, you must have forgotten how old we are," I say. I've not been to a skating rink since I was 16.

"I know, that's the beauty of it," he says, and grabs my hand, pulling me toward the building.

"Nick, we can't go in there!" I protest. "We'll be the oldest ones around."

"That's OK," he says.

"And why are we going skating?" I still can't believe we're actually together. God has sent a man who respects my celibacy. But I see this man also likes to play around and march to his own beat. I guess you really should be careful what you ask for. I asked for a man who would surprise me, and not make me choose between serving God and being with him, and God gave me that. Nick sure is full of surprises. But apparently I should have been a bit more specific. I know I didn't ask God for somebody who wanted to go around skating and whatnot.

"We're going skating because it's fun," Nick says.

"Nick, we're not kids!"

"Well, you said I couldn't see your moves in the bedroom, but surely you'll let me see your moves on the dance floor at the skating rink?"

I burst out laughing. "You are so funny! You think you are clever, huh?"

Nick winks at me. "Hey, I'm a man that just wants to have fun with his woman. And if we're not going to be doing grown folks' business, we may as well have fun at child's play."

"Oh, you are so full of jokes!"

He pauses at the door. "No, seriously, I just thought this would be a cool date. My sister is bringing her kids, and I told her we'd meet them here. We can skate for a while, then go out to eat or something. You OK with that? If not, we can change plans."

I am taken aback. He wants me to meet his family? My earlier protests evaporate in the wind and I grin. "No, this is fine. Let's go and boogie on the floor. Man, it'll be fun getting back into skates after so many years."

When we enter the skating rink, the music is blaring, but I still hear the squeals over the noise. "Uncle Nick!" Two children, about nine and ten, come flying across the floor, and they pounce on Nick.

I stand back, amused at the display. Obviously they have great affection for him.

A pretty blonde woman walks up.

She smiles at me. "You must be Candace," she says.

"Uh, yeah," I say, surprised.

"I'm Nick's sister, Summer." She grabs the girl's arm. "Celeste, let your uncle breathe. Kevin, get off your uncle's back."

The kids disentangle themselves from Nick, but not before he tickles them and sends them into fits of laughter.

Nick pulls me into an embrace. "This is Candace," he says.

His sister kisses her brother's cheek. "She is even prettier than you said. Good to see you, Nick. Glad you guys could join us."

Our attention is immediately drawn to the floor, as the children tug on Nick's arms. "Come skate with us!"

Summer beckons me. "Well, let's see how we do on those skates."

I grin. "Yeah, let's."

***

Mona

"Mona, you're eight weeks pregnant," Doctor Hansen announces.

The nurse standing next to him shares in my excitement.

"This is great news, Dr. Hansen. You've made me the happiest woman today."

"At least I could make one woman happy today. Wish it were as easy with my wife as it is with you. OK, I need you to come back and see me in three weeks."

"What should I do in the mean time?"

"I've prescribed you some prenatal pills. Get proper nutrition. You can still do all the things you've been doing before you got pregnant. I'll let you know when to stop."

"OK, thanks."

They leave me in the room to get dressed. On my way out the nurse lets me know she called my prescriptions in to Walgreens pharmacy. This is the reason I love coming to see Dr. Hansen. He is so efficient. So are his nurses.

Pier 1 should be out of candles after I go through there buying up an array of their overpriced candles. I stop by Victoria's Secret to pick up the sexiest piece of lingerie I can find. I want everything to be perfect when I break the news to John tonight. I'm feeling so full of love and joy. It's almost Thanksgiving, and I'm already in the holiday mood. I find myself even humming.

Candlelight dances to the soft music playing on the MP3 player in the living room. I prepare one of John's favorite meals, shrimp scampi with toasted garlic bread and a bottle of red wine.

Kids are something John has always wanted ever since I've known him. He and Lisa tried for years to have kids but Lisa can't have children. When Lisa was a teenager, her mother made her have an abortion, which left her infertile.

The garage door screeches to a halt announcing John's arrival. I wait patiently until the car door clicks shut before getting up to meet John at the door. On tippy-toes, I lean in to kiss him.

"Hey honey, I'm so happy you're home."

"Mmm, something smells delicious in here." John pauses to notice the candles leading from the foyer into the bedroom. "What's the occasion?" He circles both arms around my waist; the heat from his body penetrates through my dress.

I miss him when he's gone. I love it when he's here. I

hang on to him, refusing to let him go. "No occasion, you've been hard at work and you deserve a good meal."

"What's for dinner," he asks, twirling me and in a grand finale he tilts me back.

"Shrimp scampi, garlic bread, a bottle of wine and mini chocolate torte dessert."

John nuzzles my neck. "That sounds good, but I'd like to change my dessert because I'd rather have you." John strokes my thigh. My body jolts in sensual response to the demands of his.

I still John's hand with mine. "You can have me for dessert after you've had supper."

"Well then let's get started. You know baby, you've out done yourself."

"I'm glad you like it," I reply, taking my seat.

John pops the bottle of chardonnay and pours us a glass. I won't drink from mine. I don't want anything to hurt our baby. While he pours the wine, I dish out our meal. We eat in silence, except for the few bites in between where John compliments me on the food.

"What's the matter, sweetheart? You hardly touched your wine or said a word."

I blurt out, "John, I'm pregnant."

The conflict on John's face isn't hard to read. "You're what? How can this be? Weren't you on the pill?" He fires off all sorts of questions as if he's Johnnie Cochran.

The joy I expect to see on his face isn't there. Instead I see anguish, accusation, and disbelief. John throws is napkin on the table, rises from his chair and walks the floor, agitated like a caged tiger.

"Of course I was on the pill," I yell on the brink of hysterics.

"What are we going to do, Mona? You can't have this baby. If Lisa finds out she's going to kill me." John turns around too fast, and he knocks the chair to the floor. It lands with a loud thud. "Did you plan this?" he cross-examines.

"What! I'm pregnant and all you're worried about is what Lisa will do if she finds out? Get out, John!... Get dah heck outta my house, you no-good lowlife!" The anger in me rises above good judgment. I itch to punch him, but I can't bring myself to hurt him. A sense of helplessness takes control, and I burst into tears.

"Mona, baby I'm sorry. I didn't mean to say that." John fumbles for words; he never fumbles. "It's OK... um tell you what... we... a... we'll work it out somehow," he reasons. "How far along are you?"

"Eight weeks."

"Eight weeks," he repeats. The soothing rub to my back stops and his hand grows cold against the thin material. "And just how long have you known?"

"Recently."

"How recent is recent?"

"Three weeks," my voice becomes muffled and fresh tears well in my eyes.

"Three weeks!" he yells, and I jump. "And you're just now telling me?"

"John please don't be angry with me," I plead. " I wanted to wait until it was the right time, until I was sure. My doctor confirmed it this morning."

"And you think now is the right time?" He asks and his eyes narrow. "I can't help but feel like you've been setting me up."

My head snaps up so fast, it almost gives me whiplash. "Set you up? I didn't get myself pregnant on purpose, and it takes two people to make a baby. You weren't complaining when you were having your two and three orgasms up inside of me, but now that there are some consequences in doing so, all of a sudden it's my fault. I want you out of my house, right now."

"Lisa, baby don't overreact," he says and my world falls apart around me.

"What did you just call me?"

"Mona. What else would I call you?"

He doesn't even realize he called me by his wife's name. Defeated, I turn and walk away; I need to create space between us before I do something crazy. My entire well laid out plans have backfired on me. Even the best laid out plan must have a Plan B. What is my Plan B?

"Where are you going?" I notice that John did not voice his question out of concern for me, but more of the need to say something.

I can't face him. I refuse to let him see my shame. "John, I've asked you to leave, so leave."

John asks, "What did I do?"

"It's not what you did John. It's what you said. Do I look like Lisa to you, John?"

"No. Why?" he asks, looking confused.

"You called me Lisa moments ago."

John opens his mouth to deny it, but clamps it shut.

"John, I get it now. You don't want me. You never did. I was the one in your face, and I was the one forcing the issue of us. It took me getting pregnant to realize just what a rotten man you are."

His response is, "What about the baby?"

"What about it?" I ask. "This child is no longer your concern."

"Mona, you can't have this baby."

"I'm having this baby, John, with or without you and there is nothing you can do about it."

"We'll see about that. You're not having this baby," he threatens and steps toward me. I grab the knife off the kitchen counter, and John stops.

Seeing John this angry scares me. Desperation in a man is never a good thing and he is desperate. His voice betrays his appearance of being in control.

I back away from him and walk swiftly to the foyer to remove his keys from the hook. I slide my spare keys off his key ring and toss the rest to him. John catches them before they hit the coffee table.

"I'm having this baby, John."

"No you're not," he growls menacingly. "I'm warning you, Mona, get rid of this baby or else."

Baiting John when he's like this would not be a smart move. He weighs twice as much as me and can easily over power me. In this instance, I will catch more flies with honey than with vinegar. "Fine, John. I won't have the baby, but please leave me alone."

"I mean it," he points his finger in my face, giving me his final warning, and then he leaves.

Something tells me this isn't over by far. John is a winner, a conqueror and tonight he didn't win. I can't stay here.

I have a strange feeling I will not wake up tomorrow if I do. I get on the phone with Candy.

"Candy, I need to crash at your home tonight," I say through the mouthpiece.

"Why? What's going on?" I hear the alarm in her voice.

"Can I explain when I get there?" I say, knowing I don't have time to go into the story.

"OK," she says. " See you when you get here."

"I hope you have sappy movies and ice cream. I'm gonna need them."

"I'll run and get you some ice cream," Candy says. "You know where to find the spare keys."

I stuff a few toiletries into a white duffel bag. Fill my garment bag with work attire. Set the thermostat at seventy-eight then blow out the candles... what a waste.

***

Candy

I turn to Nick after hanging up. "Hey, that was Mona," I say. "She's coming to spend the night."

"What's up?" he asks.

"Not sure," I say. "Her voice sounded a little strange. She just said she would need some girl time. She wants to watch sappy movies and eat ice cream."

Nick nods. "Oh, OK," he says, and gets up from the floor. We had been lying there looking at some photos we took on a recent weekend trip to New York to attend a concert. Next on our agenda is to plan what we will do for Thanksgiving, which is quickly approaching, but it looks like we won't get to that tonight. "Well, I'll head out. Sounds like she's going to need your full attention."

"No, you can stay," I say, not wanting him to leave. "Maybe she won't stay that long, after all."

He shakes his head, though. "No, I'm leaving," he repeats. "You need to spend time with your girlfriend, especially if she is as bad off as you suspect. When a friend leaves her house to spend the night at yours, it's serious."

He's right, I know. Mona wouldn't have asked to spend

the night if she didn't have a really good reason. She's probably having man problems, though she's not been seeing anyone seriously, as far as I know. I kiss Nick on the cheek. "You're such a sweetie pie," I say. "Most men would be upset to have their evening interrupted by some crying friend of their girl."

"I keep telling you, I'm not most men," Nick says with a wink. "I'm a one and only."

"You sure are my one and only," I say.

"And you're mine," he says. He puts on his shoes. "So, I'll call you in the morning, how is that?"

"OK."

I already miss him, and he's not even left yet.

***

Mona

I throw my bags into the back seat and hop into the car. I sniffle once more, and try to just keep the tears at bay while I drive. The last thing I need is to run into somebody because I can't see through the tears John is making me shed.

I jump onto the 435 and head to Candy's house. I am so depressed I can barely think straight. I glance in the rearview mirror and almost imagine I see John's car behind me. When I look back again, it's not there anymore. A car that looks like his zooms past me.

He is such a jerk. I can't believe I actually thought I loved him, and that I convinced myself he loved me. I can't believe he was mad about this baby. I thought he'd be happy like me, that he would see that we could be a family.

He thought I was going to just agree not to have this baby, well he's got another thing coming. This baby is my chance at happiness. If he wants, we can all be a family, but if not, at least I'll finally have something that is mine. This baby will love me, and I will love it. We'll be all right, just the two of us in this world.

No, John is not going to take away this chance I have at a real family life. I'll be able to give my baby all the love, affection and attention my mother didn't give me. I won't let anyone hurt my child, and I won't make my child feel like an outsider in its own home.

I take the exit and hit a dark side street. The light is on yellow but I breeze through. No cops are around and little traffic, so it's OK. I glance into the rearview mirror and see the car behind me has shot through the light, too. I know it must have been red by the time that other car crossed.

I glance at the road in front of me and then back into the mirror. The car is speeding up behind me. My mouth opens, but the scream is stuck in my throat. I grip the steering wheel tightly and try to veer, but it's too late. The vehicle slams into the back of me and my car careens off the road.

CHAPTER THIRTY-NINE

Candy

Incident lights make a straight line down the road nearing my neighborhood. Cops block all incoming and outgoing traffic from entering. Fire trucks, police cars and an ambulance are the only vehicles they allow through the barricade.

I didn't notice the car attached to the parked wrecker truck at first glance, then I look a little closer. Read the plates on the back 5RF YKH. With my heart in my mouth, I sprint toward the accident. One of the cops grabs me as I force my way through the curious bystanders. I hear him yell, "Ma'am. Ma'am, you're not allowed in this area."

"That car belongs to my friend," I respond as I try to force my way by him.

His grip loosens, but he still secures my arm. "I'm Officer Daniels. What's your name?"

The flashing lights and wailing sirens from the police cars and ambulance increase the thumping building up in my head.

"Candace Cameron. I have ID if you want to see it."

"That's not necessary. Ma'am what's your friend's name?"

"Mona."

"Does she have family we can contact?"

"Yes, her mother. Will you please tell me what's going on? Are you going to let me through?"

"Your friend was in a car accident and was taken to the hospital. Someone drove her off the road. They did her in pretty bad, but I think she will be fine. Lucky for her a man saw the accident and called us. I am the first officer on the scene. I took his report and was able to get a good description of the car that ran your friend off the road. Do you know anyone who would want to hurt your friend?"

Officer Daniels' question is odd and I'm sure my face conveys it. "No, why would anyone want to hurt her?"

"Because this wasn't really an accident. She was hit from

behind, purposely and I have a hunch that our eyewitness knows more than he's telling us, but I can't prove it."

"So where is he?" I ask scouting the street for the mysterious witness they have.

Officer Daniels looks around with me. He says, "He's gone, ma'am."

I rub my temple and try to hold my peace at this little piece of news. "Gone, you just let him go?"

"He's not guilty of a crime ma'am. We had to let him go. Look, your friend's not dead and killers don't call in their murders and stay at the crime scene,"

"How do know? Did you check? Is this normal procedure?"

Cops are supposed to be calm in emergency conditions. They get trained to become unaffected, unemotional robots. That still doesn't give them the right to be dismissive of another person's pain.

"Yes ma'am we checked. We won't be able to do anything tonight. Do you mind if I ask you a couple of questions?"

"No I don't mind."

Officer Daniels asks a few more questions before releasing me. He wanted Mona's mother's name and a number to reach her. All of which are normal questions, except for the enemies portion. It troubles me because he asked twice.

I think about how scary this must be for Mona. Why would someone want to hurt her? They brought her to St Luke's Hospital down the street. Near death meets her five minutes from my home.

I visualize the worst in my mind. Broken limbs, possibly surgery required, or maybe she's in a coma. Oh God I hope she'll be coherent. We need to find out who did this to her.

I call Mona's mom. She doesn't care, doesn't react the way a mother should when her child is laid up in a hospital bed. I didn't expect her to care, but that didn't stop me from having hope. Mona is the mistake her mother never lived down. I call my mom, my rock and relay the events to her.

"Oh, Lord, is she all right?" My mom's voice pierces my eardrum.

"It's OK," I quickly assure her. "The police officer said she is bumped up a little, but she will live."

LOVE IS ALL WE'RE AFTER

"Well, let me get my shoes on. I'll meet you at the hospital,"
I hear her moving around.

"Thanks, Mom." Then I call Nick.

CHAPTER FORTY

Lisa

"There's been an accident," Ray Seymour says the words over the phone.

My heart immediately pounds harder. Is John all right? "What happened?"

"It was your friend, Mona."

I'm confused. Why is the private investigator I hired to follow my husband talking about my so-called friend? "I don't understand."

"The accident," Ray repeats. "John ran Mona off the road."

"Ran her off the road? Was he passing her car or—"

"No. This was deliberate."

"Ray, you're talking in riddles," I say, putting my hand to my head. "I'm trying to follow, but I don't see what you're getting at."

"The two of them must have had an argument, because John was waiting outside her home and when she got into her car, he followed her. And he rammed his car into hers and ran her off the road."

"But why would John be waiting outside her house? Why would he try to hurt her?"

"They've been seeing each other. Did you look through the photos I gave you?"

"I— no, not all of them," I say. I was so taken aback by the photos of John with his "cousin" that I couldn't look at the rest. I spent the evening crying through my heartbreak. Seeing the photos was just too hard. And I assumed the rest were just more of the same.

"Well, anyway, it's all documented in the file," Ray says. "I'm sorry to have to bring this news to you, but I know this is what you hired me for. I hope it serves you the way you need it to."

I can't comprehend anything more, so I get off the phone with Ray. I immediately snap into action. I open the envelope and flip through the photos. I come across one that shows John and Mona hugged up. Another with them standing outside her home. Another shows them naked, in each other's arms.

The numbness is replaced by searing rage. All the events from the past many weeks erupt into a volcano and like a mad woman I knock over the vanity, sending perfumes, lipsticks, jewelry, and knickknacks flying everywhere. The sound of our things shattering and clunking against the wall relieves my anguish. I've burned up my energy, hands are weak, and I can't throw another item.

From the depths of my core, I cry out in physical pain. Like a wounded animal, I whimper in my ignominy. "Dear God, dear God take this pain away from me."

Peace is what I'm after and God gives it to anyone who asks, that's what the devotional says. That's what those people at Candy's church have been saying. It's what I need to believe. I wipe my face, pop the scratchy contacts from my eyes, and run trembling hands through messy hair. I can't go to the hospital looking like I've been crying all day.

Going to the hospital to see Mona is hard, but I have so many questions. How long has she been seeing John? When did the affair start? How did it start? How could she — no, they — do this to me? I have wasted enough time trying to figure things out in my head.

The hospital they rushed Mona to is not far from Curtis' home. He lives about three blocks away. En route I change my mind about going to see Mona and take the exit before the hospital. I'm not ready to face Mona. In a state of confusion and need for human contact, I drive past Curtis' home. It's the big red brick house on the corner, white trim, and white door. His every day ride is in the driveway.

I circle Curtis' block, stop in front of the sidewalk to his house. People outside pretending not to notice, watch from hooded eyes as I put my car in park and look at the house to my right. I rehearse what I should say when Curtis comes to the door. Then I start thinking about our last confrontation. It was a disaster. Could I put my heart through that again? What if he has company? His car sits alone in the driveway.

Gaining courage from my self-talk, I approach Curtis's

house on wobbly legs. His house looks deserted. The lovely Venetian blinds I gave him endless compliments on are drawn shut.

On the first knock, sweat runs down my spine, bleeds through my silk top, down to the crease of my butt. Silence! Awful, deafening silence.

Then the rustling of the door lock. Curtis swings the door to the side. Stares at me like I'm a house bug he wants to squash. An invitation inside is not offered. He steps outside with bare feet; he has hairy toes. He looks at me. Then refocuses his attention on some distant object. Curtis doesn't speak. I assume he's waiting on me. I step closer to him, but stay at arm's length. I hug myself and wait. It's not for long.

Curtis' chest expands with a deep breath, and then he lets it out slowly. "What are you doing here, Lisa?"

His rudeness is expected, but it still stings. "I needed to talk to someone." The tears are not far behind. One more act of unkindness and they are going to flow.

"And that gave you the right to just show up at my house unannounced?"

"I-I-I'm sorry, not sure why I thought you might care. I should've called first." I say tearfully and make a move to leave, but he stops me.

"Lisa wait... Come.... Come, on in," he ushers me inside.

I sit at the edge of the sofa, lean forward so my elbows rest on my knees and wait. Curtis goes to the television set and turns it off. He throws the remote into a pile of remotes in a little black box. Someone needs to invest in a universal remote.

Curtis fidgets in the sofa near me. He looks worn out. I need to say something to fill the silence, so I say it.

I begin, "One of the ladies you saw me with at Zane's was in a car accident last night." We both sigh to blow away the heaviness from our chests. Then I go on. "An accident instigated by my husband, who was apparently having an affair with her. I was on my way to the hospital to see her, but came here instead. I'm not sure why I came here and not there. I just know that I had this uncontrollable need to see you, to have you tell me that everything is going to be

OK. I need to hear that I am beautiful and worthy of love, respect, and that it isn't my fault that my husband and friend betrayed me."

I crumble before Curtis in the most unattractive way, but I don't care. I'm hurting too much to worry about my pride. Curtis folds me into his arms, holds me tight and squeezes me. I don't deserve his kindness, but I'm grateful. I turn into the crook of his neck and let the tears I have been holding in run free. Curtis's rubbing my back gives me comfort, but I'm getting aroused. The natural aroma from his skin tempts me to press my breast into the heat of his chest. Curtis groans and explores my lips, savoring every touch of our tongues.

Curtis gently tugs my head back to ravish my neck. The touch of his mouth against my skin sends quivers down my spine, releasing the tigress in me. I tear Curtis' shirt from his body.

"Lisa, wait are you sure you want to do this? I don't want you to do this just to get even with your husband."

"I'm doing this because I want to be yours, if you'll have me."

"Lisa I love you and I was being foolish before when I sent you away. I thought you were trying to play me. I..."

"Did you say you love me?" I interrupt. I brace my hands against his chest. I need honesty and if this isn't real I don't want to play the game. He told me this before, but it was too easy for him to jump ship.

He chuckles a bit. "Yes, I love you. I have loved you from the moment I laid eyes on you."

"Then why was it so easy for you to send me away?" I ask still feeling unsure.

Curtis grimaces remembering the way he treated me the last time I was here. For something to do with his hands Curtis attempts to put the ripped shirt back on, in his futile attempt it rips even more and he throws it on the arm of the sofa.

Curtis relaxes next to me. He tells me, "I was scared. I didn't want to be involved with a married woman. I had fallen in love with you and you were telling me you are married. What kind of future would I have with you? I didn't want to share you with him, whoever he is. I figured you had your fun and now you had to go back to reality. I thought a lot of things."

I see the pain on his face and I never want to be the one to put that kind of pain there ever again. Love in my heart multiplies seeing his vulnerability.

I tell him what I've always wanted to tell him. "I love you too. I guess I've known for some time, but I was too scared to put a title on it. Every time I was with you, it felt so right as if we've known each other all our lives. You're my angel, my beautiful human being and I've been wishing for someone like you and here you are right in the midst of all this mess."

"Baby everything is going to work itself out and if it doesn't I'll be here for you. Now that I know you're mine there is no way I'm letting you go again."

"Will you go with me to the hospital?"

"Yes, you want to leave now?" Curtis asks as he makes to get up, I pull him back down next to me. That uneasy quiver I had since I received the news creeps back into my stomach.

"You go to church, Curtis?"

"Yes, every Sunday. Do you want to go with me this Sunday?"

"You think God really forgives us for the sin we commit against him?" I have been wondering this for quite a while.

"Yes. God is not like man. He is faithful and forgiving. Come to church with me on Sunday. You will like my pastor."

"You know what we're doing is wrong, right?" I remind him.

"We're going to make it right as soon as the divorce is final." Curtis' tone leaves no room for doubt.

"What do you think I should do about my friend in the hospital?"

"If you don't want to go baby you don't have to go. You can stay here tonight and think about it and in the morning if you still feel like going I'll take you to the hospital."

I rest my head on his thigh and muse over what he said. I don't want to go, don't want to see her, but I must close that chapter of my life.

"I think I'll go see her tomorrow."

Curtis smoothes my hair, when I get up one side will look like a peacock. "Let's go to bed."

"OK."

Safe and secure in his arms, I fall asleep without the nightmares of the past.

CHAPTER FORTY-ONE

Mikhail

This meeting between us is inevitable; I just speed up the process. I'd rather be on my territory, but circumstances don't permit it.

Maria's beauty makes the visit a pleasant one. Her shoulder length red hair is now short and dyed blonde. Pregnancy didn't ruin her figure. She still has a full bust, small waist and a firm butt. She hasn't sat down since I got to her flat; I watch her wash the dishes, then put away the leftovers, and wipe the kitchen table numerous times.

"Mikhail I didn't expect you to come in person," she says, standing in the doorway of her kitchen.

I take her underlying meaning as: Next time call so I can have the place decent for company. "You're not listed in the phone book or I would've called before dropping by."

"No, No that's not it. It's just that I'm not prepared and I like being prepared." She wipes her hands nervously in her apron.

Maria looks hastily around the room. Toys are scattered everywhere leaving no doubt in one's mind that a child lives here. It's hard to believe these are my child's things.

Maria opens the issue. "I'm assuming you're here because of the letter you received and you're probably wondering if this child I'm claiming to be yours is really yours. I didn't want to reach out and touch you, but I need the help."

"I am here for those reasons, but I'm also here to find out if you'd be willing to do a paternity test. When we get the results back and we find that he is mine, would I be able to see him on a regular basis or am I just a donor in his life?"

Maria looks at me suspiciously. "I would never stop you from seeing Charlie. He needs a male figure in his life and as long as you're being a father to him and being consistent with him, I don't have a problem with him visiting you or visa versa."

"Charlie," I repeat, liking the way that sounds.

"Charles. I call him Charlie. I named him after my grandfather. He was the constant male figure in my life. I don't want Charlie to ever feel rejected by his father, so if you're not in it for the long haul then you can walk out that door and send the child support check recommended by the state."

"I want to be in his life, that's why I'm here. I was afraid when I found out about him, but I'm not anymore. If we made a baby that night then I'm prepared to be a man and take care of my responsibilities."

"He's asleep right now, but you can look in on him if you'd like to."

"I'd like that very much."

Again I rise to my feet to follow Maria to the little man's room. Her hips sway like branches in a storm. I remember how her body clings to me, how it moves for me.

Inside Charlie's room the pattern on the wall are stars, moon, sun, and clouds. I bet he's never bored in this room. Maria did a good job taking care of him so far. He sleeps peacefully. Maria didn't make a mistake in identifying me as the father. Charlie is the mirror image of me. It's like looking at me in pint size. Paternity test or not, this child is mine.

CHAPTER FORTY-TWO

Mona

The nurse walks in the room just when I settle down to take a nap again. The drugs they have hooked to this IV in my vein make me groggy. She updates my chart, checks on the intravenous drip attached to the IV, and then she checks my vital signs on the screen.

"Ma'am what hospital am I in?" I sound unlike myself and my throat feels parched.

"St Luke's, they brought you in late last night. You were in a car accident." She goes on to tell me. I know I was in an accident; my face is still sore from hitting the airbag.

"Did I lose the baby?"

"I think you should wait for the doctor. I will send him in."

"Please ma'am, I need to know."

Words aren't necessary; she reveals the answer when she averts her eyes. I stifle bitter tears in the sleeve of my gown.

In my pain I ask, "Did I have any visitors?"

"Yes a young lady. She went down to the cafeteria. Can I get you something before I go?"

"No." She hesitates at the door.

She adds, "I'm awful sorry about your baby."

I wait for her to leave before I let my guard down and release the tears I've been holding.

"Weeping may endure for a night, but joy comes in the morning," Candy says and comes through the door. She leans across the bed to hug me. "I'm glad you're conscious. I was getting worried."

Candy is always on time when I need her. We have a spiritual connection. Like sisters. She is the one that picks me up every time I fall. She never lets me down. Her mom takes the pink chair behind the door. I wonder if they know about the baby. If the doctor told them before he told me.

"Hello." I cry some more. Candy continues to fold me in her arms and comforts me with soft words.

The doctor knocks on the door to announce his arrival. A short, white haired man with reading glasses, slender and has a strong likeness to Steven King.

"Hello, I'm Doctor Reynolds and how is my patient doing?"

Candy answers for me. "Little emotional, it seems."

"That's normal when someone loses a baby."

Mother and daughter's faces are priceless. Candy's eyes will me to explain. I act as if the doctor mentioned nothing about a baby.

Doctor Reynolds asks me to sit up. He listens to my heart sounds and breathing with his stethoscope, fills me in on what caused me to lose the baby. The baby was gone the instant the car crashed. Doctor Reynolds wraps up a few more things with me then he leaves me to face mother and daughter alone.

"Mind telling me what's going on, Mona?"

"Candy, not right now. I'm not in the mood."

Angry brown eyes pin me to my bed. Candy asks, "You're not in the mood? You got me and my mother up here in the middle of the night worried sick that you could've been killed and all you can say to me is not right now."

"Candy, calm down," her mom says. Turning to me, the older woman's tone is soft. "I'm sorry, baby. I'm sorry for your loss."

Candy ignores her mother's words and snatches her bag up from the bed and asks the woman, "Momma, you ready? Because I can't stay here and listen to this."

Candy's mom likes to rationalize things. Reason it out. With Candy, there is no reasoning. I know this, her mom does too, but still she makes a go of it.

Her mom speaks, "Candy sit down, maybe Mona is not ready to explain herself. Give it time baby."

"No disrespect Momma, but I'll meet you downstairs." Candy gives me a reproachful look. "Here is the police officer's card. You won't answer our questions. Maybe you'll answer his."

She drops the card onto the table beside my bed and walks out.

Ms. Norma's discomfort shows in her face when she speaks again. She is a peaceful woman, unlike her daughter who will blow up at the blink of an eye.

"Mona, don't pay her no mind. She will come back later when she has calmed down. You know her. You two have been friends for years. Candy is scared and she worries about you. I'll be at the house if you need anything." She pats my hand. I try to think up something to say. I always know what to say in every situation. Only this time I've gone blank.

On her way out Lisa appears in the doorway. Her appearance is disturbing. Ms. Norma is glad to see her and gives her a hug. They exchange polite conversation, shortly after that Ms. Norma makes her exit.

"Lisa, thanks for coming. I wish our visit to—"

Ice-cold eyes replace Lisa's pleasant demeanor saved for Ms. Norma. "Oh I didn't come here to share sympathies. I came here to let you know what you and John have been doing behind my back is finally in the light. How could you do this, Mona? What did I do to deserve this?"

Lisa's pain stricken eyes and anguish nauseate me. She put all that we've done in the name of selfishness in a spotlight and it doesn't look good.

"I wasn't trying to hurt you, Lisa. That was never my intention. I got caught up in a bad situation, and I decided to get out too late."

"When I found out that you were the one seeing my husband and making all those phone calls to our home, I was angry, then I was shocked, then I was infuriated, but I'm not any more. John and I had this a long time coming and you were just the last straw that broke the camel's back. Why did he run you off the road?"

I swallow hard. "What do you mean? John didn't run me off the road."

Lisa's eyes stare at me. "Are you that dumb? Yes he did. How do you think I know about you and John? I hired a private investigator to follow John around, Mona, and he was following behind him last night when he ran you off the road. Why is it such a surprise to you that he would do something like this? I thought you should know. That is why I'm telling you. What you do with the information from here on out is your business."

Lisa's departure is as swift as her appearance. Things seem so final between us. Denying Lisa's story is the logical thing to do, because I don't want to believe John tried to kill me and killed our baby. How can a man who told me he loved me be so cold? I gave so much to John and it took me getting pregnant to realize he gave me nothing in return; he never really loved me at all. I was only a regular piece of meat for him.

Everything is in the open now, but it doesn't excuse the shame I've brought on myself. The only good that came from this is the relief of not having to carry around this burden anymore. Before Candy walked out she had tossed the card for the officer on the scene on the hospital tray.

John you do the crime, you do the time.

"Kansas City PD," a female officer picks up the phone.

Doubt slips into my mind and I become scared. Do I really want to see John behind bars?

"Kansas City PD," she repeats.

"Officer Daniels, please."

She orders, "Hold the line, please."

Silence fills the airway and again I think of hanging up.

"This is Officer Daniels."

More silence.

His voice becomes hesitant and pressing. "This is Officer Daniels, are you still on the line?"

I blow the air from my throat and say, "Officer Daniels this is Mona Williams from the other night. I was the woman in the car accident."

"Yes ma'am, it's good to hear that you're OK."

"I also know who ran me off the road."

"That is good news. I can be at the hospital to take a statement in fifteen."

CHAPTER FORTY-THREE

Candy

Local Kansas City businessman John Boutari, arrested on attempted murder of his colleague and lover Mona Williams. When I asked Mona what the doctor was talking about she wasn't forthcoming. Now I understand why. I toss the Kansas City Star down on the table then pick up the phone to dial Mona's number. She doesn't pick up, so I hang up and call Lisa.

"Hello." It's twelve in the afternoon and she's still asleep.

"Lisa, what's going on?" I ask cutting to the chase.

She yawns. Then wrestles around in the bed. I think I hear a male voice. The air still, we both don't speak and my question still hangs in the balance.

Finally, she asks, "What do you mean?"

I pick up the newspaper and read the headline to her.

"This crap about local business man John Boutari arrested for attempted murder of Mona Williams, a local woman he's been having an affair with etc., etc., etc. What is this? Is any of this true?"

"Yes," she clucks without emotion, giving away nothing of her present state of mind.

Silence fills the air again. I flop down in my bay window overlooking the garden and let her respond settle over me. How could I have missed this? When?... How?... How could Mona do this? All these questions burn in my mind.

I ask the less inquisitive question. "How are you doing?"

She sighs and taps the phone. "I'm doing OK. I'm just taking it one day at a time."

"Why didn't you tell me?"

We're getting good at playing the silent game.

With honesty she says, "I thought you knew."

Her confession offends me. Why would I know and not tell her?

I admit, "I should've known, but I didn't. I asked her if she was seeing him the morning after we got into that spat at that bar and she said no. I believed her because I didn't have any reason to believe otherwise."

"What would make you ask her about having an affair with John?" Lisa asks suspiciously.

Open mouth insert foot. Whoever said confession is good for the soul is a liar. I never told Lisa about that night we saw John out with another woman and telling her now isn't going to make matters better. Lying also would be a betrayal of trust.

"Lisa, there is no easy way to say this, but that night we were out I saw John with another woman and I was angry with you because you were in the bar acting the same way he was, like two unmarried couples. I mentioned seeing John there with another female to Mona and she was very angry. I never understood why until now. I'm sorry I didn't tell you."

Lisa doesn't say anything for a long time; convinced she fell off the line I call out to her. "I'm here," she lets out a harsh sigh. "Why didn't you tell me?... I thought we were friends. What an idiot I've been, you knew...."

God help me.

"It wasn't like that, Lisa. I didn't want to see you get hurt and I didn't want to cause a scene at a bar. I've been trying to tell you for the longest time, but each time I tried the timing was never right. You have been through so much. How could I add more to the hurt you were already experiencing?"

Lisa curses; I've never heard Lisa curse.

"Lisa, please...."

"Candy, there is never a right or wrong time to tell someone who you've been best friends with since college that her jerk of a husband is sleeping around on her, least of all with one of her friends. If it hadn't come to this, would you have told me?"

She is making me feel low.

"I'm sorry," is all I get out before she hangs up in my face, leaving me to listen to the dial tone.

CHAPTER FORTY-FOUR

Mikhail

Pastor Matthews says, "Go with me to Exodus 1:22. When you get there say 'amen.' If you're not there, say 'not there.'" He clears his throat. "It's crucial, it's critical, and it's vital to hear a word from God."

Pastor Matthews steps down from the pulpit and walks to the middle of the sanctuary. He looks over the room full of people waiting to hear what he has to say.

He sighs into the microphone. "The preconception is that all men are dogs, but I come to tell you that is far from the truth. God did not make any human male dogs."

Someone shouts "Preach," and a few others join in.

Pastor Matthews chuckles and continues. "This morning's sermon subject is Save the boys. Our youth are ceasing to exist, because they are being raised by the streets and in the juvenile facilities. With no one to teach them how to be a man, we end up with men of different sexual orientation and immoral persuasion."

This is the Sunday before Christmas, and many people probably are expecting a holiday message. But my pastor gives one that's right on time, even if it's not seasonal.

Pastor Matthews' preaching becomes intense and everyone is moved including me, because I feel as though he is talking to me and not to the entire congregation. Amen's and hallelujah's shout down from the balcony in unison with the members standing up in the center of the sanctuary. People begin to speak in tongues. I too, shout. Thanking and praising God. For the first time I am able to keep my thoughts in the church. Now that I am someone's father it pays to pay attention. I am one of those father figures the pastor mentions.

He continues in his tell-it-like-it-is tone. "Black men need to take an active stand in the community. We need to be fathers to the children we bring into this world. Our black men use the scapegoat of the baby mama drama to not fulfill their responsibility and I say that's the cowardly way out. If you can make a child then you should be able to provide for that child. How long will we oppress our women? We are the future for this next generation and what we do now sets the course of our legacy. I say our legacy should be world changers. Too many of us are behind bars, some serving time for crimes they did not commit. I can't stress this concern of mine anymore, but we need more father figures for our boys."

I look down at the little boy lying in my lap fast asleep. Charles Raymond Lopez whose last name is about to change to Robinson is my child. The paternity test was positive. Curly hair hugs his earlobe, sweat wets his face. We weren't even in church fifteen minutes good before he goes dead to the world. It's amazing how he can fall asleep anywhere and at any time.

"You want me to take him, baby?" Momma asks.

Momma is just itching to hold him.

I shake my head, no.

"OK then, baby let me know if you need me to take him."

I smile thankful my momma is here for me. I squeeze her hand. She smiles. There is nothing like a mother's smile, a mother's understanding, and support. This is my first Christmas as a father. I feel an overwhelming outpouring of love for this child God has blessed me to know.

"It's goin' to be all right baby. You are goin' to make a good father," she says knowingly.

I have to. "I hope so, Momma. I really do."

"You are already doing the right thing by bringing him to church. It all starts with God. Continue doing this and God will lead you in the right path. Baby it takes a village to raise a child and that's what family and friends are for, listen to your momma, I know. I raised two of you and you both turned out to be fine young men."

"How do I explain what happened between his mother and me?"

"When the time is right you'll know how to answer. Now

let's pay attention to the pastor before we miss something."

"Yes, ma'am."

***

I drop little man off at his momma's house and now I'm heading toward the Acoustics, a jazz and blues club downtown. It's where a lot of people meet up on Sundays just to chill. In happier days when Candy and I were dating, I took her there many times. Tonight we're meeting there under different circumstances.

Candy is already here. Her car is the only one in Kansas City boasting a license plate with I'M PAID. Check her out. She sits in the same spot we usually reserve. Candlelight shimmers off her skin.

"Mind if I sit here?" I ask walking up to her.

She smiles easily. "Don't mind if you do."

"Been here long?"

She shakes her head, gets to her feet and hugs me so fast, I hardly have time to take a good whiff of her perfume. "No I just got here and you're on time, because I just ordered you a drink."

"You still remember what I drink?" I ask surprised.

She makes a face. "Sure I do. Crown on ice for when you're in chill mood. Long Island Iced Tea for when you're in a partying mood. Should I go on?"

"That's my girl." I pine for another hug, a real one, not one of those superficial hugs she gave me.

"Once upon a time," she corrects me, which brings up why we're here.

The waitress brings our drinks and leaves us to ourselves. I take stock of the activities around the club and try to clear my head to bring my mind into focus. Candy is right before me and all things I have rehearsed inside my head go out the window. All of a sudden, I have nothing.

She breaks my concentration. "You said you had to talk to me."

I sip on my Crown on ice. Then I ask what I drove 25 miles to ask. A phone call would've been easy, but if we've come to the end of our chapter then I want it to end on my terms. Where I can touch her one last time, see her one last time, pretend like she is mine one last time.

I ask, "Where did we go wrong?"

Candy smiles and sips her water. "I don't know." Her smile isn't for humor, she's nervous. "I was hoping you'd tell me."

"I miss you, Candy."

She looks away as if anything is better to look at than me. "I missed you, too. There were many times I rehearsed hearing you say those words, but they never came when I needed them the most. I remembered sleepless nights from crying over you. The pain and loneliness I went through. I thought I did something wrong, that I wasn't fine enough, wasn't what you want from a woman. Then one day I woke up and the pain, the doubts and confusion was gone."

"I couldn't see what I was doing when I was with you. Everything was about my needs, my feelings and me. I never stopped to think about yours. I was so caught up in me-ism."

She exhales nosily. "Mmm."

"Candy, I never meant to hurt."

"I know you didn't. I don't think any of us intentionally set out to hurt one another. We just did."

"Candy, I have a son." The emotions on her face turn from compassion to astonishment.

Her mouth hangs open then she says, "Wow, when did this happen. Who is the mother?"

"I just found out I have a son. His mother is a decent woman. She has a good head on her shoulder, no baby mama drama. It happened after we broke up. It was a one night stand."

"You slept with this woman without protection?" she asks incredulously.

I grunt. "No I didn't. I don't know how she got pregnant."

"So then how did she get pregnant?" Candy asks in a sarcastic tone then she adds. "See this is your problem, you never know. If you didn't walk around aimlessly poking everything you wouldn't be in this predicament."

Harshness slips into my voice. I ask, "What predicament? He's my child and he's here already. There ain't a thing I can do about that."

"I'm leaving. I don't know why I came here. I hoped we

could leave this on amicable grounds."

I reach for her hands on the table; they're warm, not ice-cold like her tone. "Please don't leave."

She stops to look at me and sits back down. For a good while, we don't say much. We sip our drinks. I tap the table nervously to the lyrics of Anthony Hamilton's "Can't let go."

"I love you, Candace, and I made a mistake. I came here tonight to lay it all on the table, to ask for your forgiveness. I don't want to lose you. We've had some really good times together, especially around the holidays. It's the Christmas season. It's a time for family and forgiveness. I hope you can forgive me and we can work toward building a future."

I pause but she doesn't say anything. "If you tell me you don't feel the same way about me, I'll never bother you again."

"I love you too Mikhail, but... but I can't go back to yesterday. What we had was good, but not great and now I'm in love with someone who treats me the way I've always dreamt of being treated."

The truth hurts. These empty arms will never feel her warmth again. I'll never wake up to her cocoa brown voice. Her pleasure will come from somewhere else. All the times we've made love, made plans for our future flash before my eyes and jealousy seeps into my heart. I refuse to give Candy up without a fight.

"You're throwing away what we had for the metrosexual brother who drives the Benz?"

Candy's reaction throws me. She laughs.

I glare at her. "I don't understand what's so funny?"

"How'd you know about him? Mikhail Robinson, were you spying on me?"

"No, I saw the two of you together outside your job a few weeks back. OK, maybe it has been a little longer than that by now. Anyway, I went to your job to tell you just what I'm telling you now and you two were wrapped up in each other's arms."

"That made you jealous huh?"

"Yeah I wanted to rip the brother's head off. Candy, can I have another go at it? This man can't love you like I can."

"What you want me to say, Mikhail? You left. What did

you expect me to do? Sit around and wait till you came to your senses?"

"Then I guess if you're in love with this joker there's nothing I can do about it."

"It's not him."

She puzzles me. "It's not who?"

"I'm in love with someone else. He is nice, Mikhail. He treats me real good and he is willing to wait."

"Wait for what?"

"When you left, I got saved. I gave my life to God. I've been celibate since. This man is willing to wait until we are married before he can have me and the good part is he gave his life to Christ, too."

"And you're saying I couldn't wait." I ask defensively, but we both know waiting wasn't on my agenda.

"This isn't about our past. I'm closing my past with you and opening a future with him. God has someone for you Mikhail, but it's not me. We loved each other for a while now it's time to pour ourselves into new beginnings."

"I can't say I'm happy for you, but I hope he continues to treat you right. Because if he don't I'm a coming after him."

We laugh like old times, free, and without pretence.

"You're crazy."

"It was good to see you, Candy. I'm glad we're leaving as friends, because you are such a special person."

"You too, Mikhail, I'm sorry it didn't work out."

"I wish it had."

We recall the past and pray for the future. It's hard hearing her talk about another man, hard hearing her say she loves him. Candy's Motorola lights up, vibrates then sings across the table. She flips it open; assures someone she's on her way. It's a man. She doesn't say any names. Women don't say names when it's a man.

Quick to her feet, Candy embraces me for the last time. I hold her tight and then watch the love of my life walk away from me forever. What our children would've looked like and who they would've been I'll never know.

CHAPTER FORTY-FIVE

Lisa

It's amazing to me every time I think about the last few months. From feeling beaten down by John's constant disrespect to this wonderful feeling of love, I am so thankful. When I found out about John and Mona's betrayal, I was devastated. Even though I thought I had moved on emotionally from John, the thought of Mona and him laughing behind my back was sickening. The thought of all the lies they both told me made me nauseous. The idea of them plotting against me filled me with rage.

Seeing Mona lying in that hospital bed a month ago gave me a tiny feeling of satisfaction. That's just what she gets, I thought to myself as I left her hospital room that day.

But deep inside, I knew my hard feelings were not right.

Lord, help me to be less like me and more like you, I prayed. I've been reading the Bible and the music I play in my stereo is gospel. I didn't think it was possible, but I actually do find comfort in prayer, and in church. I thought I was too intellectual for something like that.

Curtis' presence helps, too. Like today, he insisted we attend a midnight church service to welcome in the New Year. I've never attended such a service. To me, New Year celebrations are about partying and popping the bubbly. This year, it's about celebrating the blessing of a new start.

"You warm enough?" Curtis asks as I rub my hands in front of the air vents in his car.

"Oh, yeah, I am," I say, and the heated seat offers soothing warmth to my body, making me quickly forget the biting weather outside.

We're on our way to this midnight church service. "I'll pack the car tonight when we get back," Curtis says, "and we can head out first-thing so we can get to my mom's house early."

"OK, that sounds good," I say. "Do I need to take anything for the meal?"

"No, she said to just come hungry."

I laugh. Curtis' mom is constantly trying to fatten me up. But she needs not to worry. I've gained a little weight since being with Curtis. I'm not stressed out like before, so I'm feeling healthier and taking better care of myself. Plus, his cooking is so good, I can't help but gain a few pounds.

"This is the best holiday season I've ever had," Curtis says, touching my hand. "The First Noel" plays on the radio.

"Me too," I say, "And I'm looking forward to the New Year."

"Being with you is such a gift," Curtis says, and my heart fills with love.

CHAPTER FORTY-SIX

Candy

"You ready for lunch?" Nick sticks his head into my office and I smile.

"You bet!" I say and grab my purse. "I am starving."

He laughs. "You're always starving," he says. "I am constantly amazed that you can eat so much and stay so fine."

"It's my secret," I joke and lean into his kiss. I grab my coat and close the door. The months since we started dating have seemed to fly by. We spent Thanksgiving at my mom's. And boy, did she surprise us! She and her fiancé moved up their wedding from January to Thanksgiving, and we were witnesses to a simple, but very lovely wedding on Thanksgiving. They got married in the living room, then we all celebrated over a big Thanksgiving dinner.

Christmas was an amazing holiday. Nick's family even invited my mom and her new husband over, so we all hung out at the Lancaster family home. Kids ran around everywhere and there was so much activity. It felt good to be a part of something like that.

New Year was a different affair for us, though. We spent it quietly, just the two of us. We sat in front of the fireplace and talked. That wasn't really how we planned it. We had planned to go to a party, but it felt so cozy at Nick's house, just stayed in, drinking hot chocolate and enjoying each other. It was a perfect way to ring in the New Year, as far as I was concerned.

I'm not sure where the time has gone. It's now February and it seems like just the other day, we were preparing for Thanksgiving. They say time flies when you get older. I think they are absolutely right. And being with Nick seems to make time zoom by even faster.

"Hey, you there?" Nick says, snapping his fingers in front of me. "Where did you go, just then?"

I shake my head. "Oh, I'm sorry. I was just thinking about how great these past few months have been."

"Yeah, they have been pretty good," Nick says. "Let's see how much better things can get."

I don't really know what he means, but I don't press it. That's just Nick.

"I'll be back in an hour," I tell Kerrey and she smiles. If I didn't know any better, I'd think she winked. But I'm sure she didn't.

As we step off the elevator, Nick turns to me. "I feel like a walk."

I look at him as if he is crazy. "A walk? Cold as it is? And hungry as I am?"

He throws his arm around me. "Come on, baby. It's a beautiful day."

"It's 30 degrees outside!" I say.

"It's not 30 degrees," he says. Seeing my expression, he concedes. "OK, maybe 32."

He pulls me by the hand. "Let's just walk down here, just for a few minutes."

"Nick, I'm cold. And hungry," I complain. He might not be cold, but to a sister, February in Kansas City is cold.

"Just for a few minutes," he says, and I can't resist his eyes.

"Oh, OK," I say, and we enter the walking area not far from my office. He leads me to a bench and we sit.

"I thought you wanted to walk?" I ask, looking at him. This man knows how I get when I'm hungry — and cold! It may sound romantic in the movies, but sitting on a park bench in the middle of winter is not my idea of romance.

Nick slides off the bench and kneels in front of me. He grabs both of my hands in his. "What are you doing? It's—" But the look in his eyes silences me.

"Candace, you are a dream of a lifetime," Nick says. "I searched a long time for a woman like you. All that came before you pale in comparison. I never want us to be apart."

My breath catches in my throat. My cheeks are warm and my eyes water. It's not the cold. It's the emotion that brings the tears. He continues. "It was in this park that you first gave me a chance."

This is the spot where we had that conversation a few months ago. It was the conversation where he said he wanted to be with me, even if we didn't have sex. Birds stood guard and watched us then. None are here now, but the moment is perfect, even without them. I am excited at what I think his words mean, but I need to hear them to be certain. He doesn't disappoint.

"Will you give me the chance — the opportunity — of spending the rest of my life with you? Will you marry me?"

I fling my arms around Nick's neck, almost knocking him over. "Yes! Yes, I will marry you!" I squeal the words.

Nick slides a ring onto my shaking finger, and passersby clap. From somewhere in the distance, I hear someone singing. I look up, and the singer is walking toward us. I glance at Nick.

"You did all this?"

"Yes, listen to the words of the song," he says, and the soloist seems to float down the hill. The song professes love for the rest of our lives.

When the soloist finishes, the crowd applauds, and so do I. "Thank you," I say, and the woman nods and blows us a kiss.

Nick gives her a salute. "Thank you!"

The woman hands me a rose. "May God bless you as you start a new life together." She turns to Nick. "Do you need anything else?"

"No, we're good," he says. "We'll be at your concert next week. Thanks for flying in to do this special favor."

I peer closely at the woman for the first time and my eyes grow wide. I just watched this woman perform at last year's Grammy Awards! "You are something else," I whisper to Nick as the woman leaves.

"No, you are something else," he says back, and kisses me lightly.

"I can't believe you just proposed to me," I say, still shocked.

"Yeah, and in the same spot where it all started, really, for us," he says. "You were trying to make it difficult, though, at first. I thought I was going to have to throw you a sandwich."

We laugh. "Well, you know how I get sometimes when I'm hungry," I say, sheepish at the thought of my earlier complaints.

We walk back up the hill to Nick's car. I glance toward my office building. "I need to tell Kerrey I'm going to be late."

"She already knows."

"Are you serious?" I say. "You are such a little schemer, I tell you. So was everybody in on this little surprise?"

As if to answer my question, Kerrey walks across the parking lot. "Congratulations!" She says, and gives me a hug.

"Thanks!" I say, holding out my hand with the large, sparkling diamond adorning it.

"It's beautiful," Kerrey gushes. "So, Mr. Lancaster said to clear your schedule for the afternoon. I guess that means I'll see you tomorrow?"

"The rest of the afternoon?" My eyes widen. Miranda would never go for that. "Oh, no, I can't do that. Miranda will have my—"

"Miranda insists," Kerrey says, and it seems that surprises are the order of the day for me right now.

"Miranda what?"

"Yeah, she has already signed off. She says she needs the Dunaway file by lunch tomorrow."

"Wow, you must have some real influence around here," I marvel at Nick. First, he flies in a Grammy singer. Now he actually gets Miranda to be nice to me. "This is all too much."

"Nothing is too much for you," he says, and kisses me again.

CHAPTER FORTY-SEVEN

Mona

The case between John and me was brief. He got off scot-free. Amazing what money can do. Excusable homicide is what they call what he did to my baby. Running some-one off the street is excusable when committed by accident without any unlawful intent or misfortune in the heat of passion, upon any sudden and sufficient provocation, or upon a sudden combat, without any dangerous weapon be-ing used and not done in a cruel or unusual manner. I never had a chance against his money and influence.

The mail carrier sticks the mail through the mail slot. Probably more hate mail from married women cussing me out and labeling me as a home wrecker and that John should've killed me. John is a prominent man in this com-munity. His face has been on every newspaper since the accident. I even lost my job over this. I'm the victim, but he comes out smelling like roses.

Candy's calls are back to back now. She started early this morning. I had to turn off the ringer. I'm not ready for her rejection. Love and true friendship was taking for granted. Candy is the kind of friend that gives her all to the people she loves without questions or expectations. I wish I had let her in on the John and me dilemma then maybe things would've turned out different.

Since the accident, I've developed panic attacks and they are back again. The doctor prescribed crazy pills for me, tiny little green pills. They make me eat and sleep, and for a minute, they keep me sane.

"Darn it…. What?" I snap, snatching the phone from its cradle.

Prolonged silence.

"You speaking or just breathing in my phone?" I ask. "Well?"

"Mona, it's your mother."

"To what honor do I owe this call?"

"I didn't call to argue with you, Mona."

"Why are you calling then?" I ask, impatiently.

"I didn't come to court Mona, because I didn't want to see you suffer."

I laugh mockingly. "Since when have you cared about how I feel? You never gave a darn before."

Her sigh is heavy. Our bitterness runs deep. "I know I haven't been the best parent to you, but...."

"Oh wait a minute. You were never a parent. You treated me like some mistake you'd made and because of it, I'm all messed up in the head. Why didn't you love me, Mom? Why didn't you just kill me when I was in your womb? And where were you when your boyfriends came into my room, huh? Where were you a parent? Were you a parent then?"

I regret picking up the phone, regret opening old wounds. Tears of shame dampen my face.

"We're getting nowhere with this conversation, Mona. Please learn how to forgive me."

Then the phone dies. She hangs up in my face. This is what I hate about her, the immaturity and lack of respect for me. I should call her back, but calling her back would be futile. Dealing with my mom is like raising the dead. She is a heartless, selfish witch.

Lost my virginity at thirteen, one of her boyfriends robbed me of my innocence and when I told her, she called me a liar. It's not history time and I don't want to go down this tattered path right now, but history has a way of getting in your face. Confronting you with junk you want to erase.

Tiny green pills cover my floor. I must have knocked them off the when I answered the phone. I stoop down to scoop them back into the bottle then pop one in my mouth.

In my inbox I have twelve new messages. I click the first. Monty's catches me off guard. I haven't heard from him since we went our separate ways. John was the reason for that break up.

***

Re: Reaching out

"Hey beautiful how is everything? I heard about your trial from a close colleague of mine and wanted to touch base with you. I hope you're OK. I know it's been awhile and it wasn't easy tracking you down. I'm in town sometime next week and I want to see you, before I come back to Japan. Call me at Mom's, the number is still the same."

Lots of Love Monty.

***

Re: Elated

"Hey handsome, I'm thrilled to hear from you. You found me at a time when I could really use the familiar face of a friend. I would love to see you when you get into town. I hope your mom will be cool with me calling there, with what the media's been saying about me and all. I'm sorry I haven't kept in touch. I should have. Curse me. See ya next week.

CHAPTER FORTY-EIGHT

Lisa

Candy and Nick have invited Curtis and me out for dinner to celebrate the new love in all our lives. It'll be the first time we've all gone out like this. My hurt at Candy's decision not to tell me what she knew about John has dissolved. I realize I can't afford to carry bad feelings. It'll be good to see my friend and to celebrate her engagement.

When we pull up to the restaurant, Curtis bounces out and opens my door before I can even get my purse from the back seat.

"You're still such a gentleman, after all this time," I smile up at him.

"And I always will be, milady," he says and stoops in an exaggerated bow of gallantry. We both laugh. "Right this way, Madame."

It's been four months since he let me back into his life, that day I dropped by his house on my way to see Mona at the hospital. Never once has he been disrespectful no me. Never once has he cursed me or hit me or told me something I found to be untrue. Never once has he been anything like John, and for that, I am grateful.

It's been a long road for me. Sometimes, I find myself unable to believe God has shown favor on me in this way. I sometimes try to examine Curtis' words, to see if maybe there is some lie in them, but I try to keep that in check. I don't want to punish him for what John did to me — or for what I allowed John to do.

I'm hopeful the divorce can be finalized soon, but John keeps stalling. He contests every single thing I say. He calls for no reason, trying to get back in good with me, and then blows up at me when I refuse to listen. Twice he has sent the divorce papers back, unsigned.

But I don't want to think about any of that tonight. Tonight, I just want to enjoy my man and visit with my friend and her fiancé.

"Girl, you look great!" Candy checks me out and nods with approval. She turns to Curtis and kisses his cheek. "Good to see you again. Seems that you're putting some meat on her bones. I hear you're a good cook."

Curtis grins. "Yeah, I do all right in the kitchen," he says, and rubs my back. "She gives me an excuse to cook."

"Hi, Nick," I say and give him a hug.

"Good to see you again, Lisa," Nick says. He turns to Curtis. "My man! Seems that night back in September was a good one for us all. I met the woman of my dreams, and it seems that you did the same. Who knew we'd all be standing here today?"

Curtis nods. "Yeah, that's true," he says. "That night was big for us."

Candy and I exchange glances. We're both remembering the drama of that evening, but we've grown past that. Candy reaches for my hand and squeezes it. "I love you," she says in my ear and I whisper it back.

"I'm really happy for you," Candy says to me, and I know from her eyes that she means it. I can tell my friend has changed. She is not holding a grudge and I know she isn't judging me for being out with Curtis even though my divorce hasn't come through.

She introduced me to a God of love and forgiveness, and it looks that she found him herself. She's just thrilled to see me. And that's enough for me.

"You haven't seen my ring yet!" Candy squeals and before I can reach for her hand, she flings it out, showing off her platinum ring with its princess cut solitaire, with more diamonds in the band.

"Oh, it's beautiful!" I gush. The ring has got to be the most expensive thing she owns, if that diamond is any indication, but I'd expect no less for Candy. I can see Nick knows the woman he is marrying, and getting her anything less would not have gone over well.

"I'm going to get you one of those one day," Curtis says and I blush.

The hostess approaches. She smiles and says, "Your table is ready."

CHAPTER FORTY-NINE

Candy

Trials are a part of our everyday lives. They come to strengthen us, not weaken us. Mona's pity party has gone on long enough. I have been calling her for days. She had a trial and didn't tell me. Lisa was the one who called and told me. Lisa came around, we're friends again, and it's better than before. Praise God.

I step over the garden hose in the entryway of Mona's backyard, pull the latch back on her gate and close it softly behind me. I heard movements inside the house when I knocked on her front door, but no one came to the door. If Mona is home, she won't expect me to walk to the back of the house.

In the broad daylight, I'm peeping through her sliding glass door. I can see into her kitchen, but not the living room. Her laptop is on, which means she is there. I walk back to the front of the house to look under the flowerpot for her spare, but it's not there.

"What are you doing?"

I turn around to find this little old and her yapping dog ready for attack.

I stand upright.

My speech is edgy. "Nothing," I moisten my lips nervously and keep an eye on her dog. He yelps at me uncontrollably. I can see my foot straight up this pup's backside so she had better stop his barking.

"I wouldn't call peeping through someone's windows, nothing young lady."

I have a sudden urge to laugh and I do. The look on her face is scolding.

"You young people have no respect."

"I'm so sorry ma 'am, but I wasn't laughing at you. I was laughing at the situation. You see my girlfriend lives here." He eyes widen on the girlfriend part. "Not my girlfriend as in my lover ma'am, but best friend."

"Oh. No Ellen DeGeneres. Secretly, I love her show."

"No ma'am. No Ellen DeGeneres."

I explain my reason for looking through Mona's window, leaving out all the sordid details. This old woman is sharp, she still eye me suspiciously, but relaxes her grip on the dog. Then the dog licks me and tries to hump my leg. I jiggle my leg to shoo him away. I don't want to kick this dog, but I will if it doesn't go somewhere and sit down.

"He likes you. Candy you say it is?"

"Yes ma'am."

"Well Candy, I have a story to tell ya my dear." She pats a wrinkled hand on Mona's porch steps for me to sit beside her. "When I was a young woman growing up I had a very close and dear friend blow up at me over something trivial. Lot of hot air, that one had. We weren't on speaking terms, but little good did that do. We had a long history you see. Everything we did in the small town we lived in was together and we couldn't continue to do those things without bumping into one another. The experience showed us to we couldn't do without each other and we called a truce. Sadie is dead now, three years. What I'm trying to say to you is your friend may not be speaking to you right now. But later on when things are settled and she has time to think about your friendship, she'll come around."

She pats my shoulder. I think about what she said.

"I hope so, she is like a sister to me."

"Come on baby, let's finish our walk," she calls to her dog.

Her dog yelps in response.

"Have a nice day and thanks for the talk."

I take one last disappointed look at Mona's house, before heading back to my car. I can only hope the elderly woman is right, about Mona coming around. She has never waited this long to come around and we have never hidden secrets from each other. This John drama has pushed her into silence and I feel like she's a million miles away. Judgment is not for me to decide and I know she thinks I will judge her. If only she'd answer her phone, she'd see I only want to be there for her.

Nick's engagement to me is a pivotal time in my life and I wanted Mona to be a part of it. Our engagement party is tonight and it kills me that she won't be there to celebrate with us.

***

Exquisite is an understatement when it comes to describing Nick's eight thousand square foot contemporary Mediterranean style home he had custom designed and built a year ago. The entrance onto the property is breathtaking, tiles glistening like an ocean bed, pave the long driveway and surrounding us was an area of exotic trees, complimented by rich green grass, a landscaper's dream.

"Candy, oh my goodness. You didn't tell me Nick's house was this huge," Mom exclaims as she looks around in awe.

I smile. "I know right. Can you believe he lives here all by himself? I don't know why he needs some much space."

"God really blessed you in abundance. I'm happy you've found someone who truly loves you, like you deserve. Nick is such a nice man for you. I see the way he looks at you, Candy that man has it for you bad."

"Mom, I'm glad you approve. I was worried you wouldn't approve of Nick, because he is white."

"Child, please," she shushes me. "I don't care if he's black and blue as long as he takes care of you. He's OK in my book. I never judge the cover of the book before reading the contents. And I'm just glad to know his family accepts you, too. It was nice of them to invite me out to their holiday celebration last year. That says a lot about people, who they let into their home."

I reach over and embrace her. "You are the best thing in my life and I love you very much. I'm blessed to have a mother like you. My life wouldn't be complete if it weren't for you."

"Thanks to your grandmother. I was able to raise you right, because of what I learned from her."

"Grandma was a very wise woman. She was very graceful and classy. I hope to do her justice one day."

"You will, now let's going inside before you make me ruin my makeup."

I laugh and squeeze her to me then pull away. I check

my makeup in the mirror, dab some powder on, and snap the loose powder compact shut.

"OK, how do I look?" I ask.

"Beautiful."

Our engagement party is a poolside event, catered by one the best catering companies in the area. I feel like Cinderella coming to the ball. Servers float around the room carrying trays of hors d'oeuvres and champagne. Tonight is a special occasion so I grab a glass of bubbly from one of the waiters passing by for our toast.

"Hi baby," I announce, coming up behind Nick and kissing him on the cheek.

"Hey, where'd you come from?" he asks and pulls me into him.

I hug his parents. "Brenda and Joe, you guys outdid yourselves. Everything looks great."

"Anything for our future daughter-in-law. Frankly we're just happy someone wants to marry him," his mom whispers and winks. "We were starting to believe he wasn't going to give us grandchildren, but he's proving us wrong."

"Children? That wasn't part of the deal Nick," I tease and nudge him.

We laugh. Joe and Brenda Lancaster have been married to each other for thirty-nine years. How they do it is a mystery to me. What I like about them is that after all this time they are still deeply in love with each other.

Brenda asks, "Norma, so how was the trip to the Cayman Islands?"

"Wow, I had a blast. Steve and I tried all the places you suggested, too."

"Speaking of which, where's Steve tonight?"

"Working, he couldn't get tonight off."

Nick tells us, "I think it's time we go and mingle with our guests before they think of us as being rude."

I catch his hand before he walks off. "Nick, baby can I talk to you for a minute?"

"Sure, let's go in the den."

"Mom, will you be OK?" I ask.

"You kids run along, Norma and I need to play catch up," Nick's mother offers.

I tell them, "OK, we won't be long."

In the den is a huge wood-burning fireplace with a beautiful painting of a woman hanging over it. His family photos are in a neat display on the mantle top. A wall-to-wall bookshelf filled with an array of books adorns the shelves. Tired from all the running around I did today, I sink down into the plush white sofa and Nick joins me.

"I really like this sofa; it's so soft... and plush."

"You say that every time you sit in it." Nick smiles boyishly then his face becomes worried. "Baby you're not having a change of heart, are you?" Nick's stare is penetrating. He clucks his tongue. "Well?"

"Well, what?" I smile and continue to taunt him. "Getting straight to the point, aren't we?"

He frowns, and I have to quickly reassure him that I'm not changing my mind. "No silly. Why would you ask that?"

"I don't know, maybe because you have me in here away from our guests. Could be because you told me we needed to talk. I don't know. You seem a bit distant here lately. Baby what's wrong?" he asks, staring at me with those gorgeous blue eyes. Looking into his eyes is like peering into the ocean bed. I smile and then kiss him on the nose.

"Sorry buddy, you don't get off that easy. You're mine."

"I wouldn't have it any other way. Now what did you want to talk to me about?"

"Nothing, I just wanted you to myself. I need you, your kind words, and your soft touch."

"Bad day at the office?"

"No, it's Mona. I haven't seen or heard from her and I'm really worried. Honey I'm getting married in a few months and at this rate she probably won't be there. This is a special day for me, a once in a lifetime event."

"Baby, you're stressing too much. I'm sure Mona is OK. She's a big girl who can take care of herself. Give it time. Enjoy your moment and stop worrying so much."

"But you don't understa..."

"Let it go. Come here," he whispers and places his finger against my lips to silence any further protest. "Mmm, you smell intoxicating. What are you wearing?"

"Very sexy."

He flashes me a devilish grin. "That you are my little hellion. You feel good too."

He hits a button on his desk and the sound of the lock to the door leading to our guests on the other side clicks in place, shutting them out while giving us the privacy we need to delight in a few kisses.

CHAPTER FIFTY

Lisa

The divorce papers I sent John came back in the mail unsigned again. I don't know what kind of sick game he's playing, but I don't have time for it. I make corrections to the original papers based on the discrepancies he has then he finds fault with those corrections and sends them back. It's like he enjoys toying with me.

This time he encloses a letter inside, expressing to me about how sorry he is for destroying our marriage and how he wants to work it out now that the trial is over. He's right about one thing, he's sorry and dead wrong if he thinks I'm willing to give our marriage another try. I toss the papers aside and they flutter to the floor in disarray.

Seeing John with that woman and child every day in court crushed me. It was a slap to the face knowing that some other woman was able to give him the one thing I've been yearning to give him and couldn't. During the trial, John didn't even look way, not once. I can only sum it up to him being too ashamed to look at me, because the only thing he would see there was contempt, pity, and regret.

"You look like you could use a little tender loving and care," Curtis says as he walks over to kiss me on the forehead and grabs the remote off the coffee table. Curtis flips it on to TBN.

"Curtis, do you think he'll ever sign the divorce papers?"

"Where did that come from?" he stops looking at the programming on TBN and gives me his full attention.

"Well, this morning I got back the divorce papers unsigned again." I say.

"You're the attorney sweetheart, can't a judge grant you a divorce?"

"It's not that simple. All of our assets are tied up together. The only thing I was able to do was file a legal separation." I have become frustrated with John's refusal to grant me my freedom.

"Where does that leave us?" Curtis's eyes took in every inch of my face.

"You'll just have to be content with dating a married slash legally separated woman."

He grins, boyishly. "I'm already doing that."

"Well for a little while longer, because I can't continue to live this way. I was thinking that until the divorce is final, we should not sleep together anymore." I let the words out and wait for his response.

"That's fine with me, sweetheart, I understand," Curtis says easily. "You're my baby now, and I ain't letting you slide through my hands."

"I wouldn't want to," I say and slip into his lap.

"Did John ever say why he did you like this?"

I sigh and press my head into his chest. "Because he could get away with it. He said he'd been doing it so long. It became natural to him."

"John isn't a real man, Lisa. A real man doesn't do those things, only a coward. When a man finds a good thing, he holds onto that good thing. You're a real gem Lisa and a man would have to be out of his mind to mess around on someone like you. From the moment I saw you I knew you were something special."

Curtis's analysis of John is accurate. Thank God, I wasn't the failure. "Where did you come from? You can't be real."

"I'm real baby. As real as it gets and I'm going to do everything in my power to erase any doubts and fears that have been placed in this heart of yours." Curtis places his palms against my chest then brings his lips down to arrest mine. His lips are supple and engaging, urging me to lean deeper into him. Drawing heat from the depths of my core, I kiss him back with everything within me.

In my unhappiness, I never thought I'd ever find true love again. Curtis came along just in time to rescue me. In my deliberation over my previous failures with men these past few months, I have come to a realization that I don't have to worry about my shortcomings with men anymore, because this time I know deep within me that I'm a beautiful woman God has made, and I don't have to prove anything to anyone. And besides all that, I've found the real thing in Curtis.

God has really done some work on me. Last year when all this stuff broke, I wouldn't have given much thought to God or His work. I thought I could handle it all on my own. And I was so caught up in feeling sorry for myself and feeling victimized by John that I couldn't see myself for the person God has created me to be.

I heard through the grapevine — OK, through Candy — that Mona is jetting off to Japan with some man. Candy wanted me to call Mona and to offer her my forgiveness. She says Mona needs to hear it.

I'm not at that point yet. I don't hold any malice toward her, and I have actually prayed that God shows mercy to her. I have forgiven what she did, but I'm not ready to be buddy-buddy with her. Not enough time has passed.

I do the only thing I know how to do. I pray for her instead. Lord, bless Mona with safety as she crosses the seas and please come into her life like you came into mine.

"Why don't we talk to my pastor?"

"Huh?" Curtis's words jar me from my thoughts.

"I mean, as far as the divorce," Curtis says. "The pastor deals with lots of strange situations, and I'm sure he may have a suggestion."

"I don't know..." my words come out slowly. I don't want the pastor to know so much of my business, though, in all fairness, if he reads a newspaper or watches a news report, he already knows. The media had our business blasted all across the city.

"Come on, baby," Curtis says, pulling me onto his lap. "The pastor will be able to provide some counsel, and maybe even offer a solution for getting out of this situation and moving on with our lives."

I consider Curtis's statements and realize he has a point. I have a few legal maneuvers up my sleeve as well. So between what I know and what the pastor knows, I feel reasonably confident we may be able to resolve this divorce. I smile. I can almost see the future with Curtis, once this legal headache is behind me. We've talked of doing charitable work together, traveling the world, even adopting children. "OK. Let's do it."

CHAPTER FIFTY-ONE

Candy

My heart pounds in my chest as I hear the music playing downstairs in the sanctuary. My mom touches up my makeup. "Are you nervous?" she asks, and I shake my head. No, my quickened heart rate isn't because I'm nervous. It's because I feel overwhelmed with joy that this day has finally arrived. And more than a little excited at the prospect that I will be going to bed with my husband tonight.

This journey has been a long time in coming, but God's promise bore out. He told me if I just took Him at His word, I would be all right. And I am. Celibacy was hard — darn hard — but I managed to make it through. And I am a living witness that there are relationships that survive and thrive when they are built on a foundation of spiritual guidance. Seven months ago when Nick and I got serious about each other, I truly didn't know if he would stick around. But he has and today, we profess our love to all the world.

"I need all my ladies!" the wedding planner calls, and my bridesmaids scurry to her attention. Nick's sister, Summer, waves at me. Lisa, my matron of honor, gives me an air kiss.

"See you downstairs!" Lisa says, following the other girls. "You look beautiful."

And I do. I am dressed in a Vera Wang strapless mermaid gown with a lace hem. It plunges in the back, showing off my smooth, chocolate skin. It's from her latest collection and costs enough to feed a family for a lifetime. But that's OK, because I'm worth it. Today is about luxury and love.

A twinge of regret touches me though, as I miss Mona. She hasn't taken any of my calls in the past few months. She did not RSVP to the wedding invitation. I never imagined Mona would be the friend who would hold a grudge. She has always come around before, but this time it seems our friendship really is over. I've tried to apologize for the words I said to her that day at the hospital, but I guess she isn't having it.

The wedding planner comes for me now. "It's time," she says and smiles. I look at myself one last time in the mirror, and begin the walk to greet my soon-to-be husband.

As I make my way down the winding stairs, I get a glimpse of a woman rushing into the building's foyer. A smile breaks across my face. It's Mona. Always late. But today, she's right on time. Our eyes meet. She waves at me before an usher quickly pushes her to a seat so the bridal party can enter.

My friends are here. My family is here. And my man is waiting. As the bridal party enters the sanctuary, I usher up a quick prayer. Thank you, God, for this day.

Then it is my turn to enter. All heads turn and people rise to their feet. I hear a collective gasp, as they view me in all my glory. I smile, confident that I am the most beautiful bride they have ever seen.

And then I look to the end of the aisle, and I see Nick waiting for me. I can tell from his eyes, that I am indeed the most beautiful – and treasured – bride in the world.

I walk slowly and deliberately to meet my man.

CHAPTER FIFTY-TWO

Mikhail

Here I am months later and still reeling from the shock of Candy's wedding. Photographs of her and her new husband are on the front page of a local magazine company "OUT AND ABOUT." What hurts the most is that he's white and not another brother. I know I'm being a hypocrite and all, because I've dated white woman before and I've even loved a few, never fell in love with any, but loved a few nevertheless.

She looks so happy in her wedding photos, happiness I wish I were giving her and not him. They got married this summer. It seems like it was just a minute ago when I was begging her to give me another chance at Christmastime. And here she is, not only not giving me another chance, but not giving me another thought. All that's on her mind is her new life, judging by the smiles in those pictures.

She made a beautiful bride in her long, fitted white gown, though. Man did I mess up or what? Hubby had better not mess up, because as soon as he does I'll be right there to put in my bid. He can bank on it.

Today was hectic, because it was the grand opening of our new restaurant. I finally talked Pops into opening his own restaurant, but he wouldn't do it unless I went in on it with him. This morning it felt so good to push my own door keys. The last of the staff is gone and Pops and I are still here going over things for tomorrow.

"And I thought running an auto shop was hard." Pops let out a grunt.

"You tired, Pops?"

"Tired ain't the word, son. Them folks had me working today like a slave up in that hot kitchen. I know the meaning of lunch rush now, if you know what I mean."

I chuckle. "The air conditioner doesn't work in the kitchen?"

"It does, but those folks need to hurry up and install the venting system for the kitchen."

"You the one that was hurrying them and they would've finished the job if you didn't rush them to open the restaurant today." I tie a rubber band around a wad of money.

Pops huffs. "I'm not waiting for two more weeks for them to install some aluminum in the roof just because that fool builder we hired had the opening date confused. This is not the first time I've cooked in heat. I'm just not planning on doing it again. They still set to come this week, son?"

"Yep." Pops looks real stressed behind that kitchen today and it displeases me that the builder I hired didn't complete the job on the kitchen because he had the dates wrong. I would've waited the additional two weeks for the installation, but Pops was ready to get the show on the road. With all the money we invested in this building, I can't say I blame him.

"Good. You bring that grandson of mine over later."

"Man, he's real defiant, Pops. When I was his age was I like that?" I ask, hoping to gain some insight on what to expect from my little terror.

"Boy, there were times when we felt like giving you away. Michael was the quiet one, but you, you were somethin' else," he chuckles and his eyes twinkle at the memory. "Stubborn, hardheaded, and think you know too much. I used to tell you that payback was goin' to come, now look at you."

"I guess it's time to pay the piper, huh?"

"Yeah, it'll be all right son. You turned out to be a wonderful young man. You've made your momma and me proud and we love you." Pops pats me on the shoulder.

"You're proud of me?" I ask, turning around to face him.

He has a puzzled look on his face. "Yeah I'm proud of you son. You say that like I shouldn't be or you don't believe me. I've been paying close attention to you recently and I like the way you've been a man about your business, regardless of the situations that come your way."

It's all I've ever wanted to hear my dad say. "I didn't... Pops it's good to know that you're proud of me."

"Mikhail, I've always been proud of you. I'm just sorry I haven't told you until now."

"I've always thought Michael was your favorite and I

was just there."

"Your mother and I don't have any favorites. I didn't push Michael as hard as you, because I knew his limitations. I saw greatness in you at a young age and knew I had to push you way beyond your limits if you were going to exceed and today you are a success. Seeing you in action with the customers was unreal. Where did you learn this stuff?"

"I learned from you." I pause. "Hey Pops if today is any indication of how successful we're going to be then you better get ready for the second restaurant."

"Now boy you need to slow your roll. I ain't agreeing to no second restaurant," he says and shakes his head in disagreement. "Mmm, this is it for me. One restaurant, you ask me to open one restaurant and that's what I'm sticking to, my boy. I love to be in the kitchen though. Today it just filled me with joy to see all those folks eating up my food and all the compliments I received. Did you know one of the patrons asked to meet me? Can you believe that? Little old me."

I chuckle. "My old man, the overnight celebrity. I suggest you bottle up your secret recipe cause we goin' need it. If you're not planning on doing much of the cooking."

"That may not be a bad idea, it's not like I'm going to be around forever," he says and stretches. "Well, son I'm a head on home before your momma starts worrying about what's taking me so long and sends out a search party. You know how she gets when night falls and I ain't in the house."

"Do I? All right then Pops I'll see ya later. Tell Momma I'm on my way."

"You didn't need any help locking up did you son?" he asks as he limps toward the door.

"Naw, I'm cool. I got it. Go on home and get some rest."

He stops at the doorway. "You did well today, son."

My smile broadens. "I couldn't have done it without you." I shove my hands into my pants pockets then rock back on my heels. I feel like doing a rendition of Frank Sinatra's "Singing in the rain."

***

"How was the park?"

"I'm beat, that child has too much energy. He makes me feel like an old man. 'Push me higher, Daddy, Daddy higher, Daddy, Daddy faster, faster, higher, and higher.' Whew! Somebody should've warned me that kids take this much work."

I'm exhausted, but the joy I experienced today with Charlie at the park fills my heart.

Maria smiles and asks, "How long did you have to push him in the swing?"

"Forever then he gave me the guilt trip when I stopped pushing him. I couldn't get him out of that thing."

"Uh-huh that sounds like Charlie all right. I'm glad you tired him out for me. While he's taking a nap, you wanna help me go over his Christmas list? I don't want to get him anything that you guys already have in mind to get him."

I look at Maria and marvel at the way she has handled this situation from day one. She treats me with such respect and includes me in everything. "Yeah that will give me an idea of what to get him too."

Christmas is months away, but Maria is such a planner. I'm not surprised she already has a list.

"Mikhail, did you ever regret sleeping with me that night?" she asks as she fidgets with the ruffle on one of the sofa cushions.

Her question troubles my mind and I tense up. "Where did that come from?" I shift uncomfortably on the sofa.

"I've been meaning to ask you, but I kept putting it off and putting it off... I... I just don't want you to feel like this is some kind of entrapment. I didn't intentionally...."

"Wait, stop. Have I given you the impression that I feel trapped?" Maria has a valid concern and I think she does, because I've never voiced how I feel about our present circumstance.

"No, but...."

"Look Maria, I was lost until Charlie entered the picture. He taught me how to be a man and how to handle my responsibilities. If it wasn't for this divine intervention, there's no telling of what I'd still be doing."

Maria's eyes mist up. "I didn't believe that you would stick around, but you've proven me wrong. I'm glad I took the chance on you. Charlie adores you."

"I do too Maria. Will it be OK for me to take him to out of town with me in a few months? I want to introduce him to my brother and his family. Would that be OK with you?"

"Of course it would. Let me know when and how long, because Mommy needs a little break." She smiles and jumps to her feet.

"Cool. I'm going to head on home. Tell Charlie I'll come by here to see him tomorrow. Maybe I'll take him to the park again."

"Aren't you a glutton for punishment? We can go over the rest of the Christmas list then."

"I don't know what you talking 'bout, I got this thing under control."

She rolls her eyes. "That little boy has you wrapped around his little pinky and you know it."

I chuckle, but she is telling the truth. I delight in Charlie. "See you tomorrow, Maria."

Sometimes life throws you a curve ball. Charlie is my curve ball, one of the best and I intend to better the future for us both. Love for me is not in the present, but I look forward to it in my future with open arms and an open soul and mind.

CHAPTER FIFTY-THREE

Mona

Not everyone who tells you they love you means it and not everyone you love will love you back in return. I have a lot of growing up to do and living. I took Monty up on his offer to move back to Japan while he was here. I don't know where this will lead me, but I'm open to change.

Candy is four months pregnant and her little stomach is already protruding through her clothes. The girl must have been ready to get it on, because she got pregnant the night of her honeymoon. But I don't blame her; she waited a long time to get with Nick. And from the looks of it, it was well worth the wait. They are always hugged up and can't seem to stop touching each other. I have a feeling this baby won't be an only child.

It's been a year since Candy and Nick got serious, almost a year since my accident last November. So much has changed. Candy is married and soon to be a mom. I am heading over seas — and not with John.

"It's not too late to change your mind, you know?" Candy says.

"I know. I have to do this, I have to find myself and I can't do it here." I rub her stomach and rest my butt on one of the boxes. "Don't forget about the moving company, they will be here on Monday to pick up this stuff," I remind her.

"I won't. Have you said your goodbyes to your mother?" She had to ask me the one question I've been avoiding to answer for myself. I don't plan on calling my mother. We said all we needed to say to each other from our last conversion and I don't feel like dealing with her melodramatic behavior on my last days here in the States.

"Candy, you of all people should know by now that my mother doesn't care about my well being. Let alone my whereabouts. I haven't heard from her since our last blowout over the phone."

"From what you told me, it sounded as if she needed your forgiveness. Just call to say goodbye."

LOVE IS ALL WE'RE AFTER

"There's no love lost between us, her part in my life is over. Candy, your mom has been more of a mother to me than my own mother will ever be and I said my goodbyes to your mom. Help me load the luggage in your car. My flight leaves in three hours."

"I'm going to miss you." Candy hugs me. She has been doing a lot of that since I broke the news that I'm leaving.

"Well, if you can pry yourself away from that new husband of yours, you can always come and visit me in Japan," I say and give her a wink.

"Girl you know I'm there. When I get tired of being a new wife and need to get away from Nick I have somewhere to visit now," Candy says. I laugh at her last statement. If I have to wait until she tires of Nick, the wait will be long. I have never seen her like this with any man. She practically glows.

"John called me today," I say.

Candy's face darkens. "Why did he do that?"

"He wanted my forgiveness."

"Tell him to ask God," she spits the words out and shoves one of my bags in the corner of the trunk.

"I told him I forgive him."

She puts her hands on her hips and huffs. "Did you now?"

"Yes, I need to move on and I couldn't do that until I forgave him. I hope God can forgive me for the pain I've caused in all our lives."

"Mona stop, we all have fallen short in the eyes of God and he still loves us. When the time is right and you've made peace with yourself Mr. Right will show up. Until then keep your head up."

I hug her again. "You're the best friend every friend should have. I wish I could bottle you up and take you along with me."

"What I want to know is how are you going to survive in a foreign country with no knowledge of their language, culture or nothing? Girl you are crazier than I thought. I'm really, really going to miss you."

"Monty will be there," I say.

"Monty was always all right in my eyes," Candy says and

nods. "Hopefully this time around you can turn your friend-ship into something more."

"The only good thing that has come out of this whole or-deal is my promotion. I'm glad they offered me my job back. Running my own agency will be enough to keep me occupied for a long time. Do you think Lisa will ever forgive me?"

Her face clouds, but only for a moment. "Well Ms. Big Timer, don't forget us little people when you get to the top. Lisa has her own demons to deal with, we all do. Forgiveness will come with time. God has already forgiven you."

CHAPTER FIFTY-FOUR

Candy

I slip into bed beside my husband. His body is still warm from sleep. Nick stirs against my stomach. "Well good morning to you."

"Morning, baby what are you doing up this early?" he asks. Nick rubs my stomach, and then turns on his back.

"I've been up. Walked a couple of miles and now I'm ready for my husband to make sweet love to me, so wake up."

"Candy I haven't…"

"Shh, make love to me Nick." Nick is hesitant, but I know he likes what my hands are doing to him. His body's response is always so swift.

"Are you sure? What about the baby?"

"The baby will be fine. I don't know of any babies dying from the parents making love."

"Sweetheart you're going to kill me. We've made love three times before this."

"Has it been that many? Mmm, I can't recall." Running my hands across his chest, I remove the covers and kneel in bed before him.

He pulls me on top of him; his touch is fire on my skin, rekindling the flames within. We become one and I erupt like lava in a volcano. He wraps his arms around me and pulls me closer to him.

"You should go for a walk more often."

"I should?"

"Yes, I like it when you're hot and sweaty." The way he runs his fingers alongside my back is soothing. "Candy."

"Yes baby," I yawn, as I grow sleepy. I've been doing a lot of that since the pregnancy.

"Who is Mikhail?"

My back stiffens at the sound of that name. "Huh?"

"Who's Mikhail? Who is he to you? How do you know him? I don't remember him being on the guest list."

"He wasn't on the guest list. Um Mikhail… Mikhail is some-one from my distant past. Nick, Why the twenty questions?"

"Your ex-boyfriend sent you a wedding gift," he says, nonchalantly.

"When did it? He doesn't know where I live. How is that poss—?" But I interrupt my own questions as my mother comes to mind. He must have gotten the address from her.

"Apparently he does. It's downstairs." He rubs his temple. "It came in a couple of days ago."

"And you're telling me about it now." Twirling this piece of information around in my head, I quickly conclude that my new hubby did not tell me about the gift because he was jealous. "You're not jealous are you?"

He looks at me cross-eyed. "Heck yeah I'm jealous. I know you had men from your past, but I still like to think I'm the only one."

I giggle girlishly, finding it cute that he's jealous. "Please tell me you're not, baby you're the only one for me. You and Brad Pitt, didn't I prove it by marrying you?" I sit up in bed to chew on what to say next. Nick has never questioned my past relations in detail before. We both had past relation-ships that did not work out and we both moved on. Now here he is pulling a David Letterman interview on me.

He chuckles then pokes me in the side. "Why did you break up?"

"Baby, why do you want to go there? The past is the past. Let's leave it there, if you want I can return the gift." I reply, feeling uneasy.

"I don't want you to return the gift. I just want to be sure that this guy is really in the past."

I reach out to caress his face. "You're my present. You never have to worry about another man, Nick there is no one like you. You are the cream in my coffee, the ying to my yang. Baby you complete me. You make me whole. What more can I say to convince you?"

"I know, I just love hearing you say it," he says then he kisses me.

The man is still incorrigible, and I am madly in love with him. When he was willing to wait, and willing to take all the right steps to be with me, I knew without a doubt he and I were meant for each other. Nick makes things so much clearer and I know if I should ever fall, he will be there to catch me. I couldn't ask for a better half and now that I can almost hear the pitter-patter of little feet in the distance, that's just icing on top.

I went looking for love in a lot of wrong places, but God's love was there for me all along. And he showed it to me by not letting me suffer devastating consequences of my wrong choices. Instead, he protected me and guided me to the man he had for me.

I can only live each day as a testimony to the power of God's unending grace. He told me that if I would be faithful to him, he would pour out bountiful blessings. I nestle as close to my husband as I can. This is the most bountiful blessing I could want. As drowsiness takes over, I say a tiny prayer. Thank you, Lord, for watching over me.